CAT'S
PAW,
INC.

CAT'S PAW, INC.

L. L. THRASHER

A BROWN BAG MYSTERY
FROM COUNCIL OAK BOOKS

T U L S A

N

12-91 BT 14 95

Council Oak Books
Tulsa, Oklahoma 74120
© 1991 by Linda Thrasher Baty
All rights reserved. Published 1991
Printed in the United States of America
98 97 96 95 94 93 92 91   5 4 3 2 1

Library of Congress Catalog Card Number 91-70228
ISBN 0-933031-41-6

Designed by Carol Haralson

In Memory of Gregory Thrasher

CHAPTER ONE

SOMEONE WAS TRYING TO TAKE MY GUN AWAY.

I grabbed the hand and Carrie said, "Ow. Dammit, let go." I let go and was asleep again before the .38 cleared the holster.

The next time I woke up, someone was poking me in the shoulder. I rolled over and pried one eye open just enough to see Carrie's husband standing beside the couch. He looked mad. I closed my eye.

"If you ever come in here again and pass out dead drunk with that damn gun on, I'm going to beat the hell out of you," he said.

My head hurt too much to snicker rudely so I said, "I won't do it again, Tom," and rolled back onto my side.

"Zachariah?" He sounded contrite. Maybe he though he'd scared me. "I just don't want the baby to get it."

"She couldn't get it." I listened to him walk away and went back to sleep.

The next time I woke up, I was lying on my back and Melissa was sitting on my chest, stark naked. I stuck the tip of my finger in her bellybutton and jiggled it. She giggled and hit me across the face with a turquoise swimming suit.

"Am I supposed to put this on you? Where's your mother?"

"I'm peeling eggs." Carrie's voice came through the archway leading from the heavily draped family room into the kitchen. The sunlight streaming through the opening was painfully bright. I closed my eyes but it didn't help much and my rib cage was being used as a trampoline so I swung my legs over the edge of the couch and sat up, standing Melissa on the floor and pressing the heels of both hands against my forehead as my brain slammed into my skull.

"Shit," I said.

"Sit," Melissa said with the identical intonation.

"Don't repeat what Uncle Zachariah says, Missy. Uncle Zachariah is no gentleman and you're a little lady." Carrie was standing in the archway, wearing a white maternity top and bright pink shorts that seemed to be shimmering in the sunshine. After a brief squint at her, I said to Melissa, "Listen to your mother. You'll have your sex-role stereotypes down pat before your second birthday." I shielded my eyes with my hand and glanced at Carrie again. "Can't you dress her? My head hurts."

"I'm peeling eggs." There was a definite lack of sympathy in her voice. She turned and clattered, much too loudly, across the kitchen tile. I stuffed Melissa's plump little body into the swimming suit with no noticeable assistance from her. She padded off toward the kitchen, turning at the door to say her version of "Uncle Zachariah" which sounded a lot like a tape being played backward.

With a little help from the arm of the couch I made it to my feet and turned toward her, eyes half-closed against the light. "What, babycakes?"

She patted the shiny fabric stretched over her belly. "Piddy?" she asked.

"Very pretty. In a few years you'll be breaking all the little boys' hearts." There was a distinct snort from the kitchen. "I'm in favor of sex-role stereotypes," I said, too loudly. Waves of pain bounced across the top of my skull.

"All you macho types are." Carrie was back in the shaft of light.

"Slip your shoes off, cookie, and you'll be barefoot and pregnant and in the kitchen. Is there any coffee?"

There was a pause, about as pregnant as Carrie, then she said she'd make some. Melissa and I followed her into the yellow and white country kitchen which reeked of hard-boiled eggs. I opened the screen door for Melissa and watched her bellyflop into three inches of water in a wading pool.

"If you plan to yell at me, do it quietly, okay?"

Carrie didn't answer. She was making coffee and a lot of unnecessary noise. I walked carefully down the hall and up the stairs, trying to keep my head on an even keel. I rummaged around on the top shelf of the linen closet where Carrie stashed my shaving kit and anything else I left lying around her house. The only clothes I could find were a pair of shorts that had once been Levi's button-fly jeans and an old blue T-shirt with "BIGGER IS TOO BETTER" printed in darker blue across the front. No socks and no underwear but better than wearing the clothes I had slept in.

I looked into the bathroom off the hall. The tub was littered with decapitated torsos and an assortment of arms and legs. Four round pink babydoll heads were lined up on the rim, staring at me. I went through Tom and Carrie's room and checked the floor of their shower. A loofah sponge and a pink disposable razor. If I didn't step on the razor and cut a toe off, I'd be all right.

I brushed the taste of last night's tequila from my mouth, showered without cutting myself, and shaved, cutting myself only twice. Barefoot and splendidly attired in two shades of faded blue, I followed the smell of coffee back to the kitchen.

Carrie actually poured me a cup. Maybe I was going to get some sympathy after all. I sneaked a peek at her face as she sat down across from me at the glass-topped table by the window. I wasn't going to get any sympathy. I decided to try a neutral topic and asked where Tom was.

"At the hospital. He's just catching up on some paperwork. He'll be home soon."

I hoped he would hurry and save me from his wife. Carrie sighed. My stomach muscles tensed. I decided to parry before she could thrust.

"I drink less than anyone I know, including you."

Her smile was excessively sweet. "When was the last time you crawled in here at three in the morning and passed out on the couch?"

Touché.

"I didn't crawl, I walked. I might have staggered a little but I definitely didn't crawl." She knew as well as I did that it had been exactly one year ago.

"April's been gone a long time," she said.

"Yeah, time flies. Here it is almost the end of August already."

Her eyes flashed blue sparks at me. "You know goddamn well I'm not talking about the goddamn month. It's been three years."

Three years, three months, and nine days. I kept track with the obsessiveness of a man in solitary marking time on the wall of his cell. "I'm doing better," I said. It wasn't much of a defense but it was the only one I had.

"Better than what? First you were a zombie, then you played town drunk and screwed anyone who'd stand still long enough. This past year you've been about as sociable as Howard Hughes. How about a return to normal? She's gone."

"Stand still long enough?"

"Oh, shut up."

"Howard Hughes is dead anyway."

"I know, think about it. And if you aren't going to say anything, just don't talk."

Sounded like a good idea to me. I looked out the window. Melissa was sitting on the lawn beside the pool, her skin dappled with sunshine and shade from the juniper tree. She was yanking up fistfuls of grass and tossing them into the air. Her dark hair was flecked with green and so was the water in the pool.

"You shouldn't go out drinking wearing a gun anyway," Carrie said.

"I don't know why I shouldn't but I didn't anyway if that makes you feel better. I walked over here from the Honky Tonk. The gun was in the trunk and I didn't want to leave it. I'll be lucky if the car isn't stripped and up on blocks when I go get it. Or stolen."

"God, who would want it? You know what your problem is?"

"Yeah, I have a hangover."

"You have a bad case of inertia."

"Leave me alone, Carolina." The use of her given name had been forbidden since high school when she was taunted with that oldie-but-goodie about nothing being finer than being in Carolina in the morning. Since their marriage, I'd heard Tom whistle the tune a few thousand times and the looks Carrie gave him had nothing to do with anger so maybe the name didn't bother her much any more.

At any rate, she ignored my attempt to make her too mad to talk to me.

"Do you know what I'm talking about?" she asked.

"Jesus. I took physics. Inertia," I recited, "the tendency of matter at rest to remain at rest unless acted upon by an external force."

"Well, that's you. Matter at rest. And you won't let an external force anywhere near you. Why don't you ask someone out?"

"I don't remember how."

"For crying out loud. Go hang around the Starlight Club in a T-shirt. You won't have to ask."

I considered her advice briefly. "Should I wear pants?"

Carrie's laugh was pure reflex and she tried to stop it with her hands. When she stopped sputtering, I said, "There's another part to inertia. The tendency of matter in motion to continue moving in the same direction unless et cetera. I was moving downhill. I'm better off standing still."

"It isn't just women. You don't do anything. You sit out there in a half-finished house feeling sorry for yourself. And getting drunk on your wedding anniversary is just plain pathetic."

"I do my job. Which reminds me, I should see if I have any calls." I put my empty cup in the dishwasher and picked up the receiver of the wall phone. Carrie started talking so I held the hang-up button down with my thumb.

"Do you remember about a year ago we were over at your house and I was lying down nursing Melissa and I mentioned that your bed was sloshing something awful and you said you needed to burp it?"

I didn't remember but I nodded anyway.

"And last *week* we were there and Melissa was playing on the bed and it was sloshing and you said you needed to burp it?"

That I remembered so I nodded again.

"Well, in a whole year you haven't managed to burp your bed."

I closed my eyes briefly, in genuine pain. "What the hell is that? Symbolism? My life is an unburped waterbed?"

"I don't know about symbolism but it's certainly symptomatic."

With as much dignity as possible, which wasn't much, I said, "I do not believe that burping my bed will significantly improve my state of mind."

I turned to the phone and tapped out my office number. Carrie stood beside me, gripping my upper arm hard in both hands and pressing her forehead against my shoulder. The phone rang six times before it was answered. It was supposed to be picked up on the third ring but I never complained. The operators at the Main Street Answering Service had been known to do some above-and-beyond-the-call-of-duty errands for me.

Marilyn, whom I knew only by her high-pitched voice, trilled "Arrow Investigations."

"Hi. Anyone want me?"

"Yes, hang on . . . here it is. A Mr. Jason Finney wants you to call." She gave me the number, just five digits because all the phones in Mackie start with the same two numbers. I jotted the number on Carrie's wall calendar and asked if he'd mentioned what it was about.

"Well, no." Marilyn sounded hesitant. I waited. Mackie is a small town. "You want some gossip?" she asked.

"Shoot," I said.

"Bang," Marilyn said and giggled. Her giggle was an octave or two higher than her voice and set off a throbbing ache behind my eyes. "Okay," she said. "My kid hangs out with a kid named Hank Johnston and Hank Johnston has been steady-dating a girl named Jessica Finney. And Jessica Finney ran away from home a couple days ago."

Another runaway. Just what I needed. "Thanks, Marilyn. I may not replace you with an answering machine after all."

"Where are you going to find a machine that'll accept collect calls from heavy breathers?"

"You got a point," I said and told her good-bye. I replaced the receiver and rubbed my cheek against the top of Carrie's head. "You worry too much," I said. "I'm fine." She nodded and after a moment she let go of me and went outside.

I thumbed through the phone book while Finney's line was ringing. A woman answered and asked me to hold on. I found Finney's listing. His address was in Mackie's highest-priced neighborhood, which either meant he could afford me or he was in over his head and couldn't.

A man said "Finney here" into my ear. Our conversation was brief. He asked when he could see me in my office. It was almost noon so I suggested one o'clock. He said fine and hung up on me.

"If I were your kid, I'd run away, too," I told the dead phone and hung it up.

I took a bag of nacho-flavored Doritos with me and joined Carrie at the redwood picnic table in the backyard. She had *The Oregonian* spread all over the table and had the Living section open to the page where Ann Landers and Dear Abby nestled together in sisterly camaraderie. Carrie seemed to be engrossed in other people's problems and I didn't want to talk about mine anyway so I ate the chips and studied her face, an activity that provided me with endless, if somewhat guilty, enjoyment.

Her naturally straight black hair had been permed into a mass of loose curls that softened the square lines of her face. She had never liked her nose with its distinctive rise at the bridge but a lesser nose would have looked silly with the strong cheekbones and jaw and the wide mouth. Her eyes were downcast but I knew the color well — bright summer-sky blue. The long vertical creases set back in her cheeks were barely visible but would deepen considerably if she smiled. She looked up, not smiling at all, looking a bit offended in fact.

"Am I crunching too loudly?" I asked.

"You're staring too loudly."

"Oh. I was just thinking how pretty you are."

She raised a skeptical eyebrow. "That's sweet, I guess. A bit narcissistic perhaps, but sweet." She went back to reading the paper and I watched my niece who was trying to empty her pool with a spoon from a toy tea set.

A few minutes later, Melissa emitted a squeal of glass-shattering intensity as Tom came through the wrought iron gate. He plucked his daughter from the pool for a quick hug, then returned her and walked to the table, fanning the wet fabric of his shirt against his chest. He was in tennis whites and with the pale hair, blue eyes, and deep tan he looked just like a southern California tennis pro which was exactly what he had been while he was working his way through medical school. He had recently closed his private practice to take a position as a full-time emergency room doctor at Mackie General Hospital.

He greeted Carrie with "Hello, Yin" and a kiss, greeted me with "Hello, Yang" without a kiss, said "How's tricks, Junior?" to his wife's belly and asked if the fight was over.

"We didn't fight," Carrie and I said in perfect unison.

Tom laughed and Carrie said, "Well, we didn't. I just gave him some good advice."

"What advice?"

"She told me to go home and burp my fucking bed."

Tom waggled his eyebrows. "As opposed to your sleeping bed?"

Carrie and I groaned, again in unison.

"On that note," I said, "I think I'll leave."

A few minutes later, with my Reeboks on my sockless feet and last night's clothes and my gun strapped into the child carrier behind me, I pedaled down the long driveway on Tom's ten-speed.

Tom and Carrie's remodeled farmhouse on Franklin Street is the very last house at the west end of Mackie. At the edge of their big lot, Franklin ends in a T-intersection. The cross street is Bunyard Road. Six miles west on Bunyard is my house. To the east, less than three miles away, is downtown Mackie. Somewhere along the way to town Bunyard Road becomes Main Street, a name that retains its original significance since the closest Mackie comes to a shopping center is Safeway and Payless sharing a big building at the north end of town.

I slowed at the T-intersection while a blue BMW made a wide left turn onto Franklin. The driver was Carrie's next-door neighbor and my ex-boss, Robert Harkins, Chief of Police. Our eyes met briefly and without warmth. I pedaled on into town, stirring up enough of a breeze to make the ninety-plus temperature seem almost pleasant.

CHAPTER TWO

THE FINNEYS ARRIVED TOGETHER IN SEPARATE cars. Hers was a shiny new Volvo. His was a shiny new Bronco.

He was about five-ten and looked as if he did a lot of jogging. His brown hair was sun-streaked, his skin tanned to a golden bronze. He looked like a health spa ad but there was a tension in his movements that made me think his first coronary wasn't too far in the future.

She probably looked better first thing in the morning before she got the make-up on. Her nice brown eyes were overpowered by bright blue eye-shadow and the lashes had to obstruct her vision. Her hair was over-bleached and cut in a bluntly cropped style all the teenage girls were currently sporting. The white one-piece thing she was wearing over a turquoise tank top was designed to look like housepainters' overalls but the legs were short-shorts length. There was a hint of softness beneath the overalls and although her arms and legs were slim, there was no definition of muscle. I suspected she got her perfect tan from a tanning salon and her slimness from chronic dieting.

He was Jason. She was Lily. They both read my T-shirt during the introductions. Lily smiled at it. Jason didn't. While his wife checked out my legs, he checked out the office. The small room was neat and clean and smelled faintly of pine cleaner. There were two captain's chairs in front of the big oak desk and a padded swivel chair behind it. The remainder of the furnishings consisted of plants, way too many plants, most of them suspended from the ceiling.

Jason raised his eyebrows at Tom's ten-speed which I had parked beside the door. His wife raised her eyes to my thighs. I went behind the desk and gestured toward the two chairs in front of it. We all sat down. Lily's gaze moved to my chest. Her mouth was slightly open and she ran her tongue back and forth across the bottoms of her top teeth.

Her husband said, "You seem to be the only private investigator in town."

"Yeah, I am. I expect to be hit with an anti-trust suit any day now."

Lily laughed. Jason had no sense of humor. He looked at all four walls, probably checking for a no-smoking sign, then pulled a cigarette out of a pack in his shirt pocket and a thin gold lighter from his pants pocket. He lit up. I scooped the paper clips out of an ashtray and slid it across the desk to him. Lily crossed her legs and checked out my shoulders, her eyes darting rapidly from side to side.

Jason exhaled smoke and said, "I assume you can give us references."

I pulled a paper out of the file drawer in the desk and handed it to him. He glanced at the list of law offices and insurance companies for which Arrow Investigations investigated.

"What about . . . uh . . . private clients?"

"They're private."

"How much do you charge?"

I looked out the window where at least fifty thousand dollars' worth of wheels were adding a touch of class to the neighborhood. I gave him a second sheet of paper, this one giving a detailed explanation of my fees.

Lily said, "Aren't you supposed to say two hundred dollars a day plus expenses?"

I smiled at her but she didn't notice. She was finding my biceps fascinating. "I will when I get a series," I said.

Lily was easy to amuse. Jason made a sarcastic sound. I assumed he had already figured out just how much of my time two hundred dollars would buy. He continued to look at my fee sheet. Lily looked at my forearms. I looked at the two of them. They hadn't looked at each other since they'd walked in the door.

Jason took a final deep drag on his cigarette and knocked the ash off in my paper clip holder. A spiral of smoke faded en route to the ceiling. The silence stretched out. Jason drummed his fingers sound-

lessly against his thigh. Lily continued her anatomy
studies. I wondered what she would do if I told her
I wasn't wearing any underwear. I wondered what
Jason would do. I cleared my throat.

"You folks want me to look for your daughter?"

Jason's jaw dropped. Lily actually looked at my
face for a moment. I'd have to send flowers to
Marilyn. Maybe that was sexist, maybe I'd just
stop by the answering service and slap her on the
back.

"How'd you know that?" Jason immediately
looked sorry that he had asked.

I shrugged. "I'm a detective."

He shifted up on one hip to get at his lighter and
lit another cigarette. "God damn small towns anyway," he said. "Why can't the little bitch think about
someone besides herself once in a while?"

"Jason," Lily said, without looking at him. There
was a bit of warning in her tone but she didn't put
much energy into it. Jason ignored her. I had the
feeling Jason spent a lot of time ignoring her. Probably just as well though. Her eyes were half closed,
her head tilted slightly back. Unless I missed my
guess completely, Lily was in the middle of a sexual
fantasy.

I asked if they had filed a police report. They had.

"They weren't interested," Jason said. "I suppose
they have more important things to do." He
laughed without even a hint of humor. "Biggest
crime in this town is some asshole parking in a

handicapped spot. And all the goddamn drugs and the cops sure as hell aren't doing anything about that."

"How long has she been missing?"

Evidently that was Lily's department. She emerged from her reverie and wriggled her butt around on the chair. "She left Wednesday morning," she said.

"Tell me what happened."

"Same old thing."

Lily was right. It was the same old thing. Jessica Ann Finney, sole offspring of Jason and Lily, had spent the summer of her fourteenth year using her parents' home as a pit stop between outings. They set an eleven o'clock curfew; Jessica came in at twelve. They agreed to a twelve o'clock curfew; Jessica came in at one. They didn't approve of the boy she was dating; she went out with him twice as often. They fought about clothes, hair, friends, housework, homework, money, make-up, and music.

Wednesday morning had been routine. The three of them went round and round, then Jessica stomped off to her room. A few minutes later, she reappeared carrying a small backpack and her navy blue Mackie High jacket with the gold mustang on the back. With very little originality, she screamed, "I hate you both and I'm never coming back." She ran out of the house. Jason and Lily weren't particularly concerned. They expected her to return. She didn't.

"How much money did she have?" I asked.

"About a hundred dollars, a little less, I think. She's saving for her own VCR. She keeps her money in her jewelry box and it's gone." Lily looked bored with the whole subject.

I asked them a lot of other questions. They answered a few. They didn't know much about their daughter, which wasn't surprising. If there had been any communication going on, they wouldn't have been spending a sunny Sunday afternoon in my office.

Jessica had been dating Hank Johnston for three or four months. "He lives over there," Jason said, jerking his head eastward toward the part of Mackie that would be on the wrong side of the tracks if Mackie had any tracks. I jotted down Johnston's address.

The only girlfriend Jessica seemed to have was Celia Baines. I wrote her address down too when Jason gave it to me although I already knew where she lived. Jason pointed out several times that they had been looking for Jessica since Wednesday and there was no point in talking to anyone in Mackie. I got tired of listening to him.

"Do you know if she's sexually active?" I asked.

An uncomfortable silence was finally broken by Jason. "Why do you need to know that?"

"It's a matter of the options available to her."

Jason looked offended.

"Look, I know this isn't easy," I said. "I'm not asking just for the hell of it. I spend a lot of time looking for runaway kids. They all want to go to California but they don't have enough money to get there so they go to Portland where they end up living on the street. Within a month half of them are supporting themselves by prostitution."

The Finneys looked at each other for the first time. I wasn't sure their eyes met but at least they looked toward each other.

"She's been on the pill since December," Lily said.

Jason's hands clenched on the arms of his chair. The wood creaked under the pressure. Lily looked amused.

I gave them my standard I'm-not-a-child-psychologist-but-I-know-a-lot-about-runaways speech, the gist of it being that I might find Jessica and bring her home but if nothing changed, she'd run again. They sat through it without comment. When I finished, Jason said they'd worry about that when she was home again. He shifted restlessly in his chair. "Is that about it?" he asked.

"When can I see her room?"

"What on earth for?" Lily asked.

"Believe it or not, to look for clues."

"We're going home from here," Jason said. "Any time is fine."

I gave him some forms to sign. He gave me a

check. Lily gave me several photos of Jessica. Jason walked to the door and stood there briefly, jiggling the doorknob back and forth and looking at his wife's legs. He walked out without saying good-bye.

Lily was taking her time getting organized to leave. She rummaged through her purse and finally pulled out a pair of sunglasses which she put on top of her head. She stood up, adjusted the purse strap on her shoulder several times, then dug through it again to find her car keys. I was at the door by that time, politely holding it for her. The Bronco was idling roughly just outside.

Lily stopped in front of me and tapped my chest with a long pink fingernail. "Is this true?" she asked.

I looked out the door. Jason was wearing his sunglasses where they belonged. Lily flattened her hand and moved it in a slow circle over my chest. "Is it?" she asked.

The Bronco swung backward in a wild arc and bounced off the curb into the street. The knobby tires shrieked against the pavement as Jason headed home.

"Bigger is often better in a fight, Mrs. Finney. I could beat the shit out of your husband, but I don't really want to. So why don't you run along home and I'll see what I can do about finding your daughter. I know how worried you are."

She drew her fingers together, her nails raking

my chest. "Bastard," she said and walked out. Her car bounced off the curb, too.

Chapter Three

I SAT BEHIND MY DESK, RUBBING THE FEEL OF Lily's nails off my chest and studying a recent five-by-seven photo of her daughter. Jessica looked a little like each of her parents. She had Lily's brown eyes and heart-shaped face and Jason's slender nose and small mouth. Her brown hair was cropped just below the ears. Fifteen years ago I would have considered her sexy. Now she looked like a child.

I checked my notes. There wasn't a lot to go on. Jason was a consultant for a development corporation, whatever that meant, and was transferred regularly. They had lived in Mackie for eighteen months. Jessica hated Mackie. She had hated Pennsylvania before Mackie and Florida before Pennsylvania. She hadn't kept in touch with friends in either place. The relatives were all in Indiana. Jessica hated the relatives and hated Indiana, too. She also hated the sightseeing excursions her parents had dragged her on around the Northwest. But she loved Portland. They had been there three times, the last time in June for the Rose Festival.

I smiled at Jessica's permanent smile. If she was

in Portland now, she was going to find out that living on the street isn't quite the same as roughing it at the Hilton with Daddy picking up the tab. I put the photo in a manila envelope and took it with me while I went next door to get coffee.

For the past sixteen months, Fanciful Flowers had occupied the other half of my building. Before that, it had been rented by a succession of businesses memorable mostly for the rapidity with which they failed. Fanciful Flowers was thriving in spite of a somewhat unfavorable location on the corner of Main Street that separated downtown from the oldest, and now poorest, residential district.

I walked into the flower shop and caught the co-owners holding hands. They were still in the closet but kept forgetting to close the door. Once, during my year of debauchery, I spent a drunken night in bed with both of them. I had fond hopes that their memories of the occasion were as hazy as mine.

I smiled at Rosie, who said, "Hi, Zacky," in her breathy little-girl voice. A couple years ago, she was runner-up in a Marilyn Monroe look-alike contest. I'd have given her first place myself. Her partner Myrna, a tall brunette with a plain face made remarkable by a pair of astounding green eyes, had recently researched our mutual roots to figure out how we were related. She finally decided on second cousins twice-removed. Neither of us was too sure what that meant. Nothing incestuous anyway.

I included Myrna in my smile and she said, "Hi, cuz," and admired my T-shirt. Possibly she was being facetious. I said it never hurt to advertise. Rosie gave me a cup of coffee, mentioning that I looked like I needed it, and I sympathized in all the right places as they told me about some horrendous problem with a delivery of roses. After a second cup of coffee, I set out to find Jessica Finney.

I walked six blocks to the bus depot. Nobody remembered seeing Jessica and the cops had already been there asking about her anyway. I walked three blocks farther to the Honky Tonk.

My car was right where I left it. The old Chevy Nova was on its second engine and the third or fourth of just about every other moving part. The sky-blue paint had long since faded to the color of smog. I liked the car. It was dependable and inconspicuous and had been built before some fool designed away wing windows. I had locked it up tight the night before and its internal temperature was about a hundred and fifty degrees. I rolled the windows down and pushed it thirty feet across the parking lot to the nearest shade, then I went into the bar to use the telephone in the owner's office while the car cooled off.

I didn't find out much that was useful about Jessica. Ellen Finch, a counselor who had been an

English teacher when I was at Mackie High, said that Jessica, who had completed her freshman year in June, kept to herself and, except academically, stayed out of trouble.

"She's a strange one, Zack," Miss Finch said. "For the first half of each semester she did absolutely nothing but show up for classes and the failing slips went home regularly. Then all of a sudden she buckled down, aced all the tests, and did a lot of extra credit work. She ended up with C's and could be an A student if she made the effort. She was at the middle school for one semester and the pattern was the same there. I talked to her but unfortunately she didn't talk to me. Her home life seems picture-perfect on the surface but I suspect there's a lot of unhappiness there."

My other calls were to several high school students I know. I caught three of them at home. All three knew Jessica was missing but didn't know her well enough to make a guess about her whereabouts. All three mentioned that she kept to herself most of the time. Two of them said they were surprised Hank Johnston went out with her because he was a junior and the star of the track team. Before Hank, Jessica had dated nerds. There were strong hints that Hank's primary interest in her was sexual. The two of them went off by themselves, seldom showing up at parties or the usual teen hang-outs.

I decided to go see Hank.

The Johnstons lived a few blocks east of my office in a neighborhood of weather-worn houses. I parked in front of a tired two-story house and approached a man in a dirty T-shirt and olive drab work pants who was sitting on the sagging porch steps. I asked if he was Hank's father. After a long drag on a cigarette, he agreed that he was. When I asked if I could speak to Hank, Johnston flipped the cigarette butt into the yard and took another look at the business card I had handed him.

"What's he done?" he asked.

"Nothing. I just want to ask him some questions."

He studied the smoke drifting off the butt in the grass then jerked his chin toward four boys who were horsing around in an empty lot across the street. "The blond kid," he said. I thanked him and turned away. "He don't know where the little bitch is," Johnston added.

The four boys were arguing loudly about several different subjects. The only one facing me was a fat boy in loud Hawaiian-print shorts and a clashing tank top. He was leaning against a broken cement wall and as I approached he poked the end of what appeared to be an entire Twinkie into his mouth.

Hank Johnston, his back to me, said, "Hey, lard ass, didn't anyone ever tell you, you are what you eat? You're a Twinkie, man. All soft and white and gooshy. If someone squeezed you all this white goo would ooze out."

The fat kid, spitting Twinkie crumbs and cream, said, "Yeah? Well, if you are what you eat, you know what you are? You're a pussy. Hank's a pussy," he repeated, in case the others missed it the first time. The two of them, a skinny redhead and a muscular dark-haired boy, collapsed on the ground in hysterics. The redhead kicked his legs in the air, chanting, "Hank's a pussy, Hank's a pussy." Hank kicked at the flailing legs and missed.

The fat kid suddenly decided to notice me and straightened up, yanking the tank top down over his white belly and wiping Twinkie off his mouth. "Hey," he said, "I know you. You're the drug guy."

"Anti-drug guy," I said.

The two kids on the ground got up and slumped against the wall next to the fat boy. Hank stood a little apart from them and took a quick look across the street.

"I need to talk to Hank for a minute," I told the three wall-leaners. They didn't take the hint. The fat kid pulled a bag of salted peanuts out of his shorts pocket, ripped it open, and dumped the contents into his mouth. The empty bag joined the litter already on the ground.

"You aren't a cop anymore, right?" Hank said.

"Right," I said. I handed him a business card. He took it uncertainly. "Oh, yeah," he said after he finally got around to reading it, "Jess's old man sic you on me?"

"No. He hired me to look for her."

"Shit, I don't know where she is. She didn't tell me she was splitting. I didn't even know she was gone until her old man called up and ragged my ass about it. He's a real prick."

"You are what you eat," the fat kid said and all four boys guffawed lewdly. I kept a straight face out of professional courtesy to my client.

"When did you see her last?" I asked Hank.

"I dunno. Saturday. We went out." He shrugged.

"What parts of her did you see, Hank?" The redhead was grinning maniacally.

"Shut up, shithead," Hank said without looking at him. The redhead's grin faded. "I talked to her Tuesday. On the phone." He shrugged again. "We didn't talk about anything."

"You have any idea where she might go, a friend's house maybe?"

"Naw." Hank took a few steps away from his friends. I followed. The other boys seemed to get the message and drifted noisily toward the back of the lot.

"Naw," Hank said again. "Jess is kind of a . . . a loner, I guess. Celia, Celia Baines, is about her only friend and if she was over there, Celia's old man would kick her ass out into the street. He thinks Jess is a bad influence on her. Shit, Celia don't need any influence to be bad. The other girls, they think Jess is kinda stuck up, thinks she's better than them, you know what I mean?"

I nodded.

"She isn't really like that. She's kinda shy really, but she tries to act like she isn't, so people think she's snotty. She's kinda funny. Different." Hank grinned suddenly, dropping the blank mask of an adolescent talking to an authority figure. He had big dimples that he had probably hated before discovering their effect on nubile young girls.

"She wants to be an actress," he said. "One time she had this book of plays she got out of the library. Not like Shakespeare, you know, modern stuff. Anyway she was reading out of it to me and it was like she turned into someone else, into the person in the play, you know what I mean? Shit, she's probably hitching down to Hollywood." His expression became anxious. "You think you'll find her?"

"That's hard to say," I said, easily enough.

"Yeah. Well, if you find her . . . well, anyway, I wish she'd come back. Her folks are shitty but it isn't like they beat her or something." Hank shot a quick look over to the porch where his dad was puffing on another cigarette. He looked back at me with a guilty expression.

"If you hear from her, give me a call. The number's on the card."

Hank smoothed out my card which he had rolled into a tiny tube. "Yeah, sure. Listen, Jess isn't like people think. She's just, I don't know, lonely. I wish she'd come back." He watched his hands roll my card up again. "Hey, are you going to talk at the school this year? Most of that drug stuff is boring but you tell funny stories."

I said I probably was and thanked him. I walked back to my car, nodding at the man on the porch steps whose son was going to be a whole lot bigger than he was in a couple of years.

I drove over to the Baines' house, wondering whether the kids got anything but a few laughs out of the talk I gave every year for the drug abuse prevention program.

"Funny stories." I had whiled away my early teens becoming addicted to just about every illegal substance short of heroin and had spent most of my sophomore year of high school in a residential drug treatment center. When I was released, drug-free and sworn to remain so, we moved from Los Angeles to Mackie. My parents had a sincere belief that drugs would be less readily available to tempt me in the small town where they'd both been raised. They were wrong, but I stayed clean any-way, mostly because of Carrie but also because I was afraid that if I screwed up again I'd be living in a tent in the Yukon. Moving from L.A. to the back end of Oregon had resulted in major culture shock. Carrie never would have forgiven me if she hadn't felt so guilty about helping me conceal my addiction. We had both sworn, loudly and repeatedly, that we were leaving Mackie the day we turned eighteen.

We did leave, just before our eighteenth birthday in fact, but we only went as far as Portland State and we both returned four years later. I came back because Mackie's was the only police department in the state that was hiring at the time. Carrie came back because home is where the heart is and Tom Harry was in Mackie. Now our thirtieth birthday was just a few weeks away and Carrie's heart was still in Mackie. Mine wasn't but I didn't have the energy or the good sense to pack up and leave.

I cut short my musings as I pulled up in front of the Baines' house. No one was home. I decided to go look for clues in Jessica's bedroom.

CHAPTER FOUR

THE FINNEYS LIVED IN MACKIE'S NEW-MONEY SEC-
tion where most of the streets are cul-de-sacs and
most of the houses are custom-built ranches.
Theirs was a sprawling gray stone structure on a
big wedge-shaped lot. Lily let me in without a
welcoming smile.

The main rooms of the house opened into one
another through wide squared-off arches. The furnishings were ultra-modern to the point of being
futuristic, with glass and chrome predominating.
The walls that didn't have huge windows had huge
mirrors. The effect was of endless space. I'd seen
display rooms at Levitz that looked more lived-in.

Lily led me through what I guessed was a family
room although it had none of the coziness that term
implies. Jason was on the phone. He smiled and
waved as we passed. Maybe he was accustomed
to his wife sexually harassing the hired help.

After a trek down a long hall, Lily opened a door
and stood aside for me to enter. I took a quick look
and asked if she had straightened up since Jessica
left.

"No," she said. "She's responsible for her own

room. I'm sure you don't need me." She walked away. Lily was still mad at me but I was too amazed by her daughter's bedroom to worry about it. When Carrie was Jessica's age, her bedroom's decor had consisted largely of discarded panty-hose, empty record jackets, and posters of current idols. My room was the same except I had sweat socks instead of pantyhose and, since I couldn't open the closet door without moving the rowing machine, my wardrobe tended to accumulate in piles on every flat surface.

Jessica's room was large and airy, full of sunshine streaming through filmy pink curtains. The furni-ture was white wood, the carpet was deep rose, the bedspread was a rose and white print that matched the wallpaper. The only wall decorations were two oil paintings of pink flowers in white vases. The bed was made, the dresser top held only a few decorative items, there was nothing tossed casually on the floor, nothing anywhere to indicate the room had been occupied within the past few days. It looked like a guest room. A seldom-used guest room. I couldn't picture a re-bellious fourteen-year-old in it. I shrugged at my-self in the mirrored closet door. At least it would be easy to search.

I started at the door and went clockwise around the room. I found a diary in the back of a drawer full of neatly folded panties and thought "Ah-ha." Prematurely, as it turned out. She had made entries for six consecutive days. The first one, dated November 12, consisted of a list of birthday presents including the diary I was reading. The remaining entries read like an appointment calendar, "movies with Celia" being the only one that didn't involve a school assignment. I put the little book back and moved on.

In her sock drawer, I found a pack of Zig-Zags and a small amount of marijuana in an otherwise empty Tampax box. I unrolled each of the three dozen or so pairs of knee socks and anklets looking for more drugs. I didn't find any. I moved on again.

My last stop was the small bookcase next to the door. I was tempted to skip it. I had found nothing in the room that gave any real clue to Jessica's personality, let alone her whereabouts. There were at least fifty books, most of them matched sets of book club classics. I began pulling them out one by one, checking behind them and riffling the pages. I was about halfway through when I fanned the pages of a volume of twentieth-century American poetry and two envelopes fell out. One was from the Rose City School of Performing Arts. The other was from the Northwest Acting and Modeling School. Both schools were in Portland. Both envelopes were addressed to Jessica. Both had July postmarks. And both were empty.

I put them aside and went quickly through the rest of the books. The envelopes were the closest thing to a clue I found. I took them with me and found Jason and Lily in the family room, apparently doing nothing but waiting for me.

With enough sarcasm to make Jason look embarrassed, Lily said, "Well, did you find any clues?"

"Do you know anything about these?"

She took the envelopes and glanced at them. "No. I don't read her mail. I don't remember these coming." She handed them to Jason, who shook his head.

"Hank said she's interested in acting. She must have sent away for information. If she makes it to Portland, she might go by these places. Do you know if she made any long distance calls?"

Lily explained that Jason made a lot of business calls from home so she always checked the bill carefully for tax purposes. There had been no unaccounted-for long distance calls. She agreed to check with the phone company in the morning to see if Jessica had made any calls since the last bill had come.

"There's some marijuana in her sock drawer," I said.

Jason looked blank. Lily shrugged. I told them I still needed to talk to Celia Baines and found my own way out, walking through cold rooms brilliant with reflected sunlight. There's more than one kind of house that isn't a home.

I drove the short distance to Celia's house. No one was home again. I stopped by my office to pick up my gun and Tom's bike and drove over to see what the Harrys had in their refrigerator.

Tom and Carrie were necking in the backyard hammock when I arrived. They came inside and stood around exchanging meaningful looks for a couple of minutes then disappeared upstairs, leaving me with Melissa who was demanding every other bite of my potato salad.

I called the Baines' house every twenty minutes and listened to their phone ring. At five-thirty, I finally got a busy signal. Just in time, too. Melissa had been playing horsie for an hour and the horsie's knees were about to give out. I gave a loud dog-calling whistle at the foot of the stairs and after a couple of minutes Carrie came down, sleepy-eyed and wrapped in a blue terry-cloth robe.

"Have a nice nap?" I asked.

"Mm," she said. "You should drop by more often. What are you working on?"

"Runaway girl. Fourteen."

"Think you'll find her?"

"I think if I don't, she'll be peddling her cute little ass all over Portland before long."

"Why'd she run away?"

"The usual. Mommy and Daddy are too busy fucking up their own lives to keep her from fucking up hers."

"It isn't always the parents' fault, Zachariah." Carrie brushed her fingers lightly through her daughter's soft dark hair.

"No, but the parents are always several years older. That should put a little of the burden of responsibility on them. They should at least be able to recognize a problem when it's staring them in the face."

"Mom and Dad never knew what you were doing."

"I never gave them any clues. If I'd had the good sense to flunk out of school like any self-respecting dope fiend, they'd have figured it out. Besides, they never know what the hell's going on. They're always too busy trying to stop a war, or save a whale, or shut down a nuclear power plant, or paint a baby animal green. They never know what's going on right under their noses. Jesus, if you mention you're hungry, you get a lecture on Ethiopia."

Carrie had stopped listening. She'd heard it all before anyway. She was standing with her head bowed, one hand pressed against her stomach, a look of complete inward concentration on her face. She grabbed my hand suddenly and pressed it to what used to be her waist. There was a rolling swell of flesh against my palm. I felt myself grinning idiotically. It didn't matter. Carrie was grinning the same grin.

"Six more weeks," she said. "If you go to Portland, bring me a present."

"I will," I said and swung Melissa up to still her frantic "me, me" with a kiss. "I wouldn't forget you, punkin. A present for Missy and a present for Sissy and that should just about take care of my profit."

I kissed them both good-bye and drove back over to the Baines' house. They lived in a middle-income subdivision adjacent to the Finney's ritzier neighborhood. Donna Baines, a vaguely pretty, easily-rattled brunette, answered my knock and became confused.

"Oh, dear. Well," she said. "It hasn't fallen off the walls." She laughed uncertainly.

"That's good," I said. I had hung all the wallpaper in the house during Donna's frenzied remodeling two years ago. I handed her a business card to remind her that hanging paper was only my sideline and explained what I wanted.

"Oh, dear. Well. You want to talk to Celia?" She solved the problem the way I suspected she solved all life's problems. "You'll have to talk to Joe," she said.

She motioned for me to follow her. The house was a cluttery hodge-podge of styles and colors that I liked much better than the Finneys' showcase. Donna's burly husband was in the kitchen, drinking a Bud Light and reading the *Mackie Mirror*. Yesterday's, I assumed, since the paper was only published on Wednesdays and Saturdays. Donna busied herself with the brown bags of groceries that were sitting on the counter without explaining my presence to Joe. It didn't matter. Joe

Baines was not easily rattled and knew exactly why I was there.

"Celia doesn't know where Jessica is," he said, without wasting words on a greeting.

"I'd like to talk to her anyway."

He mulled it over for a bit then said, "She's out back." I followed him out the sliding glass door. Behind me, Donna said, "Oh, dear, dear."

Celia was indeed out back and most of her was visible. Like her mother, she was pretty in a vague way. Her face was childish and was light years behind her body, development-wise. The tiny coral bikini served only to call attention to what it was supposed to conceal. Joe stood behind her the whole time we talked, looking at me look at his daughter. I worked very hard at keeping my eyes on her face.

If Celia recognized me as the nice man who had pasted pastel rainbows all over her bedroom walls, she gave no sign of it. She stared at the grass between our feet and denied knowing anything about Jessica. Few people are good liars and Celia wasn't one of them. She was lying through the braces glinting on her teeth.

I considered her father briefly, then said, "If Jessica's out on her own someplace, she could be in big trouble. She could be raped. Or murdered."

Joe glowered and took a step closer to his daughter. Celia, true to her heritage, said, "Oh, dear." She chewed on her lower lip and shot a quick look over her shoulder at Joe. "Wait a minute," she said to me and headed for the house.

Joe said "Shit" and spit into the grass.

We stood silently until Celia returned with an envelope in her hand and a completely non-functional white lace cover-up over her bikini. She handed the envelope to Joe who pulled a sheet of notebook paper out of it. He read it quickly then handed it to me saying, "When the hell did this come?"

"Yesterday." Celia was pouting prettily.

"Goddammit, her dad's called here a dozen times."

The note was brief: "Dear Celia, I couldn't stand it any more. I hate my parents and I hate Mackie. I'm never coming back. Don't tell anyone you heard from me. Love, Jessica." The I in the signature was dotted with a tiny star.

The letter was typical of runaways, a pointless contact with home serving no purpose other than reaffirming the writer's existence. The envelope was postmarked Thursday. The zip code on the cancellation was for Portland's main post office. There was no return address.

"I'd like to show this to her parents," I said.

"Sure." The looks Joe was giving his daughter boded ill for a peaceful Sunday evening at the Baines'. I thanked them both and left by the side gate to avoid Donna who was probably "oh dear"-ing herself into hysterics in the kitchen.

Five minutes later I was back at the Finneys' house. Jason was obviously shaken by the evidence that Jessica had actually left town. For the first time, Lily seemed to take her daughter's disappearance seriously. I embarrassed her by catching her staring across the room at a portrait of a much younger Jessica. With very little discussion, we agreed that I would leave for Portland in the morning.

I went back to my office where I unlocked the heavy fire door behind the desk. The back room was much larger than the front room but not nearly as neat or clean and smelled faintly of old paper. One of the battered file cabinets against the left wall contained current records. The rest were full of thirty years' worth of Jake Matthews' records. At the rear of the room, two closed doors concealed a bathroom with a shower stall and a storage closet I had stopped using the second time I found a black widow in it.

Beneath a barred opaque window on the right wall, a long work table was cluttered with three or four telephones, a guitar with two broken strings, a wadded-up Taco Bell bag, an electric typewriter, and a two-year-old computer that I was going to learn to use someday. I tossed the Taco Bell bag into a wastebasket and sat down to type Jessica's description on a missing person form that discreetly mentioned a reward in two-inch high letters. Beneath a space for a picture were the words

"Arrow Investigations" followed by my post office box address and telephone number. Beneath the phone number, in bold letters, were the words "CALL COLLECT." Mackie is a toll call from everywhere but Mackie. People could watch Amelia Earhart make an overdue landing on an interstate in rush hour and wouldn't report it if it ran up their phone bills. I taped the three-by-five photo of Jessica into place and walked down to the print shop to get copies made.

By seven o'clock I was home. I tucked the Nova into the space next to the four-wheel drive that summered in the garage and earned its keep getting me through Mackie's miserable winters. I checked the Nova's oil and water, kicked a couple of tires, opened the trunk and checked the tool box. Everything was in order for my trip to Portland.

I wandered around the garage, straightening a few tools on the pegboard and peering into the freezer. Then I pulled the tarp off Carrie's birthday present and ran my hand along the smooth wood. I had found the carousel horse in the back lot of a junk store. I had cleaned it up and sanded it down and painted it gleaming sky-blue and gold. All I needed to do was get a pole and cement it into Carrie's back yard.

I opened the freezer again and picked out a pint of strawberry cheesecake ice cream which I ate standing up with a spoon from my camping gear.

When I finished, I tossed the carton into the garbage can, stuck my hands in my back pockets and rocked back and forth on my heels. That got old in a hurry. I couldn't think of any other way to stall. I got my gun and the bundle of clothes from the car and unlocked the connecting door to the house.

I stepped into the hall.

The soft swell of classical music greeted me.

Home sweet home.

Shit.

I tossed my clothes into the laundry room to my left. Next to it was a bathroom with a shower stall. To the right was a big pantry. Directly ahead was the kitchen. I walked quickly through it, putting my gun down on the long curving counter that separated it from the dining area of the family room. I walked the length of the family room and switched the stereo to a station playing hard rock, turning the volume up so the driving beat would make it hard to think. I went down a short hallway, past the closed door of a half bath, and then I was in the front entry.

I stopped dead.

After a moment, I leaned back against the front door. To my left was the hall I'd just come down. To my right, a curved arch opened into the living room which was full of heavy oak furniture that April and I had found in second-hand stores and spent months restoring. The gleaming hardwood floor was bare except for a couple of area rugs.

The far wall was old brick surrounding a big fireplace. In the back wall were closed French doors. The room behind the doors was supposed to be a den but I used it as my bedroom.

In front of me, a curved stairway led to the second floor. Upstairs were two medium-sized bedrooms, a bathroom, a small room perfect for a nursery, and a master bedroom suite with an enormous tub in its bathroom. April had wanted a tub big enough to play in, big enough for two.

The house was a lot more than half-finished. The downstairs had been complete when April and I moved in three and a half years ago. Three months later, April was gone and the upstairs was still as it had been then. Beyond the top step, the floors were plywood, the walls were aging sheetrock mud, the light switches and electrical outlets had no covers, the ceiling lights were bare bulbs. Only the bathrooms had doors. I had hung cheap curtains so the house looked normal from outside.

I pushed myself away from the door and touched the cool smoothness of the oak bannister. As if in response to my touch, the light at the top of the stairs came on. Another light flicked on in the living room.

Ghosts.

I didn't want to be there.

I packed a lot more clothes than I thought I would need. There's nothing worse than needing to sidetrack to the laundromat when you're hot on someone's trail. On my way to the garage with the luggage, I stopped at the closet beneath the stairs. Pushing some jackets aside, I ducked under the clothes rod and turned a concealed latch. The paneling on the back wall snicked open. I stepped into a small room with reverse stairsteps for a ceiling. Built into the back wall was a gun cabinet containing enough of an arsenal to make a survivalist's eyes gleam. Also built into the wall was a safe. I spun the dial and the door swung open silently. After taking out some stacks of bills, I locked everything up again and made a quick check of the house. The stereo had gone off and the television was on, the volume slightly too high. A lamp was on in the family room. The late summer sunset was just beginning to color the sky but dusk comes early beneath the big trees surrounding the house.

Fifteen minutes later, I rang the bell on a gingerbready house in one of Mackie's stately older neighborhoods. Mattie Hagen opened the door. Her plump curves were wrapped in a worn red velour housecoat and she had a pencil sticking out of her salt and pepper curls over each ear. She had another pencil in her hand.

She said, "Oh, hi." I followed her inside and joined her at the dining room table where she was revising her latest manuscript. I started reading through the stack of finished pages. The heroine, whose name was Felicity, seemed to spend an inordinate amount of time running into strange men in her underwear. She was in the underwear, not the men. The men were all macho studs of the highest order and were given to casting sardonic looks at Felicity. I didn't think I could manage sardonic if I ran across a voluptuous raven-haired beauty in flimsy lace. Dumbstruck, possibly. Hopeful, undoubtedly. But not sardonic.

It was about eight-thirty when Mattie removed all her pencils and stood up. I tore myself away from a steamy bathtub scene and followed her upstairs to a gold and white room where a big brass four-poster gleamed coldly in the fading glow of the long summer sunset filtering through gauzy curtains.

Between the hellos when I arrived and the good-nights an hour or so after we went upstairs, we exchanged maybe two dozen words, few of them containing more than four letters. With Mattie asleep at my side, I stared at the swirling pattern on her ceiling and thought about April. When it started hurting too much, I turned and pulled Mattie into the curve of my body. She felt soft and warm and she murmured something that might have been an endearment but probably wasn't. Better than nothing. But not much.

I fell asleep just after the grandfather clock downstairs bonged ten times. Six and a half hours later, while I was nudging Mattie awake enough to be compliant — if not exactly enthusiastic — about early morning sex, a murder was committed in Mackie.

Chapter Five

Mattie was asleep again when I rolled out of her bed at five o'clock. I hadn't told her I was leaving town. If I didn't show up eventually, she'd replace me. Mattie considered men an expendable commodity. She put it a bit more graphically — "Men are good-for-nothing-but-fucking bastards."

Showered and shaved and perked up by a cup of instant coffee, I revved the Nova up twenty minutes later. The fastest way to Portland was to head north and pick up Interstate 84 just outside of Pendleton. I chose the less traveled road which was Bunyard.

In the early morning light I passed Carrie's house where the arc light on the cupola was still glowing weakly. Six miles later I passed my own house, barely visible in the small forest surrounding it. A light was on upstairs. Soon, it would go off and the kitchen lights would come on as my electronic gadgetry tried to make an empty house look lived in.

The air conditioner would purr on occasionally to keep the plants from dying of heat. The sprinkler system would water the lawn. All the mail I wanted went to the post office box in town. I had eliminated the junk mail problem at the house by removing the mail box. If anyone phoned the house, which didn't happen often, they could leave a message after the beep. Just before leaving Mattie's, I had called Fanciful Flowers and left a message after its beep. Myrna and Rosie had a key to the front door of my office and would take care of the plants. If I wasn't back in a few days, Carrie would water the houseplants and clear the perishables out of the kitchen. If burglars showed up, a deafening alarm would sound and another would silently summon the county sheriff to save my worldly goods. When you got right down to it, I wasn't very necessary.

Beyond my house, Bunyard Road bumps and grinds its way westward. Just past Allentown, which was my immediate destination, the road makes a long slow curve north, intersecting I-84 forty miles west of Pendleton. From there, it's a straight shot into Portland, a hundred and seventy miles farther west in the Oregon tourists know about.

I was still five miles from Allentown when I heard about the murder. Johnny Cash and I had just finished a day-late rendition of "Sunday Morning Coming Down" when the DJ, in the middle of a yawn, gave the time and temperature, adding unnecessarily that it was going to be another hot one in eastern Oregon. Sounding more interested, he announced the lead story of the local news. I turned the volume up.

At the Mackie Arms, the small, handsomely restored hotel in the center of town, guests had been rudely awakened at four-thirty in the morning by the sound of gunshots. After what sounded like a considerable amount of confusion, the police found the body of a sixty-eight-year-old man in a third-floor room. His name was being withheld pending notification of next of kin. There were no witnesses, but the police, as usual, were investigating a number of leads. I was advised to stay tuned for updates. I did, but there weren't any before I pulled up to the Allentown gas pumps.

Allentown's hand-lettered welcoming sign proclaimed a population of four hundred and thirty-eight. Someone had used spray paint to change the last digit to a nine. A few pot-holed roads led south off Bunyard past saggy-roofed houses. The north side of Bunyard was lined with old trees tangled in undergrowth. The town's business district consisted of a large veterinary clinic, the Allentown Cafe, and a rambling store that had no name as far as I knew but stocked most of life's necessities and a few of its luxuries. The gas pumps were in front of the feed section of the store. Off to one side was a garage that had once been a barn.

The garage and gas pumps had been managed for several years by Russell Garvey, a legless Vietnam vet known to everyone as Sarge. I knew him only slightly, having made his acquaintance several years earlier when I refused to arrest him for popping wheelies in his wheelchair in the middle of Mackie's busiest intersection. He was creating a hell of a traffic jam in a one-man demonstration protesting the fact that several of Mackie's older businesses had narrow doors, skinny aisles, lots of stairs, and no ramps.

I mentioned a few of the laws he was breaking and asked him to get out of the street. He refused, showing me a copy of the letter he had sent to City Hall and to the offending businesses. After two months, he had received no replies, not even a single form letter acknowledging receipt of his complaint. I used the radio in my patrol car to inform my superiors — as well as several hundred citizens who had nothing better to do than monitor police calls — that they'd have to send someone else to arrest him because I wasn't going to do it.

The next two cops who arrived on the scene had both done time in Southeast Asia. They joined me in my traffic management exercise and we soon had a detour around the block. By that time, Sarge had a couple hundred supporters cheering him on. Half of them had no idea what was happening but they knew a good time when they saw one. Hastily lettered protest signs sprouted like weeds in side-walk cracks. A lot of the signs sported anachronistic peace symbols and a lot of the peace symbols were really the Mercedes-Benz logo but, what the hell, it had been a few years.

Ten blocks away, the high school dismissal bell clanged. Scenting excitement with the uncanny sixth sense peculiar to adolescents, a hundred or so students spilled into Sarge's demonstration. Vietnam was history to those kids but a party is a party. Guitars materialized and a group of teenagers with designer jeans and a fair knowledge of old-fogey music sang sixties' protest songs with a disco tempo. "Blowin' In The Wind" had never sounded so upbeat.

A television camera crew, fresh from filming a fire in Pendleton, began thrusting cameras and microphones at faces in the crowd just minutes before Chief Detective Robert Harkins and the mayor arrived on the scene. The two of them took turns ad-libbing speeches full of motherhood and apple pie and remember-our-war-heroes.

With Sarge in the lead, the demonstration was formed into a disorderly parade and moved three blocks to Main Street Park where it turned into a picnic that broke up some time after dark.

Sarge triumphed. The *Mackie Mirror* printed several guilt-inducing editorials and the town's unemployment rate dropped briefly as work crews were formed to do some overdue remodeling. Mackie received some nice publicity as a small town with a heart of gold. But Chief Detective

Harkins, whose heart was dross, was not a happy man.

At the end of my shift, I reported, as requested, to his office. Thin-lipped and shaking with anger, Harkins told me that from now on I would by God enforce the laws I had sworn to uphold and if the goddamn media wouldn't make a goddamn circus out of it, he'd throw that goddamn pathetic little cripple into jail and kick my goddamn ass right off the goddamn force. It wasn't the first time I heard the latter threat from him and it wasn't to be the last.

Since the day of the demonstration, I had seen Sarge maybe once a year when I stopped in Allentown on my way to somewhere else. One of his lanky redheaded sons was pumping gas into the Nova when Sarge rolled down the ramp from the feed section and headed my way.

"Hey, how's it going?" he asked. "Why aren't you in town solving the big murder?"

"I'm not a cop any more."

"No kidding. What are you doing now?"

"I'm a private investigator."

"No shit. Just like *Magnum*, huh?"

I grinned. "It isn't much like *Magnum* at all."

"I guess not. This sure as hell ain't Hawaii either." Sarge had stopped just in front of me, his head bent awkwardly back. "Shit, you're tall," he said and rolled back a couple feet to improve his angle. "I used to be six foot even," he said.

"So did I."

Sarge bellowed with laughter, his shaggy copper hair and beard sparking in the sunlight. After he stopped laughing, he asked where I was headed.

"Portland, as soon as I have some breakfast." I glanced down the street at the Allentown Cafe then took a much longer look at the tall blonde who was busy looking out of place on the cafe's long porch.

"Foxy chick," Sarge said.

"Mm hmm. Does she live here?"

"You gotta be kidding. All the women in Allentown look like Miss USSR of 1956. Except for my wife. I thought she was a mirage at first."

"How long's she been there?"

"I dunno. I saw her about five-thirty when I unlocked the pumps. Maybe she's meeting someone for breakfast."

The Allentown Cafe seemed like an unlikely place for a breakfast date. I'd eaten there before on my way west. The food fulfilled the "home-cooking" promise on the peeling sign above the entrance but the customers, at least at six in the morning, were mostly ranch hands and laborers.

I talked with Sarge a few minutes longer then paid my gas tab and drove the fifty yards to the cafe. The Nova's tires spit dust and gravel as I pulled into a parking place twenty feet away and got my first good look at the girl.

She didn't belong in Allentown. Allentown was faded denim. The blonde was silk. She was gold.

She was fine leather. She looked like money with a capital M and elegance with a capital E. She also looked like hell.

I'd have bet the rent that no one had ever called her cute and few people would call her pretty. Her face was too unconventional, too full of planes and angles, too lacking in softness. Her forehead was high and wide, her cheekbones prominent and almost horizontal. She had a long, incredibly straight nose and a delicately tapered jawline. Her dark eyes were deeply lidded beneath pale straight brows. Her wide mouth tightened every thirty seconds or so as she yawned with it closed. I've never been a fan of conventional prettiness. I thought she was beautiful, even with fatigue draining her face of color.

She was young, not more than twenty, I thought, and had the fragile slenderness that results from the body having recently spent several years concentrating on upward growth. The upward growth in her case had been considerable. She was at least five-nine.

A thin line of gold glinted on her neck, a narrow band of gold circled her left wrist, a slender hoop of gold hung from each earlobe. Her thick light-honey hair was piled on the crown of her head and secured with an intricately twisted clasp of gold. Several strands had escaped and hung almost to her waist. A thick loop of hair drooped against the nape of her neck.

If the pale blue dress wasn't silk, it was close enough. It had a softly draped neckline and over-sized sleeves gathered at the elbows. In spite of having the deep diagonal creases that come from hours of careless wear, the skirt fell with flawless grace from a wide shirred waistband.

A run down her left leg revealed skin a shade lighter than the silky hose. Her low-heeled strappy sandals were white leather with a fine coat of dust. The matching shoulder bag was big but apparently not quite big enough. It was bulging badly and looked heavy enough to qualify as a lethal weapon. It must have felt it, too. She switched it from shoulder to shoulder and finally dropped it onto her right foot, the long strap dangling from her hand. In her other hand she was gripping a bulky-knit white sweater. Its hood brushed the dusty floor-boards as she shifted her weight from foot to foot.

While I was busy checking out the most interest-ing sight I'd ever seen in Allentown, the parking lot filled up with pickup trucks, four-wheel drives, and assorted rattletraps. The Nova fit right in. I didn't know where they all came from but the Allentown Cafe never lacked for customers. A cou-ple dozen men and two women in white uniforms had joined the blonde's vigil, leaving a small empty circle around her as if in fear of standing too close to the flame.

I got out of the car and joined them, standing at the inner edge of the circle, about three feet away from the girl. I revised my age estimate down a year and my height estimate up an inch and, when she finally looked my way, I changed my on-a-scale-of-one-to-ten rating from nine and a half to about a zillion.

I was wrong about there being no softness in her face. It was there, all concentrated in her eyes. They were blue, but not everyday, ordinary blue. They were dark blue, deep blue, twilit-sky blue, newborn-baby blue, so blue the color spilled over and tinted the whites, so dark the pupils were an almost undelineated deepening at the centers.

In the half second or so that our gazes held, I felt a swooping sensation just beneath my diaphragm, a feeling I associated with bending over in an upward-bound elevator. A feeling I also associated with the transient, frantic passions of adolescence. Maybe I was just hungry.

The cafe opened promptly at six. The blonde entered first through a door held open by a man with cracked-leather skin. I thought he was going to bow as she passed but he settled for touching the bill of his green John Deere cap. I filed in with the rest of the peasants.

The blonde took the first stool at the counter right next to the cash register. Possibly she was too tired to walk any farther. She had her head propped up with both hands when I passed behind her. I made no attempt to sit near her. In fact, I sat as far away from her as I could get, at the last stool around the bend of the L-shaped counter. So I could see her face.

With brisk efficiency, the waitresses filled coffee cups and took orders. The blonde was served first. Hot tea and English muffins don't require a lot of preparation time. She swished the tea bag around listlessly then folded her hands in front of her and stared at the muffin. My order arrived — steak and eggs and hash browns, orange juice, and a second cup of coffee. I didn't waste any time staring at it.

The next time I looked at the girl, she was nibbling around the edge of a muffin half. She put it down on the plate, carefully adjusted the position of the plate in relation to her tea cup, then abruptly got up and headed for the ladies' room. Her sweater slid off the back of her stool when she stood up and I thought she looked down at it but she didn't stop to pick it up. The old man sitting next to her retrieved it, carefully arranging it over the back of the stool.

When she came out of the restroom a few minutes later, the girl had a bright spot of color on each cheek and her hair was still a mess. In fact, it was worse. The loop on the nape of her neck had worked loose and she now had about as much hair straggling down as she had caught up in the clasp.

Curiouser and curiouser. From years of intense study, I had gleaned three hard facts about women.

If the temperature drops below seventy, they're cold. If they get more than a block away from the nearest bathroom, they immediately have to pee. And it takes a whole lot of trouble to make them forget about their hair.

The girl didn't sit down again. She paid her bill, grabbed her sweater, and left. I looked out the window and watched her walk to the end of the parking lot. She looked carefully in both directions, crossed Bunyard, and headed west. There was nothing in that direction but several miles of lonely country road.

Well, it was none of my business.

I sat there for five minutes telling myself it was none of my business. I might have sat there longer if I hadn't thought of Cindy Amsberry who was sixteen and naked the only time I ever saw her.

That had been on another hot summer day after I drove down another lonely stretch of country road with a rookie cop named Dan Fogel chewing off his thumbnail beside me and two green-faced young brothers and their mother huddled on the back seat behind the wire barrier. I parked where the boys told me to and Fogel and I left them with their mother in the patrol car.

Two hundred feet into the woods we found the BB guns the boys had dropped in their haste to get away from Cindy. Another twenty feet and we found Cindy herself. She wasn't hard to find. A blind man could have found her and she looked worse than she smelled.

Dan Fogel vomited into the dry brush behind me as I looked down at the low-budget horror movie corpse. Only the blond curls bore any resemblance to the pretty cheerleader who had been reported missing several days earlier. A gentle summer breeze lifted the curls and rustled Cindy's scanty blanket of old leaves, giving a gut-churning illusion of movement to her body. I pulled Fogel to his feet and headed him toward the car to call for the men with the body bags.

Cindy Amsberry could ruin anybody's appetite. I signaled the waitress for my check.

CHAPTER SIX

SHE WAS A FAST WALKER. I WAS BEGINNING TO think she had gone off the road into the woods when I rounded a curve and there she was, on the right, walking quickly up the gentle slope of the road with her head down.

I slowed as I passed but didn't stop because another driver rounding the curve would have plowed into the Nova's rear end. I went another two hundred feet before the shoulder was wide enough for me to pull off the road. I started to shut the engine off but decided to leave it running, thinking it might reassure her. A rapist wouldn't waste gas while he dragged a tall blonde into the woods, would he?

I got out and stood by the car door. The girl had stopped walking. She looked back over her shoulder, took a couple steps toward me, then stopped again.

"Do you need a ride?" I called to her.

She shook her head. Something shiny fell to the ground and the rest of her hair fell around her shoulders. She stooped to retrieve her hair clasp and shoved it in her purse.

I walked to the rear of the car. She looked into the woods. They didn't look very inviting. I started toward her, walking slowly, wishing my car looked a little more upwardly mobile and that I was wearing something else instead of a white T-shirt tucked into faded jeans. And that I wasn't so damn big.

I covered about half the distance then stopped and asked again if she needed a ride. The long golden hair swung from side to side. She looked into the woods again.

"This isn't a very good place to be walking," I said.

She looked across the road. More woods. I started toward her again. She waited, not quite looking at me, until I was about thirty feet away and then she started running. But not away from me. She ran diagonally across the road then toward me and past me on the other side of the pavement.

I had some vague idea that if I just stayed put, she'd realize I was harmless. So I stood there. And I watched her run. And I watched her legs flashing in an easy long-legged lope. And I watched her blue skirt swirl up above her knees. And I watched her come even with my car which was idling nicely.

My car! I said "Oh, shit" and started running, knowing it was useless. Without slowing, the girl veered across the road, yanked the door open, and got in. I saw her push the locks down on both doors. I stopped running. There was no way I could get there before she got it in gear and took off.

The Nova's brake lights lit up. I turned toward Allentown. The state troopers would pick her up easily enough on the Interstate. There was nowhere else for her to go. The troopers weren't going to like hearing about the gun in the suitcase. After a few steps, I turned around and walked backward. She was taking her time.

The brake lights went off and the car rolled backward and the lights lit up again as the car stopped suddenly enough that I saw the girl's head jerk forward. The lights went off and the car rolled backward again and came to another jolting stop. I laughed and started jogging up the hill. God looks after old cars and fools.

Just as I reached the car, the girl managed to find some gear and instead of rolling backward, the Nova bucked forward and its engine died. I felt around inside the back bumper, pulled off the strip of tape, and peeled the spare key off it. The engine started. After a rough gear-grinding noise, the car bucked and died again.

I peered into the window. She had the brake and the clutch pressed to the floor and was jiggling the gear shift. It looked like neutral to me. She glanced my way without meeting my eyes then turned the key. The engine started smoothly. The car rolled downhill. At the rate she was going, she'd be back in Allentown before long.

She was fiddling with the shift again when I caught up with the car. Even if she found first, she'd never get it going on a hill but I wasn't sure how much abuse the old car would tolerate. I waited until she ground the gears again and killed the engine, then I unlocked the door and swung it open.

The door handle jerked out of my hand as the Nova rolled down the hill, engineless and damn near driverless. I followed it at a trot. The girl hit the brake, yanked the swinging door shut, and punched the lock down. I sighed, unlocked the door again, opened it again, and said, "Keep your foot on the brake."

She didn't look at me. She had her lower lip clamped in her teeth, a death grip on the steering wheel, and both pedals pressed to the floor. Her knees were shaking. She didn't really seem to be afraid of me or maybe she was just more afraid of moving her feet and letting the car loose. I squatted in the open doorway and reached inside to set the parking brake.

"I'm going to put it in gear and then it won't go anywhere, okay?"

She didn't answer but she dropped her hands from the steering wheel. I reached across her and shoved the shift into first. "You can move your feet now," I said.

She moved her feet, cautiously, and pressed her hands hard against her knees, bending her head so her hair swung forward and hid her face from me. I rested my elbows on my knees and my chin on my hands and waited patiently. The dress sure looked like silk to me. Her jewelry had the gleaming depth of good gold. The slender watch had probably cost ten times as much as my very functional-looking digital. Money can't buy everything. Her watch had the wrong time.

My legs were starting to cramp by the time she finally pushed her hair behind her shoulder and turned those wonderful midnight-blue eyes to me. Sounding like a tired child, she asked, "Why couldn't you have an automatic?"

I almost apologized.

"How about sliding over and I'll do the driving." It sounded like a reasonable suggestion to me. She thought it over for a bit then asked, "Are you taking me to the police?"

"No. I don't want to be laughed at this early in the morning."

She slid over and I got behind the wheel. "Where to?" I asked.

The question must have been harder than it sounded. She stared at her clenched hands, then out the windshield, then out the side window into the woods.

"How about home?" I suggested. "Where do you live?"

Another hard question. I'd almost forgotten what I asked by the time she said, "Portland."

"Portland, it is," I said. "Buckle up, babycakes."

She reached automatically over her right shoulder and I felt pleased when she found the strap right where she expected it to be. It had only been a few weeks since I had finally had the worn lap belts replaced with new seatbelts with shoulder harnesses. She was the first person to use the passenger belt. For some obscure reason, that also pleased me.

"Are you really going to take me all the way to Portland?" she asked. "In your car?"

"Yeah, well, my Lear jet's in the shop for a tune-up."

She regarded me quite seriously. Maybe Lear jets were an everyday fixture in her world. Her voice was low and pleasant and she had no particular regional accent as far as I could tell but her speech was a bit more clipped and precise, a little more cultured-sounding, than the soft Northwestern dialect I was so accustomed to hearing, and speaking, that I no longer noticed it except in its absence.

I told her I was on my way to Portland anyway and asked what part of town she lived in. While she thought that one over, I got us back on the road. During its backward travels, the Nova's right side tires had gone off the shoulder and sunk into soft dirt. The car didn't want to make the effort but I coaxed it along and got all four tires on the pavement.

We were about a mile down the road when my passenger said, "If you could just take me downtown, I can get home from there."

"Okay by me. What's your name?"

"Allison . . . Smith."

I grinned out the windshield. "As good a name as any. How old are you?"

"Nineteen."

Nineteen and definitely five-ten. Damn, I was good. "Aren't you going to ask what my name is?"

Apparently she hadn't planned to. Several yawns and half a mile later, she said, "What's your name?"

"Zachariah," I said. "Smith."

I glanced over at her, smiling. She didn't look as though she believed me. Smiths get that look a lot. I steered one-handed while I pulled my wallet out and flipped it open so two credit cards showed. She squinted at them and sighed heavily.

"What's your real name?"

"Allison. Not Smith."

"Well, Miss Allison Not-Smith, there's a down jacket on the seat behind you. Why don't you grab it and use it for a pillow and I'll wake you up when we get to Portland."

It took her at least thirty seconds to fall asleep.

The next couple hours were uneventful except for the time I almost drove into the Columbia River because my leggy passenger shifted in her sleep and I became so entranced with the curve of her thigh that I forgot I was hurtling through space faster than the speed of legal travel. Soon after that, I pulled off the Interstate.

Allison slept through a stop at a gas station. I parked by a restaurant and shook her gently. She uncurled and blinked at me.

"Hi, remember me? We're in Hood River. You think you can try to eat something?"

She said "Mm" and opened her big purse. I could see Crest toothpaste in a pump dispenser, Johnson's Baby Shampoo, Secret deodorant, and a tube of aloe vera lotion. And that was just the top layer. The edge of a blue leather wallet was visible down amongst all the tubes and jars and bottles. She found a natural bristle brush and yanked it through her hair a couple times. It didn't help much. She shoved the brush back into her purse and folded her hands in her lap. After a moment, I got out and opened the door for her.

While I worked my way shamelessly through my second breakfast of the day, Allison ate half a piece of toast and the whipped cream off the top of a cup of hot chocolate. When I was waiting for a final coffee refill, I asked if she had a pen in her purse. I expected something gold-plated at the very least. She handed me a blue plastic EraserMate minus the cap. I printed WILLAMETTE neatly on a paper napkin and slid it over in front of her. "Read that," I said.

She looked at the napkin then looked at me suspiciously.

"Why?"

"Why not?"

She studied the napkin, searching for tricks and failing to find any among the innocent letters. She shrugged slightly and said, "Willa-met."

The waitress appeared to refill my coffee cup. After she left, Allison asked, "What does it mean?"

"It means you don't live in Portland. Or anywhere in Oregon." I tapped the napkin. "It rhymes with dammit. WilLAMette. The Willamette River runs right through downtown Portland. It's a big river. You can't miss it. There's also Willamette Valley, Willamette Falls, Willamette Boulevard, and a few hundred businesses all called Willamette something-or-other. Out-of-state tourists say Willa-met."

Allison had been busy destroying the evidence of her deceit. She put the shredded shibboleth in the ashtray. I asked how much money she had.

"I can pay for my food if that's what you mean."

"I don't want you to pay for your food. I want to know how much money you have."

"I'm not sure."

"Well, count it."

She picked up the salt and pepper shakers from the center of the table and lined them up neatly on her side of the napkin holder. "I have thirty-seven dollars," she said, without counting anything.

"Any credit cards?"

"No."

"What are you planning to do in Portland with thirty-seven dollars and one blue dress?"

She pushed the shakers a quarter-inch closer to the napkin holder. "I'll be all right."

"What were you doing in Allentown?"

"Nothing."

"How'd you get there?"

She put the salt shaker on my side of the napkin holder, poking it gently back so it balanced the pepper shaker.

"Were you with someone who went off and left you there?"

"No."

"You walked?"

"No." She put both shakers in front of the napkin holder, aligning them with military precision. "I asked a man to give me a ride."

"Why'd you want to go to Allentown?"

"I didn't. I mean, I did. Well, I didn't exactly. I heard him say he was going there. I thought it would be bigger." She gave the pepper shaker a vicious little jab. "I don't know why they call it a town anyway."

"Mr. Allen was an optimist. If you were already hitchhiking, why try to steal my car? I offered you a ride."

"He was old."

"Jack the Ripper could have been ninety for all

anyone knows. Where were you when he picked you up?"

She reached for the shakers and drew her hand back quickly when she found my hand in the way.

"I was in Pendleton," she said.

"What were you doing there?"

"Nothing."

"You do a lot of that. Do you know someone in Pendleton?" She shook her head and I asked, "How did you get there?"

"On a bus."

"From Portland, right? You flew into Portland from somewhere in the eastern time zone and you took a bus to Pendleton." She looked at her watch then covered it with her right hand. "Am I right?" She nodded, just barely. "Why go to Pendleton if you don't know anybody there?"

"Just . . . because."

"Nobody goes to eastern Oregon just because."

She stared out the window and chewed on her lower lip. I finished my coffee and picked up the check. "You ready to go?"

She turned to face me. "I went to Pendleton to meet someone. It didn't work out. So I left."

"Without your luggage?"

"Yes. I mean, no." Her gaze dropped to my chest. "The airline lost my suitcase."

"We can stop by the airport when we get to town and see if they found it."

She turned a nice shade of pink. When she spoke,

she stared at the wall behind my head. Maintaining eye contact while lying is an acquired art. "I already called them. I told them to send it back to . . . to where I live." Her hand hovered over the pepper shaker briefly then she made a minute adjustment of the napkin holder's position. "I told them I was going home. I want to but I don't have enough money." She twisted a strand of hair around her finger then yanked it loose. "I don't suppose you could lend me some money," she said, looking me right in the eye. "I can pay you back."

"I could do that." The look of relief on her face was painful to see. It was even more painful to watch it fade as I said, "There are some conditions though. I want to know your real name and where you live and I want to talk to your folks and be sure they know what you're doing."

"You can't go home again" is the runaway's creed. She resumed her lip-chewing and window-gazing. I tapped the check on the table and considered what she had told me. If she'd gone to Pendleton to meet someone, the someone was undoubtedly a man and he could have made her mad enough or upset enough to walk off without her luggage. If there wasn't anyone in Pendleton, she had either left home in a mighty big hurry or she couldn't leave with a suitcase without being stopped. I was inclined to believe there was someone in Pendleton. Otherwise, it would have made a lot more sense for her to stay in Portland when she got off the plane instead of wasting money on a bus trip to the boondocks. Either way, she was alone and broke and thousands of miles from home. And she was wrong. She wouldn't be all right in Portland.

She turned from the window. "You aren't responsible for me."

"Who is?"

"No one. I am."

"You're doing a piss-poor job of it, babe. Let's go."

When we were back in the car, I started the engine, then shut if off again and turned to face her. "I'll take you on to Portland but you listen to me first. I don't know what you're running from but I know you're running and I know what happens to runaways. You have no money and no way to get any. If you think you're going to get a job in Portland, you're wrong. The economy's been depressed around here for years and jobs are hard to come by. And it's pretty damn difficult to get work anyway when you don't have enough money to live on until the first paycheck comes. People will get a little suspicious when you show up in that same dress every day.

"And you have another problem. Unless they're crazy as hell, your folks are going to be looking for you. If you're serious about staying lost, you can't get a job. Your social security records will lead them right to you. So you'll have to do what all the other runaways do — live on the street. It's a hard

life and I don't think you have the necessary sur-
vival skills." Allison was concentrating hard on
looking bored. I persevered.

"What are you going to do tonight, when it's dark
and you're all alone out there? There are hundreds
of homeless kids in Portland, a lot of them younger
than you are. They sleep in abandoned buildings,
in parks, doorways, under bridges. In cardboard
boxes, for Christ's sake. You think you can do that?
And there aren't any bathtubs with gold fixtures
on the street. Street people stink. When was the
last time you went a month without a bath? I bet
you've never gone a whole day without washing
your hair."

She smoothed the blue skirt over her thighs, her
face expressionless. Perseverance is one of my
best qualities.

"Street kids survive any way they can. Some of
them steal, some of them beg, most of them hook.
You'll end up on your knees in cars giving blow-jobs
for grocery money."

That got to her.

She turned to me, her face tight with anger. "I
will not," she said, her voice shaking.

"You will when you get hungry enough."

"I would *never* —" She took a jerky breath and
doubled over, wrapping her arms around her waist.
"I'm going to be sick."

"Open the door and lean out."

"I'm not going to throw up in a parking lot," she

wailed, then she opened the door and threw up in the parking lot. I handed her my handkerchief and told her to slide out my side. "Go back inside and rinse out your mouth, splash a little water on your face. You'll feel better."

She shook her head. "I'm not going back in there."

"Nobody saw you."

"I am not going back in there."

She sounded like she meant it. I drove to the gas station, got a funny look and the key to the ladies' room from the attendant, and got Allison out of the car. She leaned heavily on my arm as I helped her inside. After some deep shuddery breaths against my shoulder, she pulled away from me. She frowned at herself in the mirror over the sink then looked my reflection right in the eye and said, "Go away."

I went away and leaned against the Nova's fender until she emerged. She was pale and had those bright spots of color on her cheeks again but her hair was brushed smooth and tucked behind her ears.

We headed off on the last leg of our journey. The temperature had been dropping steadily since before Hood River when we left the high arid plateau behind and entered the Columbia River Gorge. Sixty miles ahead of us, under leaden skies, was Portland. The City of Roses. Stumptown. River City. Crime Capital of the Northwest. I was looking forward to a little Portland mist after Mackie's long dry summer.

I flipped the radio on just in time to catch the news. Mackie's murder was still the top story. There were few new details. The dead man's name was Carl Anthony Vanzetti. He was from Chicago and had been at the hotel for three days before he was murdered. The police still had no suspects. The announcer finished by casually mentioning that the FBI was involved in the case. He either didn't know why or wasn't telling. He went on to a story about a big drug bust in Clackamas County which I didn't hear because Allison suddenly developed a bad case of the dry heaves and was doubled over, gasping and moaning. When I suggested stopping at a hospital, there was so much fear in her face that I didn't press it.

Chapter Seven

By THE TIME WE REACHED PORTLAND, THE WIND-
shield wipers were slapping at a light rain and
Allison was restlessly asleep, bent over awkwardly
with her head on my wadded-up jacket on the seat
between us.

I rented a room at my usual motel which was just
off the Interstate, close enough to downtown to
be convenient and far enough away to be cheap
enough to keep my clients' blood pressure within
the normal range. I found a parking place near a
rear entrance and left Allison sleeping in the car
while I carried my luggage inside.

All the rooms opened off blue-carpeted corridors
that smelled faintly of chlorine although the motel
had no pool. Room 210 was on the second floor,
the second door from the stairwell. I pulled the
covers down on the first bed and left the door
standing open while I went back outside.

Allison started and grabbed her purse when I slid
my arms under her. I ignored a very feeble protest
and carried her upstairs. Just as I reached the door,
a couple came out of the next room. The man
grinned and gave me a thumbs-up gesture. I forced

a smile back at him, feeling an old familiar despair as I remembered the last time I carried a woman over the threshold.

I put Allison on the bed where she curled up into a ball, her purse clutched to her stomach. I took her sandals off and twitched the blankets over her.

After making a couple of phone calls, I opened my suitcase on the second bed and stared at my gun for a while. I had no immediate plans to shoot up downtown Portland. I kept the gun handy partly out of habit and partly because of the paranoia that comes from getting used to having a gun around. There's a persistent little voice that says, hey, you had it with you a thousand times and didn't need it, leave it behind this time and you'll be sorry. Still, I seldom wore it any more. I had used it only once since I'd been a PI, brandishing it at a pimp to convince him that the world was full of girls and he really didn't need the one I was taking away from him.

Most of the time, the gun was strictly window dressing for my clients, useful when someone wanted a courier or a bodyguard. I could say, see, I'm licensed, I'm bonded, and I have a gun. Your body/money/negotiable securities/sexy young daughter couldn't be safer. Ordinarily, I would have left the gun in the suitcase during the day. Ordinarily, I wouldn't have had a roommate. Locking it in the car didn't seem like a good idea, what with car thieves running rampant all over the place. I stuck the gun in a pile of clothes and went into the bathroom to change.

When I came out, I surveyed myself in the bureau mirror which neatly decapitated my image at chin level. Dark brown pants, pale blue shirt open at the throat, light brown cotton canvas sportcoat artfully concealing a .38 in a shoulder holster. Yuppie to the max. I stooped to grin at myself in the mirror, rubbing the earlobe with the hole in it. Maybe Allison would lend me a gold hoop.

I was pulling on socks when she rolled over and sat up. I stood up, shoving my feet into brown tassel loafers. Allison was sitting cross-legged, the blankets over her lap, staring hard at nothing. She had a look on her face that I had seen before on the faces of people in police stations and hospital waiting rooms, a look that says something bad has happened and something worse is coming and there isn't a damn thing to do but wait for it. I asked if she was feeling better.

She gathered all her hair in front of her left shoulder, twisting it into a thick snarled rope. "Are we in Portland?"

"Uh huh."

She nodded slightly and looked around the room. There wasn't much to see. A motel room is a motel room is a motel room. This one had two double beds covered with blue fleur-de-lis bedspreads and separated by a nightstand holding a telephone and a fake brass lamp with a tan shade. Just inside the

door was an open-air closet, then a long bureau-
desk combination with a television bolted onto a
Lazy-Susan base at one end. The open bathroom
door revealed a small vanity and a tub with a glass
enclosure. In front of the single window, another
fake brass lamp was suspended over a small round
table that was flanked by two blue upholstered
chairs. The drapes were tan, the walls were white,
the flat carpet was a busy blue and gold print to
conceal the stains. The framed prints over the
beds were better not looked at too closely. Every
flat surface in the room held an ashtray with a book
of matches folded to stand upright in it. There was
bound to be a Bible in a bureau drawer. The room
cried out for plants.

While Allison was checking out the room, I
checked my pockets. Wallet, handkerchief, keys,
quarters for the phone, Buck knife, and the disposable lighter I had carried religiously since the
time I was stranded overnight in the Blue Mountains without a match to light a fire. I quit Scouts
after fifth grade. We never got to the rubbing-two-
sticks-together lesson.

Allison cleared her throat and twisted the rope
of hair tighter. "How did you sign the register?"
she asked.

"You mean like in the movies? Mr. and Mrs. John
Smith with a furtive glance at the clerk? It isn't like
that. There's just a card to fill out. Name,

Zachariah Smith. Number in party, two. They don't care who's with me."

If she gave her hair another half-twist, she would yank it all out by the roots. I was working out a polite way to tell her I had no intention of jumping her bones, not without an invitation anyway, when she decided to take matters in her own hands.

"Am I supposed to sleep with you?" she asked.

"No one is ever *supposed* to sleep with anyone. And no, I don't expect you to. I brought you here because I don't know what else to do with you. You're in no condition to be wandering around a strange town by yourself."

She let her hair go and began working her fingers through the tangles.

"I'll be going out for a while," I said. "I'll come back later and get you some dinner. In the meantime, there are some fast food places down the street and there are vending machines down the hall. I left some change on the desk. And a key. Be sure to take it with you. The door locks automatically."

"I thought you lived in Portland."

"I live in Mackie. East of Allentown. You would have passed through it on your way from Pendleton."

She shrugged. "I don't remember. I think I was asleep part of the way. Why are you here?"

"I'm working."

She didn't ask what I was working at and I didn't

volunteer the information. A runaway wasn't likely to be reassured to find out she was in the hands of a private investigator. People tend to think PI's have something to do with law enforcement.

"How long will you be here?" she asked.

"I'm not sure, a couple days anyway. You can catch up on your sleep and maybe figure out what you want to do with the rest of your life. Something a little more sensible than wandering around accepting rides from strange men. You've done it twice already and your luck won't hold."

"I'm quite capable of taking care of myself."

"No, you aren't. I have to leave now."

"Wait — are you married?"

"Am I married?"

"I heard you telling someone on the phone where you are. I was just wondering if I should answer it if it rings. I mean, if your wife called . . ."

"You can answer the phone."

"So you aren't married?" I said no and she frowned and asked how old I was. "I'll be thirty next month."

"Why didn't you ever get married?" She made it sound as if marriage after thirty was highly improbable if not downright illegal.

"I've been married. Twice, as a matter of fact, although the first time didn't really count."

"Why not?"

"We were in high school. She got pregnant, we

got married, she miscarried, we got unmarried. We didn't even live together."

Allison nodded slowly. "What about the second time?"

What about it? It had counted. "We were married three years." Or five years, depending on how you wanted to figure it.

"Did she die?"

After a moment, I said, "Why would you think she died?"

"You looked sad."

"Oh. Well, I really need to work." I picked up my black zippered binder full of Jessica Finney fliers. "Behave yourself while I'm gone. And don't run off. I don't want to spend the rest of my life wondering what happened to you."

"I don't have anywhere to go." She sounded lost and hopeless and made me want to scoop her up in my arms and murmur the kind of inanities I murmured to Melissa when she fell down and bumped her head.

"You'll be all right here," I said.

She nodded and I went out to look for my other runaway.

CHAPTER EIGHT

BY ONE O'CLOCK THAT AFTERNOON I KNEW WHERE
Jessica Finney wasn't. She wasn't in Juvenile Detention, she wasn't in a hospital, she wasn't at any
of the youth shelters, she wasn't in a morgue. I
left fliers at the street clinic and the social service
agencies I thought a fourteen-year-old might contact if she had enough sense, or got scared enough,
to ask for help.

I had taken a break at twelve o'clock to have a
beer and catch the noon news on a tavern's television. It must have been a slow day in Portland.
Mackie's murder was still the headliner. The television station had dispatched its novice reporter to
the scene and after a brief introduction by the
anchorman, the screen flicked to a view of the brick
facade of the Mackie Arms.

A woman with a microphone in her hand was
standing in front of the ornately carved wooden
doors. A man's arm and shoulder were visible beside her and, as she made her opening remarks,
the camera panned back and the rest of Phil Pauling
came into view. He was looking at a sheet of paper
in his hand. As he looked up into the camera, he

moved his hand down to his side. There was a faint sound of paper crumpling. I grinned at the television screen. He had just wadded up the official statement he was supposed to read.

Phil was between haircuts, as usual. His dry sandy curls looked as if he had combed them with his fingers the day before yesterday. He was wearing his customary uniform — a blue chambray work shirt with the cuffs rolled back and faded jeans with a big bucking bronco on the belt buckle. His feet weren't visible on the screen but I knew what was on them — a pair of well-worn cowboy boots that added two inches to his lanky six-foot frame. He had freckles and east Texas all over him.

You had to know him well to see the pain behind the country bumpkin exterior. I knew him well. I had seen him too drunk to crawl, let alone walk. I had seen him through pre-binge desperation, mid-binge mania, and post-binge mortification. I had listened, a thousand times, to his rambling memories of a war and of the Vietnamese girl he had loved and left behind, her belly swollen with his child.

Five years ago, another baby's death stunned him into sobriety. Since then I had sat through enough AA meetings with him to have the Twelve Steps memorized. And I had, as he liked to remind me, benefited immensely when his fight against the craving drove him to obsessive hyperactivity. The house I had been slowly building rose from the ground in record time. Night after night, I had fallen into exhausted sleep on a pile of dropcloths, lulled by the rhythmic sound of hammering. Night after night, I woke in the darkness to see Phil silhouetted against the floodlight, hammering in nails, hammering out guilt, hammering back his consuming fear that the tiny daughter he and his wife Patsy buried had been taken in retribution for the child he had left to live or die in a war-ravaged village half a world away.

On the television screen, the woman wrapped up her summary of the murder and announced that she was speaking with Detective Philip Pauling who was heading the homicide investigation. Phil's deceptively innocent pale blue eyes crinkled as he smiled the slightly buck-toothed little-boy grin that made women want to run home and bake cookies for him. The woman beside him was no exception. She started to smile back then remembered her professionalism and gripped her mike harder.

"Detective Pauling, can you describe what happened here this morning?"

Phil grinned harder. The woman had just given a detailed description of the murder scene. "Why, sure thing," Phil said with the east Texas twang he could shut off whenever he wanted to. He seldom wanted to but people learned to tread softly when he did. "A man was murdered here," he said.

The woman held the microphone expectantly in front of him. Nothing further was forthcoming. Phil pursed his lips and whistled soundlessly. The woman's mouth tightened as her live interview died on-camera. I could have warned her. Phil would have been charming as all hell off-camera but his distrust of the media bordered on paranoia.

The woman straightened her shoulders. "Detective Pauling, this has been described as an execution-style murder. Do you have a comment on that?"

"No, ma'am. It sure does make it sound more interesting, though."

The woman's face was stony. "We have been informed that the victim was involved in black market prescription drugs. As I'm sure you recall, the Mackie Police Department was involved in a lengthy investigation three years ago when one of its own officers alleged that the department was in some way involved in black market drug trafficking or in the cover-up of drug trafficking. Do you —"

"I also recall that all the allegations were disproved." There was a commotion off-camera and Phil glanced to his left, looking peeved. "Looks like the Chief has something to say," he said without a trace of Texas in his voice.

Phil moved aside and another man took his place. He was tall, dark-haired, blandly handsome, with a smooth big-city sophistication that contrasted sharply with Phil's country casualness. The woman with the mike looked slightly frazzled as she said,

"I'm speaking now with Chief of Police Robert Harkins."

"Thank you," Harkins said. "I just want to make it very clear that there is absolutely no connection whatsoever between the homicide that occurred in our town this morning and the investigation into police corruption over three years ago. Those charges were made by a disgruntled police officer who resigned shortly afterward. Following a thorough investigation, all the allegations were dismissed as unfounded. I consider it an insult to the fine officers of our town to have this matter brought to public attention again. We're trying to solve a murder here."

Very hastily, the woman wrapped up her broadcast and the station's newsroom reappeared on the screen.

Throwing my bottle of Henry Weinhard's at the tavern's television would have been childish as well as a waste of good beer. I took a drink from it instead and cursed Harkins silently.

Disgruntled, my ass. I'd been mad as hell.

It was during my last year on the force that Mackie first earned its reputation as the black market drug capital of eastern Oregon, a reputation it still maintained. The effort to put an end to the sudden, inexplicable increase in the quantity of illegal prescription drugs flowing in and out of town had been hampered by a series of events that began to seem less and less coincidental as case after case was thrown out of court or never made it that far. Reports disappeared, evidence was misplaced, mishandled, and, in my biggest case, destroyed in a fire that may or may not have been caused by faulty wiring in the police property room.

Phil and I became suspicious and began handling all drug cases with a secrecy unmatched since D-Day. And we came up with the big one, the bust that would put an end to Mackie's thriving drug business. Backed up by most of the Mackie Police Department, Phil and I entered a garage at the edge of town. Sure enough, the four men we wanted were inside. But instead of interrupting a major drug transaction, we interrupted a pinochle game. There wasn't so much as an aspirin on the premises.

I went straight from the garage to Harkins' office, certain that we had been burned by someone within the department. Harkins didn't want to hear it. The city fathers were politely waiting for old Chief Hightower to finish dying of lung cancer before officially replacing him and Harkins didn't want his status as shoo-in for the job screwed up by allegations of corruption. He also didn't like me and had considered me a troublemaker for years.

If Phil had been with me, Harkins might have listened, but Phil had just been going through the motions for months. Patsy was divorcing him and he was compulsively attending every AA meeting within a hundred miles of Mackie. He would have been hard-pressed to work up a little righteous indignation if he had seen Mackie cops, en masse and in uniform, peddling pills on a grade school playground.

By myself, I went over Harkins' head to the mayor who was surprisingly quick to agree to an investigation. Surprisingly until I belatedly realized it was an election year and he needed an issue to spice up a dull mayoral race. Instead of a quiet investigation, a committee was formed and for eight months an investigation of the police department was carried on with all the hoopla of a Barnum and Bailey grand finale.

The committee's report exonerating the police department from any wrongdoing was made public early in November, just before the election. By that time, I no longer cared. April had been gone since May and on Halloween night I had thrown a pumpkin through a second story window of the police building and had tendered my resignation by flinging my badge out after it.

I finished my beer and left without watching the rest of the news. After I completed my official inquiries about Jessica Finney, I set out to follow my clues.

Chapter Nine

THE ROSE CITY SCHOOL OF PERFORMING ARTS WAS in an elegantly restored turn-of-the-century house not far from downtown. The small foyer was lush with ferns, thick carpeting, and deep-green flocked wallpaper. I rang a silver bell that was on a delicate Queen Anne desk. Before the tinkle faded, a small middle-aged man with an ascot and a pompadour stepped through a doorway to my left and asked if he could be of service.

He raised his already high brows at my business card and assured me that the Rose City School of Performing Arts did not harbor runaways. I was at least a foot taller but somehow he managed to look down his nose at me. A very versatile nose. He also talked through it.

"We do get the odd transient wandering past," he said. "Isn't it just awful the way those people are just everywhere now? God. I just loathe going downtown any more. You can't walk five feet without one of them asking for money. I just don't know what the police are doing, letting that kind of riffraff wander around. Why, the taxes —"

I didn't want to hear his views on taxes. I waved Jessica's envelope at him.

"We do, of course, send brochures to persons who request information, but we don't accept applications from just anyone. Our students don't *choose* to come here. *We* choose to let them come. We have a small enrollment and each of our students is hand-picked and comes most highly recommended. We have the most stringent —"

I stemmed the flow of bloodless rhetoric by shoving Jessica's picture under his elite nose. It wrinkled disdainfully.

"Oh, her," he said.

"She's been here?"

"Well, not *inside*. I was just appalled. She was sitting on the steps when I arrived, let me think . . . yes, it was Thursday. About six. I always arrive early. I do think morning is the best time of day, don't you? Everything is so fresh. A brand new day and all that. Well, anyway, as I said, she was sitting on our steps and, I just hate to think it, but it looked as if she might have slept there! Can you imagine? Right on our steps! She had our brochure and wanted to enroll, of all things. I sent her on her way very quickly, I can assure you. We can't have that type of . . . I mean . . . God! She looked . . . unkempt. She was wearing jeans and the most awful jacket with a horse or something on the back. She looked as if she belonged to one of those street gangs you read about."

"How was she?"

"What do you mean?"

"Happy, sad, nervous, scared?"

"I believe she was crying when she left." The son-of-a-bitch smirked.

I stared at his nose, imagining it crunching under my fist. "She's fourteen," I said and left him shaking his head over the decline of elegance in the world. Poor little Jessica had followed her dream and found it intimidating.

The Northwest Acting and Modeling School didn't look intimidating. Or impressive. Or prosperous. It was sandwiched between a second-hand store and a video rental place on one of Old Town's sleazier streets. The windows were plastered with posters announcing aerobics classes which led me to believe that future Meryl Streeps and Christie Brinkleys were not exactly clamoring to get in.

Just inside the door was a long counter. Behind it was one of those walls that open and close accordion-style. Through the narrow center opening I could see into a long, carpeted room. At the far end, a ballet barre dissected a wall of mirrors. Reflected in the mirror were several lights on poles, a video camera, and a clutter of other electronic equipment I couldn't identify. I could hear a low hum of speech but couldn't see anyone in the mirror or out of it. There was no silver bell. I knocked on the counter.

The hum broke off abruptly then there was another brief murmur followed by the sound of a telephone receiver clattering into its cradle. A woman came through the opening in the wall. Her face lit up with pure delight when she saw me and her smile made me think I was the best-looking thing she had seen all day. Considering the locale, I probably was. I had stepped over two winos on the short walk from the car.

She turned her back to the counter in front of me, hitched herself up on it, and spun around on her fanny to face me, crossing her legs in mid-spin.

"Virginia Marley," she said. "Manager."

"Zachariah Smith," I said. "Private eye."

She gurgled with laughter. "I suppose you're gay," she said.

"Not that I've noticed."

"Oh, goodie. All the gorgeous men I've met in this town are either gay or cheating like crazy. Are you really a private eye?"

I said I really was and gave her one of my cards.

"Mackie?" she said. "Where the hell is Mackie?"

A couple years ago half the population of Mackie was wearing T-shirts emblazoned with that question. "Out east," I said. "Near Pendleton."

"Mm. Cowboy country. I went to the Pendleton Round-Up last year. This friend of mine said I'd have the time of my life. Do I look like sitting on bleachers with a bag of popcorn and a styrofoam cup of beer watching cowboys fall off horses would just tickle me to death? Some of the cowboys were cute though."

Virginia Marley was cute, too. She was my age, give or take a couple years, and had big brown eyes and a cute little turned-up nose sprinkled with freckles. There was a space between her two front teeth that her curvy upper lip couldn't quite cover. Her light brown hair was in a fashionably cute frizz that looked as if the curl had been produced by combing out hundreds of tiny tight braids. Her body was very, very cute in a bright blue leotard cut low in the front and high on the thighs. She was wearing hot pink tights with stirrup feet. Even her bare toes were cute.

"So," she said, "what can I do for you?"

I had the impression the possibilities were limitless but I was on Jason Finney's time at the moment so I stuck to business. She shook her head at Jessica's picture.

"We send a brochure if anyone asks for one. Not a brochure, really. It's just a sheet of paper listing some of the classes, costs, that type of thing. I'm almost always here and I don't remember seeing her. I'll show this to the instructors when they come in. We don't start until ten so lunch break is late and you missed everyone."

"Thanks," I said. "You can leave a message at the number on the card. How long have you worked here?"

"About a year. I'm afraid I'm not a very good

manager. The place loses money every month but no one seems to care. I think it's some kind of tax write-off for the owner. I'm not complaining. He pays me more than I'm worth."

"I doubt that," I said and Virginia gurgled again.

She said, "Believe it or not, the aerobics classes do pretty well. We videotape them so the fatties can see what they look like. Very motivating."

"Sounds like it would be."

A cute pucker formed between Virginia's brows. "You know, there was a girl outside. Um, Thursday. I remember because I came in late. Had a little trouble getting out of bed." Her eyelashes fluttered. "Anyway, there was a girl sitting on the sidewalk out front. The thing is, I didn't really look at her. There are always street kids hanging around. They're usually stoned and most of them are panhandling. And they can get pretty obnoxious if you don't give them money, so I just ignored her and came inside. I noticed her a couple times after that, just sort of hanging around." She looked at Jessica's picture again. "The hair is about right but I never really saw her face."

"Do you remember what she was wearing?"

"Well, let's see. Jeans, I'm sure of that. Oh, I know. A jacket, a high school jacket, you know? With the school name or something on the back. And a horse or something."

"The Mackie Mustangs. That was Jessica."

"Oh, God, now I feel bad. I thought she was just

a street kid. If I'd known she was somebody's little lost child, I'd have done something."

"Most of them start out as someone's little lost child."

Virginia looked hurt.

"I wasn't criticizing," I said. "Just thinking out loud. They get hard fast on the street and they're not very likable. And I don't do anything about it either. Except look for the ones I'm paid to look for."

Virginia nodded. "We can't all be Albert Schweitzer," she said. "What are you going to do now?"

"Keep looking. She doesn't have much money and I don't think anyone would rent her a room anyway. She's bound to be around town somewhere. She doesn't know her way around Portland so I'm hoping she hasn't made it out to 82nd Street."

"It sounds hard, finding one little girl in a town the size of Portland."

"Finding kids is mostly a matter of luck. Grown-ups are easier."

"Why is that? It seems to me grown-ups would be better about staying out of sight."

"They would be but they take all their habits with them. And their credit cards half the time. If you can find out what town an adult is in and you know he plays the horses or bowls or likes antiques, you hang around the tracks or bowling alleys or antique shows and sooner or later you stumble right over him. Habits are hard to break."

"Kids don't do the same things they did at home?"

"They might, but the ones who end up running are usually pretty secretive and no one knows what they like to do. Jessica wants to act so bad she can taste it and her parents didn't even know she was interested. Well, look, I'd better get going. I'm already five days behind her."

"I'll walk you to your car." Virginia spun around on the counter again and hopped off. She got a hooded sweatshirt and a pair of aerobics shoes from beneath the counter and put them on, leaning over to tie the shoes without bending her knees. Virginia was definitely cute. She slipped her hand around my arm as we walked outside and looked up at me. "You sure are big," she said. "I suppose you get tired of people pointing that out."

"It doesn't bother me much."

"It must be just a little difficult for you to do sneaky undercover work."

"Yeah, but there's not a lot of call for it anyway. Private investigating isn't nearly as sneaky as it sounds."

We stepped over the same two winos. The second one looked dead and Virginia gurgled when I nudged him with my foot and he snored loudly.

When we reached my car, Virginia looked at it a bit dubiously. She walked around to the front and looked some more. "Well," she said, "I guess you really aren't the Porsche type anyway."

"Would it impress you if I told you I have a four-wheel drive at home?"

"Now that's more your style. Or maybe a pickup with those great big tires. What year is this?"

I told her and she said, "Guess what I drive."

"A little red Jag."

She laughed. "An old Volkswagen bug. An orange one. It's a sixty-nine. My favorite . . . year."

"Good year," I said.

"There's a bar called Tonita's over by Portland State. I live nearby and I usually stop in for a nightcap. If you get a chance, drop by. About eleven. I'll buy you a drink."

I said I'd try to make it and waved to her as I drove off.

The remainder of my plan for finding Jessica Finney had all the subtlety of a triple-X movie — show her picture to as many people as possible and hope that someone had seen her and would be concerned enough or, more likely, greedy enough to tell me where she was.

I wended my way through downtown, Old Town, and Chinatown, showing Jessica's picture to clerks, customers, tourists, loiterers, white collar workers, blue collar workers, cops on foot, cops on horseback, cops in cars, little old ladies, dirty old men, sweet young things, up-and-comers, down-and-outers, three-piece-suited yuppies, time-warped-in-from-Woodstock hippies, hucksters, buskers, hookers, johns, junkies, pushers, pimps, bums, blacks, whites, Asians, Orientals, Hispanics, two Indians in full tribal regalia, and one young man with his face painted blue. I didn't ask him why.

I was smiled at, frowned at, nodded at, winked at, blinked at, stared at, ignored, rebuffed, questioned, shied away from, fondled, flirted with, and told to fuck off. No one admitted ever seeing Jessica Finney.

At six o'clock I headed back to the motel to see what Allison was doing.

CHAPTER TEN

WHAT ALLISON WAS DOING WAS SLEEPING. THE
covers were tucked up beneath her chin. The
honey hair strewn across the pillow had the heavy-
stranded look long hair has when it dries without
being combed. She didn't stir when I entered the
room. The television was on, the volume low.

I went into the bathroom and became highly distracted. Allison's blue dress was dripping dry on
one of the motel's hookless, theft-deterring hang-
ers that she had balanced over the shower head.
Draped over the shower door, also drying, were a
pair of panties, a bra, and a slip — all three white
and lacy — and a pair of pantyhose. By my calcu-
lations, Allison was sleeping in the nude. I told
myself not to think about it.

Myself didn't listen. I checked the label on the
bra. I could rationalize looking. I might have to run
an ad — Found: One tall blonde. Eyes like the sky
of a moonlit mountain night. Bra size 32C. Identify
to claim.

I remembered why I was in the bathroom then I
went back into the other room and watched Allison.
She was definitely asleep. And dreaming. I could

see the movement of her eyes beneath the long lids. The only other person I knew who could sleep that deeply in a strange bed in a strange room with a strange man wandering around was nineteen months old.

Her purse was on the bureau and it was no longer bulging. Her toiletries and cosmetics were lined up neatly next to the bathroom sink. I stood facing the bed so I could keep an eye on her while I went through her purse.

It contained her hairbrush, a blue plastic comb, the EraserMate pen, a big white compact, an eyeglasses case, a small zippered leather case, the blue leather wallet, and an X-Acto knife which seemed odd but I'd been through too many women's purses to be surprised at anything I might find in one.

The wallet contained thirty-seven dollars in bills, a dime, and three pennies, all stuffed into the coin compartment. The place in the middle where the plastic flip-flop window insert should have been was empty. I smiled at the back of Allison's head. Obviously she thought I was the kind of man who would go through a woman's purse while she was sleeping.

The eyeglasses case contained a pair of glasses with frameless beveled lenses, the earpieces attached near the bottoms of them. When I held them up to my eyes everything looked watery.

Reading glasses, I decided. I remembered her squinting to check the name on my credit cards.

The leather case contained a manicure set.

I opened the compact. Powder and a puff.

In a zippered compartment in the purse I found a small Hallmark calendar book. The only marks in it were circles around a single date about every four and a half weeks. The last circled date was ten days ago. I decided I could rule out pregnancy as an explanation for her condition. The back cover of the little book was torn in half. The missing piece would have had the name of the store giving out the free calendars.

The wastebasket beneath the desk was empty. So was the one in the bathroom. She must have ripped the book cover up and flushed it. None of her toiletries were suitable for concealing identification.

Her sweater was tossed on the foot of the empty bed. I checked it out and came up empty-handed.

Well, hell. She probably had her ID under her pillow and nobody slept that deeply. I stood beside the bed, watching her sleep and considering my options. I could turn up the thermostat and wait for her to kick the covers off. Or I could go get her some dinner.

She frowned suddenly in her sleep and made a small sound, almost a whimper.

I went out to get her some dinner. I was hungry anyway.

I brought back styrofoam cups of vegetable soup, turkey sandwiches on soft rolls, and fruit salad from a deli down the street. The smell of food must have penetrated Allison's dreams. I had just placed the containers on the table when I heard movement behind me. I turned around just in time to watch her sit up. The blankets fell to her waist. I tried to keep the disappointment off my face.

She stared at me for several long seconds, her wide-eyed, unfocused gaze making me wonder if she was really awake. Apparently she was. When I smiled, she frowned and said, "I took it out of your suitcase. It was open. Is that okay?"

I said it was fine. After the initial letdown, Allison in my T-shirt was a whole lot better than fine. The neckline sagged into a V, the shoulder seams were halfway to her elbows, the thin white cotton clung very nicely to her breasts.

I asked if she was hungry. She asked if I had a robe. I had one at home, about eight years old and in mint condition. I handed her a blue wool Pendleton shirt which I had actually purchased in Pendleton. She took her time, buttoning every button and carefully rolling the cuffs up several times. She got out of bed and took her purse into the bathroom with her. Water started running full blast immediately.

I checked under the pillows and ran my hand between the mattress and box springs. Nothing.

Eventually the water stopped running and Allison

came out of the bathroom, her face shiny clean, her hair gleaming in a thick golden cascade down her back. With the oversized shirt and the Alice in Wonderland hairdo, she looked about twelve. Except for the legs. No twelve-year-old ever had legs like that.

The pocket of my shirt looked a little stiffer than it should have. She must have slipped the ID from beneath the pillow while I was trying not to be obvious about watching for her to do it. Getting it out of the breast pocket of the shirt without her noticing didn't seem likely. Outsmarted by a nineteen-year-old girl. Well, it wasn't the first time.

I got her a Seven-Up from the vending machine and we sat down to eat. The television was still on and the sound from it kept the silence from seeming too awkward. When I finished, Allison was still picking at her food. I decided to see what was going on in Mackie. The last news report I had heard was a rehash of the earlier broadcasts.

I propped pillows against the head of my bed and pulled the telephone off the nightstand. After studying the directions on the phone, I dialed the twenty or so digits that would connect me with the second floor of the Mackie Police Station and charge the call to my credit card. Technology can wear a man out.

Someone picked up the phone on the other end and I listened to half a minute's worth of background commotion before Phil Pauling said, "Yeah, well, screw you. Not you, hello."

I said hello and Phil said "Hang on, Bucky" and the line clicked. I listened to a minute of hollowness before the line clicked again and Phil said, "Where the hell are you?" There was no background noise and I knew Phil had moved into one of the interrogation rooms where he could discuss official police business with a civilian without worrying about who overheard him.

"In Portland," I said.

"Well, that figures. What are you doing, chasing underage pussy again? You looking for the Finney kid?"

I said yes and Phil said, "I kinda figured her daddy would decide to hire some outside help. He wasn't real pleased with the amount of time and energy we were willing to put into dragging his kid home for him."

"So how's it going there? You looked good on the tube."

"Shit, we're really pissing into the wind on this one, Bucky. And Harkins is about to can my ass. He says the TV bitch never would have brought up the corruption investigation if I'd minded my P's and Q's and read the goddamn statement he gave me. Shit, that woman was all over me about it before we went on the air."

"What's with the execution-style story?"

"Pure media hype. The man was just plain shot to death."

"You don't think Vanzetti had anything to do with drugs in town?"

"Hell, no. We managed to keep the reporters in the dark about his profession for a couple of hours. The first thing I did was haul in everyone in town I ever even suspected of dealing. I never saw such a bunch of blank stares in my whole life. I'd bet my badge none of them ever heard of Carl Vanzetti until his name showed up on the front page."

"How'd you find out he was in the business?"

"Ran him through the computer and came up with a federal warrant. For tax evasion. I called the Fucking Bureau of Investigation and they were pissed as hell that we let Vanzetti go and get himself killed. The tax charge was good. Vanzetti'd been living high on the hog and hadn't filed a tax return in fifteen years. But the Feds didn't give a shit about that. They wanted to work a deal. They knew he was some kind of high-class errand boy in a big black market pharmaceutical operation and they wanted him to name some names and in exchange they'd hit him with some back taxes and penalties to make it look good and drop the charges against him. Of course, they didn't bother to explain the game plan to Vanzetti and he already did twenty years' hard time and the thought of going back apparently didn't set too well with him. So he ran. That was six months ago. He lit out of Chi town one jump ahead of the law and nobody's seen hide nor hair of him since. Until this morning."

"So you don't have any leads at all?"

"Leads? *Leads?* Oh, we got leads, Bucky. They just ain't leading us anywhere. Lemme start at the beginning, okay?"

I switched the phone to my other ear and said, "Okay."

"Things started hopping down at the Arms about four twenty-five when the switchboard lit up like a Christmas tree and all the guests started complaining about their beauty sleep being ruined by gunshots. The night clerk heard the shots but he thought it was a truck backfiring. The guests were pretty panicky though, so he tells them all to stay in their rooms and calls us.

"Jackson and Malcolm get over there and they fart around in the lobby for a while before they decide to mosey upstairs. They get on the third floor and discover the definite odor of gunpowder lingering in the hallway. So they think 'hot damn' and start checking rooms. The killer was a polite son-of-a-bitch and closed the door behind him.

"They finally get the right room and find Mr. Vanzetti who wasn't a whole lot of help on account of he'd been shot four times in the chest at point blank range with a .38 and he was deader'n a doornail. What the hell is a doornail, anyway? So Jackson and Malcolm seal off the scene of the crime, meaning the hotel in its entirety, and I had to drag my weary ass out of bed at five o'clock in the A.M. and go down there.

"We ID'd the deceased easily enough. He had an Illinois driver's license and a passport, both saying he was Carl Anthony Vanzetti. So we set out tracking down John Thornton."

Phil paused, possibly for a breath.

"Who's Thornton?" I asked.

"Just what we wanted to know. Room 301 — that's where the body was — was registered to him. We wasted maybe twenty minutes trying to find someone who could tell us about him. Finally some of the day shift hotel people get down there and I stick Vanzetti's passport picture under their collective noses and they all say, oh, that's John Thornton. Which pretty much ruled out our prime, not to mention only, suspect."

"None of the guests saw anything?"

"Shit, middle of the night in a hotel you think someone's going to step out into the hall in his jammies to see who's playing with firearms? None of them saw anything. None of them heard anything, except for the shots. And the guests all checked out okay. Jesus, I never saw such a bunch of upstanding citizens in one place in my whole life. All the couples were married, for fucking out loud. I don't know what this world is coming to when you can shake down an entire hotel and not come up with one good case of fornication."

"They're all down at the Woodland Inn. The Arms doesn't have hourly rates."

"Well, that's true." Phil sounded relieved to be reminded that sin was alive and flourishing. "In the meantime, some interesting items were turning up in Vanzetti AKA Thornton's room. Item number one was a suitcase containing his clothes. It wasn't real interesting except that just one of his shirts probably cost more than I've spent on clothes in the last five years. Item number two was a corker — another suitcase, smaller and padlocked. Guess what was in it."

"Drugs?"

"Guess again."

"Money."

"You got it. Almost a hundred and fifty thou of Uncle Sam's finest. Small, unmarked bills, non-sequential serial numbers."

I whistled.

"That's just what I said," Phil said. "So instead of just a dead man, we got a dead man traveling under an assumed name and carrying one colossal amount of folding money. He also had close to a grand in his wallet, which pretty much ruled out robbery as a motive.

"Then we find item number three which confused the shit out of us. You want to guess? You'll never guess. A nightgown! A goddamn woman's nightgown hanging on a hook on the back of the bathroom door. Vanzetti was in one of those big rooms the Arms calls suites and they all have two beds but he checked in alone and ordered meals for one from room service all three days he was there. Nobody ever saw him with a woman. Nobody ever heard him with a woman. The cleaning ladies say only one bed was ever slept in. Except for the nightgown and item number four there was nothing to indicate double occupancy."

"What's item number four?"

"Found it in the bathroom trashcan. Some Kleenex smeared with cold cream and mascara."

"Maybe Vanzetti liked to dress up."

"We thought of that. You think we're a bunch of small town hick cops who never heard of perverts? The nightgown was way too small and there wasn't any cold cream or mascara in the room. So I ask you, who — not to mention where — is the woman who took her nightgown and mascara off in Vanzetti's bathroom?"

"Beats me."

"I talked to our higher-priced ladies of the night but they were all wide-eyed innocents at least as far as Vanzetti is concerned. Both beds looked like they'd been slept in but I know funky sheets when I see funky sheets and neither one of those beds was used for any heavy-breathing activities. Besides, who ever heard of a hooker wearing a nightgown? And this wasn't any Frederick's of Hollywood come-and-get-it-big-boy number either. Looked like something your sister would wear.

Well, not *your* sister. I always kinda picture Carrie in black lace. Not to give the impression that I spend a whole lot of time thinking about your sister in sexy nighties, her being a married lady and all. Come to think of it, how come I never did think about Carrie in black lace back before she latched onto young Doctor Kildare?"

"You were married."

"Oh, yeah. Funny how a little thing like six years of holy wedlock can just kinda slip your mind. Speaking of which, did I happen to mention that Philip the Second hit the winning run in his ball game Saturday?"

"No, you didn't," I said. "That's great, Phil."

While Phil gave me a play-by-play description of his son's game, I studied Allison who had given up on her dinner shortly after I left the table. She was sitting very still, hands clasped in her lap, legs tucked under the chair, head and shoulders bowed. She seemed to be trying to displace as little air as possible.

I wondered idly what her problem was. My best guess was that the man in Pendleton didn't meet with her parents' approval and she had run off to be with him. I didn't know what happened in Pendleton but I figured it was some variation of the usual. She showed up unexpectedly and caught him with the girlfriend. Or maybe with the wife and kids. Or maybe when he found out she ran away and jeopardized the inheritance, he made it clear that he had expected a package deal — her and the old man's money. Whatever happened, I couldn't believe it was more than a minor problem in the long run. She got hurt, but everyone gets hurt. All she needed to do was swallow her pride and call home. She had to be Daddy's little darling and all would be forgiven soon enough.

And yet, I sensed an undercurrent of desperation that seemed out of proportion to her situation. Whoever paid for her clothes and jewelry had enough money to get her home posthaste and first-class. She had to feel uncomfortable accepting the hospitality of a stranger and yet she was in no apparent hurry to make other plans.

Her attempt to steal my car didn't bother me much. Her options at that point were to walk, accept a ride with me, or try to take the car. Going for the car made a lot of sense under the circumstances, especially when I had made it so easy for her. But the fact that she had opted to walk out of Allentown troubled me. If ever there was a time when she should have called home, that was it. Long walks on lonely country roads don't usually appeal to young women. Especially wealthy young women who have probably never walked anywhere outside of a shopping mall.

Phil wrapped up the ninth inning and said, "Where was I?"

"Is there an item number five?"

"Sure is, fingerprints on a water glass. Thumb

and first three fingers. Best damn set of prints ever lifted. Looks like an illustration in a how-to-classify-fingerprints manual. And the only thing we know about them is they aren't Vanzetti's. There's no item number six. Oh, hell, I have a date with that little redhead over at City Hall and now I'm late on account of you calling up and bending my ear. What did you want?"

I grinned into the receiver. "I didn't want anything."

"You should've come and kept me company Saturday night instead of tying one on down at the Honky Tonk."

"I'm hanging up now."

"Okeydokey," Phil said and hung up. The silence was startling.

CHAPTER ELEVEN

WHEN I JOINED ALLISON AT THE TABLE, SHE didn't look up and when I asked if she would like to talk about it now, she jumped visibly, looking startled, as if my presence in the room had been forgotten and my return to the table had gone unnoticed.

"About what?" she asked.

"About why you ran away from home and why you can't go back."

"Oh." She sounded as if it were the very last subject she expected. She straightened a bit, combing the fingers of both hands through her hair, drawing it back from her face. "No," she said. "I really don't want to talk about it."

"I think you should."

"I'll leave in the morning. You don't mind if I stay here tonight?"

"No, but where do you plan to go in the morning?"

"California, I think."

A great state to get lost in. "How? Hitchhiking? Chivalry really is dead, babe. There are men out there who'll have you hooked on drugs and hooking

so fast you'll be under your hundredth john before
you figure out what's happening."

"I wish you'd stop talking about that. You make
me sick." Her tone was oddly perfunctory, as if
her thoughts were on something else entirely.

"So I've noticed," I said. "And I'm one of the
good guys. I don't seduce young girls with drugs
and sex and turn them out to sell their goodies on
the street so I can wear silk shirts and snort coke
all day. Think how sick the bad guys would make
you feel."

"Honestly, you make it sound like every girl who
leaves home becomes a prostitute. Women can
take care of themselves."

"I'm not talking about women in general. I'm
talking about young girls — or boys, it doesn't
matter — who are unprepared to be on their own,
who cut themselves off from their families and
friends, who are either afraid or unwilling to go to
the authorities for help, who just plain don't have
a chance. I've never met a hooker yet who just
woke up one fine morning and said, well golly gee
whiz, I think I'll go out and be a prostitute. It just
happens. It beats starving."

"I would never do that."

"Maybe not. You're smarter than the average
hooker. But you'll do what you've already done.
You'll go with the first man who seems to offer
some kind of security, no matter how temporary.
If I told you sleeping with me was the price you

had to pay for a roof over your head and food to eat, would you do it?"

"No, I wouldn't," she said, with a little honest emotion in her voice finally. "And if you had any sense you wouldn't go around telling people you consort with prostitutes."

"Is consorting as dirty as it sounds? My association with prostitutes has always been strictly business — my business, not theirs. I used to be a cop."

She paled to roughly the color of the paper napkin she suddenly pressed to her mouth.

"Are the police after you?" I didn't get an answer. "Look, my only connection with the cops right now is trying not to let them catch me breaking any laws. I won't turn you in. But if you've done something besides attempted car theft, I might be able to help. If you're just worried about your folks filing a missing person report, you might as well forget it. If some cop stumbles over you, he might take you in but they aren't out looking for nineteen-year-old runaways. They don't have time to look for ten-year-olds. There's no law against running away from home anyway."

"I haven't done anything wrong."

We sat silently for several minutes. Allison seemed to be doing a lot of swallowing. Finally she asked, "Where were you a policeman?"

"In Mackie."

She nodded. "I watched the news on television.

There was a story about a murder there. You were talking about it on the phone, about the man who was killed . . ."

"I was talking to the detective who was interviewed. He's a friend of mine. I was just curious about the case. I promise I'm not a cop any more. I quit almost three years ago."

"Why?"

"Why did I quit?" Why *did* I quit? I told her the truth. "I didn't like the Halloween decorations they had at the police station."

That answer got just the look it deserved, truth or not. I half expected her to ask what I did now but she didn't. She examined her fingernails, which were long and slender like the rest of her, unpolished but carefully manicured.

After a few minutes, I said, "Doesn't it bother you that they're probably worried sick?"

"Who?"

"Your parents," I suggested.

"Oh. No."

"Well, it should bother you."

"I meant nobody's worried about me. I don't have any family."

"What happened to your parents?"

The look she shot me was almost lethal. "They died," she said. "Obviously."

"I understood that. I meant —" I broke off and reached a hand across to her as she turned ashen and inhaled sharply. "I'm sorry. Did it happen recently?"

She shook her head no, nodded yes, shook her head no again and stood up, shoving the chair backward. It didn't shove well on the carpet and tipped over, the legs coming up and catching her behind the knees. She toppled over with it. I stood up to help but sat down again — very abruptly — to give Allison, who was definitely a natural blonde, a chance to get her legs untangled and my shirts pulled down.

When she was on her feet, I stood up and started to apologize again. She brushed past me. The bathroom door slammed. I sat back down and listened to her vomit, feeling like I just drop-kicked a kitten.

She was even paler when she came out. She headed straight for her bed, crawled in, and pulled the covers up to her chin. When I crouched beside the bed and touched her forehead, she told me to leave her alone. Her skin was icy and damp. After a moment, I figured out what the funny noise was.

"For Christ's sake, your teeth are chattering," I said. "Scoot over."

She looked a bit wary but she scooted. I lay down beside her and pulled her close. "Body heat," I said. "Mother Nature's miracle drug." She felt stiff and resistant beside me. I cast about for a topic of conversation in a brain that was suddenly dealing only with tactile input. The best I could do was the weather.

"This rain is typical Portland weather. They call it Portland mist. If you live here, you learn to ignore it. Residents of Portland are called Webfoots. There are mountains all around, the Cascades to the east and the Coast Range to the west, but usually there's so much cloud cover you can't see them. So when a nice clear day comes along, guess what people here say."

She raised up on her elbow to look at me. "Look, there are mountains over there?" she suggested.

"Close, but no cigar. What they say is, 'The mountains are out.' "

For the first time, Allison smiled at me, a smile like sunshine in Portland — well worth the wait.

"The mountains are out," she said. "I like that."

"So do I."

She lay down beside me again, banging her elbow against my gun in the process. She looked a bit puzzled but didn't ask what the hunk of metal against my side was. Maybe she thought I had some weird prosthetic device to keep the old ticker going. The old ticker was thudding heavily, coping with the stress of repressed lust.

I felt around under the covers and found her hand. Her fingers were cool but not icy. I held her hand until it warmed up in mine then I pulled her a little closer. Her waist felt impossibly slender beneath the soft wool of my shirt. She no longer felt cold. In fact, her thigh resting against mine seemed to be generating a phenomenal amount of heat. I moved my head a bit to see if maybe she was thinking about how good I felt against her.

She wasn't.

I got my arm from beneath her without waking her and, after clearing away the remains of our dinner, I changed into jeans and a waist-length denim jacket over a blue chambray shirt. If I left the jacket unbuttoned, the gun wasn't obvious except to anyone who was looking for it. The western boots I pulled on made me six and a half feet tall and the cowboy hat added a few more inches. As Virginia Marley had pointed out, surreptitiousness isn't my strong suit.

I faced the mirror, drew two six-shooters, and shot my reflection twice. I blew smoke off the barrels then twirled the guns elaborately, which is easy with make-believe guns, then slapped them into invisible holsters. There was a smothered laugh from behind me.

"I want to be a cowboy when I grow up," I said, turning to face the bed.

Allison was raised up on one elbow. She brushed her hair back from her face and asked where I was going. I told her back to work.

"You work funny hours."

"I have a funny job. Get some rest. It'll be late when I get back. Leave the dead bolt off and I won't have to wake you to get in."

She nodded. "Mr. Smith?"

"Zachariah."

"Just . . . thank you."

"You're welcome," I said and went out into a misty rain to look for Jessica Finney.

CHAPTER TWELVE

I SPENT THE EVENING HOURS ON SOUTHEAST 82ND Street, where the cops' latest efforts to curb the cruising didn't seem to be working. School was still several days in the future and the kids were out in force. The ones in cars were mostly suburbanites out looking for kicks.

I was more interested in the kids in the shadows of the street, the runaways who wouldn't go home and the throwaways who couldn't go home because Robert Frost was wrong — they don't have to take you in. Some of them would be on the street briefly then go on to something else, something better if they were lucky. Others would live out their lives in this shadow world where a warm bed was a dream and a loving touch was no longer dreamed of. Still others would die on the street before they were old enough to understand that death was possible. There but for the grace of God and my parents' money . . .

There are no palm trees on 82nd Street but in the ways that matter, it's no different from the street in L.A. where I sojourned in the shadow world half my lifetime ago. The street seduces with the illusion of freedom and the price of the illusion is isolation. I had watched muggings, had seen the aftermath of rape and murder, had watched someone whose name I knew — as close to friendship as you get on the street — die with the needle still in the vein. None of it touched me. And I didn't want to leave.

I had to be locked up to be kept off the street and it was years before I felt any gratitude toward the people who had turned the key in the lock, years before I even acknowledged the simple fact that my parents might have had other uses for the thousands of dollars it cost them to get my act cleaned up. Years before I felt any guilt over what I had done to them or to myself. My only guilt back then was for Carrie and it was her guilt that she hadn't broken the code of our childhood and betrayed me that kept me from returning to the street. Carrie's guilt and the thin scar on her left wrist that was a constant reminder of that guilt.

I didn't want to find Jessica on 82nd Street and I didn't. About a quarter to eleven I decided to see if I could find Virginia Marley instead.

Once I located Tonita's, finding Virginia was a cinch. She was sitting at the bar, wearing a sizzling red dress and a matching smile. We had time for one quick drink before she asked me to walk her home, which turned out to be just around the corner. Her little orange bug was snug in a carport beneath her living room. The small apartment was haphazardly furnished and had a temporary look to it. Virginia hadn't struck me as the homebody type.

She confessed to having three wine coolers and one carton of yogurt in her refrigerator. "Would you like a drink?" she asked. "Or a joint? I don't have any coke. I started worrying about my nose and gave it up."

"Thanks, I don't want anything."

She was standing very close to me. She tilted her head and smiled and said, "Nothing?"

I smiled back at her. "I can't stay. I have to get back to work."

She eliminated the few inches of space between us, sliding her arms around my neck and pulling my head down toward her. After a long kiss, she whispered those three magic words in my ear. "Quickies are fun."

I picked her up. "The bed's that way," she said. She didn't indicate any direction at all but any half-way decent detective can find a bed in a three-room apartment.

I left Virginia shortly after midnight. I had spent the evening watching the young kids doing their buying and selling of booze and drugs and bodies. Now I set off to watch the grown-ups do the same thing. Drugs and bodies anyway. They could buy the booze at any state liquor store.

Portland doesn't have a well-defined red light district like Boston's Combat Zone. Late at night, downtown is largely the domain of the male prostitutes, some of them gay, some of them gay-for-pay, all of them virtually immune from arrest because cops don't like the role-playing necessary to get evidence against male prostitutes.

The girls tend to work semi-residential streets close in to town. They work one street until the residents make enough noise to force the cops to roust them, then they move their operation a few blocks one direction or the other. I found the current "O's Stroll" by the simple expedient of asking a cop where the hookers were. He looked disgusted but he told me.

Since prostitutes are pretty sure they know a cop when they see one, my conversations with them invariably began with the girls saying "Oh, fuck" in tones of deep disgust. Once they realized I wasn't going to take them out of commission for the couple hours it took to be processed and released, they were usually friendly and helpful. None of them had ever seen Jessica Finney.

It was about two o'clock when I called my office number for the dozenth time. Dora, who was the girl most likely in my high school class, was delighted to tell me I was wanted by the police. I laughed obligingly. The message was to call Detective Bundy at the Justice Center. I decided to go see him instead.

I drove downtown with an uneasy feeling in the pit of my stomach. The last time the cops found a runaway I was looking for, she was dead.

CHAPTER THIRTEEN

JESSICA FINNEY WASN'T DEAD AS FAR AS ANYONE knew, but the girl in the photo Bundy slid across his desk to me definitely was. She had frizzy blond hair, a pug nose, and a bullet hole in her forehead.

"Ever seen her?" Bundy asked. He was a medium-tan black man with short graying hair and light brown eyes behind gold-rimmed glasses. Anyone who overlooked the hard line of muscle beneath his shirt would have called him skinny.

"No," I said.

He drummed his fingers on the desk and stared at me for a while then his phone buzzed and he spent several minutes saying "uh-huh" into it, staring at me the whole time. By the time he hung up, I was ready to confess to anything.

Without looking at any notes, he said, "Zachariah O'Brien Smith. Age twenty-nine. Currently single. No military service. BA from Portland State in Administration of Justice. Six years with Mackie PD, four in uniform, last two as a detective. Two citations for meritorious service. Resigned three years ago citing personal reasons. Co-owner of C & Z Paperhanging, Incorporated. Sole owner and operator of Arrow Investigations for the past two and a half years. That about do it?"

"Story of my life," I said. Currently single. Interesting way to put it. Diplomatic.

"What were the citations for?"

"Why didn't you ask?"

He tilted his chair back, clasped his hands behind his head, and stared at me.

I cleared my throat. "Mackie's a small town. They give those things out all the time. Gives the newspaper something to print."

He kept on staring. I looked at my knees. Back at Bundy. Still staring. I checked out his desk. The nameplate said he was Jefferson Bundy. Good name.

"One was for rescuing some people in a nursing home fire. The other one . . . some hopped-up kid tried to hold up a drug store. It turned into a hostage situation." It turned into a bloodbath.

Bundy lowered his chair legs to the floor. "Oh, yeah," he said. "That's where I've seen you before. Knew you looked familiar. You're the cop in the picture."

The cop in the picture. My claim to fame. The picture had been in a lot of newspapers, in a magazine, and finally in a book after it won the photographer some kind of award. I had a copy at home but I never looked at it. It was a good picture in high contrast black and white that for some reason has a gritty realism missing from color photographs. A very good picture of a big tough cop with blood on his hands, caught in the act of crying.

"Who's C?" Bundy asked.

"Who's what?"

"C & Z. The paperhanging business."

"Oh. My sister. She's management. I used to be labor but we have four guys working for us now and they handle most of it."

"So what do you do now?"

I thought it over briefly. "Public relations," I said. Carrie would have laughed herself sick.

"What were the personal reasons?"

"Why?"

"Just curious. Four years in school, six on the force, and six months after you quit you get a PI license. You must like the work. So why quit?"

"What's with the dead girl?"

Bundy touched the photo in front of him. "Diane Dobbs AKA DeeDee Dobbs. Part-time waitress, part-time night school student. Ex-hooker. Shot entering her apartment about nine this evening. Weapon was a .22. No witnesses."

"I don't carry a .22."

Bundy grinned. "Smith and Wesson thirty-eight. You want the serial number?"

I shook my head. "What's it got to do with me?"

"Maybe nothing. She had one of your pictures of the Finney girl in her purse."

I looked at the photograph again. "I didn't give her one. She must have picked it up somewhere.

They're probably blowing all over the streets by now."

"Why do you suppose she kept it?"

"How the hell would I know? Maybe she saw Jessica and was thinking about calling me. Maybe she needed a piece of scratch paper. Maybe she doesn't like littering."

"Didn't like littering. She turned seventeen last month."

"Yeah. I've never seen her."

"No military service surprises me."

"The draft was over. I offered to do my patriotic duty anyway but Uncle Sam didn't want me."

"What was the problem, they didn't have boots big enough?"

"They didn't want an ex-junkie."

Bundy wasn't surprised. Whoever gave him his information had been thorough. "Shit," he said, "the only time I did drugs was in Nam."

"You have any more questions? I've been up since five this morning and I'd like to get a little sleep if it doesn't inconvenience the cops too much."

"Where were you at nine this evening?"

"When did they repeal Miranda-Escobedo?"

"Couple weeks ago. It was in all the papers. Jesus, wouldn't that be the day?" Bundy laughed, his laugh turning into a yawn. "I hate these hours. I miss my wife poking me in the ribs all night, telling me to roll over and stop snoring." He took his glasses off and massaged the bridge of his nose.

"I just like to know who I'm dealing with. Keep in touch. I'd like to know if you find your runaway."

I stood up and held onto the back of the chair. "I quit . . . I don't know why I quit. My wife left me." Understatement of the century.

Bundy nodded. "See you around," he said.

It had been a long day. I decided to call it a night.

Allison slept through my homecoming. She had left the bathroom light on and I did the same in case the light was for her instead of for me. I pulled my clothes off and rolled into bed, thinking that for once I was surely tired enough to sleep.

Thirty minutes later I was still staring at the ceiling, deep in my nightly litany of April memories. Damn April to hell anyway.

CHAPTER FOURTEEN

SLEEPING DEEPLY IS ONE OF SEVERAL THINGS I'M lousy at. I was aware of Allison getting out of bed early the next morning. I heard her in the shower and I heard her moving around the room afterward. It wasn't until her movements took on a stealthy quality that I really woke up.

I was on my stomach, my face turned toward the window. I kept my eyes shut and concentrated on breathing deeply. She seemed to stand at the foot of my bed for a long time then I heard the soft rustle of her dress close by.

I opened my eyes just in time to watch her slide my wallet out of the back pocket of the jeans I'd dropped on the floor the night before. She had her lower lip caught up in her teeth and a look of fierce concentration on her face. When she looked my way and our eyes met, she jumped about six inches and exhaled loudly. She also blushed, probably all the way down to her bellybutton but I could only see as far as the hollow in her throat.

I took my wallet from her limp fingers, shoved it under my pillow, went back to sleep, and dreamed tortuous dreams in which I pushed through crowds of faceless people in pursuit of a dark-haired woman in an emerald green dress. She seemed to be very close but I could never reach her and when she looked back at me, she had a maddening habit of changing from April to Allison to Virginia Marley. When she turned into a frizzy-haired blonde with a bullet hole in her forehead, I struggled awake, with Jefferson Bundy on my mind.

He must have thought I was crazy. I decided to believe I overreacted to his questions because I was tired. I was as sane as the next person. Of course, the next person was a runaway blonde who was a bad car thief and a worse pickpocket. Not very reassuring.

I rolled over and sat up. Allison was sitting cross-legged at the foot of her bed watching "Wheel of Fortune" with the sound off. At the sound of my movement, she tipped her head forward so her hair made an effective screen between us. I stayed in bed long enough to figure out the puzzle — "WALK DON'T RUN" — then I pulled on my jeans, gathered up some clean clothes and my wallet and went into the bathroom. I came back out immediately to get my gun out of the bed where it had nestled next to me all night. I concealed it in a shirt to carry it into the bathroom. Hiding it wasn't really necessary. Allison had apparently decided she was never going to look at me again.

When I finished in the bathroom, I checked myself out in the bureau mirror, considering a tie and deciding against it. I was wearing blue pants and a navy blazer over a white-on-white shirt. I looked at Allison's mirror image. She had turned the volume up on the television and was watching a commercial for Stayfree Maxi-Pads as if her life just might depend on it.

"Would you like to go downtown this morning?" I asked.

She shook her head then said, "Oh, yes. Of course. I'll get my things." She untwined her legs and went into the bathroom, leaving the door ajar. I heard the clinking of jars and bottles. When I looked in, she was reloading her purse.

"I didn't mean I want to get rid of you. I just thought you might not want to sit around here all day. Portland's a great town for a walking tour. I have a map you can take and we can meet somewhere later and I'll bring you back here."

She managed to meet my eyes in the mirror for about half a second. "All right," she said.

"Would you feel better if I told you I committed burglary on a regular basis when I was younger than you are?"

"No." She looked at me in the mirror again. "Is that true?"

I said it was and she asked how a burglar could get a job as a policeman.

"You're only a criminal if you get caught," I said.

"Why would you do that?"

"Steal? Same reason you would. I needed money."

She unloaded her purse and got her sweater and we headed out. After a quick stop for Egg Mc-Muffins which Allison insisted on eating in the car, we crossed the Willamette. When I told her what river it was, she smiled and said it would be hard to miss.

I found a parking spot downtown and spread my map across the steering wheel. Allison put her glasses on and slid over to look at it.

"You'll be better off staying downtown. That's this area where we are, mostly high-rise buildings. Old Town is this part." I pointed it out on the map. "You'll know it if you wander into it. It looks just like it sounds. You'd be all right there in the daytime but you might not like it. All this area around here is called Fareless Square. You can ride the buses and MAX for free."

"What's MAX?"

"The light rail system. Metropolitan Area Express. Like a subway but above ground. And cleaner. You'll see it." I made a big X on the map. "This is Pioneer Courthouse Square. Meet me there about two o'clock. You can't miss it; it's a plaza, paved with brick, and it has a lot of stairs. You got all that?"

She said yes and put her glasses and the map in her purse.

"Ignore the drunks and the panhandlers. Don't

give them any money. If you need to ask directions, go in a store and ask someone who's working. Don't talk to strangers on the street."

She smiled. "I've been shopping in Manhattan. I think I can survive in Portland, Oregon."

I tried to figure out how many states she could live in and go shopping in New York. She must have read my mind. "I don't live near there," she said.

"I'll walk you down to the Galleria," I said. "You'll like it. There are about fifty shops."

I left her gazing into shop windows and spent the next few hours traipsing around not finding Jessica Finney.

At a quarter to two I arrived at Pioneer Courthouse Square and took full advantage of the fact that I had a legitimate excuse to closely scrutinize every female there. There wasn't a one of them who wasn't worth looking at. As Phil Pauling once said, they don't call Oregon the Beaver State for nothing.

A couple minutes after the hour, I saw the best looking one of them all heading my way. I noted the changes in her appearance with interest. Her hair was tucked up beneath a big floppy-brimmed straw hat with an attached white scarf that was tied in a bow under her chin. Her eyes were hidden behind very large, very dark sunglasses. When she got closer, I saw that she had also bought new pantyhose. The run was gone.

She took off the sunglasses when she reached me and did the standard tourist's double-take at the man with the umbrella who was a few feet away from me. She laughed with delight and walked over to take a closer look at him.

"He's wonderful," she said, gingerly touching his arm as if he might object. He was fairly wonderful, life-sized and life-like down to the wrinkles in his metal skin. He was frozen forever in mid-step, one hand upraised to hail a cab or a friend, the other hand holding an open umbrella over his head.

"Does he have a name?" Allison asked.

"Officially it's called *Allow Me* but most people just call it the man with the umbrella."

We took a quick tour of the Square. Allison was intrigued by the bricks beneath our feet, which were imprinted with the names of people who had donated money for the development of the Square.

I suggested lunch at the restaurant on the upper level. Allison preferred hot dogs and Cokes from the vendor at the bottom of the stairs. I'm easy. We had hot dogs. We sat near the fountain to eat them. The clouds cooperated by blowing apart, providing what the weathermen in Portland like to call a sunbreak. The Square filled up with Webfoots scurrying out to take advantage of the break in the gloom.

I asked Allison how she liked Portland. She loved it, which wasn't surprising. Most people do. Portland has all the problems that plague any metropolitan area but it's easy to forget the problems when you can turn just about any corner and find a park or a fountain or a statue or a work of art disguised as a building.

She had ridden a bus and MAX and preferred MAX. She had also ignored my advice and wandered through Old Town, spending some time window-shopping at the Skidmore Fountain Building.

"What's the Saturday Market?" she asked. "I saw a sign."

"That big empty area under the foot of the Burnside Bridge is set up as an open-air market every weekend except in the dead of winter. You'd like it. The merchandise is all hand-crafted and there are lots of food stalls. Maybe you can go Saturday. In the meantime, why don't we go buy you some clothes."

She balked politely until I assured her she could consider it a loan. She hadn't mentioned her purchases. In addition to the hat and sunglasses, she had a big flat bag from a stationery store. When we stood up to leave, she saw me glance at it and said, "Scratchboard." While I was pondering the significance of that, she started babbling.

"I know I shouldn't be buying things I don't really need when I hardly have any money and you're paying for my food and everything, but, well, it's windy here and my hair blows all over and . . . um . . ." She looked upward. The clouds had regrouped. Failing to find an explanation for the sunglasses, she fell silent.

"The hat's pretty," I said.

"Thank you."

I drove us out to Clackamas Town Center where Allison could shop while I gave Jessica's picture to the security people. Allison read all the freeway signs out loud on the way and asked if Milwaukie wasn't spelled wrong.

"Only if you're in Wisconsin," I said.

When we arrived at the mall, Allison checked the directory and decided on Penney's. I wondered if she had ever been inside a J.C. Penney's but I didn't argue. When we got to the women's clothing department, she suddenly became very shy about spending my money. She didn't know what to get.

"Pretend you're going away for a weekend and get what you'd take with you. A weekend in Portland, not Paris, okay?"

She said *"Oui, monsieur"* and headed into the racks of clothes.

On my way to and from the security office, I checked out the young girls. They were there, noisy droves of them, all sizes, shapes, and colors, but not a Jessica Finney among them.

Back at Penney's, I found Allison looking at panties. She told me to go away. I went to the luggage department and bought a medium-sized canvas suitcase. By the time I got back, Allison had her selections piled up at a checkstand. Her weekend wardrobe consisted of a pair of already-faded jeans, a pair of dressier dark blue pants, a white woven belt, three blouses — one blue, one pink, and one in blurry rainbow stripes —, three pairs of white panties, one bra, three pairs of blue cotton knee-high socks, a package of three pairs of pantyhose, a pale blue cotton nightgown, and a gathered, light-weight blue denim skirt with a wide ruffle around the bottom. I handed over three hundred-dollar bills and got back enough change to pay for a pair of white and blue Adidas in the shoe department. Size ten, which made Allison blush.

We stashed her purchases in the suitcase and then walked the length of the mall because she wanted to see it. We took a break midway and ate frozen yogurt while we watched the ice skaters on the level below us.

On the way back to the entrance nearest where I'd parked, we stayed on the second level. We were walking on a wide balcony. There was a matching balcony on the other side of a wide open space revealing the lower level of the mall. On the other balcony I spotted a definite Jessica Finney type in the center of a group of girls who looked as if they didn't have mothers to nag at them. I stopped and leaned against the railing, waiting for her to turn toward me.

She didn't cooperate. The nearest connection between the two balconies wasn't close and involved going downstairs and then up again. The makers

of malls don't believe in the closest distance between two points.

Allison was fidgeting beside me. I whistled my
very best, very loudest male chauvinist pig wolf-
whistle. Every female face in the place turned
toward me. The girl wasn't Jessica. I waved at her
anyway and the whole cluster of girls giggled, wig-
gled, waved, and blew kisses.

Allison was looking faintly aghast. I grabbed her
arm. "Let's get out of here before I'm mobbed by
a horde of sex-crazed teenyboppers."

All the way to the car, Allison shot me little
sideways looks as if she had serious doubts about
my sanity.

I stopped at a Fred Meyer on the way back to
the motel and bought fruit and snack food and junk
food and beer and soda pop to stock the room.
Allison chose to sit in the car while I did the
shopping.

She had kept her hat on all day but had removed
the sunglasses at the mall. When I pulled into a
parking place at the back of the motel, she put
them on for the ten-foot walk to the building and
didn't take them off again until we were safely in
the room.

While she was in the bathroom, with the water
running full force as usual, I peeked into the stationery store bag. Scratchboard was heavy paper,
more like cardboard actually, with a glossy black

coating on one side. There was also a metal straightedge in the bag.

She emerged from the bathroom and I went into it to change into jeans and my denim jacket. When I was ready to go, I told her I wasn't sure when I'd be back. She nodded absently, intent on cutting the price tags off her new clothes with the tiny scissors from her manicure set.

I picked up the Monday *Oregonian* as I was leaving the room. I had barely glanced at it but Allison had done the crossword. I stopped in the lobby to buy the Tuesday edition then I sat in the car and went through both papers page by page. I went through the Monday edition a second time looking for missing pages. There weren't any. There was also no picture of Allison and no story about a missing nineteen-year-old blonde.

So why the disguise?

Chapter Fifteen

I RESUMED MY SEARCH FOR JESSICA FINNEY, TAKING a break to have dinner with Virginia. Our plan to go to her place afterward was foiled when I checked in with the service before we left the restaurant. I had two messages. Call Hank Johnston and call Jefferson Bundy.

Hank answered the phone on the first ring. Jessica had called him thirty minutes earlier.

"She wants me to give her old man a message," Hank said. "I didn't call him yet. She knows about you. She said to tell her dad she doesn't want to come home and he should tell you to stop looking for her."

"Did she say where she was?"

"She said Portland and I asked whereabouts and she said downtown. I asked her if she was sleeping on the street and she didn't answer. I told her I could send her some money if she gave me an address, trying to find out where she was, you know. Well, I would send her money. But she said she didn't need any and then she said she was at a pay phone and couldn't talk any longer and she hung up."

"Does she know who I am or just that her dad hired a detective?"

There was a short silence then Hank said, "I guess I blew it. She knew a detective was looking for her and I said I knew because you talked to me. And I guess I kinda told her about you being the guy who talks at school. She remembers you okay. The girls think you're a real hunk. They practically drool while you're talking." Hank sounded bitter. "I guess I shouldn't've told her, huh?"

"Don't worry about it. It probably won't make much difference. You want me to talk to her dad?"

"Yeah. I don't want to call him. He acts like it's all my fault. Shit, I didn't want her to leave."

I told him to call me right away if Jessica contacted him again then I called Jason Finney. After some lengthy cursing, he asked if I thought Jessica had told Hank the truth about being downtown. I didn't point out that he should know his daughter a little better than I did.

"It makes sense," I said. "She was seen at both those acting schools Thursday and she knows I'm here. I've spent a lot of time downtown."

He said, "Shit."

I told him I'd call again as soon as I had some news. He said "yeah" and hung up on me. Maybe he just didn't like good-byes.

I dropped Virginia off at her apartment and drove to the Justice Center. This time the picture Bundy slid across his desk was of a young black girl with two inches of blond at the ends of her dark hair and a thin scar like a whipmark down the side of her face. The bullet had shattered the bone beneath her right eye.

I shook my head. "Did she have Jessica's picture, too?"

"No, but the gun was the same one used on Diane Dobbs. This one is Karen Baylor, sixteen, ex-hooker. She quit the business about six months ago and moved in with her sister. The sister and her husband work graveyard shift. They got home this morning and found her on the floor. Time of death is within two hours of the time Dobbs was shot."

"Did they have the same pimp?"

"No. Dobbs' pimp is still around but he has an ironclad alibi for Monday night. He was here waiting to make bail. If he didn't do Dobbs, there's no reason to think he did Baylor. Baylor's pimp OD'd and she jumped at the chance to get off the street. The sister says she was in a drug rehab program and was planning to go back to school next month." Bundy picked up the picture, shaking his head slightly.

"Maybe you have a psycho killing hookers."

"So why ex-hookers? Why not the girls on the street?"

"Maybe some john didn't like them quitting. Did

you want to know where I was when Baylor was shot?"

"Not unless you plan to confess so I can wrap this up."

"Maybe later. I need to find Jessica first."

I called Virginia from a pay phone and told her I wouldn't be over. The dead girls didn't have anything to do with Jessica but knowing she was out in a world where young girls were being shot to death on a regular basis took my mind off sex.

I wandered the dark streets and the darker parks of Portland for hours, looking for Jessica. As the night grew later and lonelier I became aware that I was also looking for April. But then, I always looked for April. I didn't see her nearly as often as I used to.

At one in the morning, I decided coffee might help. I found an open cafe and checked the sign in the window. The place had met the health department standards. I would have preferred a sign that said "Exceeded" but in some neighborhoods it doesn't pay to be choosy.

I walked on in. The clientele was eclectic. I got some "woo-woo's" and a lot of batting eyelashes from the group in the first booth. The drunks were in the back, shaky hands wrapped around coffee mugs. Two working girls at the counter gave me a visual frisk and decided to set up shop elsewhere. They departed with elaborate nonchalance.

I chose a booth midway between the drunks and

the gays so as not to offend anyone. A waitress came and snapped her gum at me. I ordered black coffee. She said the cherry pie was good. I ordered cherry pie. She fished down the sleeve of her blouse for her bra strap and plucked it into place. It made the same snapping sound as her gum.

I slouched down in the seat, stretching my legs out beneath the table. There was a kid at the counter with a bleached mohawk and no less than five earrings piercing the one ear I could see. He was wearing a black leather vest with nothing under it and jeans that looked older than he did. Next to him, a pale boy in a green fishnet shirt and Spandex pants was whispering sweet nothings into the ear of a man even I wouldn't have wanted to meet in a dark alley. A tired black woman in a tireder white uniform was propping her head up down at the end of the counter. Next to her, in a turquoise and gold caftan, was the most beautiful person in the world.

I was caught staring and received a smile of infinite sweetness. The vision slid off the stool and floated my way, the caftan swinging gracefully from side to side, giving me glimpses of tiny feet in blue satin dance shoes. Above the glimmering gown, the face was exotically Eurasian with big round dark eyes, broad cheekbones tapering to a fragile chin, and a full, heart-shaped mouth, all framed by silky, shiny black hair in a deliberately ragged lost-waif style. The perfect face for a "save-this-child" poster. I was smitten. I was also stumped.

I tried to check for breasts. The caftan wasn't giving anything away. Neither were the hands which are usually a dead giveaway. The fingers were slender with rosy, perfectly manicured nails. One of them pointed questioningly toward the bench across from me. I nodded and unslouched.

What do you say to a person of indeterminate sex? I tried "hello" and got the same back. The voice was light and breathy and no help at all.

The snappy waitress plunked coffee and pie down in front of me. "Would you like a soda or something?" I asked my guest.

"No, thank you." The lashes fluttered. "May I have some pie?"

The waitress had walked away. I pushed the plate across the table and drank my coffee while I studied the exquisite child eating my pie.

The face was even better up close, lightly, flawlessly made-up with a bit of emphasis on the eyes. The lashes were long, the lids painted a faint tint of the blue in the caftan. The caftan looked expensive and was backed up by jangling bracelets and dangling earrings that looked as good as Allison's jewelry.

"What's your name?" I asked.

A tiny pointed tongue licked cherry juice off the back of the fork. "Nikki, N,I,K,K,I, darling."

The spelling didn't help. Neither did the endearment.

"Is that short for something?"

"Just Nikki." The smile was impish. "I haven't seen you around here before."

"I'm from out of town."

"What are you doing here?"

I smiled, choosing my words carefully. "I'm looking for a young girl."

The lovely, androgynous face fell with disappointment. Whatever Nikki was now, he had started life as his mother's bouncing baby boy. I felt on firmer ground. "Actually, I'm looking for a specific girl." I gave him a flier from the binder.

"Oh, perfect," he said. "A private detective. What's your name?"

"Zachariah Smith."

"Zachariah is nice."

"Zachariah is downright Biblical."

A tiny line appeared between Nikki's brows. "I don't remember who he was. In the Bible, I mean."

I wondered how much time a boy in make-up and dance slippers spent reading the Bible. Maybe a lot, he seemed genuinely distressed over his failure to place the name.

"The father of John the Baptist," I said. "A bit part."

"Oh, yes. The Book of Luke. An angel told him he would have a son who would be great before the Lord. Do you believe in angels?"

"No, but if there are any, they should look just like you."

Nikki's laugh was light and tinkly, like a windchime made of thin glass. He looked at Jessica's picture again.

"I don't think I've ever seen her. I don't really pay much attention to the girls. I'll keep this. I have some friends. . . . Would she be hooking?"

"Maybe."

"I don't. I have a friend." Nikki touched the golden bracelets on his wrist.

"Do you have parents?" I asked.

"Well, I did." The impish smile flashed. "I don't think an angel warned them about me." His eyes widened with glee. "I would have been aborted."

"That would have been a shame."

"Sometimes," Nikki said, "I have more than one friend."

I shook my head. "Not that kind of friend anyway. I need to get going. You want to come with me? I'm going to check out the park."

Nikki couldn't think of anything he would rather do. We left the cafe amidst a flurry of lewd comments from the fluttery bunch at the first booth. "They're just jealous," Nikki said.

The top of his head came to about the middle of my upper arm. He took two or three steps to every one of mine. We walked through the north end of Waterfront Park, disturbing several sleepers, none of them Jessica. Nikki kept up a running patter about people he knew.

On the way out of the park I was shaken down by a cop who examined my identification at length but didn't ask a single question of the child by my side who was in flagrant violation of the state curfew laws. As he was leaving, the cop said "It's getting late" to the air above Nikki's head.

Nikki made a call from a pay phone and within five minutes a long silver-gray limo with tinted windows slid up to the curb. Nikki blew me a kiss before disappearing into the back seat of luxury. A friend indeed.

It was almost three in the morning. I decided to call it quits. I called the answering service first. No one wanted me. Good.

Chapter Sixteen

Allison was asleep, her hair glimmering in the light coming through the half-open bathroom door. I took a quick shower. I didn't have any reason to think the sound of a man taking a shower ten feet away would wake her, so I just wrapped a towel around my waist before I left the bathroom, leaving the light on and pulling the door mostly closed behind me.

I turned toward my bed, took one step and stopped, doing a pretty good imitation of a man walking into a glass wall.

Allison was standing just in front of me.

She was wearing the white slip I had last seen dripping dry over the shower door. It was silky and wonderfully clingy against the bare skin beneath it. Her eyes were downcast.

I felt my heartbeat quicken and my breathing deepen. I had time for one completely rational thought — "This isn't a good idea" — and one semi-rational thought — "I should have shaved" — before my brain shut down all areas relegated to reason.

She raised her eyes to mine. I took a step toward

her. She didn't scream or faint or run away so I took another step. She tilted her head up and I bent to kiss her, a nice long kiss that gave me plenty of time to get my arms around her and pull her close. Nothing feels as good as bare skin under silky fabric. Except bare skin under nothing. A concept that was sufficiently motivating to make me pick her up and carry her to my bed. I adroitly lost the towel en route.

For several minutes I was aware of nothing but the feeling of Allison's mouth against mine, the pressure of her body against mine. It was after I trailed kisses down her throat and found the swell of breast below that I began to get an uneasy what's-the-matter-with-this-picture kind of feeling.

She had seemed to enjoy the kisses but now she was very still, flat on her back, hands at her sides, legs straight. I had no particular objection to passive submission if that was what she liked, but I was being forcefully reminded of the time April read something about necrophilia and decided it would be fun to play dead. It hadn't worked out. Corpses aren't supposed to giggle.

Allison wasn't giggling. Allison was trembling. Passion, I assured myself. I found the hem of her slip and raised her slightly to slide the slip up above her breasts. She neither resisted nor assisted the maneuver. I circled a nipple with my tongue. She put a hand briefly on my shoulder. It wasn't a caress. There was too much pressure, almost as if she wanted to push me away but decided against it.

All right, not passion. She was nervous. We hardly knew each other, after all. So help her relax, I told myself. Talk to her. I would have been hard-pressed to yell "fire" if the bed burst into flames so I talked to myself instead. She's young, she's not very experienced. She's been with kids her own age. Nineteen-year-old boys aren't known for finesse and tend to think foreplay has something to do with tennis doubles. Living in a small town, I constantly run into women who were once the young recipients of my adolescent ardor. I always have to squelch an urge to tell them I've improved since then.

She's nervous, I assured myself again. Well, she'd relax soon enough. Onward and downward. I kissed my way to her bellybutton.

Sounding very distant, Allison said, "Mr. Smith?"

I pressed my mouth hard against her abdomen, trying not to laugh and laughing anyway. I sputtered loudly against her skin which she must have found either ticklish or disgusting as hell because she suddenly pushed herself backward and upward to a sitting position. Wondrous body parts slid past my face then her knee connected with my chin, clacking together a lot of very expensive dental work.

With a body-arching wriggle any sane man would have died to see, Allison tugged her slip back down where it belonged. I felt like a little kid watching his ice cream roll off the cone and plop in the dirt.

"I'm sorry I laughed. Mr. Smith sounded a little formal, under the circumstances. It's Zachariah, okay?"

She was intent on the wall beside the bathroom door. She said, "I changed my mind."

"Does it work better now?" I couldn't help it. I was suddenly under a lot of stress. I always react to stress with grade school humor.

She turned to look at me, her face blank. Then her eyes widened and she pressed her lips tightly together. And then she whooped, screeched, howled with laughter. I tried to shush her but started laughing myself. When I could, I gasped, "S-h-h! They're going to kick us out of here."

She reached over her head for a pillow and covered her face with it. I sobered up considerably watching her body shake with laughter under the thin slip. Eventually she got it under control and got rid of the pillow.

"Where have you been all your life?" I asked. "That joke's at least twice as old as I am."

"I never heard it before." She raised up on one elbow, facing me. She was still breathing raggedly, gasping back giggles, but when she glanced down the length of my body, her face became very serious. She lay down quickly and stared upward.

I twirled a long strand of honey hair around my

finger. "Why did you change your mind? You didn't like what I was doing?"

"It was all right," she told the ceiling.

"All right" sounded fairly uninspired. I'd been hoping for rave reviews. I didn't know what to say so I waited for her to think of something. She thought of the very last thing I expected to hear.

"I'm a virgin."

"You're a *what*?"

"A virgin?"

I shook her hair loose from my finger. I sat up. I stood up. "A virgin! A *virgin*!" If they didn't hear me back in Mackie, they weren't listening very hard. Allison slid over to the far edge of the bed, pulling all the covers up around her for protection against the maniac bellowing at her. "Are you crazy? Are you completely out of your mind? What kind of stupid stunt is this? Are you nuts? Virgins don't waylay strange men outside bathroom doors. You could get hurt. You could get *pregnant*." I worked several variations on the theme until I finally had to stop to breathe. When I did, I felt very naked — which I was — and made a grab for the sheet. Allison wasn't about to relinquish it and when I tugged, she resisted and toppled backward off the bed in a tangle of blankets. She hit a chair and it toppled too, striking the wall hard enough to make the window glass rattle.

The telephone rang.

In the spaces between the first three rings there

was dead silence in the room. Allison was on her feet across the bed from me, wrapped in a sheet, a blanket, and a blue fleur-de-lis bedspread. She was looking everywhere but at me. I ripped the bedspread off her bed and wrapped it around myself before picking up the phone on the fourth ring.

I assured the night manager that, no, there was no problem and, yes, we would keep it down and, of course, I realized it was four in the morning and, certainly, I understood that some of the guests were trying to sleep and, no, it wouldn't happen again. I replaced the receiver very gently.

Allison and I, in matching bedspreads, faced each other across the stripped bed. "We will discuss this in the morning," I whispered.

I unwrapped my makeshift toga and slid between the sheets of what had been Allison's bed. Still in all her wrappings, she flopped face down on what had been my bed. I gritted my teeth for a while, listening to her trying to be quiet. When I couldn't stand it any more, I pulled some jeans on and tugged her loose from her cocoon. I straightened the blankets out a bit and lay down beside her, pulling her close. "Stop crying. You should be spanked." Mindful of the neighbors, I whispered.

She wiped her wet face across my chest a few times and drew some sobbing breaths. "I'm sorry," she whispered.

"Well, you should be." I stroked her hair until she quieted down. She used my chest for a hanky several more times, the only use I've ever found for chest hair.

"Don't try that again, Allison. Some men are in a big hurry. You could have stopped being a virgin before you ever got around to mentioning it. What did you think you were doing anyway?"

"It's just . . . I need you to help me and I thought if you liked me . . . "

"I like you just fine. And I've offered to help. Several times."

"I know. But what I really need is money."

I sighed. "The going rate wouldn't get you very far."

She shoved hard against my chest with both hands. I didn't move but she did, sliding away from me and sitting up. She forgot to whisper. "Every time I think you're going to be nice, you say something absolutely disgusting. I hate you. Get out of my bed."

"Quiet down. I don't want to be kicked out of here. You can hate me all you want but the way you're going, you're going to end up hating yourself and that makes for a very unhappy life. Why don't you tell me why you're on the run and I'll see what I can do."

"I can't."

"Fine. Go to sleep."

I returned to the other bed. The light from the bathroom was right in my eyes. When I asked if she minded if I turned it off, she said. "I don't care.

I'm not afraid of the dark." There was just the slightest emphasis on the last word, making it sound as if there were a whole lot of other things she was afraid of.

It was a long time before I fell asleep but I never once thought of April.

CHAPTER SEVENTEEN

AN AWKWARD MORNING AFTER DIDN'T SEEM FAIR somehow. We sidestepped around each other while I was getting ready to go out. When I suggested breakfast, or an early lunch since it was almost eleven, Allison said she had eaten some of the fruit before I woke up and didn't want anything else. She never quite met my eyes.

I had the feeling her discomfort had little to do with her aborted seduction attempt and a lot to do with the fact that she was trapped in a small room with a man who had seen her naked. What we needed was an icebreaker. I didn't have any liquor or candy. Which left sex. Always in plentiful supply.

She was sitting at the bureau. I took away the brush she had just pulled through her hair for about the thousandth time and put my hands on her shoulders. After a moment she raised her eyes to mine in the mirror.

"Last night, did I get around to mentioning that you're beautiful?" She shook her head, looking just a bit skeptical. "I thought it," I said. "I was rendered speechless. Happens to me a lot."

Her mouth twitched. "I hadn't noticed that."

"Yeah, well, I'm great at reading people the riot act, not so great at other things."

She stood up, turning to face me. Since she was so close anyway, I kissed her, intending it to be a nice semi-brotherly, just-friends kiss. It started out all right, got muddled up in a hurry, and was becoming downright torrid when Allison slid her hand inside my jacket and ran right into my gun.

"That's a gun," she said, pulling her hand away quickly.

I pulled my jacket aside to check. "Well, I'll be damned, how did that get there?"

She was not amused. "You said you aren't a policeman anymore."

"I'm not." I unzipped my binder and handed her a Jessica Finney flier. "That's me, Arrow Investigations. I wanted to change the name to Cat's-Paw, Incorporated but my sister said no one would get it."

Carrie was probably right. Allison obviously didn't get it.

"It's from an old fable about a cat and a monkey. The cat was sleeping by a fire where the monkey was roasting some chestnuts. When the nuts were done, the monkey used the cat's paw to pull them out of the fire so he wouldn't burn his own fingers. People hire me to pull their chestnuts out of the fire."

Allison frowned at Jessica's picture. "You never really answered me the other day," she said.

"About what?"

"About if your wife died."

I had spent too much time in the company of women to wonder how she made the mental leap from a cat and a monkey to a wife. "She didn't die. We're divorced."

"Why did you get a divorce?"

"Irreconcilable differences are the only grounds you need."

She nodded. "What was the problem?"

Persistence, thy name is Allison. I bit back my anger. My divorce had no more immediacy to her than a story in a book. She didn't realize she was picking at scabs over deep wounds.

"Desertion. The ultimate irreconcilable difference."

She looked faintly shocked. "You deserted your wife?"

Now there was a sex-role stereotype if I'd ever heard one. "The other way around," I said.

She looked definitely shocked. "Your wife deserted you? Why would she do that?"

It was the question I went to bed with every night and woke up with every morning. I gave her the only answer I had ever come up with. "I don't know."

"You mean she just left without saying anything?"

"That's what I mean. That's what desertion is. We didn't discuss it in advance. I came home from work one day and she was gone. I haven't seen or heard from her since."

"But —"

"Allison. I don't want to talk about it, okay?"

"I just wondered how you could divorce her."

After a moment, I said, "I waited two years. That's a long time to be married to someone who isn't there."

"I meant, I thought you had to wait seven years or something if someone disappears."

"Oh. No, you just have to prove desertion. It wasn't hard. She took her clothes and the money from our savings account and left her wedding ring on the kitchen counter. Later on, I found out she cashed in her life insurance policy two weeks before she left. It obviously wasn't a spur of the moment decision."

"Did you try to find her?"

I had spent two years driving myself and everyone else crazy with my attempts to find April. "I looked for her myself and I hired a detective. Neither of us ever came up with anything. She doesn't want to be found. She hasn't used her social security number or filed a tax return since she left. She's either using phony identification or she's out of the country or someone else is supporting her." Or she was dead, which sometimes, late at night, was the choice that seemed least painful to me.

"Is that why you became a detective?"

"Not if you mean so I can spend the rest of my

life searching for her. I'm not looking for her any-more. But in a roundabout way it is. When I quit the cops, I worked part-time for a detective named Jake Matthews. He's the one I hired to look for April. Arrow Investigations was his then. Jake's way up in his sixties and he wanted to quit but couldn't afford to. He's the worst compulsive gam-bler I've ever known. If someone gave him good enough odds, he'd bet on the sun shining at mid-night. He used to drive across the state line every week and buy fifty bucks worth of Washington lot-tery tickets. And he hit it. Almost two million dollars. He signed the business over to me and the last I saw of him he was heading out of Mackie in a thirty-foot-long motor home. I get a postcard from him every now and then. Nice guy, but he ruined the lottery for me. Oregon started its own lottery after that but I can't get too interested in it. I figure the odds on two people who know each other both hitting the jackpot are astronomical."

Allison, who could fixate on strange details, said, "April's a pretty name."

"Yeah. I need to get to work."

"You don't like to talk about yourself, do you?"

I raised an eyebrow at her. "You won't tell me your last name."

"That's different. I can't tell you."

"Why not? Would I recognize it? Are you a run-away Rockefeller?"

She smiled. "No. I'm not rich either."

I tugged on the thin gold chain around her neck, pulling the stone into view. I noticed it last night but had been too distracted by the slip and what was under it to give much thought to a diamond the size of a pencil eraser. "Somebody's rich," I said.

She took the diamond from my fingers and twisted it slowly, catching the light. "It was a gift. I suppose I should sell it." She clasped the stone tight in her fist.

"Never sell anything with sentimental value. Look, I have to find Jessica or at least keep looking for her until her dad gets tired of paying me. Maybe afterwards I can help you out. In the meantime, you're doing all right here, aren't you? You haven't thrown up in at least twenty-four hours."

"Do you lift weights?" Another mind-boggling mental leap.

"Sometimes. I carried you up here, didn't I?"

She grinned. "How much do you weigh?"

"Oh, about two twenty. How much do you weigh?"

"Two hundred and twenty pounds!"

"Really? You don't look it."

She fell backward on the bed, laughing. She looked so good stretched out in her brand-new faded jeans that I joined her. Several minutes later she pulled her mouth away from mine.

"Zachariah?"

"Mm?"

"Do you think I'm sexy?"

We were pressed about as close together as two people can get with clothes on. "If you have to ask, I'm going to start worrying about being underendowed."

Her cheek warmed up beneath my lips. "Well, I suppose men always . . . well, I mean, if we weren't . . ."

"I thought you were sexy when you were up-chucking in the parking lot in Hood River."

She wrinkled her nose. "I'm not very pretty."

"You're way past pretty. You'll realize that when you get over wanting to be cute. Pretty doesn't have much to do with sexy anyway."

"I wouldn't mind being cute."

"Cute doesn't last, beauty does. You're beautiful. Trust me, I'm an expert."

"You can be very nice when you want to," she said.

I nuzzled her ear. "You're nice all the time." Allison chose that moment to move against me in a way guaranteed to turn any man's mind to Silly Putty. "Getting naughtier every minute though. Let me up, babe, before I forget how innocent you are."

While we were dallying, the light patter of rain against the window had changed to a hard splatter. I decided to give Jessica Finney credit for having enough sense to come in out of the rain. I wanted to see how Mackie's murder investigation was progressing anyway.

The Chief of Police answered the phone. I asked for Phil and Harkins asked who was calling. I gritted my teeth. I had learned years ago that it was impossible to disguise a distinctly rumbly baritone. Harkins knew my voice as well as he knew his own. I thought about hanging up but instead I said "Smith" and spelled it for him, slowly, as if I were speaking to someone with the IQ of a banana peel. Two grown men. I consoled myself with the fact that Harkins was twenty years my senior which had to make his behavior worse.

The phone clicked. I wasn't sure if he hung up or put me on hold. I waited and there was another click and Phil said, "Hey, Bucky. What's up?"

"Nothing. Just wondering how you're doing."

"Oh, I'm just hunky-dory. You know what we got here? We got us a locked room mystery, only it's a locked hotel. The night clerk swears up and down no one came in the hotel after midnight. The restaurant closed at eleven. None of the customers in the bar were hotel guests and they all left by the street exit. The clerk didn't see a living soul after midnight. Which means the killer came in earlier or came in through the parking lot entrance. That door's locked after eleven o'clock but all the room keys open it. Last winter when the Arms was having trouble with vandals spray-painting the halls in the middle of the night, we figured some kids got hold of a room key somehow and were using it to get in. So the Arms called in a locksmith and changed all the locks. Ever since then they've been keeping track of keys like they're gold bricks at Fort Knox. They even have signs in the rooms asking the guests to turn them in at the desk instead of leaving them in the room when they check out. Every goddamn one of the keys was accounted for Monday morning. Vanzetti's key was in his pants pocket. So what do you think?"

"Either the killer was in the hotel for several hours or Vanzetti went downstairs and let him in the back door. Or maybe Vanzetti went out and they came back together."

"That's a whole lot of tramping around the halls. The Arms is pretty small. None of the guests remember hearing anyone walking around. And the people in the room next to Vanzetti's are pretty sure his television was on for an hour or so before the shots. The woman's a light sleeper and she woke her husband up about four o'clock to bitch about the TV waking her up. You want to hear Harkins' theory?"

"Sure."

"He thinks the nightgown and the Kleenex are some kind of red herring. He thinks Vanzetti was smoked by a hit man from Chicago who was hired by his ex-bosses so he couldn't finger them if he got picked up on the federal warrant."

"You mean he thinks a hit man left a nightgown

and some dirty Kleenex to throw you off the track?"

"Shit, even Harkins isn't that dumb. He just thinks they don't have anything to do with the murder. I could almost buy the nightie as a coincidence. The cleaning ladies could have been careless. And Vanzetti was alone. He could've been there for three days without ever closing the john door. Or maybe he wouldn't bother complaining if he did see it. But there's no way in hell the Kleenex was in the trashcan for three days and the nightgown and mascara go together like a hooker's knees at the sight of an empty wallet."

"And you have the fingerprints. Someone was in the room long enough to get a drink."

"Yeah, too bad we don't have one of them super computers like the cops on TV have. We could zap those babies through it and come up with the owner's name, address, and favorite food in about five seconds flat. The only other new stuff I have is a bunch of worthless shit about Vanzetti. That man was a high-class transient. Lived in ritzy hotels, didn't have any personal belongings except a bunch of expensive clothes. Regular customer of a classy call-girl operation. Sounds like a real loner. Didn't socialize much even with his criminal buddies. They didn't like him because he was an unfriendly bastard but they tolerated him because he did his job."

"How did he get to Mackie?"

"If you mean how did he come about picking Mackie as a place to die, we don't know. How he got here was in a car. He left his brand-new Caddie behind in Chicago, bought an eighty-three Chevy off a used car lot. Paid cash and registered it under the name of John Thornton."

"You said he did twenty years. What was he in for?"

"Homicide. I wish some of these assholes we arrest would get twenty years. That was a while back though. Vanzetti was sent up when he was twenty-nine, got out when he was forty-nine. Hell of a way to spend the best years of your life, isn't it?"

"Sure is. Why hasn't there been any mention of a woman in the news reports?"

"Aw, that's the fucking Feds. They think they're running some kind of covert operation or something."

Phil was silent for a moment. Not exactly silent, he was whistling softly, a sure sign that his thoughts were elsewhere. I tried to see what Allison was doing. She had taken the stationery store bag out of a drawer and put her glasses on. She was sitting at the table with her back to me and was doing something that produced a tiny repetitive scratching sound. I couldn't figure it out.

"Did Vanzetti have a gun?" I asked Phil.

"No, and that's a hell of a note. Seems to me an ex-con running from the Feds would carry one. He had a shotgun and a rifle in the trunk of his car but nothing in the room. And no handgun in the car. Which makes me think maybe he was shot with his own gun and the killer took it with him. Or her. The other thing that's bugging the hell out of the Feds is where did Vanzetti get the hundred and fifty thousand. He wasn't paid enough to have that much petty cash lying around and he had a reputation for not putting anything away for a rainy day. So how are you doing? I haven't seen Jessica Finney down at the old malt shop."

"I'm still looking."

"Is it raining there?" Phil sounded wistful.

"Pouring, as a matter of fact."

"Jesus, I wish it would rain here. It was a hundred and two yesterday and the fucking air-conditioner went on the fritz. We had prisoners upstairs trying to confess to felonies just so's we'd transfer them to the county jail. We'll be lucky if one of them doesn't file a suit for cruel and unusual punishment. We finally took them outside and turned the hose on. You shoulda seen it, Bucky, a bunch of hungover drunks running through the sprinkler like little kids. And the photographer from the *Mirror* showed up, of course. Someone's yelling for me, I gotta go. Call me later."

I said okay and hung up. The telephone immediately rang.

It was Marilyn. "Well, it's about time," she said. "The motel operator had me on hold for ten minutes. Hank Johnston wants you to call. You have his number?"

"Yeah," I said. "Thanks." I broke the connection and called Hank. Same song, second verse. Jessica had called again to tell him to tell her dad to tell me to stop looking for her.

I called Finney. He swore lengthily, asked a few pointless questions, and hung up on me. He was consistent anyway. Since he hadn't fired me, I decided I'd better go out and look for his daughter.

But first I wanted to see what the scratching sound was. I walked over and stood behind Allison's chair. She had one of the tourist brochures that had been in the room open to a page with a picture of a full-blown rose. She was duplicating the flower on a piece of scratchboard she had cut to about five by seven inches. The rose, black like its background, was defined by the white highlights she was etching onto the paper. Each tiny movement of the X-Acto knife scraped off a bit of the black coating, revealing the white beneath it. I realized I had seen scratchboard drawings before and had admired them without having any idea how they were done.

"You're good," I said. "Are you an art student?"

She shook her head. "It's just a hobby."

I moved around so I could see her face. "What are you crying about?"

She took her glasses off and brushed a hand

across her wet cheeks. "Nothing. I was just feeling sad."

I crouched beside the chair. She leaned her head on my shoulder, wrapping her arms tight around me.

"I wish you'd let me help," I said.

She let go of me and straightened up. "I'm all right, really. I think it's the rain. It always makes me feel sad."

"It always makes me feel wet." She smiled, just a little. "And I have to go out in it now," I added. "Are you going to be okay?"

She nodded. I kissed her on the forehead and left.

Chapter Eighteen

THE STEADY RAIN DIDN'T MAKE IT ANY EASIER TO find Jessica but it didn't make it any harder either. I had my usual amount of success. I called my office number every thirty minutes out of sheer boredom. No one called in response to my fliers. Hank Johnston didn't call to betray any new confidences from Jessica. Jefferson Bundy didn't call to invite me down to look at pictures of dead girls. Jason Finney didn't call to hang up on me. In fact, the whole world didn't call.

Late in the afternoon, I was in the neighborhood so I stopped by the Justice Center to see if Bundy was around. He was.

"You're dripping all over the floor," he said by way of a greeting.

"It's raining." I shook the water from my cowboy hat and sat down on the chair in front of his desk. "Did you figure out who killed Dobbs and Baylor yet?"

"Hell, no. Did you find the Finney girl?"

I said no and told him about Jessica's calls to Hank.

"So you're looking for her and she's looking out for you. Maybe you should consider a disguise."

"I do a great Michael J. Fox impersonation. Listen, I met a boy late last night. He's about twelve, dresses like the Tooth Fairy, and lives with a 'friend' who gives him limo service home."

Bundy said, "You mean Nikki, darling?"

At least that's the way I heard it and in the instant before I heard it right, I felt my jaw drop. I started laughing so hard I almost tipped the chair over. Bundy crossed his arms and glared. After a moment, his shoulders were shaking. He gave up and started laughing too and then we were lost. Every time our eyes met we laughed harder, like two kindergartners caught in a giggling fit. Bundy finally walked out of the room. I deep-breathed for a while and managed to meet his eyes, straight-faced, when he came back.

"You mind telling me what I'm laughing about?"

I told him about Nikki introducing himself and my assumption that the "darling" was directed at me. "And when you said Nikki Darling . . ."

"Don't start up again. I got a stitch in my side already."

"Is that his real name?"

"He says it is. Who knows? What's your problem with him? Did he proposition you?"

"Yeah, but that's not the problem. I don't like the way he lives."

"And you think we should do something about it?

What do you suggest? We could bring him in for curfew any night of the week but he's safer on the street. We got kids in Detention who would rip him to shreds. We can't put him in with the girls. Shit, some of them would rip him to shreds. Juvie's talked to him. He won't say who his people are and you can bet your ass they don't want him back anyway. So what happens if we start him through the system? You know any couples waiting to adopt a racially-mixed thirteen-year-old with a severe gender-identity problem who dresses in drag? They probably couldn't even get a foster home to take him. So he'd be placed in an institution. That's if he stuck around, which he wouldn't. He'd split the first chance he got."

"Whoever owns that limo isn't taking care of him out of the goodness of his heart."

"No, but the question in Nikki's case isn't whether it's right for him to be some rich old pervert's plaything. The question is whether that's better than him turning twenty tricks a night for some pimp. He's fed, he's clothed, he's sheltered. I don't think he does drugs. He goes to private school. He goes to church, for Christ's sake. We got upwards of five hundred minors living on the street in this town. Hell, you've been out there talking to them. They're hungry, they're sick, they're scared. Nikki isn't hurting. His keeper's up in his sixties and I don't think there's a whole lot of action going on. So Nikki cheats a little on the side. At least he's selective."

"Should I take that as a compliment?"

"Take it any way you want. But take it out of my office. I got work to do. And forget about Nikki. Stick to saving the one you're being paid to save."

"I'm not making much headway there."

"Welcome to the club."

"Okay if I use your phone?"

Bundy shoved it toward me and I called the motel to see if Allison was hungry. She was starving. "Put your blue dress on and I'll take you out to dinner," I said.

She asked if I could bring something to the motel instead.

"Sure, I'll be there in about an hour."

I hung up and looked at Bundy who was grinning broadly.

"Must be one fine-looking dress to rate a smile like that over the telephone," he said. I wasn't aware of any smile and I used the back of my hand to remove any lingering trace of it. "Or one fine-looking woman," he added.

I muttered something about her just being a friend and left Bundy laughing over his homicide reports.

I used a pay phone to make my second dinner date for the evening.

"Do I get dessert?" Virginia asked.

"Only if you eat all your veggies."

"I love veggies," she gushed.

I told her I'd pick her up about seven and headed to the motel, stopping on the way to buy ham and swiss sandwiches on onion rolls, pasta salad, and one piece of cheesecake. I figured I'd skip dessert since I was having dinner again in less than two hours. There was a T-shirt shop next to the deli and I picked out a shirt for Allison. It was blue with a cartoonish, disgruntled duck in a raincoat on the front. Above the duck it said "Oregon Rain Festival" and below the duck it gave the dates of the festival — January First through December Thirty-first. I felt the typical eastern Oregonian's irritation at the assumption that all of Oregon was in the wet spot west of the Cascades, but I figured Allison would like the shirt.

She did. She met me at the door, wearing my T-shirt over a pair of her panties.

"I thought I bought you some clothes," I said.

"You did, but this is comfortable. And you're early. You said an hour."

"From now on I'll be absolutely sure not to let you know exactly when I'm coming."

She nodded then blushed prettily when she realized what I had said. When she joined me at the table, wearing her jeans and the new T-shirt, she looked relaxed and happy, very different from when I first found her. I hadn't given much thought to searching for her ID again and since she was, for once, eating as if she were hungry, I kept my mouth shut and didn't bring up her past or her plans for the future.

About halfway through the meal, she asked if I had a girlfriend in Mackie. "Not the way you mean it," I said.

"How do I mean it?"

"Dining and dancing, hearts and flowers, billing and cooing."

She looked puzzled. "What do you do?"

"We sleep together now and then."

"That doesn't sound like much fun. Stop laughing at me. It doesn't sound very friendly anyway."

"We aren't friends."

"How can you sleep with someone who isn't even a friend?"

"I know her better than I know you."

Her cheeks reddened. "That was different. Besides, we didn't do anything."

"You were considering it seriously enough at first. I think a long-term unemotional arrangement is a little better than a one-night stand in a motel."

"It just seems so cold. Is that the way she wants it?"

"It was her idea. She's been married three times. Twice to drunks and once to a man who spent all her money on presents for his girlfriends. She doesn't like men very much. She likes sex."

"And what about you? You don't like women?"

"I think women are God's masterpiece. I just don't want one screwing up my life at the moment."

"Like April did?"

"Like April did," I agreed.

"What did she look like?"

The past tense irked me. Carrie always talked about April as if she were dead, too. The one time I complained, Carrie told me I was crazy, people always talk about people in the past tense when they are no longer in contact with them. She was right but it irked me anyway.

"She has dark hair, big brown eyes. Kind of an Audrey Hepburn face."

"Was she tall?"

"About five-six. Short, from my point of view."

"I'm five-nine," Allison said. "And a little bit."

I grinned. "That makes me six-three and a little bit."

She took a bite of her cheesecake. "This is good." She cleared her throat. "How tall are you?"

"Six four."

She sighed. "Five-ten just sounds awful. It's almost six feet tall."

"There's nothing wrong with being tall."

"I don't really want to be a virgin anymore."

"You sure can change the subject in a hurry. There's nothing wrong with being a virgin either. In fact, it's nice. I wasn't sure they even made nineteen-year-old virgins anymore."

"Do you mostly look for runaways?"

"There you go again. Mostly I do very routine, fairly boring work for lawyers and insurance companies. I get quite a few missing persons but most of them have skipped out on creditors or are trying to dodge child support payments. Sometimes it's a long-lost relative who shows up as the beneficiary of a will or insurance policy. I've had a few adoption cases, people looking for their natural parents or parents looking for the kid they gave up. Let's see, what else do I do? Bodyguard, occasionally."

"That sounds interesting. Whose body have you guarded?"

"Usually just some man who's carrying around a lot of cash. A writer who lives in Mackie hired me to go to Paris with her last year. She wanted to get some first-hand information on the seamier side of Parisian nightlife and didn't want to go alone. So I had a very well-paid vacation and all I had to do was keep the Frenchmen from pinching her fanny."

"Did you sleep with her?"

"Did I sleep with her?"

"Well, it sounds romantic. A lady writer and her handsome bodyguard in the City of Love."

"I see."

"Does that mean yes?"

I smiled. "I think that probably means none of your business, babycakes."

"Which means yes. Oh, is she the one who isn't a girlfriend the way I mean it?" I didn't answer which must have meant yes again because Allison asked, "Is she famous? What's her name?"

"She sells a lot of books but you wouldn't recognize her name. She writes romance novels under three or four silly-sounding pen names. Nanette Nightingale is the only one I can ever remember. The others are worse, believe it or not. I need to change. I have to get going."

Allison had cleared the table by the time I came out of the bathroom. She watched with interest while I made a neat knot in a tie. When she told me I was doing it backwards, I checked the tie — which looked just fine to me — and asked what she was talking about. She said I usually dressed up in the daytime and wore jeans at night.

"It was pouring down rain today. And I have a business appointment this evening." Maintaining eye contact while lying is an art I acquired years ago. Being good at it didn't make me feel any less guilty. I pulled her down on the bed for a quick cuddle which turned into a long cuddle because she felt so good. I was starting to worry about being late picking Virginia up when Allison pulled away from me in the middle of a perfectly good kiss.

"I'm not really anyway," she said.

I rolled my eyes at her. "You're not really what anyway?"

"A nineteen-year-old virgin."

I thought that over very carefully, looking into deep blue eyes in a face that was not at all childish.

"An eighteen-year-old virgin?" I asked.

"In April."

I sat up. "This past April?"

"Next April. Of course, I might not be a virgin by then."

I got off the bed in a hurry.

"Jesus Christ." It was pretty close to a prayer. "You're seventeen. Jesus Christ. Seventeen! Seventeen is . . . Seventeen is . . ." I knew exactly what seventeen was. Second degree sexual abuse. "Holy shit, this is child molest."

"I'm not a child," Allison said, very huffily, and then she started laughing.

"There is nothing funny about this. I don't believe it. I checked into a motel with a minor. My god, are you in high school?"

"No, I already graduated." She had stopped laughing but she was having trouble looking serious. "I don't know why you're so upset. It's only two years' difference."

"That's not the point. You're seventeen. You're a baby. I'm almost thirty. I have no business messing around with a nineteen-year-old but at least it's legal. Jesus, why did you lie to me?"

"I felt safer being nineteen. And I wasn't sure you'd give me a ride if you knew how old I am."

"How young you are," I corrected.

She frowned, watching me pace in the space between the beds. "Does this mean you're never going to kiss me again? I wish I hadn't told you." After a moment, she added, "People always think

I'm older than I am. I think it's because I'm so tall."

I checked my watch. I was going to be late. "You and I are going to have to have a long talk. In legalese, you're a CINS, a Child In Need of Supervision. You aren't old enough to be on your own and you sure as hell aren't old enough to be with me. You said your parents died. You must have a guardian."

She shook her head. Her chin quivered. Tears brimmed over her lashes. "I don't have anyone," she sobbed.

I sat down beside her and put my arm around her. "Don't, Allison. You'll make yourself sick again."

She sobbed out something about the police and I promised I wouldn't turn her over to them and I promised she could stay with me for now. She didn't ask me to promise to kiss her again but I did anyway — kiss her, not promise to. It was a very chaste peck on the cheek as I was leaving the room and she botched it up completely by turning her mouth to mine and clinging hard against me. Seventeen!

CHAPTER NINETEEN

IF VIRGINIA FOUND ME DISTRACTED DURING DINNER, she didn't mention it. I had a hard time thinking about anything but Allison's age although after a couple glasses of wine the plunging neckline of Virginia's slinky blue dress began to demand more and more of my attention.

We topped off Italian food with dessert in her apartment, after which we played in the shower long enough to drain the hot water heater.

Virginia had been on a shopping spree. The refrigerator was stocked with a bag of apples, four cartons of yogurt, and a bottle of Paul Masson Brut. We drank the champagne lounging naked on her bed which led to more dessert. After a second very fast, very cool shower, guilt got to me and I decided to check in.

I stretched out on the bed beside Virginia who was toweling her hair dry and reached across her for the phone on the nightstand. Dora answered my line. I said hello and she said, "Where the hell have you been and who's the girl in your motel room?"

"Out and none of your business. Who wants me?"

Dora lowered her voice to a breathy purr. "Brandy would like you to meet her at the Skidmore Fountain at midnight."

"Did she say how we're supposed to recognize each other? Red carnation on the lapel or something?"

"I don't think I've ever seen you in lapels, blue eyes." Dora laughed, probably because she had seen me in nothing on several distant occasions. "She just said meet her. She sounded like a hooker."

"What's a hooker sound like?"

"Her gum-popping almost broke my eardrum."

"That should narrow it down. A gum-popping prostitute. How many of those can there be in Portland?" I told her I'd call again later and replaced the telephone, nuzzling Virginia's flat belly in passing.

"I have an appointment with a prostitute in thirty minutes."

She grinned. "Are you sure you're up to it?"

"He needs must go whom the devil drives. Whatever the hell that means. Where did I drop my clothes?"

"By the front door. You were in a hurry."

"I thought I did pretty well. I kept my clothes on in the restaurant. That dress should be rated X."

"It is," Virginia said. "No one under eighteen admitted."

I didn't laugh as hard as I might have if her comment hadn't reminded me of my underage roomie. Virginia followed me into the living room, curling up naked on the couch to watch me dress. When I crouched beside her for a good-bye kiss, she stroked the creases in my cheeks with her index fingers. "You could come back later," she said.

"I'd like to. But don't wait up. If this woman knows something about Jessica, I may get tied up."

"Never let a hooker tie you up."

I laughed and kissed her again and headed off to Old Town to see what Brandy had to offer.

Back in the 1880's when Stephen Skidmore bestowed the fountain bearing his name on the City of Portland, Southwest First Avenue and Ankeny was the center of town, but even before the turn of the century, fires and floods had convinced the businessmen and the city fathers that it made more sense to build on higher ground away from the banks of the Willamette. Downtown shifted southward and the Skidmore District shifted downhill until it was more of a Skid Road district.

The Willamette has long since been tamed by a seawall and in recent years Old Town has been making a comeback. MAX tracks now dissect First Avenue. Lower rents and a renewed interest in the historical value of the area have lured businesses back into the neighborhood. On weekends, hordes of shoppers throng to the Saturday Market which has grown too big to be contained in its original location under the foot of the Burnside Bridge. The open-air market now spills out into the adjacent open areas right to the Skidmore Fountain itself which sits off-center in a brick plaza formed by a widening of First Avenue. The big octagonal pool of the fountain has a short flight of steps on four sides and horse troughs on the other four. In the center of the pool, two vaguely Grecian ladies stand back to back on either side of a column, holding aloft a large basin from which the water spouts and flows.

Mr. Skidmore's fountain is inscribed with the words GOOD CITIZENS ARE THE RICHES OF A CITY. Even with the renewed civic interest in the area, not many of the people loitering there at midnight meet the criteria.

I parked a block away and approached the fountain on foot, thinking as I always think when I see it that the fountain would look more at home in Paris or London than in Portland. The girl standing by the fountain would have looked more at home out on O's Stroll.

Even for a hooker, Brandy was blatant. She was short and twenty pounds underweight with unnaturally blond hair moussed into a mass of wet-looking curls. A white fake fur jacket was thrown across her shoulders. She was wearing a black vinyl micro-miniskirt, black lace stockings, and red shoes with four-inch heels. Her breasts were too big for the rest of her and were unrestrained beneath a red and white striped top. She looked like a bad caricature of a Parisian whore.

I had never seen her before but she knew who I was. As soon as I reached her, she flapped Jessica's picture at me, saying, "How much you paying, man?"

"Depends on how much you know."

"Shit, man, I know everything."

"You know where Jessica is?"

"Huh? Oh, the girl. Yeah, kinda. I know who knows. So how much?"

Brandy had a month's worth of makeup on her face. Her mascara was in thick clumps and her lipstick had worn off, leaving a thin scarlet outline. She was jittering badly, toes tapping, fingers twitching, tongue darting out to moisten her cracked lips. Her pupils had shrunk the irises to a thin circle of brown. She looked thirty and probably wasn't old enough to vote.

"I'll give you fifty bucks now, more later if your information's any good."

"Fuck. Shit, man, I gotta have real money." She turned angrily away and teetered up the steps at the base of the fountain. She sat on the broad curved rim and crossed her legs. Bright red panties showed in the gap where the skirt stretched across her crotch. Pale flesh rippled above the elastic tops of the stockings. She leaned toward me, her eyes widening melodramatically. "I gotta get out of town, man. They're gonna kill me if they find out I told."

"Who's 'they'?"

"Huh?"

"Never mind. I'll give you a hundred bucks up front." Information from junkies is questionable at best, but no one else was offering any.

"Fuck you," Brandy said. She pulled a thin brown cigarette out of her purse and placed it between her lips, raising her eyebrows at me. A real lady. I flicked my Bic for her, grateful for the acrid tang of the smoke. Brandy's last bath had been a few johns ago.

A long tendril of smoke curled out of her mouth. "So how much?"

"A hundred."

"Fuck. Didn't you hear what I said? They're gonna fucking *kill* me, man."

"Nobody's going to kill you," I said and there was a loud sharp crack and Brandy fell backward into the Skidmore Fountain.

I had my gun out before she splashed and I spun around in a crouch, the .38 in front of me. Two dozen people were running in three dozen different directions. I didn't see anyone with a gun. I didn't see anyone standing still enough to aim a gun. I straightened up and took another good look around. The last person in sight was a drunk who was just rounding a corner, his legs wobbling, unused to such speed.

MAX was coming, its white sides gleaming sur- realistically in the light mist, its wheels whirring quietly against the track. As the train slowed for the stop, the driver leaned forward, peering at me and my gun and Brandy's legs sticking out of the fountain behind me. The train picked up speed, passed me by. I heard angry protests from unob- servant passengers who had just missed their stop.

And then MAX was gone and we were all alone, just me and Brandy at the Skidmore Fountain and when I turned around to look, I knew it was just me.

Her legs were bent at the knees, the calves protruding over the fountain's rim. Her mouth and eyes were open under the water. Her hands were floating.

I pulled her out anyway, checking for a pulse just in case, and arranged her neatly on the ground, straightening her arms and legs and tugging the wet skirt down to cover her panties. One of her fake nails had come loose and was dangling from a thin shred of adhesive. The nail beneath was bitten to the quick. I pressed the scarlet plastic back into place as I crouched beside her amidst the scattered clutter that had spilled from her purse.

The entry wound in her right temple looked oddly benign and was bloodless, cleansed by the cool water of the fountain. In its search for an exit, the bullet had turned the left side of her head into a mass of torn tissue and shattered bone. I looked elsewhere while I waited for the cops.

Bundy wasn't going to like this.

Chapter Twenty

Bundy thought it stank.

"This stinks," he said.

That pretty much summed it up. "I suppose you aren't buying coincidence?"

"I been a cop a lot of years. If there's one thing I've learned it's that coincidence sucks."

"That was no .22 tonight."

"No, but we got two girls shot with the same gun and one of them had your runaway handbill and we got another girl shot while she's talking to you. Start at the beginning and don't leave anything out."

I started at the beginning and told him about Jason and Lily and Hank Johnston and Celia Baines and the supercilious son-of-a-bitch at the Rose City School of Performing Arts and Virginia Marley at the Northwest Acting and Modeling School and about all my traipsing about town. I diluted my relationship with Virginia to a couple drinks at a bar and left Allison out completely.

When I finished, Bundy said, "Well, shit."

"I don't see what Jessica could have gotten herself into in a week that would be worth three homicides. She's fourteen years old."

Bundy glanced at some papers on his desk. "Brandy was seventeen. Brenda Weinstein AKA — you want to guess?"

"Brandy Wine?"

"Yeah. Original. Chronic runaway since she was twelve, been hooking for at least three years. Her pimp's down the hall but we're cutting him loose. His alibi's tight."

"You have any ideas?"

"I think the dead girls were into some bad business and someone didn't want them talking."

"Brandy wanted money. She said she had to get out of town or they'd kill her." *Nobody's going to kill you.* I rubbed my hands hard down my thighs.

"Yeah," Bundy said. "So maybe whoever's in charge of this bad business — let's call him Mister X — recruits Jessica and then finds out you're spreading her picture all over town. He starts worrying about someone talking. Hookers can be hard to find, no permanent residences, no phone listings. But Dobbs and Baylor were living halfway normal lives. They were easy to find. So maybe Mister X figures that with you stirring things up, two ex-hookers trying to go straight might decide to blow the whistle on him. So he gets rid of them, just in case."

"Why not — No, I was going to say why not kill me. But I can be replaced. Kill me and someone else comes along asking questions. Kill the girls and there's no one to answer the questions."

"And maybe he figures we'll take a little more interest in a PI getting blown away than in a few dead hookers. Not that we would. Homicide is strictly equal opportunity around here."

"So how did Mister X find Brandy tonight?"

Bundy grinned. "I think he was tailing you."

There was no point in trying to pass myself off as Super Sleuth of the Year. "Could be, I wouldn't have noticed."

"No reason for you to be watching for a tail," Bundy said graciously. He laced his fingers behind his head and tilted his chair back.

"So what do you think?" he asked.

"I think I'd better find Jessica in a hurry." I could see him thinking it over. "I can put a lot more hours into looking for her than you can. I'll stay clear of the homicide investigations. You don't have any concrete evidence connecting Jessica with them."

He thought it over a bit longer then brought his chair legs down hard against the floor. "Okay. You look for her, but if anyone contacts you I want to know about it right away. And if anyone stops you on the street claiming to know where she is, for Christ's sake, grab them and take cover. And watch for a tail. Why do you drive that old heap?"

"My car? I like it. Why?" He didn't answer. "Have you been snooping again?"

"I'm a cop. I don't snoop, I ask questions. We

got some guys in the Bureau who put in some time with Mackie PD before Portland hired them. They tell some interesting stories. Ten acres of prime Oregon land and a big house, all paid for. I got twenty-three more years on my mortgage."

"The land was a wedding present from my parents. And I built the house."

"Why'd you throw the pumpkin through the window?"

"What kind of business do you think Mister X is in?"

"I don't know. Drugs, most likely. That's where the money is." Bundy drummed his fingers against his desk then rapped his knuckles hard against it once. "I got this funny little coincidence with Dobbs and Baylor and I don't know what to make of it. I asked Dobbs' pimp why he let her go. Pimps don't usually like their girls taking early retirement. He said about six months ago she took a couple weeks off, said she had to visit her sick mother, which was a lie. Her parents live in Idaho and hadn't seen her in years. When she came back, she was nervous, jumpy, acted like she was scared to death. The johns didn't want anything to do with her so he let her go. She told him she'd been raped. And Karen Baylor told her sister she'd been raped."

"Rape's an occupational hazard for prostitutes."

"Yeah. It happens. But it doesn't make them quit hooking. Dobbs and Baylor were raped and they got out as fast as they could. Which makes me think there was more to the rapes than some guy ripping them off for a freebie."

"Brandy didn't strike me as the type who would be concerned about Jessica's welfare. She was looking for a stake to get out of town."

"Yeah. So we got three scared hookers who didn't want to hook anymore."

Bundy left the room briefly to talk to a uniformed cop who had beckoned from the doorway. When he returned he said, "No luck at the fountain. They rounded up a dozen or so people who were there. Most of them thought you shot her. They didn't see anyone else with a gun. Damn, I hate this job. Three homicides and not a clue in sight."

"Lead," I said. "Cops have leads. Private eyes have clues."

"Yeah, well, if you stumble over a clue, let me know. Get some sleep, you look like hell."

I had arrived at the Justice Center in a patrol car. Nobody offered me a ride back to my car so I walked. Rain riding on a strong east wind pelted my face. I didn't mind the rain. Brandy would never feel it again.

I stopped briefly at the Skidmore Fountain where some cops were still doing cop things. Brandy's fake fur was a sodden heap on the steps. The rain dimpled the water in the pool. I wondered how they cleaned the fountain. I walked quickly to the car and headed off into the night.

I made it an entire block before indecision took hold. I stopped at an intersection and watched the wipers sweep rain off the glass. Left turn to Virginia's, a warm bed and a warmer body. Right turn to the motel, a cold bed and a sleeping seventeen-year-old.

A car pulled up behind me, its lights glaring harshly off the rearview mirror. The driver honked impatiently.

Virginia or the virgin?

I let the clutch out and turned right. I knew one seventeen-year-old who wasn't going to end up dead in the Skidmore Fountain.

CHAPTER TWENTY-ONE

ALLISON ROLLED OVER WHEN I ENTERED THE room but she didn't wake up. I stood by the bed for a while and watched her sleep. Then, in the heavy silence of the wee hours, I searched her purse, her suitcase, the clothes she had hung in the closet, and the paper bag of art supplies. She had finished the picture of the rose and started another. A conch shell was emerging from the blackness of the scratchboard.

I was pulling out the first drawer to check behind it when I decided to use a little common sense. She would keep her ID where she could get it in a hurry if she decided to run. What would she take? The suitcase if she had time. If she was in a big hurry, she would take what she came with — her purse and her sweater. And I already checked both of them. I yawned at myself in the mirror. Bundy was right. I did look like hell.

I looked at the sweater again. It was hanging up, pressed between the wall and my suitbag. Bulky-knit white sweater, big white buttons, big empty pockets, hood. *Hood.* I slid my hand into the hood and pulled out a plastic wallet insert. Nothing to it.

A Connecticut driver's license was right on top. The name on it leaped out and hit me right between the eyes. I blinked. Looked again. Same name. My heartbeat was suddenly audible in the still room. I flipped through the rest of the little packet. Blue Cross card, library card, social security card, card from a dentist's office reminding her of an appointment last March. Every card with the same damn name. I looked at the driver's license again. The address was in a town I had never heard of. The name refused to change.

I returned the packet to its hiding place and sat on the edge of my bed to watch Allison sleep. I seemed to be spending a lot of time watching Allison sleep. But then, Allison spent a lot of time sleeping. The great escape.

She was facing me, one hand curled against her chin, her hair a halo of gold across the pillow. Sleeping like a baby. Somebody's beautiful baby girl, trusting, angelic, innocent.

Innocent.

Mary Allison Vanzetti didn't look anything like a killer.

I slid to the floor and leaned my back against my bed, resting my arms on my upraised knees. I sat there for a long time in the darkness putting together the few facts I knew and the half-truths Allison had told me.

I tried, hard, to come up with a scenario in which she wasn't the killer. The facts didn't lend themselves well to an alternate theory. Vanzetti was shot at four-thirty in the morning. By five-thirty Allison was in Allentown and in bad shape.

Could she have been a witness? Not likely. The killer would have shot her, too. If she somehow managed to witness the murder without being seen, why did she run? If she panicked and ran, why was she still running?

Could she have been an accomplice? Also not likely. If someone else killed Vanzetti with Allison's complicity, he never would have let her go off on her own with thirty-seven dollars, no place to hide, and enough information to put him on death row.

The conclusion was inescapable. My sleeping beauty was a murderess.

Opportunity, means, and motive.

Opportunity was easy. She flew to Portland and took a bus east, just as she said. But she went to Mackie, not to Pendleton. And she met someone, just as she said. The someone was Carl Vanzetti. And just as she said, it didn't work out. With a vengeance.

I spend enough time chasing people on the run to have the bus schedules memorized. Allison arrived in Mackie at eight Sunday evening. She walked the three blocks to the hotel. She went to Room 301 without calling any attention to herself. Eight and a half hours later she picked up a gun and shot Carl Vanzetti four times in the chest at point blank range.

She got out of the room and out of the hotel without being seen. She found a nice old man and asked him for a ride to wherever he was going, which turned out to be Allentown. Allentown wasn't much of a place to hide so she tried to steal a car belonging to a kind — if not overly bright — private investigator who carried good Samaritanism to the limit by aiding and abetting her escape and taking her to the big city where he hid her away in a motel room and fed her and clothed her and hugged her and kissed her. Another fine mess I had gotten myself into.

Means. She couldn't get a gun past airport security. And she couldn't buy one in Oregon. So the gun was Vanzetti's. She took it with her and got rid of it later, probably in the woods outside of Allentown before I picked her up.

Motive. I didn't have a single good guess as to why a seventeen-year-old girl would stick a nightie and a few necessities in her purse and fly across the country for a clandestine meeting in a hotel room with a sixty-eight-year-old male relative. I didn't have even a bad guess as to why she would shoot him.

What had they done in that room for eight and a half hours? What were they doing up and dressed at four-thirty in the morning anyway? Allison had obviously missed at least one night's sleep. What happened in that room that drove her to murder?

I ruled out sexual misbehavior on Vanzetti's part, not because of his age or their apparent relationship, but because of Allison's subsequent behavior toward me. A victim of rape or molestation wasn't likely to snuggle up to a stranger a couple days later. No matter how much she wanted my help, she would have been unable to disguise her fear and anger. And I had seen enough of Allison to know there wasn't a bruise anywhere on her body. Whatever struggle had taken place in that room had been a war of words, of wills, of conflicting wants.

Motives for murder: greed, passion, fear, vengeance, and anger. Not greed, she left the bag of money. Not passion, whatever relationship they shared had to be one of blood and not of love or lust. Not fear, Vanzetti had been in Mackie for three days. Allison came to him. Fear should have kept her away. Not vengeance, vengeance meant premeditation and I couldn't believe Allison would deliberately, cold-bloodedly, set out to commit murder. Which left anger. What did Vanzetti do, or fail to do, that made Allison mad enough to kill?

What were they to each other anyway? Mary Allison Vanzetti, age seventeen. Carl Anthony Vanzetti, age sixty-eight. Husband and wife was unthinkable. Brother and sister was pretty much impossible. Father and daughter was possible but highly improbable. Grandfather and granddaughter made the most sense.

Why would she kill her grandfather? Not that Vanzetti was a typical grandfather. He was an ex-con and a criminal and he was on the run from the law. Did Allison know that already or did she find it out in Room 301 of the Mackie Arms? Was Vanzetti an idolized father-figure whose feet suddenly turned to clay? Did she kill him out of outraged disappointment? Could be. People killed with less reason every day.

I studied the sleeping girl and tried to picture her with a gun in her hand. Other pictures intruded. Allison, a slender figure in pale blue running up the gentle slope of a lonely country road. Allison, hands clenched on the wheel of a car she couldn't drive. Allison, doubled over in pain after I casually flipped on the car radio to catch the latest news about a murder in Mackie. Allison, sitting very still, listening to me get my vicarious cop-thrills by discussing a homicide case on the telephone. Allison, long honey hair hidden beneath a floppy-brimmed straw hat, raindrops on her sunglasses. Allison, trying to survive, trying to steal a car, trying to steal a wallet, trying to steal a heart, a sacrificial virgin offering her body to a stranger in desperation. But she changed her mind. *Does it work better now?* Allison, blue velvet eyes, soft satin skin beneath my lips. Brandy's skin was warm and wet when I pulled her from the cool water of the fountain. I had to find Jessica. I felt myself sliding floorward.

CHAPTER TWENTY-TWO

I WOKE UP WHEN ALLISON STEPPED ON MY CHEST. She seemed a bit surprised to find me underfoot. Holding my T-shirt tight against her thighs, she asked what I was doing.

"I *was* sleeping."

"On the floor?"

"It's good for the back." I sat up slowly, groaning. "Maybe it isn't good for the back."

She grinned and asked if she could have the bathroom first.

"Sure," I said. "It'll take me half an hour to walk that far." I made it to my feet, arching my back to realign the vertebrae. Allison collected some clothes and locked herself into the bathroom. Water started running immediately. I smiled at the closed door. I could remember being young enough to worry about people hearing me pee.

I eased down on the bed and stared at my old friend the ceiling. What does one do when one discovers one has a killer in one's motel room? One calls the cops. One might; I wasn't going to. I had, in my sleep I think, arrived at a decision.

If I hadn't found her identification, I wouldn't know

who she was. I wasn't going to tell her I knew and I wasn't going to tell the cops. I was going to remain officially unaware of her identity until her picture made the front page, which I suspected would be any day now. My conscience has always been more flexible than it probably should be and wasn't going to trouble me. The fact that I would derive a bit of perverse pleasure from watching Chief of Police Robert H. Harkins flounder in a puzzling homicide investigation was something I acknowledged but chose not to dwell upon. The fact that my best friend would flounder along with Harkins bothered me a bit, but Phil was a lot tougher than Allison. He'd get over it. Eventually, he would find it funny. Eventually, he would even forgive me. He always did. Besides, the way things were going, they were never going to solve the case and Phil would be so damn glad to have the perpetrator handed over to him that he would be willing to overlook a few irregularities. In the meantime, I could give Allison some time. She might have killed once but she was no danger to anyone now. Except to me and it wasn't bodily harm I was worried about.

The telephone jangled, interrupting my thoughts. It was Marilyn. "Call Hank Johnston. Call your sister. Is it raining there?"

"Yeah, it's been in the low seventies."

"It was eighty degrees at seven this morning here."

"Enjoy it while it lasts. We'll be trudging through snow in a few months."

"That sounds good."

"No, it doesn't. I'll check in later."

I dialed Carrie's number and talked to her answering machine then I called Hank Johnston. Same song, third verse. I broke the connection and called Finney. After relaying Jessica's latest message, I told him about the three dead girls.

There was a deep silence before he said, "What are you saying?"

"I'm saying three girls have been murdered and the cops think Jessica might be mixed up with the same people."

Another deep silence. "Maybe I should come out there," he said.

I was as discouraging as I could be without coming right out and telling him to stay the hell in Mackie and not fuck things up any worse than they already were. "I'll call you as soon as I have any news," I said.

He hung up on me. The man definitely didn't like good-byes. Maybe he just didn't like me.

Allison emerged from the bathroom, wearing my Pendleton shirt and looking clean and shiny and slightly damp and innocent as a new-born babe. With incredible guile and cunning, I asked, "What time have the cleaning ladies been showing up? I don't want to be in the shower when they get here."

"I don't really know." She unwrapped the towel she was wearing turban-style and shook her hair loose. "I've been going for a walk every day after you leave. They come before two o'clock because I've been back by then."

"I guess I'm safe in the shower then," I said.

I stood under the hot spray for a long time, thinking about the hitches in my not very well-laid plan for turning Miss Vanzetti over to the cops.

I didn't want to turn her in to the Portland police, partly because they wouldn't let me stay with her. Mostly because I wanted to give her to Phil. And not just to placate him. Allison would look into Phil's faded blue eyes and see compassion and understanding and just the slightest trace of humor at the messes people get themselves into. She'd like Phil and she'd trust him. And Phil could talk a confession out of just about anybody.

As soon as her picture hit the front page, I wanted to put her in the car and drive straight to Mackie without passing Go. But I couldn't leave Portland until I found Jessica. If the cops ID'd Allison before I found Jessica, I might be able to stall for a day or two if I could keep Allison hidden and keep her from running. I could claim I had been so busy searching for Jessica that I didn't read a newspaper or hear a news report. No one would believe it but it didn't matter what they believed. It only mattered what they could prove.

There was also the problem of Allison having a

very memorable face. Once her picture made the six o'clock news, people were going to start calling the cops. It didn't matter how many people remembered seeing her as long as they couldn't connect her with me or with the motel. Allison had been skulking about being sure no one at the motel got a good look at her.

If someone who saw us together gave the Mackie cops a halfway decent description of me, it would all be over. I thought over the places we had been together. Downtown Portland was no problem. Neither was Clackamas Town Center. The salesclerk in Penney's clothing department had customers three deep around her register and had barely glanced at me. The shoe salesman had been busy trying to talk Allison into going out with him and didn't realize I was with her until I paid for the shoes. He was so embarrassed he never looked at my face. The cafe in Hood River was no problem either. I hadn't thought much about it at the time but I remembered now that Allison had let me order for her and had made a point of looking out the window whenever the waitress came to the table. We had been in a corner booth with a wall behind my head. I was pretty sure none of the customers got a good look at the face behind the tangled hair.

Some people would remember seeing Allison with a man but I had questioned enough witnesses to know that I would be remembered as a tall white male, period. Without a picture of me to jog their memories, I was faceless.

Allentown was the big problem. No one at the cafe knew me and no one would remember me being there after this many days. But Sarge knew me and knew I was interested in the mysterious blonde. If he mentioned my presence to the Mackie cops, Phil Pauling would jump to the right conclusion in two seconds flat. I was going to have to do something about Sarge.

When I came out of the bathroom, Allison was chatting on the phone so animatedly that I thought for a moment she had called whoever she had in Connecticut. Then I realized she was in the middle of a what-to-name-the-baby conversation. She handed me the phone and I said, "Hi, Delly."

I could hear the smile in Carrie's voice as she said, "Hi, Dabby. What are you so cheerful about?"

"I'm always cheerful. It's part of my not inconsiderable charm. Are you in labor?"

"I just called to warn you that Mom and Dad are coming up for our birthday and they're throwing a party for us." After a long pause, she said, "If you don't show up I'll never speak to you again. I don't like birthday parties either but we are their only children and this is our only thirtieth birthday. It won't kill you to be civil about it. I told her to put 'no gifts' on the invitations." She waited a while then said, "I mean it, Zachariah. I'll be eight and a half months pregnant and if I can do it, you can do it." After another wait, she said, "Who is she?"

"She who?"

"She who answers your phone while you're in the shower."

"Oh, her. That's Allison Wonderland. I found her down a rabbit hole."

"She sounded like an external force to me."

"Bye bye, Delly."

She was smiling again when she said, "Bye bye, Dabby."

I hung up the phone and said to Allison, "My sister, in case she didn't tell you."

"What's her name? I thought she said Carrie."

"Carrie, short for Carolina. We're twins. We didn't learn to speak English until the speech therapist got hold of us in grade school. We had our own little language. She was Delly, I was Dabby, but don't you dare tell anyone."

"Twins." Allison barely breathed the word, as if it were a secret incantation. "I wish I had a twin."

I thought it might be a little late to arrange. "You can have Carrie."

"She's going to have a baby," Allison informed me as if it might have escaped my notice. "I'd like to have a baby," she added.

"You're too young." And in too much trouble. I put my holster on and pulled a tan sportcoat on over it. Allison was looking faintly worried. She did something to my shirt collar then smoothed my lapels.

"Do you think I'm normal?" she asked.

"Normal? As in sane?"

"No, as in . . . sexually."

"Uh. You seem pretty normal to me."

"If someone does something . . . well, the thing is . . . well, I did something once that wasn't exactly normal."

Tears were threatening to spill over her lashes. She was going to confess. That grandfatherly son-of-a-bitch Vanzetti had forced her into some kind of perverted, incestuous relationship and she shot the bastard. I decided I needed to sit down for this. I sat on the foot of her bed and took her hand. "Would you like to tell me about it?" I asked. Dr. Sigmund Smith.

She suddenly didn't look at all as if she wanted to tell me about it. She fidgeted and cleared her throat and made several false starts then she blurted, "I kissed a girl."

Wrong confession. I did not laugh. "I see. That doesn't sound so bad. Kissing girls is one of my favorite things."

"You're supposed to." She blinked a tear down each cheek.

"Was this a girl your age?"

"Yes. Well, it was two years ago. We were fifteen."

"Did you go to boarding school by any chance?"

She nodded and I said, "I don't think a little adolescent experimentation with another girl if you didn't have any boys handy makes you abnormal. Probably makes you very normal. I don't think it's unusual."

She nodded, not looking very convinced.

"When I'm kissing you, do you close your eyes and pretend I'm a woman?"

"I close my eyes and hope you won't stop."

I grinned. "I think that makes you certifiably heterosexual, babe. I know a couple lesbians. They also sleep with men and they enjoy . . . uh . . . I assume they enjoy it, strictly from a physical standpoint. But their emotional attachments, their falling-in-love feelings, are for women."

Allison's smile was blinding. I read the mind behind those magnificent eyes. Her falling-in-love feelings were for me. And I had no one to blame but myself. I had encouraged her and now I had a seventeen-year-old murderess in love with me. I was going to have to cool the relationship somehow. She had enough problems without having to cope with an unrequitable passion for a man who was much too old for her.

She sat on my lap. I was going to have to stop this. Her arms went tight around my neck. I rolled us both over onto the bed. I was definitely going to have to stop this. Her lips parted beneath mine. Tomorrow. Tomorrow I'd think of a way to discourage her.

I tore myself away a few minutes later, wondering fairly desperately if Virginia would have lunch with me. And dessert. No, I'd better skip it. I had to find Jessica.

I went out looking but I had the feeling I was never going to find Jessica. I had spent so much time on the street that the regulars greeted me like a long-lost friend and several people I didn't remember talking to inquired about my progress.

I wasn't making any progress. In her latest call to Hank, Jessica had again said she was downtown. Hank was sure she was calling from a gas station because he heard the sound of the bell cars drive over to alert the attendant. He had given me the information triumphantly, as if he had just pulled off the coup of the century. I wondered if the kid had any idea how many gas stations there are in Portland. He had been stuck in Mackie for too many years. So, was Jessica really downtown or was she hoping Hank would pass the information on to me so I would think she was downtown? I didn't know how devious Jessica was. I also didn't have any idea where she might be if she wasn't downtown, so I decided to believe she trusted Hank. Besides, she seemed to know I was still looking for her and I had spent the majority of my time downtown.

When I checked in with the answering service in the middle of the afternoon I had a message to call Virginia. She invited me to have lunch with her.

When I got to the school, an aerobics class was in full swing in the big room. Virginia took me by the hand and pulled me into a small office.

She locked the door and locked her arms around my neck. When we came up for air, she asked if I had any objection to floors.

"No," I said, "but it looks a little hard. You'll have bruises on your backside."

"No, I won't. But you might."

A while later I was back at the motel, delivering Chinese food to Allison. She gave me a second to set the food down before she put her arms around me, snuggling her face against my neck. I was definitely going to have to do something to discourage her. I nibbled on her ear. Very discouraging.

She said, "You smell like Charlie."

"Charlie who? I hope he bathes regularly."

"It's a cologne. *Charlie.*"

"Oh." I pressed my lips to her forehead and stared across the room, trying to think up a good lie and then wondering why I thought I needed one. I finally just let it pass.

Allison didn't. "Do you have a girlfriend in *Portland?*" she asked.

I smiled at her. "Not the way you mean it." That should cool her off in a hurry. Let her think — well, let her know — that I was a no-good bastard with a woman in every port. Unfortunately, Allison appeared undaunted. She asked if I planned to eat with her and when I said no, she opened the small white boxes, asking what it all was.

"It's a number three on the take-out menu. Just eat it, it's good for you."

When I left, she was deftly wielding chopsticks, looking as though she didn't have a care in the world. Once she had caught up on her sleep and kept a few meals down, she seemed amazingly untroubled. She could get all worked up about a minor indiscretion but murder didn't seem to trouble her. She had to be worried about being caught but she didn't seem to be carrying around a heavy load of remorse. It occurred to me that maybe Allison wasn't completely normal. As in sane.

CHAPTER TWENTY-THREE

I LOOKED FOR JESSICA AGAIN BUT MY HEART wasn't in it. Neither was my head. The only way I could have found her that night was if she had walked up and kicked me in the shin.

My thoughts were on a murder back in Mackie. I was digging myself a deep hole and it was likely to cave in on me. I was smack dab in the middle of an ongoing police investigation, a license-losing place for a PI to be. And not just some minor investigation — a homicide investigation. And not just any homicide investigation — the one both my best friend and my worst enemy were doing their damnedest to solve. I was aiding and abetting and withholding evidence and doing a few other things that added up to several counts of Hindering Prosecution, a Class C Felony. Well, I couldn't worry about it now.

Sometime after dark while I was loitering outside a club featuring female impersonators, Nikki walked up behind me and slid his hand around my arm.

"Hi," he said. "You haven't found her?"

"Hi. No."

"I'm glad you're still here." He grinned wickedly. He was wearing lavender Spandex pants that made it obvious he was a boy and a top made of layers of drifting lavender chiffon. He extended one arm in front of him, moving it in a slow sideways figure-eight. Yards of sleeve floated in the air. "Do you like it?" he asked.

"Enchanting. You look like you live under a mushroom."

His forehead creased. "An elf, you mean? I don't think I like that. I'm trying to look sophisticated."

I removed his hand from my arm. "There is nothing at all sophisticated about a twelve-year-old —"

"Thirteen-year-old."

"— boy dressed in a purple cloud."

His chin puckered and a tear slid down one cheek. He sobbed.

"I'm sorry," I said. "I'm in a bad mood. You look very . . . pretty."

The sobs got louder. I put my arm around him and pulled him close to muffle the noise against my chest. People were staring. I said "Fuck off, shithead" to some passing asshole who thought smirking was the proper response to the sight of a giant macho stud with his arms around a little boy in lavender chiffon. Nikki giggled against my chest. I pushed him away.

"I'll forgive you for being mean if you let me walk with you for a while," he said.

"Why don't we get something to eat instead. I don't want you walking with me."

His tears were gone, his makeup suspiciously undamaged by the crying bout. "I hear the girls are just *dying* to meet you," he said.

"Not funny. And if you know that, you know hanging around me isn't a good idea. Where did you hear about it?"

"Just here." He made a sweeping gesture encompassing street life in general. "Everyone knows what you're doing and they know about the girl who was shot at the fountain. You're quite famous."

"If everyone knows so goddamn much, why don't they tell me where Jessica is?"

"'Discover not a secret to another,'" he said. "That's from Proverbs."

"'Nothing is secret, that shall not be made manifest.' The Book of Luke, I think. And if you say anything about the devil quoting scripture, I won't buy you anything to eat."

He laughed and took my arm again as we walked down the street to a coffee shop.

After I left Nikki, I called Bundy. He wasn't making any progress either. "You been watching for a tail?" he asked.

"Yeah, I haven't spotted anyone. Keeping tabs on me in town would be easy though. All the street people know what I'm doing."

"The price of fame," Bundy said.

I checked in with the answering service next. No

messages. Jessica Finney was getting to be a royal pain in the ass.

It was close to midnight when I jaywalked across a dark street in Old Town to check out a group of kids who were about to sack out in a doorway. There were five of them, the youngest a boy who hadn't hit puberty yet, the oldest a skinny girl with straggly brown hair who was dressed in layers of thrift shop clothes. She was the spokesman for the group.

She looked at Jessica's picture briefly, said they had never seen her, and turned her back to me. The others stood mute and motionless, colorless in the drab night light. They looked like a sepia still of Depression-era Appalachia. One of them, a fragile, pretty girl with long dark curls, had tears streaming down her face. More out of habit than anything else, I asked if she needed help. She said her contact lenses were bothering her. Maybe they were. I turned and walked away. I was tired of joyless, leaden-eyed children.

I wandered aimlessly and soon found myself approaching the Skidmore Fountain. I skirted around it, walking through an opening between two buildings. I stopped when I was beneath the arching underbelly of the Burnside Bridge.

On weekends the big space beneath the foot of the bridge would be bustling with the activity of the Saturday Market. On Thursday night it was eerily still, the occasional slapping whine of tires on the pavement overhead punctuating the silence. There was a soft continuous snore from somewhere in the shadows. The cavernous space was filled with a light mist, not quite a fog, that muffled sound and limited vision. My scalp prickled at the skittering of leaves or litter blowing in the darkness.

"Sir?"

The syllable shivered on the air, seeming to come from all directions at once. I thought for a moment I had imagined it. Then it came again.

"Sir?"

I turned full circle before I saw her. She was thirty feet from me in the shadow of the stairway leading up to the bridge. She moved, seeming to float toward me through the mist.

A rush of adrenalin sped up my heartbeat and switched the external world to slow motion. I jerked my gun out, yelling "Get down!" The snoring stopped. The girl began turning in a slow pirouette, seeking the source of danger. A shot shattered the stillness and the underbelly of the bridge exploded with echoes of the blast. At the periphery of my vision I was aware of the girl falling slowly to the ground as I fired two shots into the shadows where the flicker of the muzzle flash had been. A darker shadow detached itself, staggered forward, fell. A rifle with a short barrel clattered across the ground, landing beside a big packing crate that suddenly rose straight up from the ground then flew toward me. The man who had been sleeping under the box ran toward light and safety.

I shouted something after him as I ran to the crumpled form of the girl.

CHAPTER TWENTY-FOUR

I WAS BACK IN BUNDY'S OFFICE, SHIRTLESS AND shaking, with an empty holster slung over my shoulder.

The legs of my jeans were thick with blood that had pooled around me while I knelt by the girl, frantically constructing pressure bandages from my shirt and T-shirt, tucking my jacket around her to try to keep the warmth of life in her body, compulsively checking and re-checking for a pulse. She was alive, but just barely, when they took her away.

I had stood in the mist, bare-chested and freezing, while some young cop who seemed to be very far away told me my rights and asked me questions I couldn't quite answer, like what was my name. The few times he got through to me, I told him to get Bundy. He finally gave up and delivered me to Bundy in a patrol car, uncuffed but with my gun confiscated.

Bundy handed me a cup of coffee. My teeth chattered against the rim of the cup. "Give me a minute," I said.

He nodded and sat on the edge of his desk. "A few years back," he said, "my youngest boy had a birthday coming up so I asked him what he wanted. He looked me right in the eye and said, 'I want an evil whore.' My first thought was to knock him sideways but LuAnn — my wife — is big on child psychology and I knew knocking the kid through the wall wasn't the way I was supposed to handle it. So I went and asked her what I'm supposed to do when my first-grader tells me he wants an evil whore for his birthday. Took her about ten minutes to stop laughing long enough to explain it to me. Seems it was a toy. The Evil Horde." Bundy leaned heavily on the finally consonant. "One of He-Man's enemies. I told Matthew he could have it when he learned to say it right."

I surprised myself by managing a genuine laugh. "How many kids do you have?"

Bundy sighed. "LuAnn wanted a big family so we had four, two of each. Four wasn't too bad. I could almost afford to feed them. Then a couple years ago, LuAnn gets this funny look on her face and says, wouldn't one more baby be nice? Shit, our youngest was six. The oldest was thirteen. We just reached the point where we could go out to dinner without taking out a loan to pay the babysitter. But what are you going to do, right? So I said okay, one more, then don't ever mention it again. So guess what she went and did."

"Had twins?"

"Yeah, identical girls. Eight months old now and

cute as anything but, Jesus Christ, six kids on a cop's pay."

"I'm a twin."

"You mean there's another one of you running around loose somewhere?"

"Not exactly. Our mother used to tell people we were identical twins of opposite sexes."

"Oh, yeah, your paperhanging partner. How'd you get the scar? If you put another line at the bottom, you'd be monogrammed."

"I've thought of that but I can't reach and I haven't found anyone kinky enough to do it. I got it in a fight in a bar. Fell through a window."

"Ouch." Bundy went behind his desk and sat down. "So what happened?" he asked.

I put my cup down on the desk. "I saw the girl earlier. Ten minutes, maybe fifteen. She was with four other kids. I showed them Jessica's picture. They said they'd never seen her. The girl was crying, said her contacts were bothering her. She must have followed me down to the bridge. And the man was following me, too. Maybe I'm in the wrong line of work."

"You're in the right line of work but you should be carrying a badge. You're one hell of a shot. Twice in the chest in the dark and at twenty-five feet with a thirty-eight. That's damn near impossible."

"Mostly luck."

A woman came into the room to hand Bundy

some papers and a ragged gray sweatshirt which he tossed to me. I pulled it on. Its sleeves had been cut short unevenly and it had several small holes in it but it was warm. I flapped the loose fabric against my chest. "Who does this belong to? King Kong?"

"We got some cops who make you look like Tom Thumb." Bundy quickly scanned the papers he was holding. "Guy's name was Richard Bolin. Several AKA's. California record a mile long. Mostly petty stuff. The L.A. cops say he fancied himself a big-time hit man but he was mainly a kneebreaker for loan sharks. Did some time as a mercenary in South America. Guerrilla warfare crap. Could be why he was so good at staying out of sight.

"Ballistics will take a while but the gun's sure to be the one used on Brandy. And he had a twenty-two in his jacket pocket. So. We have three girls dead and one dying and the man who did it is down at the morgue. Which leaves the big question. Why?"

"Jessica has to be mixed up in it."

"Yeah. Tell me about the kids the girl was with."

About halfway through my description of the motley group of children, Bundy nodded his head toward the open doorway. "Is that them?"

I turned to look. The girl who had spoken to me in Old Town was talking to a uniformed cop, her three ragtag companions huddled close to her. The other kids stayed behind as the cop led her to

Bundy's office. I stood up to give her my chair and leaned against the doorjamb.

She struck her bargain first. "I'm eighteen," she said. She would tell what she knew but not if a warm bed and a hot meal in Juvenile Detention was the price she had to pay.

"All right," Bundy said. "What's your name?"

She thought it over carefully and decided to be Kimberly Jones.

"The girl who was shot didn't have any ID. You know her name?" Bundy asked.

"Peggy. I don't know her last name. Is she dead?"

"She's hurt pretty bad. The doctors are doing everything they can."

Kimberly didn't receive Bundy's words with any apparent optimism about the medical profession's ability. She separated a thin strand of oily brown hair and pulled it between her lips. Her skin had the gray matte look of malnutrition and poor hygiene. An infection was gooing up the corners of her eyes and she wiped at them every couple minutes with the cuff of her worn jacket sleeve.

"Do you know why she was shot? Does it have something to do with the girl Mr. Smith is looking for?"

She nodded. "Jessica Finney. I never seen her but Peggy did. The others, they don't know nothing about it."

"Where did Peggy see her?"

"I dunno. I can tell you what happened to Peggy."

Bundy nodded and Kimberly crossed her ankles and clasped her hands in her lap, a schoolgirl reciting her lesson. She said, "This is what happened to Peggy." She stared at the wall behind Bundy for several seconds before she started talking.

"Peggy, she run off from home. I dunno when. She got here, I think it was in May. I dunno for sure. We didn't know her then. She's thirteen, fourteen, I dunno for sure, and she had a hard time. She didn't know nobody on the street. Some nigger pimp —" Kimberly suddenly sat up straighter and some color came into her cheeks. Bundy's face was expressionless. "Some black guy, a pimp, put her to work but she was scared and she run off.

"Then she met this woman, name of Molly. Molly took good care of her. Put her in a motel and gave her clothes and food. Took real good care of her. Peggy's real pretty." Kimberly touched her own plain face briefly. "Anyway, this Molly said she could help Peggy make lots of money. Said all she had to do was make a movie. So Peggy says okay and some men, some friends of Molly's, take her out to this house in the country. Old house with a barn. Peggy didn't know where it was. Said it was a long drive."

Kimberly's voice was getting rough, rusty-sounding, as if she didn't use it much. Bundy asked if she would like a soda and we waited silently until someone brought her a Coke. She popped the top and took a long swallow.

"The movie," Bundy said. "They made a porno movie?"

"Yeah, I guess, only it wasn't real bad. It wasn't . . ."

"Hard-core?"

"Yeah, hard-core. It was just . . . Peggy was naked and there was some man in it but there wasn't no real sex. Just make-believe. Acting, you know?"

Bundy nodded.

"Then," she said, "the next night, they did it."

"What did they do, Kimberly?"

"Peggy, she was sleeping in this room upstairs. There was a big mirror on the wall. The whole wall was a mirror, you know? She was asleep and all these lights come on in the ceiling. There was like sheets of plastic on the ceiling so you didn't know the lights was there. Anyway, all these lights come on, real bright, and Peggy woke up and there was two men in the room. Naked, except they was wearing ski masks. And they raped her. Both of them. She was real scared. She thought it was real, you know, and she tried to fight. She didn't know about the cameras behind the mirror. She didn't know it was just a movie and she was real scared."

The secret, made manifest.

Kimberly took another long drink of her Coke

and wiped her eyes. "They kept her there, maybe a week longer. Until the bruises was gone, you know. Then they put her back on the street here. Didn't give her hardly any money. They said she couldn't tell nobody about the movie, the rape movie, because they had the other movie, the one she did first. And everybody'd think she knew what she was doing, like she knew being raped was just a movie, just acting, you know? So she didn't tell nobody. We met her in July. She's been with us since then."

"She saw Jessica?" Bundy asked.

"Yeah, with Molly. She saw them together somewheres. I dunno where. She told me all this a couple nights ago, real late. She was crying and everything and it was hard to understand her." Kimberly turned to me. "We saw the picture before. This guy who's with us sometimes had it and Peggy saw it and got all upset and that night when everyone else was asleep, she told me about it."

Bundy questioned her for a while longer, carefully, gently, the way I could imagine him questioning one of his children about some schoolyard squabble. She told him that Peggy was from somewhere in the South but had never talked about her family or her reasons for running away. Peggy had not described Molly. There were three or four men at the house in the country but she hadn't named any of them or described them, except for the man in charge. "She said he was real fat, a real pig.

Gross, you know? Can I go now? I don't know nothing else. And they're tired. We gotta find some place to sleep."

Bundy gave her the addresses of a shelter and the street clinic. She took them politely but would probably never use them. As she was leaving, she said to me, "You know why she was going to tell you?"

I shook my head and Kimberly said, "She said you look just like Superman. In the movies, you know? Just like Superman in the movies." She laughed harshly. "Guess she thought you could do something."

She left, collecting her ragged band of surrogate children. Minus one. I sat down in the chair she had vacated. "So now what?" I asked Bundy.

"Shit, I don't know. You know, she's right. If you slicked your hair back a little, you would look —"

"I don't look anything like him. And I can't fly worth a damn."

Bundy locked his hands behind his head and tilted his chair back. "Molly and a fat man and an old house with a barn somewhere out in the country."

"Any chance of getting a line on the movies?"

"I doubt it. They're sure to have a very private list of customers." He brought his chair legs down and ran his hands roughly through his hair. "Rape movies. I wish it shocked me. I've been at this too many years. Jessica Finney was with Molly. Which means she's probably with the fat man. Which means . . ."

"That killing her would be the smartest thing they could do. I'm tired. I'm going to get some sleep and then I'm going to find Jessica."

"She could be dead already."

"Then I'll find the fat man." I stood up, picking my gun up from his desk.

"Sit down," Bundy said. He stood up. I didn't sit down. He was about five-ten but I had the impression my size wasn't intimidating the hell out of him.

"I'm looking for her," I said.

"Sit down."

I sat down.

Bundy seemed to take a dim view of an armed civilian wandering loose in a killing mood, but eventually he agreed that I could look for Jessica. On his terms. From ten at night until two in the morning with two undercover cops dogging my footsteps.

"If you weren't our only lead, I'd tell you to get back to Mackie and stay there. But you're all we have. If we're lucky, they'll send someone else to tail you and we can spot him."

"Or another girl will stop me on the street and we can keep her alive long enough to talk."

"Yeah. I want you off the street the rest of the time. If anyone calls you, I want to hear about it right away. Try anything on your own and you'll be hanging wallpaper full time. Get some sleep. Come in at eight tomorrow night and I'll introduce you to Garcia and Wilson. They're good. If anyone can spot a tail, they can."

"Maybe they can give me lessons."

"Get some sleep."

I got up and walked to the door. "Bundy?"

"Yeah?"

"You think you could give me a ride to my car?"

"Anything to keep you off the street."

CHAPTER TWENTY-FIVE

I WATCHED ALLISON SLEEP FOR A WHILE THEN I counted raindrops on the window. When that got boring, I pulled off the ragged sweatshirt, dropped to the floor at the foot of my bed, and did a hundred and twenty and a half push-ups. The half was agony. I lay flat on the floor, my forehead pressed to my crossed wrists, and counted heart-thuds until I got to a hundred. Then I raised my head and looked at the feet in front of me. I rolled onto my back and looked up at the legs attached to the feet.

Allison pressed my T-shirt tight against her legs. "What are you doing?" she asked.

"Sweating like a pig at the moment. Did I wake you up?"

Stupid question. She didn't bother answering. I raised my arms over my head and slid my hands up her calves, tugging gently. She obligingly dropped to her knees, leaning her face down to mine, her hair forming a golden curtain around us. Nothing fits quite right in an upside down kiss but it was good anyway.

She stretched out on her back on the floor behind

my head, putting her head on my shoulder and flinging honey hair all over my sweaty chest.

"Is that blood all over your pants?" she asked, exactly the way a wife would ask, "Is that lipstick all over your collar?"

"If you fall asleep down here, you'll have to stay. I'm too tired to pick you up." I nudged her head off my shoulder and rolled over for another upside down kiss. "You should have a Surgeon General's warning tattooed on your forehead."

She smiled. "Am I hazardous to your health?"

"You're highly addictive."

"You killed someone tonight, didn't you?"

Takes one to know one. Her eyes were every bit as beautiful upside down. "I'm going to take a shower," I said. I got to my feet and held out a hand to her. "How come you never wear your nightgown?"

"I like your T-shirt."

I liked it, too, especially when she was flat on her back and the thin fabric clung to every curve and hollow. She held the shirt down with one hand and gave me the other and I pulled her to her feet.

"I never realized how good I am at resisting temptation," I said.

She sighed. "You're too good at it."

I got an old sweatsuit out of my suitcase and went into the bathroom, locking myself in and temptation out.

The shower didn't help. I came out feeling as

wired as I ever felt on speed. The soft fleece of the sweatsuit felt prickly, as though my skin had become hypersensitive. Allison was in bed but awake. I joined her, tucking the covers around her and then pulling her into my arms. She snuggled her head against my shoulder.

I told her all about Jessica and the three dead girls and Peggy who might be dead by now. She never said a word and by the time I finished, she was motionless and heavy against me. I was pretty sure she was asleep but I wasn't going to let a little thing like that stop me. I was on a roll.

I went straight from The Great Jessica Finney Caper into The Life and Hard Times of a Deserted Husband. "I couldn't believe she left like that. Literally couldn't believe it. I still can't believe it. I had all kinds of crazy thoughts, like it was some kind of bizarre kidnapping or she was sick, had a brain tumor maybe and wasn't thinking right. Or somebody told her lies, told her I was cheating or something. She couldn't just leave. It didn't make any sense. We were happy. I was happy anyway and she sure acted happy. We didn't fight. We didn't really have any problems at all. We were . . . best friends. I thought I knew her better than I've ever known anyone. And I didn't know her at all. Divorce is easy. If she wanted out, I couldn't have stopped her. Why do it that way? And it wasn't just me. Her parents, her brother and sister, all her friends — she just walked out and left us all. No note, nothing. Why would she do it?"

No answer was forthcoming. I went on to an unnecessarily graphic description of the trips I had made to morgues to see if a Jane Doe was really an April Smith. The morgue trips made a great lead-in to I Was a Teenage Dope Fiend. I explained the finer points of burglary and shoplifting and ripping off family and friends to support a few habits. I ended where it had ended.

"My parents never knew what was going on but Carrie did. She covered for me and lied for me and occasionally stole for me. Right after school was out for the summer, Mom and Dad came home when they weren't supposed to and found their only son zonked out of his mind. Even then, they didn't realize how deep I was in. They grounded me for the rest of my life so I climbed out my bedroom window and spent the rest of the summer on the street.

"I stayed in contact with Carrie and she was catching hell at home because they knew damn well she knew where I was. Then one night one of my doper friends slipped me a joint laced with PCP I think I dropped some speed, too. I don't remember anything after I smoked the joint. They told me later the Highway Patrol picked me up on the Santa Monica Freeway. I was eastbound in the westbound lanes, playing chicken with the cars. I was on a skateboard. Fortunately it was about four in the morning and traffic was light. Some cars scraped the guardrail trying to get away from me but no one got hurt. I've always been glad I don't remember it.

"I woke up three days later, strapped to a hospital bed. There wasn't any other furniture in the room and Mom and Dad were sitting on the floor, crying. I had the distinct impression that I had really fucked up. I spent the next eight months in a private rehab center. I haven't been on a skateboard since."

That was funny. I laughed but my laugh sounded strange so I stopped it and went on. "They didn't tell me about Carrie for a long while. I wasn't carrying any ID when I was picked up so it took them a while to figure out who I was. When a cop showed up at the house the next day and told them where I was, Carrie went into the kitchen and slit her wrist with a butcher knife. It wasn't much of a suicide attempt. There were three people practically standing beside her. She says she doesn't remember doing it. She just remembers thinking it was all her fault. Carrie always thinks I'm her fault. Anyway, there we were — me in a detox ward and Carrie in a psych ward and Mom and Dad having a grand old time running back and forth between us."

I was silent for a moment then I went on to the story I wouldn't tell Bundy — the sorriest story in what seemed like a lifetime of sorry stories. Why I quit The Cops by Zachariah O'Brien Smith.

"April had been gone for a few months and I didn't really give a damn about anything. I went to work because it was better than being at home. It was Halloween night. Mackie celebrates Halloween the old-fashioned way — lots of tricks. We were busy as hell and it was about midnight before I ever got to the police building and I never did get over to my desk.

"Someone had decorated the place. There were jack-o'-lanterns all over, spiderwebs hanging from the ceiling, all kinds of crap. I noticed a big pumpkin on my desk but it was facing the other way. Then the guy who was Chief of Detectives back then put some papers on my desk and started laughing like crazy. He doesn't laugh very often so after he left, everyone else in the room went over to see what was so funny.

"The pumpkin was carved to look like a house, with a door and some windows. There was a mailbox painted on it. My name was on the mailbox." I shut up for a minute to let the pain in my throat subside. "Had a wife and couldn't keep her. Shit. I threw the pumpkin through the window and threw my badge out after it. It seemed to make sense at the time."

"Did you find out who did it?"

I jumped about a foot off the bed. "Jesus Christ, I thought you were asleep."

"You were talking to me."

"Well, I still thought you were asleep. You didn't say anything."

"You sounded like you just wanted me to listen."

"Are you sure you're only seventeen? I knew who did it. There was a cop named Porter who was a real nut-case. He pulled practical jokes constantly. None of them were funny."

I didn't tell Allison the rest of it. Carrie knew most of my sins but I had never even told her how I deliberately set out to charm the pants off Porter's lonely, homely wife. It wasn't hard to do and I whiled away several days of unemployment in the Porters' chintzy bedroom waiting for the day I knew would come, the day Porter would slip away from work and come home for a snack or a nap or a quickie, the day I was going to break every bone in his body if he didn't shoot me first.

The day came. Porter didn't shoot me and I never laid a hand on him. I pulled my clothes on and watched his wife's face as he explained to her exactly why I had found her charms so irresistible. I left them both crying on the marriage bed I had recently defiled. They moved to California a month later. If there's a hell, Betty Porter's tears bought my ticket.

Allison moved restlessly inside her swaddling blankets.

"Zachariah?"

"Hmm?"

"Would it be all right if I tell you I love you?"

"For crying out loud, it's four o'clock in the morning."

"What does that have to do with it?"

"I don't know. I guess it's all right as long as you promise not to believe it."

I could tell she was smiling as she said, "I promise." Then, very solemnly, she said, "I love you."

The statement, incomplete as always without a response, hovered above the bed. I didn't know what to say. Fortunately, Allison did.

"I promise not to believe you either."

I kissed the top of her head. "I love you. Now go to sleep."

She did. I couldn't, so after a while I got up and undressed and got into my own bed.

Chapter Twenty-Six

I MANAGED TO GET ABOUT FIVE HOURS' SLEEP before Allison woke me up by sitting on my pillow. I opened my eyes to the sight of a creamy thigh so close I could see the fine pale gold hairs on it. There isn't much you can do with a thigh that close except kiss it, so I did and felt goosebumps rise beneath my lips. When I curved my hand around her leg just above the knee, Allison shivered.

"The mountains are out," she said.

They were. The room was awash with sunshine and she had opened the window to let in a fresh breeze. A perfect day for a picnic. A loaf of bread, a jug of wine, and Allison in my arms. And I didn't have to do anything until eight o'clock. I nuzzled the thigh again while visions of Allison in a motel room with me for ten hours danced through my head.

"How would you like to go to the zoo?" I asked. "I can drop you off and pick you up this afternoon. You'll like it. And there's the Western Forestry Center next to it and OMSI. That's the Oregon Museum of Science and Industry. You'll like them all."

She thought it was a wonderful idea. I told her to turn around so I could put my pants on.

"What are you wearing?"

"Nothing."

She smiled. "I saw you naked the other night."

"You were older then. Turn around."

I was ready to go twenty minutes later but Allison was still in my T-shirt so I called Phil. He seemed distracted and after he called me Zachariah for the third time, I asked him what was wrong.

"Aw, shit, Harkins is driving me nuts. That man's about half a bubble off plumb on a good day and ever since this murder went down he's been acting like a man in need of a rubber room. First big case since he's been Chief and we're running around like a bunch of jackasses who couldn't arrest a jay-walker if he stepped on our toes."

"Don't let him get to you. You been to a meeting lately?"

"Last night. Don't worry, it'd take a better man than Harkins to drive me to drink."

"If I remember correctly, it usually takes a woman."

I didn't join in Phil's laughter. The solution to his problem, and to Harkins' problem, was on her knees on the bed beside me, threading one of her gold hoops through the hole in my earlobe.

"You haven't come up with anything new?" Phil said no and I asked, "How about relatives? They're always a good bet." Guile and cunning again.

"Yeah, but Vanzetti didn't have any. He never married and he was the only child of two only children. We'd have to go back three generations just to find some kind of cousin. Bucky?"

"Yeah?"

"Aw, nothing. It'll keep. I gotta get back to work."

I hung up the phone, smiling at Allison who was related to a dead man who had no relatives. She sat back on her heels, tilting her head to the side.

"You look like a pirate," she said.

"You aren't going to ask why I had my ear pierced?"

"No," she said and very primly added, "I'm not going to ask about the tattoo either."

I laughed. "I forget it's there. And don't you go telling anyone you know about it. I could go to jail for letting a minor see it."

"I would like to know how you got the scar."

The scar she was referring to was the same one Bundy had asked about. It was shaped like a number seven, stretching between my shoulder blades and angling down to the small of my back. It looked as though Zorro had made two-thirds of his mark on my back with a very shaky rapier.

"You know how in the movies when there's a big fight someone always crashes through a window and gets up and walks away? In real life you don't get up and walk away. You lie there and bleed all over the sidewalk."

"You were knocked through a window? Was that when you were a policeman?"

It was when I was a drunk. "After I quit. I was in a bar and I took exception to the way a man was treating a woman. I didn't notice he had three friends with him."

"That sounds romantic. Protecting a lady's honor."

The lady sold her honor nightly, hourly if she could find the customers, and her beef with the man stemmed from the fact that her minimum was fifteen dollars and he only had ten. She was drunk, he was drunk, the three friends were drunk. I was drunker than all five of them put together and had spent several hours looking for something to hit.

I gazed into Allison's midnight blue eyes and said, "Yeah, it was romantic. But it hurt like hell and I ended up paying for the window. Are you going to the zoo in my T-shirt? All the animals will stare at you. And I don't mean the ones in the cages."

She retrieved her earring and went into the bathroom. When she came out, she was wearing her dark blue pants with the pink blouse which had a deep V neckline and enormous sleeves. She liked sleeves. All three blouses she had chosen had big ones. On the run from the cops and she picked out clothes she would look good in. I supposed it made some kind of sense. What woman wants to get arrested looking less than her best? She pinned her hair up and tied her hat on. As we left the room, she put her sunglasses on. For once, she needed them.

On a clear day in Portland, you don't need to see forever. The day itself is sufficient. The wind that had blown away the marine layer during the night had gentled to a perfect summer breeze. As we crossed the Willamette, Portland was spread before us, a multicolored jewel in a setting of green hills and blue sky. Sunlight played upon concrete and steel, brick and glass and water. Tall buildings with mirrored facades reflected the scene with crystal clarity.

The water of the Skidmore Fountain would be dancing in the sunlight with no memory of the heavy splash of a suddenly inanimate object. To the water it was all the same — fallen leaves, tossed coins, discarded gum wrappers, blood and brains and bits of Brandy.

Just beyond the fountain, the Burnside Bridge would arch toward blue skies for its leap across the Willamette. The impartial sunshine would spill into the space beneath the bridge, warming, drying, bleaching. To the sun it was all the same — morning dew, urine and vomit, spat tobacco, spilled whisky, Peggy's blood.

When we arrived at the Washington Park Zoo, I gave Allison enough money to enjoy her day but not enough to run on. The third time I reminded her to save taxi fare in case something came up and I couldn't come get her, she said, "Honestly, I'm not totally incompetent."

"Sorry. Carrie says I have a mother-hen complex."

"She's right." She kissed me quickly and got out of the car. I watched until she waved at me from the ticket booth then I drove straight back to the motel.

I called the answering service to see if anyone knew the name of the store in Allentown. Someone did. I should have just guessed. It was the Allentown General Store. Marilyn got the phone number for me. I gave my name to the kid who answered and asked for Sarge.

He came on the line immediately, saying, "Hey, how's it going?"

"Fine," I lied. "I need a favor."

"Sure thing. Whatcha need?"

"I think you're going to be asked some questions about Monday morning, who was at the cafe, that kind of thing. It would be helpful if you forgot I was there."

"Are we talking cops?"

"Yeah. I don't want you to lie. If they know I was there, go ahead and tell them you talked to me. But if they don't know, don't volunteer the information."

"Shit, the last thing I volunteered for was Nam. You got it."

"Thanks, I owe you one."

"No, you don't. This makes us even."

I called Finney who listened to my story in incredulous silence then said "I'm coming out there" and hung up on me as usual. My next call was to Bundy. He wasn't at work but I left a message and he called me back within five minutes. Peggy was in intensive care and hadn't regained consciousness. There was no other news. I told him I'd see him at eight.

The motel room seemed too quiet. I turned the television on, flipped through all the channels, and turned it off again. I called Virginia.

"Hi," she said. "Is there another private investigator from Mackie in town or is this you in the paper?"

"Shit. What does it say?"

"Not much. An unidentified girl is in critical condition following a shooting in Old Town. Her assailant was shot and killed by a private investigator from Mackie who witnessed the shooting. The incident may be connected with the recent shooting deaths of three other women."

"Shit."

"You sound like you could use some cheering up. I can get away from here for a while. Why don't you meet me at my place in about an hour."

"That's the best offer I've had all day. All year."

As soon as I hung up the phone, it rang. Phil said, "What the fuck is going on, you closemouthed son-of-a-bitch. Carrie just called and read me an interesting item in *The Oregonian*. She's all upset and she just knows you're going to get your tattooed ass blown off."

"Shit. Call her back and tell her everything's okay. I don't want her calling me every five minutes."

After I gave him a quick summary of events, Phil said, "Sounds like you got yourself a whole lot of trouble right there in River City. Try to remember you're not required to die in the line of duty anymore. I got something I need to talk to you about and I'd hate like hell for you to kick the bucket before I get a chance to do it."

"Just keep Carrie off my back."

"Last time you killed someone, you took a nose-dive off the deep end. That's one thing that's worrying her."

"This wasn't a kid, he was a hired gun. And I'm not going off any deep end so just tell her to leave me alone."

"I'll give it my best shot."

"How's the Vanzetti case coming?"

"We're *cherchez*-ing the woman as hard as we can. Nothing about the damn case makes sense. I keep feeling like I'm missing something and I just don't know what it is. It's gotta be the woman though. Damn, why couldn't she take her fucking nightgown with her so I could buy into Harkins' theory. A nice simple case of one bad guy getting offed by another bad guy and we could set it on a back burner and forget it."

"What is it you want to talk to me about?"

After a long pause, Phil said, "It'll wait. Talk to you later."

I hung up, wondering what his problem was and wishing I didn't know he had one so I wouldn't have to worry about it. I checked my watch, making a bet with myself that Carrie would call within ten minutes. I stretched out on the bed and worried about Phil and worried about Allison and worried about Jessica and worried about Peggy. When I started worrying about a birthday party I didn't want to go to, I sat up, totally disgusted with myself. The phone rang. Eight minutes.

I listened to the concern in my sister's voice as she made small talk at long distance rates. When she ran out of newsy chatter, I said, "Everything's fine. I have two undercover cops keeping an eye on me. I'll be home in a few days."

"I had a scary dream last night."

"Don't pull that twin intuition crap on me. If you have it, why don't I?"

"You do. Remember when you showed up at the hospital at four in the morning when I was in labor with Melissa?"

"Jesus Christ, I was on my way home and saw your car in the parking lot."

"The hospital isn't on your way home from anywhere."

"So I was out sightseeing. You're a real pain in the ass, you know that?"

"I love you, too. Be careful, Dabby."

During the drive to Virginia's, I watched my rearview mirror carefully, trying to spot a tail. When I missed the rear end of a Tri-Met bus by about two inches, I decided to look out the windshield instead. If I could walk down a dark, deserted street with two people behind me and not notice, I sure as hell wasn't going to be able to tell if one of the hundred cars going my way was following me.

Virginia's plan for cheering me up had to do with getting my clothes off as fast as possible. She didn't have to bother with hers. She was naked when I got there.

"Feeling better?" she asked when we were stretched out on the bed catching our breath.

"You do have a way of taking a man's mind off his problems."

She grinned. "Guess what! I have food! Are you hungry?"

I said I was and she went to the kitchen and returned with a tray of cold cuts and crackers and two bottles of Michelob. After we finished eating, she cheered me up again.

I left her place at three-thirty and drove to the zoo to get Allison. She was waiting by the entrance, surrounded by two sailors. She frowned fiercely when she saw the Nova. I drove past her and found a parking place at the far end of the lot. I got out and stood by the car. The sailors trailed after her until she stopped and said something, shaking her head firmly. They turned, reluctantly I was sure, and headed back to the zoo entrance. Allison walked quickly to the car, checking over her shoulder a few times to be sure her admirers weren't persisting. She got into the car and sighed heavily. Life is hell for killers on the run.

Once we were safely away from the zoo, she chatted happily about polar bears and penguins and baby elephants and museum exhibits until I stopped at a pizza parlor. She was suddenly very tired and thought she would sit in the car while I went inside. That suited me just fine. I was glad she had enough sense to realize that being seen with me was a bad idea.

Back at the motel, we sat on my bed to eat the pizza. When we finished, I propped all the pillows against the headboard and leaned back, pulling her close to me. My head was buzzing pleasantly from the cumulative effects of the beers I'd had at Virginia's and the ones I'd washed the pizza down with. We had been talking about my family and Allison asked if I had any pictures. I handed her my wallet. I had two or three pictures of Melissa at different ages and one of her with her parents. Allison thought Melissa was adorable, Tom was handsome, and Carrie was fascinating.

"She looks just like you, only she's pretty."

"I'm not pretty?"

She slanted a look at me. "I don't think pretty is quite the right word for you."

"When I was a kid I used to worry that I was going to look just like my sister for the rest of my life. Except for haircuts and clothes, you could hardly tell us apart. Then along came puberty and the hormones worked their magic."

Talk of hormones and puberty seemed to embarrass Allison. She looked away from me and after a moment she asked what Carrie's last name was now.

"Harry," I said.

She grinned. "Carrie Harry?"

"And she used to complain about Smith. Now, Tom's name has a lot of potential. I offered to pay the legal fees so he could have his middle name changed from Ryan to Dickon, but he refused."

"Tom Dickon Harry?" Allison collapsed against me in a fit of giggles. While she was distracted I slipped my hand up under the Oregon Rain Festival T-shirt she had changed into when we got back to the motel. I unhooked her bra then slid my hands up her sleeves, found her bra straps and pulled them down through the sleeves and over her wrists. I plucked the loose bra from beneath her shirt and tossed it on the other bed. She ignored the whole procedure but I was pretty sure she noticed. The giggles ceased abruptly.

"What's your middle name?" she asked.

"O'Brien. So is Carrie's. It's our mother's maiden name."

She was resolutely ignoring my caresses. "You don't look Irish. You should have red hair."

With my hands on Allison's breasts and my brain God only knows where, I opened my big mouth and said, "That's a nice bit of ethnic stereotyping coming from a blond Italian." I added a very heart-felt *"Shit"* as she pulled away from me, her face pale and stiff with fear.

"I've known since Wednesday night," I said quickly. "I haven't done anything about it."

She drew a long shaky breath. "How did you find out? That policeman you talk to . . ."

"I found your ID. The cops don't know about you yet. Not who you are anyway. They're looking for a woman. You left your nightgown behind."

She started to get off the bed but I grabbed her wrist and pulled her back against me. "Don't get all upset, babe. You'll make yourself sick again."

"Why haven't you told the police?"

"I'm not sure. I wanted to give you some time. You weren't in very good shape."

"But you're going to make me to go the police, aren't you?"

"I don't want to make you do anything." I stroked her hair. She wasn't crying but she felt rigid against me. I held her quietly and after a while she seemed to relax a bit although she was clutching my hand tightly.

"Allison? Who was Carl Vanzetti?"

"My father."

I looked at her in surprise. "Your father? He would have been over fifty when you were born." She nodded. "What about your mother?" I asked.

"She was much younger, of course. Oh, you mean where is she. She died in a car accident when I was five."

"What about other relatives?"

"I don't have any."

"Aunts, uncles, cousins?"

She shook her head. "There's no one on my father's side. I don't know anything about my mother's family. I think when she married Daddy she didn't have anything to do with them anymore. I don't remember much about her. She had blond hair and blue eyes and I don't look like her. I remember her laughing a lot. She always seemed happy. I hope she was. She was only twenty-four when she died."

Twenty-four. Nineteen when her daughter was born. And more than thirty years younger than her husband. An unusual marriage. I hoped she had been happy, too.

We were quiet for a few minutes. Allison was probably thinking about her mother. I was thinking about the question I didn't want to ask and the answer I didn't want to hear.

I slid downward in the bed so I was no longer sitting but lying on my side. Allison followed me.

She was facing me, very close to me, her head on my arm. I put my other arm around her waist and looked into those beautiful night-sky eyes.

"Did you kill your father?"

She didn't answer. She turned her face against my shoulder and wept.

CHAPTER TWENTY-SEVEN

SHE DIDN'T CRY FOR LONG. SHE GOT SOME KLEE-nex from the bathroom then stretched out beside me again.

"I don't know what to do," she said.

"You should start by telling me about it."

"I don't want to."

"I don't think you have much choice. I'm all you've got on your side right now. The cops are sure to ID you one of these days and you're going to need some help."

She sighed. "I didn't kill him."

"Who did?"

"It doesn't matter who did it."

My turn to sigh. "Start at the beginning, babe."

She took me literally. Allison was born in New York City and lived in a Manhattan penthouse until her mother's death. She had few memories of those years. "I remember a park my mother took me to, with swings and a slide, and a Christmas tree with silver bells all over it, little things like that. She died in May so I had just turned five. I know we had a cook and a housekeeper. And a chauffeur. He died in the accident, too. I think

Daddy lived with us but he was gone most of the time. I remember him coming home after the accident and telling me I was going to live with his mother. And I remember the airplane trip to Grandmother's."

"Where did she live?"

"In Minnesota. Near St. Paul. I stayed there for two years, until she died. She was very old and she never left her room. I went to a private school during the day and the servants took care of me at home. I only saw Grandmother on Sundays when I had tea in her room."

"Where was your father then?"

"I don't know. He didn't live there. He visited once in a while. When Grandmother died, he came to get me."

"Where did you go then?"

"To school," Allison said bitterly. "For the rest of my life."

"In Connecticut? That's the school's address on your driver's license?"

"Yes. You know the kind of place you think of when you hear someone threaten to send their son to military school?" I nodded and she said, "That's Fanhaven Academy, except it's for girls. It's small and I think it's very expensive. All the students are rich. Their parents are rich anyway. They're movie producers, foreign diplomats, business tycoons, the Jet Set." She sat up, turning to face me. "The newspaper said Daddy was a criminal. The FBI was looking for him."

"You didn't know that before?"

"I didn't know what he did."

So much for my idol-with-the-feet-of-clay theory.

"So you lived at the school," I prompted.

"Yes. One of my girlfriends described it pretty well. She said people send their daughters to Fanhaven so they'll grow up untouched by human hands." She smiled. "Some of the girls call it Fannyhaven. It doesn't really work, of course, because the girls go home during the summer and on holidays. You'd be surprised how wild their lives are when they're not at school."

I didn't think I would be surprised at all but I didn't say anything.

"I'm the only one who lived there permanently," Allison continued. "I don't mean I was all alone during vacations. There are always girls who have to stay for a summer or at Christmas because their parents are working or went abroad or something. But I'm the only one who never left." She traced one of the fleur-de-lis patterns on the bedspread. "I didn't have a home to go to. Daddy took me there when I was seven years old and I never left until Sunday."

He put her in a private school and there he kept her very well. "Where was he all those years?"

"I don't know. He never told me anything about

his life. He said he was in the import business and traveled all the time."

"How often did you see him?"

"Twice a year. Once during the summer and once at Christmas. He'd show up in the afternoon and take me out to dinner then he'd leave and I wouldn't see him again for six months. He never wrote or called and I never knew how to get in touch with him."

She lay down beside me on her back. I supported myself on one elbow and watched her face.

"I got presents from him on my birthday and at Christmas. When I was younger, I thought he actually sent them to me. Then I realized the school bought them. He just gave them the money. Except for my diamond." She tugged the stone from beneath her shirt and looked at it, turning it so the facets caught the light. "He gave it to me last Christmas. He said it's from my mother's wedding ring.

"I know I shouldn't complain. I was taken care of. No one was ever mean to me. I don't even remember anyone ever being mad at me. I had everything I needed. And if I wanted anything, all I had to do was ask. Daddy gave the school a lot of money, I guess. I got anything I wanted. Except for a car. I asked him for one last Christmas and he said I had to wait until I leave school. Anyway, I was treated very well. It's just that there was no one . . ." She swallowed hard, blinking back tears.

I expected her to say "No one who loved me," but she said, "No one I belonged to."

After a moment, she said, "So, that's where I've been all my life."

"Until Sunday. Tell me about Sunday."

"It started before that actually. I finished all the high school courses in May but you don't have to leave Fanhaven just because you graduate. I think they'll keep you forever as long as someone pays the bills. But I wanted to leave. I was just so tired of being there. I wanted to live in a house, or an apartment, a *home*. I thought Daddy would come for my graduation, but he didn't.

"I waited all summer to see him so I could talk to him about leaving school. He usually came at the end of June but he never showed up. There's a lawyer who handles the money. I talked to him but he didn't know how to get in touch with Daddy. All he had was an address in New York and it was one of those mail-forwarding places. I wrote but he never answered.

"Then, last Saturday, he finally called. He told me he was leaving the country and he didn't know how long he would be gone. He told me I have to stay at Fanhaven until I'm eighteen and then I can go to college or do whatever I want. He said he'd support me as long as I needed him to, but he didn't know when he could see me again."

Allison separated a thick section of her hair and began to braid it tightly. "I was really upset. I asked if I could leave school and get an apartment and he said no, I'm not old enough. He said I had to stay at school until April. I was upset, I was crying and I couldn't talk very well. I asked if I could call him back when I was calmer and he gave me the number. Area code, telephone number, and room number. I didn't think anything about it until later, when I was ready to call him. Then I realized I could find out where he was. For the first time in my life, I could find out where he was.

"I called the telephone operator and she told me the number was in Mackie, Oregon, and I got the name of the hotel when the desk clerk answered the phone. I told Daddy I'd do what he wanted, I'd stay at Fanhaven until my birthday. He said he'd write to me and maybe in a year or so I could visit him."

She threaded her fingers through the braid she had made and worked it loose. "I hardly slept at all that night. I kept thinking about knowing where he was. And I decided to go see him. I don't really know what I expected him to do. Take me with him maybe or at least I could make him understand that I just couldn't stay at school any longer.

"I had some money. I get an allowance every month but the school supplies everything I need so I don't spend much of it and I just keep it in my footlocker. I couldn't take a suitcase so I stuck some things in the biggest purse I have. Sunday morning I told Mrs. Mayhew — she's the headmistress — that I wanted to go to an art show. I go places by myself a lot. It's a small town and they trust me. I've never been in any trouble at school. So I took a cab into town then I took the train to New York and went to the airport."

At the airport, Allison was told there were no commercial flights into Mackie. The closest they could get her was Pendleton but she would have a layover in Portland. She had never heard of Pendleton so she bought a one-way ticket to Portland. From the Portland airport, she took a cab to the bus depot where she bought a ticket to Mackie. She had less than forty dollars left by then.

"What were you going to do if your father was gone when you got there?"

"Call Fanhaven. They'd make sure I got home."

"I don't understand what the school's doing. It seems to me the mysterious disappearance of a student at a ritzy private school would rate a little news coverage. For all they know, you were kidnapped."

"Well, no. I left a note in my room."

"Ah. You left that part out."

"Well, I did. I just said I was going away for a few days by myself and they shouldn't worry about me."

"Even so, they would have filed a missing person report, just to cover their asses. They must be going crazy by now."

She nodded. "Daddy started to call them when I

got to the hotel but then he said something about letting them sweat it out overnight. I guess he was mad because they let me get away."

She closed her eyes. She was pale and looked tired. I let her rest for a minute. A private school that had misplaced a rich man's daughter was going to be trying hard to find her. Vanzetti's death probably hadn't made the news east of Chicago but eventually someone in Connecticut was going to find out that Allison bought a plane ticket to Portland. Portland Police Bureau would be routinely notified to be on the lookout for a runaway named Allison Vanzetti. It would take the Portland cops about half a second to connect her with Mackie's murder case. I was surprised it hadn't happened yet.

"Allison?"

She looked at me, her eyes the color of the sea on a stormy night. The skin beneath them had a faintly bruised look that hadn't been there before. "Tell me what happened in Mackie."

"It was about eight o'clock when the bus got there but it was eleven o'clock to me and I was exhausted. I hardly slept Saturday night and I couldn't sleep on the airplane. I saw the hotel when we drove through town so I just walked over from the bus depot. Daddy's room number was 301 and I was sure it would be on the third floor so I didn't talk to anyone in the lobby. I just took the elevator upstairs and went to the room. He was . . . he wasn't angry really. He was shocked to see me, of course, and he seemed almost frightened. I didn't understand that. First he told me I had to leave right away then he decided I could stay overnight but I had to go back to Connecticut in the morning. We didn't really talk very much. He seemed nervous and I was so tired. And I felt awful because I came all the way out here and it didn't do any good. He was sending me back to school."

She pulled the pillow from beneath her head and put it lengthwise on top of her, gripping it hard with both hands. "I went to bed but I couldn't sleep very well. I kept waking up. Daddy was pacing around the room and he had the television on part of the time. Once when I woke up, he was lying on the other bed. He had the covers pulled down but he was dressed and he was just lying there. I asked him what was wrong and he said . . . he said, 'I wish I had done things differently.'" She squeezed the pillow tighter until her fingers met in the middle.

"I guess I fell asleep because the next thing I knew, he was shaking me and telling me to get dressed. It was about four o'clock and I felt really confused and sleepy. I got dressed in the bathroom and then he told me to stay behind the curtain and be very quiet. Do you know how the rooms are there? With the curtains?"

I nodded. I had been in the Mackie Arms plenty of times. The rooms they call suites are just larger than average hotel rooms. The beds and bathroom are at the end away from the door. The front part of the room is furnished like a sitting room. Mounted on a ceiling-hung traverse rod between the two sections of the room are wall-to-wall, floor-to-ceiling drapes that can be closed to separate the two areas.

"I stood behind the curtain like he told me to. Everything was so strange, Zachariah. I didn't know what was happening and Daddy seemed so scared. The lights were off where I was but they were on in the other part of the room and there was a little gap where the curtain didn't come together completely in the middle and I could see into the room where Daddy was. He was standing by the door. Nothing happened for a long time. At least it seemed like a long time. Then, he must have heard footsteps in the hall because he opened the door and a man came in. They stood right inside the door and talked, not for very long, just a minute or two. I couldn't hear what they were saying. Daddy had the television on again and they were very quiet. But I could tell they were arguing. Then the man left.

"Daddy told me he was going to take me to a hotel in Pendleton. I put my sweater on and picked my purse up and then there was a tap on the door, very quiet. And Daddy . . . he looked so scared and he told me to stay behind the curtain and be absolutely quiet. So I did. There was still that little gap and I saw what happened."

Allison's fingers were bloodless, skeletal against the white pillowcase.

"What happened, babycakes?"

She took a deep breath and spoke in a rush. "Daddy opened the door and it was the same man again and he pulled out a gun and shot Daddy. A lot of times. Four times, it said on the news. And then he left and Daddy was on the floor and his eyes . . . he was . . . there was blood and his eyes . . . I knew he was dead. I walked through the curtain and he was . . . he was . . . lying there and I knew he was dead and the door was standing open and I walked out and closed the door and went down the stairs and then I was outside in a parking lot. I saw a restaurant across the street. I don't remember its name."

"Sparky's. Mackie's only twenty-four-hour restaurant."

She nodded. "I went inside and I stayed in the restroom for a while and then I sat at a booth and ordered tea. Nobody paid any attention to me. They were all looking across the street. There were police cars at the hotel. And an ambulance.

"I think it was about five o'clock by then. I heard an old man talking to the waitress. He told her he was going to Allentown to babysit his grandchildren because they had the chickenpox and his daughter couldn't afford to take time off from work to stay home with them. I went outside and waited and when he came out I told him my car was broken down and I needed a ride to Allentown. He drove me out there in his truck. He didn't ask me any questions. He talked about his grandchildren all the way. I felt sick when I saw Allentown. There's nothing there. I told him to let me out at the gas station and he did. And you know the rest."

I knew the rest. What I didn't know was how much of her story was the truth. I believed everything up to the point where the other man came into the picture. Allison's eyes were closed, her hands still squeezing the pillow hard. I got off the bed and stood at the window. Beyond the parking lot was a neat row of columnar arborvitae. The mountains were no longer out. Flat gray clouds covered the sky.

Allison said, "You don't believe me, do you?"

I turned to face her, leaning back against the window sill. She was sitting up, her arms wrapped around her bent legs. She rested her cheek on her knees, looking at me with beautiful, innocent eyes.

"When a person witnesses a murder, the usual response is to scream or faint or run for help or pick up the phone and call the cops. You're telling me you just walked away."

"I wasn't supposed to be there." She said it in a toneless, dreamy voice. It was the excuse of a child who sees something frightening, something incomprehensible, something adult, and believes it will go away if its existence is denied. I thought of Melissa, covering her eyes and thinking no one could see her.

"You saw a man kill your father and you can identify him and you're letting him go, letting him get away with it? Why not go to the police and describe him and help them find out who he is?"

"I know who he is." She spoke again in that dreamy voice as if what she was saying was of no consequence at all.

"You mean you know his name?"

"I know his name." Dreamily, dreamily.

"How?"

"Daddy told me." She suddenly shifted to a crosslegged position, her back very straight, her wrists on her knees. She spoke brusquely. "After the man left the first time, when Daddy told me he was taking me to Pendleton, I asked him who he was and he told me. Maybe he thought it would reassure me."

"He might not have told you the right name."

"He did."

"How do you know? Had you seen him before?"

"I never saw him before." She was speaking in that dreamy voice again.

"Then how do you know it's the right name?"

She shrugged. "I just know."

"Why won't you tell the police?"

Very patiently, as if I should have known, she said, "Because if I tell anyone, he'll kill me, too."

I sat on the bed beside her and took her hand. "No, he won't, honey. He won't even know you talked until after he's arrested. The police won't let him anywhere near you."

"He will kill me. I don't want to die."

She lay back on the bed and closed her eyes. I got up and looked out the window again. Down in the parking lot a woman was trying to put a little boy about Melissa's age into a child's carseat in the back of a small tan hatchback. The baby kept stiffening up, struggling against the restraints. His mother finally yanked him out, smacked him on the backside, and then stuffed him into the seat, fastening the belt around him. The little boy was screaming, his face contorted. The woman crossed her arms on the top of the car and lowered her head against them. After a moment she straightened and leaned in to kiss the sobbing child. Then she got in the car and drove off.

I leaned my forehead against the cool glass and thought about motives for murder.

Family ties bind with steel that is often barbed. In every way that matters, Allison had been orphaned at the age of five. But unlike a true orphan, she would have been unable to dream of adoption; unable to hope for placement in a loving foster home; unable, out of loyalty to an absentee father, to form an attachment to a surrogate parent of her own choosing; unable, finally, to turn a face of cold indifference to the world and say, "There is no one."

Any other man she saw only twice a year would have been a stranger. But Carl Vanzetti was her father. No matter that he sent a bereaved child to the home of a dying old woman to be cared for by servants; no matter that he abandoned her at a posh school to be cared for by teachers; no matter that he abdicated all but financial responsibility for her — he was her father. I could only imagine the mixture of loyalty and betrayal she must have felt.

Her anger would have grown as she grew older and compared her life to the lives of her friends, as she realized how odd her own life was, as the depth of his betrayal became apparent to her. And she finally rebelled, as all teenagers rebel. But she didn't want a later curfew, or more money, or more freedom. She wanted a home. Vanzetti had slipped up and revealed his whereabouts to her, underestimating the daughter he hardly knew. She had seen an opportunity to force the issue, to confront him, to demand her rights, to ask him to be a real father and give her a home.

And he refused.

And she shot him.

A physically and emotionally exhausted child, face to face with the father who didn't want her. As a motive for murder, it wasn't bad.

I turned from the window. Allison was asleep, her hands loosely grasping the pillow on top of her.

I took the pillow away and covered her with the blanket from the other bed and let her sleep until seven o'clock when I lay down beside her and kissed her awake, not feeling guilty about it any longer because the last thing I wanted to do was discourage her. Now that she knew that I knew, I wanted her in love with me so she would stay. She was going to panic when the police identified her and she was going to run if she could, but until then she would stay because staying was easier than running and because running meant leaving me.

"I have to go to work now," I said. "Promise me you won't leave."

She moved her head restlessly against my shoulder. "I can't leave. I don't have any money. I don't have anywhere to go. And I'm afraid. Monday, I could have done anything, slept in the woods, robbed a bank. It wouldn't have bothered me. I wasn't afraid then, not of being alone anyway. I just knew I had to get away and I could have done anything. But now, I don't know. What happened in Mackie seems so far away, like it never really happened, and being alone with no money and no place to go is so scary."

"You're not alone. I'm here. And I'll help you, but right now I have to find Jessica." I kissed her again then got up and put on my holster and my denim jacket. "I'll be back about two-thirty. You get some rest, okay?"

She clung hard to me at the door. I left but was back ten minutes later. On impulse, I had stopped at a store a few blocks from the motel and bought her a big, soft, understuffed teddy bear. When I re-entered the room, she was sitting up in bed, wearing my T-shirt and watching television. She took the bear and smiled and thanked me. "I think I'll name him Mr. Smith," she said. She snuggled down against the pillows, Mr. Smith clasped to her breast. Freud would have loved it.

I drove down to the Justice Center and met my two babysitters. Bert Wilson looked more degenerate than any wino I had ever seen and smelled as if he had poured a bottle of Thunderbird on his clothes. Ernesto Garcia was small and wiry. In dim light he could pass for a street-tough eighteen-year-old. I thought I did a fine job of keeping my expression noncommittal during the introductions but something must have shown in my eyes.

"Go ahead," Wilson said. "Say it once then don't say it again."

I grinned. "Bert and Ernie?"

"That's right, Big Bird. And it's only funny the first few thousand times."

I hit the street at ten o'clock. With Bert and Ernie somewhere in my wake, I tramped all over downtown and Old Town. It might have been my imagination but it seemed to me that the regulars on the street thought of something pressing to do in the opposite direction when they saw me coming.

I didn't blame them. I was a walking death warrant. Typhoid Smith on the loose in Portland.

Nikki found me at midnight, running to me on slippered feet, a black and red caftan swirling around him. He flung his arms around my neck, his feet leaving the ground, and kissed me. On the cheek, for which I was grateful. I disentangled myself from him and told him to go away.

"I just want to walk with you," he said. "I promise I'll behave myself."

"I'm bait for a killer at the moment, Nikki. Go away and stay away."

"Would you be sad if I got shot?" he asked.

"Nikki, I think you're a very nice boy and I like you and I guess your lifestyle is your own business but I'm not gay and I'm not going to suddenly turn gay and I think you should give that some thought. Now go away. Yes, I'd be sad if you got shot."

He smiled and blew me a kiss and left. I passed Ernie farther down the block. He was leaning against a storefront, his shadowed face a sullen mask of adolescent arrogance. Our eyes met briefly and I saw the laughter in his. I winked at him. Let him wonder. I had been rebuffing advances from homosexuals since I was a kid and had learned not to let it bother me. It was the price I paid for being the flip side of my beautiful sister.

I stayed on the street until two in the morning. Absolutely nothing happened.

CHAPTER TWENTY-EIGHT

THE MOUNTAINS WERE OUT AGAIN ON SATURDAY and I bent Bundy's rule a bit to spend the morning at the Saturday Market. Allison and I separated at the parking lot. I kept catching glimpses of her in the crowd of shoppers. Besides the hat and sunglasses, she was wearing her denim skirt with the blue blouse which had a high collar and, of course, huge sleeves. Even in denim, she had a well-bred air and a cool elegance that made her about as inconspicuous as a nun in a whorehouse.

The open-air market had grown even larger since the last time I was there. Hundreds of booths were set up, providing an impressive array of hand-crafted merchandise and an assortment of food that I sampled liberally. I bought a miniature carousel horse mounted on alabaster for Carrie and a wooden train and a fuzzy blue jacket with bunny ears stitched to the hood for Melissa. After picking out some things for Allison, I worked on my surveillance technique by tailing her.

She collected admirers and gifts as she moved through the jostling crowds. A young man selling silk flowers presented her with a red rose, flourishing an imaginary hat as he handed it to her. An old man gave her a sample of chocolates and gazed after her with nostalgia for his youth plain on his face. An artist did a quick sketch of her as she watched a magician working a crowd by the Skidmore Fountain. She accepted all gifts with polite delight, seemingly unaware that none of the other shoppers were being showered with free samples.

The admirers were more of a problem to her than the gifts but she finally got the hang of it and sent them all away clutching scraps of papers with what I assumed was a phony name and phone number on them. She was leaving a trail of broken hearts behind her as well as a trail of evidence that the police were going to find frustrating.

A young Marine who had left his hair behind at boot camp talked her into having lunch with him. They sat at a table beneath a canvas roof and ate pita sandwiches. I ate teriyaki-on-a-stick while I leaned against a tall counter nearby and listened to the Marine's war stories. Allison pretended very hard that I wasn't there. When they finished eating, she told him a long involved lie about how she absolutely had to leave right this minute. He reluctantly settled for a paper napkin. I moved closer to see what she wrote on it. Allison Smith at the Hilton. A nice hotel. And as good a name as any.

The Marine stayed at the table after Allison left.

He carefully folded the napkin and tucked it in his pocket. I felt bad for him.

I met Allison, as planned, at the parking lot at one o'clock. It was a pay-as-you-enter lot. When we arrived that morning, I had dropped her off around the corner. Now, the attendant was busy at the entrance as we made a clean getaway out the exit.

When we got back to the motel, Allison told me not to look and busied herself doing something mysterious at the table. When she finished, she presented me with an oak picture frame holding one of her scratchboard drawings. It was an ancient gnarled tree made of thousands of tiny lines. In minuscule letters that formed part of a twisted root were the date and the words "From A to Z."

I thanked her and kissed her and kissed her some more until the telephone interrupted us. Marilyn said hello, asked if it was raining, sounded disappointed when I said no, and gave me my messages. Call Phil Pauling. Call Jason Finney at the Hilton. Call Bundy at home.

I talked to three of Bundy's children before word finally got to him that the call was for him. "Peggy's still hanging on," he said, "but the doctor doesn't sound optimistic. We found Bolin's car and the motel where he was staying but all we got out of them was an airplane ticket from LAX to Portland Monday afternoon. The fat man worked fast if he got him up here because of you. The ballistics report came in. Same gun on Brandy and Peggy and the twenty-two was the one used on Dobbs and Baylor. Smith?"

"Yeah?"

"For what it's worth, the doctor said your first-aid under the bridge is the only reason she wasn't DOA at the hospital."

"My brother-in-law's an emergency room doctor. He talks shop a lot."

"Like hell. Listen, I got three kids wailing that their social lives are going down the tube because they can't get to the phone. Come in at two and I'll buy you a cup of coffee."

I called Phil next. He didn't seem to remember why he wanted to talk to me unless it was just so I could listen to him call Chief Harkins foul names.

I finally interrupted him. "Take it easy, Phil. Why don't you just tell the son-of-a-bitch to fuck off. He can't fire you. You're the only cop in town who knows it's still against the law to spit on the sidewalk in the city limits."

Phil laughed and said, "Oh, shit. Okay, Bucky. You're right. I got a lot on my mind and I'm letting him get to me. Son-of-a-bitch, you'd think I arranged to get Vanzetti killed just to piss Harkins off. That man is losing it, mark my words. He's going to have himself a good old-fashioned nervous breakdown if he doesn't learn to relax a little bit."

"What's on your mind?"

"When are you coming home?"

"It won't be long now."

"It'll keep. I gotta go, kemo sabe. *Adios.*"

"Wait. What about phone calls? Did Vanzetti make any calls from his room?"

"You're a few days behind me. He didn't make a single call from his room, but this is interesting. Two different hotel people remember him using the pay phone in the lobby. Now why would he want to stand up to gab on the phone when he could stretch out on a nice bed to do it? And this is even more interesting. The clerk on duty Saturday says he got ten bucks' worth of quarters and left the hotel. I can't see an old geezer like Vanzetti feeding quarters into Pac-Man down at the arcade so my guess is he used a pay phone somewhere else. Real secretive, huh?"

"Yeah, what about incoming calls?"

"No one remembers anyone asking for him by name. If someone asked for the room number, nobody's going to remember that."

When I got off the phone, Allison was looking worried.

"They haven't identified you yet," I said. She continued to look worried. I sat across from her at the table. "You know, if I had wasted my time trying to guess your last name, Vanzetti would have been way down on the bottom of my list."

She smiled wanly. "I'm not really very Italian. I never even thought about it until I read something about Sacco and Vanzetti. I asked Daddy the next time I saw him. He said my great-grandfather was an Italian named Carlo Vanzetti who came to the United States and married an American girl. I don't know anything about her but they had one son, also named Carlo Vanzetti. He was my grandfather, of course, and he married — well, obviously he married my grandmother, the one I lived with. She was from Sweden and was very fair. Daddy was their only son and, of course, my mother was a blonde. Daddy called me an American mongrel."

"I'd call you a genetic work of art myself."

She smiled, not quite so wanly.

"What did he look like?" I asked. There had never been a picture of Vanzetti in the paper or on the newscasts I had seen, maybe just because he wasn't local or maybe the FBI was being covert again. The only picture I had seen was of his covered body being removed from the hotel.

"He had brown hair and his eyes were sort of greenish-brown. I don't look like him." She rearranged the clutter that had accumulated on the table and sighed. "I've been thinking about my mother. I told you I don't know anything about her family. I've been wondering if I even know her real name. Guess what her maiden name is on my birth certificate."

There was only one possible guess. "Smith?" She nodded and I added, "There are a lot of us. That's why the name is such a joke."

"Everything else he ever told me was a lie. Why

should I expect him to tell the truth about my mother? This probably wasn't even hers." She yanked hard on the thin chain around her neck, snapping it in two at the clasp. She threw the broken necklace against the wall. "I'm not going back to Mackie. I can't."

"You can't spend the rest of your life running. Nothing terrible is going to happen. You're a minor. There's no public outrage over your father's death. No one is going to insist on trying you as an adult. Any lawyer with half a brain can get you off. You might have to spend some time in a hospital for psychiatric evaluation but that's it. It'll all be handled in juvenile court and you can start over."

"But I didn't kill him."

"Then, for Christ's sake, tell them that."

"They won't believe me. You don't even believe me."

"I'll believe you if you tell me who he is."

"I can't. Don't you see, he committed the perfect murder. He got away with it. No one suspects him and he's sure to have an alibi worked out and I don't have any proof he was there. They'll think I'm making it up. I've heard you on the telephone. They have my nightgown and my fingerprints and when they find out how I got out of town . . . well, it all looks so *guilty*. If I hadn't been there, no one on earth would ever know he did it. The perfect murder. Except that I was there. And if he finds me, he's going to kill me."

When she talked about it, I almost believed her. Almost, but not quite. It was too coincidental that Vanzetti would be killed within hours of his daughter's unexpected arrival. Too coincidental that not one but two people got in and out of the Mackie Arms without being seen. And it was impossible to commit a perfect murder. Phil Pauling's rattletrap mouth concealed a steel-trap mind. Even with evidence pointing to a woman, he would have kept searching. The fact that he hadn't come up with a single shred of evidence pointing to someone else meant there wasn't anyone else.

"Are you Catholic?" I asked.

"No. Why? Oh, you want me to confess. Well, I'm not confessing, not to a priest and not to a lawyer and not to the police. I'm going away and I'm never coming back here again."

"All the states extradite murder suspects, Allison. You'll be running for the rest of your life. You'll never be able to tell anyone the truth. What are you going to do when you fall in love and want to get married? What if you have children? You'll be lying to everyone you care about for the rest of your life. You'll never be able to tell anyone who you are."

"Who am I? I'm nobody. I'm a dead man's daughter. If you take me back to Mackie I will not say one single word to anyone. Not one word. They'll think I'm crazy and they'll think I killed him and they'll lock me up somewhere. But maybe he won't kill me then. I've been locked up all my life anyway so it doesn't really matter. And no one would care."

"You're being ridiculous. And I would care."

"Then why won't you help me? All I need is some money, not much, just enough to get away from here, out of Oregon. I read a book about a woman who was hiding from someone. She got a birth certificate for someone about her age who died when she was a baby and she used it to get a social security card and then she had a new identity. I could do that. And I can get a job. I'm smart and everyone thinks I'm older than I am. I'll pay you back, honest."

"Goddammit, it isn't the money. I have plenty of money. I could mortgage my house and the land it's sitting on for enough to support you for the rest of your life. But I'm not doing it. I'm not giving you one goddamn penny to run on."

"I hate you." She didn't scream the words, she said them in a hard cold voice that was worse than an angry scream. She got up from the table and got into her bed, taking Mr. Smith with her. Within five minutes she was sound asleep.

I picked up her necklace and stuck it in my pocket. Then I called Jason Finney. He had already talked to the cops and he wasn't happy. I finally interrupted his tirade.

"You're right," I said. "All they have is a story told by a street kid. That and the fact that people who want to talk to me have a way of dying. I've watched two girls get shot already and I don't care to make a habit of it. There's a limit to how much time the cops are going to spend following me around and when they stop, that's it. I'm out of it. If no one contacts me soon, the only way Jessica is going to be found is in the course of the homicide investigations and I can't get involved in them. Even if I wanted to risk losing my license or going to jail, it would be pointless. I don't have the resources. And if you think the cops are going to let me have access to their records, you've been watching too much television."

There was a lot more I wanted to say but he hung up on me. I slammed the receiver down then picked it up again and called Hank Johnston.

"She hasn't called again," he said, sounding worried.

"How did she sound when you talked to her?"

"She sounded okay, not scared or anything, if that's what you mean. She sounded . . . she didn't really sound like herself. I mean, it was Jessica okay, but she sounded like when she was reading those plays to me, like she was being someone else, you know what I mean?"

I knew what he meant. She sounded like someone was listening to her, like someone was forcing her to make the calls, like someone was holding a gun to her head. I had the feeling that little Jessica Finney was one hell of an actress.

Carrie called, apparently just to be sure she still

had a brother. When I told her I hadn't forgotten about bringing her a present she made some non-committal response, sounding very guilty.

"You been out to the house?" I asked.

"Yes, I watered the plants and got rid of some of the stuff in the kitchen."

"And snooped around until you found your birth-day present. Well, figure out where you want me to put it."

"I wasn't snooping. I was looking for the watering can."

"Uh huh."

"I love it. We'll put it on that little hill near the big tree."

We talked a while longer then I sat on the bed beside Allison and shook her awake. She didn't want to wake up. She was angry and confused and she said her stomach hurt but I made her get up anyway.

"Tell me what happened at the hotel again."

"Why? I don't want to."

I insisted and she resisted but I got my way after reminding her the cops were only a phone call away. She told me the story again quickly, leaving out details, but it was the same story and not so pat as to sound like something she memorized.

I interrupted her with questions, trying to trip her up, but she answered them all easily. She ended with the shooting. "Daddy opened the door and it was the man again and he pulled a gun and shot Daddy."

"From where?"

"From the door. He didn't come into the room."

"I mean the gun. You said he pulled a gun. From where?"

Her face became very still, almost blank. She looked past me toward the window and licked her lips. "From . . . from his pocket. What difference does it make?"

"What was he wearing?"

"A suit." And then because she was only seventeen and she wasn't very good at what she was doing, she turned to look at the closet where my jackets were hanging. Some of them had pockets you could put a gun in. She looked back at me and blushed.

The jury was in and the verdict was guilty but I wasn't going to let her sentence herself to life imprisonment, so I set about making her like me again. It wasn't hard. Women are putty in my hands. It helps if they're dead set on getting their hands on some money. Allison wasn't ready to abandon her plan to have me finance her escape. As long as there was a chance that I would change my mind — or leave my wallet where she could get it — it was in her best interests to like me.

As she snuggled against me on the bed, smiling, her dark eyes soft and warm, I wondered how much of it was an act. Then I wondered why it mattered.

When I left at six o'clock, I took her necklace with me. Her watch and earrings wouldn't bring enough at a pawn shop to get her very far and there was nothing of mine in the room that she could sell easily.

I had a dinner date with Virginia but she didn't feel like going out so we whiled away the time in bed. I left in time to get something to eat before I showed up at the appointed place to pick up my tail. As soon as I spotted Bert and Ernie, I started walking.

It was a clear summer night but there were clouds on the horizon and I was pretty sure there was a big dark thundercloud right over my head. This wasn't going to work. No one was going to contact me. No one was going to be discovered tailing me. Bert and Ernie would go on to some other assignment and I would go back to Mackie and Jessica Finney would die, if she hadn't already, at the hands of a fat man who raped young girls for profit.

What we needed was a big stroke of luck.

CHAPTER TWENTY-NINE

LUCK IS BLINDER THAN LOVE OR JUSTICE.

Shortly after eleven o'clock I was walking down a street in Old Town when a couple lurched out of a bar halfway down the block. The man was my size and was all duded up in his best urban cowboy duds. His hand was under the sweater of the woman beside him. In a loud, obviously phony southern drawl, he said, "Y'all jest come with ol' Tex, sugah, and ah'll give you the ride of yo' life on mah great big ol' holly."

Holly? I'd never heard it called that before.

The weaving twosome made it to the curb where a motorcycle was parked. A great big ol' Harley. My steps slowed, stopped. The man threw his leg over the bike and the big engine roared. The woman climbed on behind him, flipping her skirt up and giving me a flash of white bikini panties. I hardly noticed. With a drunken rebel yell, the cowboy headed the bike into traffic. I didn't wait to see if he kept it upright. I went into the open store beside me.

"I need to use your phone," I told the greasy man behind the counter.

He shifted a wad of tobacco around in his mouth. "Pay phone's down on the next block."

"This is police business."

"You got a badge?" he asked sarcastically.

"I got a gun," I said and moved my jacket aside to show him.

He slammed a phone down on the counter in front of me and backed off several feet. I looked around while the line rang. I was in a dingy shop specializing in obscene T-shirts. My genial host was spitting tobacco juice into a Tab can held close to his lips. He was wearing some of the store's merchandise. The front of his white T-shirt had a pink fluorescent design that was similar to a Rorschach inkblot. Looked at one way, it was a pleasingly symmetrical abstract design. Looked at another way, it was a stylized drawing of the female genitalia.

Bundy answered the phone.

"It's me. Listen, you remember the acting school I told you about, run by a woman named Virginia Marley?"

"Yeah, she said the Finney girl was hanging around last week."

"Right. Virginia took quite an interest in me that day, even walked me to my car and got a good look at it. And I've seen her since. She's asked a lot of questions, how I go about looking for a runaway, what part of town I was checking, that kind of thing. I thought she was just being polite, taking an interest in my work. I think she's involved in this."

"Sounds a little short on probable cause. You got a clincher?"

"Kimberly said Peggy was from the South. Say Virginia Marley with a southern accent."

Bundy drawled "Vuhginia Mahley" and added "Holy fucking shit!"

"Yeah. Peggy said Marley and Kimberly heard Molly and thought it was a first name. And how about an acting and modeling school as a front to recruit girls for dirty movies. Jesus Christ, am I stupid. And she would have admitted seeing Jessica in case someone else in the neighborhood told me she'd been hanging around. Bundy?"

"Yeah?"

"I was at Virginia's apartment the night I got the message to meet Brandy. I've been with her just about every day, in fact. She could have set up the tail. And she knows I'm working with the cops now."

"Jesus. Is there anything you didn't tell her? Didn't you think it was a little coincidental that some woman who'd seen Jessica couldn't wait to hop into the sack with you?"

"No."

After a pause, he said, "I guess not. You know her number?"

I gave him the numbers for Virginia's apartment and the school and he put me on hold. A T-shirt on the rack beside me asked the burning philosophical question, "If we aren't supposed to eat pussy, why does it look like a taco?"

"Who buys this crap?" I asked the greasy man.

"Lotta assholes in the world," he said. I stared pointedly at his chest, mentally making a solemn vow to burn my "BIGGER IS TOO BETTER" T-shirt. It had been given to me by my mother who was oblivious to any sexual connotations that could be read into the shirt's message. At least I thought she was.

Bundy came back on the line. "No answer either place. I'll get on it. You want to come in?"

"No, I might as well stick it out tonight in case you can't locate her."

"Okay. Watch your back. I don't like the feel of this."

"Bert and Ernie are watching my back, aren't they?"

"They're good but they aren't faster than a speeding bullet. Be careful. I'm getting goddamn sick and tired of writing up homicide reports."

I left the shop without thanking the man in the dirty T-shirt and headed down the street, my step buoyant, my heart light. The cops would pick up Virginia and she'd tell them where Jessica was and it would be over.

It was all up to Bundy now. I was out of it.

I was wrong, of course.

Chapter Thirty

I WAS WALKING DOWN A DARK STREET NEAR THE stadium when I heard my name being called. I stopped and waited for Nikki to catch up with me. He ran gracefully in spite of the fact that his silver shoes had stiletto heels. The gown swirling about him tonight was gauzy silver. When he reached me, he clung breathlessly to my arm and said, "God, you walk too fast. I have a message for you."

"What message?"

"A man, I never saw him before. He said you should go sit in your car and someone will come talk to you."

"What did he look like?"

"Blond, about twenty, short but really built. Muscle-y. A real jock, you know. He was wearing white jeans and a blue windbreaker. White tennies, I think." Nikki giggled. "I wasn't looking at his feet."

"Where was he?"

Nikki gestured down the street. "About three blocks." His face puckered with worry. "Zachariah, he knew I know you and he told me where to find you."

"Okay, don't worry. You run along. In fact, it

might be a good idea for you to get off the street for a while. Can you do that?"

He nodded. "I have some friends waiting for me. I'll tell them I have to go home and I'll call for the car."

He headed back the way he had come, turning once to blow a kiss. I waited until his small silver shape disappeared into a crowd of Saturday night loiterers then I headed quickly to my car. I passed Ernie on the way but I barely glanced at him. Any of the authentic-looking teenagers holding up the wall with him might have been watching me. I had the feeling half of Portland had me under surveillance.

The Nova was at the curb on a dimly lit street. I sat behind the wheel, feeling just like the sitting duck I was. I had my gun in my hand but it wasn't going to do a whole lot of good if someone drove by and blew my head off with a shotgun.

In a doorway half a block behind me was a heap of rags I was pretty sure was Bert. I couldn't see Ernie anywhere now. I had both windows down and was listening hard for footsteps while I tried to see into passing cars.

Five minutes later, a dark blue Buick passed slowly beside me. I couldn't see the driver.

But I could see Nikki clearly.

His face was pressed against the rear passenger window.

Tears were ruining his makeup.

Someone's hand held a gun against his neck.

I started the Nova and forced my way into traffic three cars behind the Buick. I looked over my shoulder. An incredibly spry drunk was pounding down the sidewalk in the opposite direction. A slim figure joined him. Their car was at the end of the next block. They'd broadcast a description of the Nova in a hurry but they wouldn't have noticed the other car.

The Buick made a right at the corner. I did the same just in time to see it hang a left at the next intersection. I followed and then there were no cars between us. A series of confusing turns took us away from town and through a deserted industrial area and then, much sooner than I had thought possible, we were out of Portland and traveling down a dark road. For once, I had managed to lose a tail. Bert and Ernie were long gone.

Thirty minutes later, paranoia began to set in. I was behind the wrong car. I was following a carload of tourists who were fulfilling a lifelong dream of seeing rural Oregon by night. I had lost Nikki. And Jessica, if she was out there somewhere. I slowed the Nova to a crawl. The Buick slowed, too, keeping the same distance between us. I was behind the right car.

The paranoia deepened. I was being led into an ambush. Somewhere up the road an army of bad guys was waiting for me. With machine guns. Grenades. Mortars. Maybe a nuclear bomb or two. I told myself to stop being stupid and came up with a more realistic, if equally scary, idea. They were going to drive around until I ran out of gas then they'd double back and kill me. Or maybe they'd just go off and leave me to wander around Oregon for days, looking for civilization.

I began to watch the fuel gauge compulsively. I hadn't gassed up since Hood River and the needle was wavering ominously just above empty. Maybe three gallons. Twenty miles to a gallon was optimistic but easy to compute. Another sixty miles and it would all be over. I thought longingly of all those gas stations in Portland and cursed myself for not filling the tank.

I also cursed myself for not having a car phone. Or at least a CB. I had committed the Buick's license plate to memory but it was a sure bet that the plates were stolen — if not the whole car — and the number would lead the cops to nothing but a dead end. We passed dark houses set back from the road but if I stopped, the Buick would get lost in a hurry. My only choice was to follow them, which was what they wanted. I was making no effort to be inconspicuous. I was back there and they knew I was back there and that's the way they wanted it.

It wouldn't have been so bad if I had been following them through familiar territory, but I was lost. The Buick's driver knew every back road in the state. We passed tiny towns with unfamiliar names where the sidewalks were already rolled up and we drove through miles of farmland and miles of forest. An hour after we left Portland, the only thing I would have sworn to was that we were east of the Pacific Ocean.

We were on dark winding roads with trees thick on either side. For several miles, the only signs of life I saw were dead possums. The night was black and silent. The darkness on either side of the car became tangible, claustrophobic. I seemed to be driving through a luminous, ever-lengthening tunnel formed by the Nova's headlights.

Being unable to place myself within a geographic frame of reference gave me an eerie feeling of vague dread. I didn't like being a stranger in a strange land. I longed for some point of reference — a signpost with a familiar name, a distant mountain range, the pounding of surf against rock. I'd have settled for a glimpse of the moon through the clouds although I knew I was kidding myself if I thought I could figure out where I was by the position of the moon.

The red lights ahead of me began to seem friendly, a beacon in the darkness signaling a haven ahead, a hospice for the weary traveler. I wanted, more than anything else, to get wherever we were going. Men with guns were a danger within my realm of experience, a danger I could handle better than the irrational fear of being lost and directionless. Real danger — and real fear — would send adrenaline coursing through my veins, heightening my senses, sharpening my reflexes, demanding action, exorcising the numbness that was spreading through me as the endlessly telescoping tunnel of light and the low drone of the Nova's engine became hypnotic.

I needed to do something, anything. I unbuckled and leaned over to rummage through the dashbox, steering awkwardly with my left hand. Credit card receipts, maps, straws and paper napkins fell to the floor as I searched for the comforting feel of stiff leather over hard steel. I found it and clipped the sheathed hunting knife onto my belt. I rummaged some more. A ring of colorful plastic keys — Melissa's — and a Phillips screwdriver I had misplaced months ago joined the litter on the floor. My fingers closed over a small heavy carton. I straightened up in front of the wheel and shoved the box of bullets into my jacket pocket, feeling a little foolish because if I got into a situation where I needed to reload, I would probably be dead before I could do it.

The action, however futile it might turn out to be, broke the trance-like state I had been slipping into. I began to wonder what their plan was. Their plan was obvious. They were going to kill me. Virginia was Peggy's Molly and they knew the cops were tailing me. They kidnapped Nikki so I would follow them into the boonies. And not for a friendly chat. They were going to kill me. And Nikki. They'd have to kill him, too.

I felt, belatedly, a cold hard anger building up inside me. Anger for Jessica who, if she hadn't been murdered, had probably been raped and had almost certainly made a movie she wasn't old enough to watch. Anger for Nikki, whose friendship with me had made him a pawn in the fat man's game. Anger for Diane Dobbs and Karen Baylor and poor pathetic Brandy who had also been pawns, casually forfeited to keep the game going. Anger for Peggy, another pawn, who would probably die, unidentified and unmourned, a lost child whose family would never know what happened to her. Anger, an intense burning anger, at Virginia Marley, cute little Virginia, whose willingness had been a strategy in the game. And anger at myself for accepting that willingness without thought, without question, because they had always been there, an endless supply of willing women attracted by my size and my looks. I wondered, not for the first time, what odd quirk of ego it was that made me feel obligated, almost duty-bound, to take advantage of that willingness. The constraints of marriage had come as a relief, giving me a legitimate excuse to refuse without feeling guilty. Zachariah Smith, God's gift to women. But the ones I wanted to keep always slipped away.

The needle on the fuel gauge was bobbing crazily at the E. We had been on the road for almost two hours. The lights ahead of me disappeared and I found myself making a hairpin turn. The ground to the right of the car dropped away. I was going up a moderately steep grade. To the left were hills densely covered with trees. To the right was a deep ravine. I could see the tops of trees rising beyond it. The road became a series of S-curves. Two or three times I spotted a stationary light in the distance.

I crested the hill and the road straightened out, giving me a good view for a couple miles ahead. I geared down and the distance between the cars increased. The Buick was approaching another series of S-curves and didn't slow this time. They weren't worried about losing me now. There was nowhere for me to go.

Just beyond the curves ahead was the light I had seen, on a building of some kind in a big clearing set back from the road. The tail lights disappeared and reappeared as the Buick negotiated the curves. I was still on the straight stretch of road when the Buick approached the building. The tail lights intensified then the left one began blinking rhythmically. A real creature of habit. Not a car but mine for miles and he was signaling his turn.

I slowed until the Nova was barely moving. Turning around and going for help was out of the question. Nikki would be dead and the fat man would be in Argentina before I found my way out of the maze of country roads. They were waiting for me.

I wondered what made them think I would be stupid enough to go up to that building by myself. Did they know me that well?

A second later I stopped wondering about anything. Being a creature of habit myself, I had been making periodic checks into the rearview mirror. As I approached the first S-curve, I glanced into it again. And took a longer look. Just topping the hill behind me and starting down the straight stretch of road was another car, traveling with its lights off. I wondered how long it had been there. It didn't matter. I knew what their plan was now. I was boxed in.

I pushed the accelerator down and increased the distance between the Nova and the dark car. I tried to picture the road ahead. There had been two or three S-curves. I was making the last turn on the first one. The hill beside me hid the building from view and the curve of the road hid the dark car behind me.

Now or never.

I stomped on the brake, shoved the gearshift into reverse, and jerked the steering wheel all the way to the right. I let the clutch out and as the car started to move, I opened the door and bailed out, low and rolling to avoid the swinging door and the front tires. I scrambled up and ran for the trees across the road. The Nova backed to the edge of the road and went over, its headlights stabbing the sky.

The night was filled with the sound of metal crumpling, glass breaking, tree limbs snapping. The Nova's engine coughed out and then there was a settling silence. I heard the dark car approaching and dropped to the ground beneath some low, dripping bushes.

Just as the car came into sight, there was a dull *whump* that I felt more than heard, then my Nova went out with a bang. An orange glow lit up the road. I could hear flames but couldn't see them. The ravine must have been deep as hell. The glow was already fading as the car stopped and two men got out.

They walked to the edge of the road and looked into the ravine, their heads bowed as if they were praying over my departed soul.

One of them said, "Takes care of that asshole."

They probably hadn't been praying at all.

"Think we should go down and see if he's alive?" the same man asked.

"I ain't going down there," the other man said. "No way he's walking away from that. We'll be gone in a few hours. Take him that long to crawl up here if he's alive." They stood silently for a moment then the man added, "Must've been trying to turn around." He yawned loudly.

I considered shooting them to even up the odds. I decided against it. Being called an asshole probably wasn't sufficient grounds for justifiable homicide. Besides, the shots would be heard for miles

and if these men didn't show up, the ones up the
road would know I was alive. I was better off dead.

CHAPTER THIRTY-ONE

THE MEN GOT BACK IN THE CAR AND DROVE OFF, with the headlights on now. As soon as the car rounded the curve, I ran into the woods until I was even with the building then I headed toward it. The undergrowth was thick. A lot of it was Oregon's killer blackberries that escaped from cultivation decades ago and have been terrorizing the populace ever since. I kept an arm in front of me but still felt the stinging slap of the vines against my face. They twined around my legs and arms, their big spines catching in my clothes and ripping my skin. The ground was soaked from recent rain and within seconds my shoes were heavy with mud. I felt like I was slogging through wet cement and I was trailing blackberry vines behind me. Anyone witnessing my dash through the woods would have gone to his grave swearing he'd seen Big Foot.

I made good time by eliminating the curves of the road. Car doors slammed just before I reached the clearing. I took cover behind a tree and tried to catch my breath while I disentangled myself from the vines. The last one was a tenacious bastard. By the time I got it off my leg, it had wrapped itself around my arm. I finally stood on one end of it and jerked my arm upward. My sleeve ripped but I was free.

I sucked at the worst scratches on my hands while I crouched to peer around the tree. The building was an old two-story house, set in a big clearing of mowed weeds. There were bushes and small trees near the house. Lights were showing at the downstairs windows, most of which were partly open and missing the screens. Curtains billowed from them, pulled outward by a light breeze. The upstairs windows were dark. One of them was shuttered and a long board appeared to be nailed across the shutters. The driving beat of hard rock drifted across the clearing.

Staying back in the trees, I ran to the front of the house. They weren't worried about security. The front door was standing open. Its old warped screen door was only partly closed. A big window with the drapes open gave me a good view into the living room which was sparsely furnished in Early American. Several packing boxes were stacked up against one wall. The floor was strewn with open cartons and video and electronic equipment. At the far end of the room was an open archway into a dining room. A dinette set sat beneath a hanging light fixture. On the other side of the table was a door that should lead into the kitchen, a wooden swinging door with a small round window at eye level. I couldn't see any people in the house.

Three cars were parked in the front yard. I made a snap decision. The chance of me getting a set of keys and Nikki and maybe Jessica out of the house was a lot slimmer than the chance of the men getting to the cars and leaving me stranded. I unsheathed the hunting knife and slithered around on my belly, moving from car to car and slashing both rear tires on each one. The night was sibilant with the sound of escaping air.

I peered over the hood of the Buick and checked the house again. No one in sight. I ran to the far corner of the house. And there was the barn, what was left of it. Part of the roof seemed to be gone and boards were broken at intervals along the side. The big doors leaned open at crazy angles.

I crouched low and ran along the side of the house to the back. The windows were dark on this side. I peered around the back corner. Light was streaming from an open door and a window. An overgrown hedge formed a fence around a small section of back yard. I crept around behind it until I was even with the door. There was a break in the hedge where a walk made of cement circles led up to the house.

I was looking into an old-fashioned kitchen with painted wooden cupboards and an uneven linoleum floor. The screen door matched the one at the front, old and warped and tattered. The window just to the left of the door was open, its cafe curtains ruffling in the breeze.

The kitchen was crowded. A man with a full black beard was leaning against the wall next to the swinging door. Next to him, a redhead with glasses and a bad complexion was straddling a chair. I recognized them as the men from the dark car.

Nikki's jock, in tight white jeans and a black T-shirt stretched across over-developed pectorals, was leaning against the sink which was to the right of the door. A fourth man had his back to me. He was leaning back against the doorjamb, partially blocking the screen door. He was smoking and after every puff he moved his arm across in front of the door to flick ashes into a brown grocery bag overflowing with garbage that was sitting to the left of the door beneath the window.

The fifth person in the room was the fat man. "Gross," Kimberly had said. "Grotesque" was more like it. The man was a blob, a misshapen pile of human flesh. Short but very big around. Four hundred pounds, minimum. His body was so monstrous that his head seemed several sizes too small. He had tiny piggy eyes and a wet red mouth. A series of chins led down to his swollen chest. He was wearing shapeless black pants and a white shirt, untucked. I couldn't tell if any of the bulges beneath his clothing was a gun.

The other men were armed. The redhead had a pistol stuck in his waistband. The smoker had a hip holster on the back of his belt. Blackbeard and Nikki's jock were wearing shoulder holsters. Four armed men, maybe five. Bad odds.

The men weren't talking but the scene was easy to interpret. The underlings had made their report and were waiting for the head honcho to give them their orders. The fat man tapped a sausage-shaped index finger against his pursed lips for a few moments, then clapped his hands three times as if he were calling a class to attention.

His voice was high-pitched and wheezy. "Here's what we do," he said. "We finish packing. Tony'll be here with the van in a couple hours. We'll load up and clear out tonight. We'll take the little cunt down to the dick's car. Throw some gasoline around and light it up again. It'll look like he found her and then ran off the road. We'll take his little faggot friend with us and get rid of him later. Make it look like he picked up the wrong boyfriend. Once we're out of here, no one can connect us with any of it. The house is in a phony name. We'll dump the Buick. The other cars are clean."

"What about Virginia?" Blackbeard asked.

"She's ready to go. They haven't tipped to her. The dick was humping her earlier today. They don't know shit about the set-up."

The fat man lumbered to the swinging door and pushed through it, his body squeezing through the opening. The other men followed quickly except for the smoker, who lagged behind taking quick deep drags on his cigarette, flicking ash at the garbage bag. After a final drag, he knocked the live ash off against the rim of the sink. And threw the dead butt into the bag. And left.

The swinging door was still moving on its hinges when I stuck my hand through a hole in the screen and thumbed my lighter. I touched the flame to the edge of the garbage bag and ran back to my hedge.

Within seconds, the paper bag was a column of fire. The curtains above it suddenly turned to a sheet of flame. Bits of burning fabric dropped to the window sill and flames ran quickly along the wood. The garbage bag tipped over, spilling flaming papers past the door to the counter. Layers of old paint on the cupboards bubbled, the wood caught, flames licked upward toward the counter top. The kitchen must have been covered with a quarter-inch-thick layer of old grease. It was going up like a stack of kindling.

I watched my handiwork with a growing sense of panic. I didn't want to burn the whole house down. I could hear the flames and smell the smoke but the men would be in the living room with a closed door and the dining room separating them from a kitchen that was going to be an inferno in a few more minutes.

I was at the window, planning to smash it with my knife hilt and hope they thought the heat broke it, when the door swung open. The puzzled look on the smoker's face turned quickly to panic. He shouted over his shoulder and suddenly the kitchen was very full of men fighting a fire. I counted five of them then ran to the front of the house.

At the front steps, I kicked my muddy shoes off and into some bushes, then crossed the porch and entered the house. I wasn't worried about noise. The radio was blaring and the firefighting was creating quite a commotion. The fat man's voice was raised nearly to a scream. The smoker was getting a royal chewing-out.

I took a quick look through a set of open French doors to the right. They led into a large room with obvious signs of recent remodeling showing it had once been two smaller rooms. The room was completely empty except for a mattress on a platform base. A prop for dirty movies.

The stairs were also to the right, between the living room and dining room. I stepped over the clutter on the floor and headed up them. There was a landing halfway up where the stairs turned at a right angle. At the top was a hallway that ran the width of the house. A ceiling light on the landing provided enough light for me to see by. At the far end of the hall, a door was standing open. I could see a toilet just inside it.

The rest of the upstairs was divided into four rooms, two on each side. The first door on the left was open. I glanced in, saw it was an empty room, and tried the door on the right. It led to a bedroom, plainly furnished, with the occupant's belongings strewn all over.

I went to the next door on the right. Another bedroom, similarly furnished but with a difference. This one had a gleam of silver on the bed.

Nikki was facing away from me, his hands tied behind him. His breath was coming in soft sobbing gasps. His shoulders hunched as I approached the bed. I put my hand over his mouth and rolled him toward me as I sat on the bed beside him. His eyes were wide with terror then they filled with tears of relief. I told him to be quiet then sat him up to cut the rope from his wrists.

"They said your car blew up," he whispered.

"I wasn't in it."

Nikki shook the rope from his hands and threw himself at me. I held him a moment, rocking him gently. Whatever else Nikki was, he was a victimized child at the moment.

"I want to get you out of here," I whispered. "Do you think you can drop to the ground if I lower you out the window?"

He nodded against my chest. "Go into the woods and stay there. Don't come back here unless I call you. If you think something's gone wrong, follow the road down but don't flag down any cars. They could be headed up here. Try to get to a phone. Call Jefferson Bundy, he's a homicide detective at the Justice Center. Take your shoes off."

Nikki let go of me and pulled off the ridiculous

silver heels. I rolled them up in a blanket. The old sash window opened with little noise. There was no screen. Nikki perched on the sill and we clasped each other's wrists. I leaned out, lowering him as far as I could without overbalancing. He looked up and nodded and we let go. He dropped to the ground, rolled over, and immediately got to his feet. I tossed the blanket to him and watched until he disappeared into the trees. One down.

Chapter Thirty-two

I STOOD IN THE HALL, LISTENING. THEY WERE still busy in the kitchen. I tried the door across the hall. The knob turned freely but the door didn't budge. A dead bolt was set into the wood just above the doorknob.

I went down the hall and into the empty room, closing the door part way. A big window was set into the wall to the right of the door. On the other side of the window was the locked room. It was a bedroom, dimly lit by a nightlight. Nightstands holding lamps flanked a double bed. A bureau stood near the door. An open closet door was on the far wall. The single window above the bed was covered with frilly white curtains. Behind them would be a shuttered window with a board nailed across it. Someone was in the bed. All I could see was dark hair above a patchwork quilt.

I looked around the room I was in. There was a single light switch just inside the door. Next to it was a bank of four switches with no switchplate covers. The sheetrock was cut out around them in a rough rectangle. I flipped the first of the four switches and a section of the ceiling in the locked room lit up. The person on the bed sat up quickly.

Jessica Finney. Alive and well enough to get out of bed in a hurry. She was wearing yellow babydoll pajamas. She stood still for a moment, looking at the door, her arms crossed protectively across her breasts. Then she turned, dropping her arms, and looked at the window. On her side, it would be a mirror and all she would see was her own reflection.

Her face was expressionless. There was a dark line along her jaw, and marks on her upper arms and on her thighs. Jessica knew all about the camera behind the mirror. *"She thought it was real, you know, and she tried to fight."*

Jessica sat on the foot of the bed, her head bowed.

I went back into the hall. The noise had abated but they were still in the kitchen. I returned to the room, closing the door behind me, and flipped the single light switch, turning on the ceiling light in my room. On the other side of the window Jessica raised her head and stared, surprise then recognition and relief on her face.

There's no magic to a one-way mirror. It's just a window with a reflective coating on one side. It works the same as any window. The one-way effect depends on the relative lighting on either side of it. If you're in a lighted room at night and look at a window, you see your own reflection and darkness beyond. If you're outside in the dark, you can see into the lighted room clearly. If you equalize the lighting by turning on a light outside, you can see into or out of the room with equal ease. Jessica and I now had equal lighting in our rooms and were looking at each other through the glass.

I put my finger to my lips. She nodded. I gave her a thumbs-up gesture and turned out all the lights. I disappeared from her view but she was visible in the dimly lit bedroom. She sat back against the headboard of the bed and pulled the quilt up to her chin.

I opened the door and stood behind it in the darkness trying to figure out how to get Jessica out of the locked room. The dead bolt had a key-hole on each side. The window would be nicely finished on her side but on this side it was rough. The wall was about ten feet long and the window took up most of it. The glass was held in place by a frame of unfinished one-by-fours. I might be able to pry the boards loose with my knife but there was no way I could handle a sheet of glass that big by myself. If it broke, no amount of firefighting would cover the noise.

It occurred to me that I wasn't in a very good position. I could get out a window but that would put me outside with five men between me and Jessica. Eventually someone was going to come upstairs to check on Nikki. Once they discovered he was gone —

Someone was coming up the stairs. I drew my gun and moved so I could see through the crack at the hinge side of the door. A shadow moved along the wall, then a man passed by. The smoker. If he looked in on Nikki, all hell was going to break loose.

I stayed where I was, barely breathing. His steps continued down the hall. Stopped. I heard, clearly, the sound of a zipper. Then the sound of urine streaming into a toilet.

I holstered my gun and walked quickly down the hall. The bathroom door was partly closed. I pushed it open. The smoker was standing at the toilet, his back to me. He looked over his shoulder, nothing but mild curiosity on his face. Before his expression could change, I had him in a chokehold that's been banned by police departments everywhere. His feet lifted off the floor, his full weight hanging from my arms. I ruined his aim completely. My socks grew hot and wet then cold and wet as he struggled silently against me.

After an eternity, his hands stopped clawing at my arms and face. He seemed to be fumbling in front of him. He wasn't trying for his gun. It was digging into my ribs. His right hand came into view. A switchblade flicked open. His brain must have been screaming for oxygen by then. His movements were slow and clumsy but he got the knife turned toward me. I increased my pressure and gave a quick hard jerk to his head. I felt an odd snap and he collapsed, his body dangling from my arms. The knife fell, hitting the rim of the toilet with a loud clang.

I lowered him to the floor. The bathroom suddenly smelled like an overused cat litter box. I grabbed a towel off a rack and pressed it against my nose and mouth, breathing deeply into it. I dropped the towel and peeled my wet socks off as I stepped into the hall, closing the bathroom door behind me.

I stood in the hall. My arms were aching and I was shaking with reaction. My brain was non-functional. I just stood there.

Eventually, I became aware that the noise from downstairs had changed. Over the sound of the radio, I could hear paper crumpling and something heavy sliding across the floor. They were finished in the kitchen and had gone back to packing.

A shadow leapt up the stairwell, making me flinch.

Someone called, "Hey, Bill! Didja fall in?"

The fat man's voice wheezed, "He's probably buggering the little faggot."

Laughter followed his remark. The shadow receded.

I managed a complete thought — they expect him to come downstairs.

So go downstairs.

After a moment, my feet moved. I went into the bathroom and flushed the toilet, ran the tap briefly.

I drew my gun.

Walked down the hall.

Down the steps.

When I reached the landing, automatic pilot took over. I spun around the corner in a crouch, fanning the thirty-eight in front of me. Without my willing it, my voice said, "Police! Freeze!"

Nobody froze.

The fat man was standing in the archway to the dining room. He lurched backward, disappearing into the darkness.

The three men crouching by packing boxes went for their guns.

I shot Nikki's jock and Blackbeard while they were fumbling at their holsters. The redhead and I fired within a half second of each other. His shot slapped into the wall beside me. He had jumped to his feet and my bullet hit his leg. Blood spurted out in a thick stream. He screamed, dropped his gun, fell to the floor, clutching his leg, frantically trying to stop the blood pulsing from an artery. The scream gurgled out. He lay, white-faced and silent, bleeding to death.

Without being aware of doing it, I had backed into the corner of the landing. I crouched there, my heart racing. There had been a fifth shot. From the dining room. The bullet had hit the living room wall just in front of the stairwell.

The fat man had a gun.

I pressed my ear to the wall at my side. All I

heard was my heart pounding and an amplification of the bass notes of the music. One of the men on the floor began to moan softly. The song on the radio ended and the DJ began his inane patter, oblivious to the fact that he was speaking to a room of dead and dying men. I shot the radio. It exploded, splattering plastic fragments against the wall. A thin column of black smoke rose from the ruins.

The sudden silence seemed absolute. I pressed my ear to the wall again and felt a faint shudder. The fat man was moving but I couldn't tell whether he was in the dining room or the kitchen. Then I heard the swinging door moving on its hinges. I crept down the stairs. Just before I reached the archway, I heard another sound. The slap of a screen door closing.

He was going for the cars.

I ran to the front door, leaping over boxes and bodies, my feet sliding on the bloody carpet. I vaulted the porch railing and crouched at the corner of the house, listening for the sound of the fat man coming. Four hundred pounds can't be moved quietly and he would be breathing harder than I was. I didn't hear anything. I looked around the corner. Nothing but the old barn.

I ran to the other side of the porch and looked down the side of the house. Nothing.

I ran to the back of the house, staying close to the wall. At the corner I stopped and listened hard.

Nothing. I swung around the corner. Nothing. Light streamed from the screen door. I looked around, confused. I was faster than a fat man. He couldn't have made it to the woods.

From the trees where I had hidden earlier to fight with blackberries, Nikki's voice came, clear and pure, "No one came out."

It took an instant for it to sink in, then I jerked the screen door open and ran for the stairs. Never underestimate a fat man. The screen door slamming had been a trick to get me out of the house. He wasn't going for the cars. He was going for a hostage.

The hall at the top of the stairs was empty. Light from the open door of Jessica's room made shadows leap and weave wildly on the walls. The upstairs was filled with the sound of raucous breathing, his, hers, and mine.

I went into the empty room and closed the door. I hit the four light switches with the side of my arm and the room beyond the window lit up like the movie set it was.

Jessica and the fat man froze for an instant in mid-struggle. They jerked around to face the mirror, eyes blinking against the sudden brightness. The fat man had one arm around Jessica's waist. His other hand was jamming a gun into her side. He pulled her tight against him, dragging her backwards a few feet. They were staring into the mirror, but my room was dark. They were seeing their mirror image.

I moved back until I was against the wall opposite the window then I took careful aim at the fat man's nose and waited for something to happen.

Acres of blubber bulged out on either side of Jessica. As Bundy had said, I'm a hell of a shot. I could have dropped the fat man with an elephant gun without much danger of hitting the girl by mistake. But if I fired, his gun hand would clench, voluntarily or involuntarily, and a bullet would tear through Jessica.

The fat man's voice wheezed faintly through the glass. "Throw your gun out in the hall. I'll let her go."

Fat chance, fat man. I kept quiet. He couldn't be sure I was still in the room, couldn't be sure I wasn't sneaking down the hall toward the open door. As if he read my mind, he took a quick look at the door then shifted his weight so he was facing it.

I kept on waiting, not knowing what I was waiting for but I couldn't think of anything else to do. The phrase "Mexican standoff" drifted through my mind.

Jessica was staring in my direction. She smiled gaily.

I was so surprised I smiled right back at her.

She went limp, her torso dropping across the fat

man's arm, her head almost to the floor, arms hanging loose, legs splayed out rag doll fashion.

The fat man buckled under the sudden unexpected weight on his arm then he heaved her upward. Her arms swung loosely, her head lolled. The fat man heaved again, hard enough to snap her back against his huge belly. She flopped forward again.

All he had to do was keep the gun pointing toward her. But he didn't. He shoved his right hand under her arm, the gun in front of her, and before he got the leverage to yank her upward, I shot him. Right through the looking glass.

For a fraction of a second, the thick glass held, cracks spiderwebbing out from the bullet hole, then it fell with a noise like the final crack of doom. Somewhere in the midst of all the glass breaking there was a second gunshot then a thunderous shudder as the fat man hit the floor. Jessica was on her knees, then on her feet. She kicked the fat man twice, her foot sinking into his flesh, then she headed toward me.

"Don't," I said. "You're barefoot."

Come to think of it, so was I. We picked our way through broken glass to our respective doors. Jessica stopped before she got to me, treading water, but I kept going and when I reached her she put her arms around me and pressed her face against my chest. She wasn't crying but she was trembling violently. I left her for a moment to look at the fat man. I didn't bother checking for a pulse. No one could be alive with a hole like that in his head. Jessica was slumped against the wall in the hall. I picked her up and took her downstairs, putting her on the couch which I pulled away from the wall, angling it so she wouldn't have to look at the men on the floor.

I went out to the porch and yelled "Ollie-ollie-outs-in-free" and was rewarded with a shimmer of silver coming my way. I had my arms full of Nikki for a minute then I peeled him off and we went inside. I introduced the two kids and explained Nikki's presence briefly to Jessica who had seemed a bit confused at the sight of him. I sent Nikki upstairs to get linens and Jessica's clothes. I headed for the phone with a tremendous sense of relief. It was over.

The telephone was on a small table near the dining room door. I picked the receiver up and put it to my ear, the dial tone as welcome as a warm fire on a cold day. I poised my finger to dial then stood there staring stupidly. There was no dial, just a smooth black surface where one should have been. I picked the phone up and turned it over. No dial on the bottom either. I slammed it down and slammed the receiver on it, muttering some of my best obscenities.

"There's another one," Jessica said. "They always unplugged it and hid it. It's one of those little one-piece things, just a receiver with the buttons in the middle. It's white."

Nikki appeared with Jessica's backpack and an armful of sheets and towels. I stationed him at the door to watch for headlights while I did what I could for the wounded men. Blackbeard was shot just below the shoulder and was semiconscious and moaning softly. He moaned louder when I asked him where the telephone was. Nikki's jock had a bullet through his gut. His pulse was thready and his breath was coming in slow rasps. The redhead was very dead, most of his blood soaking into the carpet around him. I tossed a sheet over him.

Jessica had pulled jeans and a sweatshirt out of her backpack and put them on over her babydolls. She shoved her feet into some sandals and said she would look for the phone. I took Nikki's place at the door and sent him to help her. I retrieved my shoes and scraped mud off them while I watched the road.

The kids returned, shrugging and shaking their heads. Nikki watched the road while I checked a few obvious hiding places then gave it up. It would take hours to systematically search the house for a small white telephone.

Jessica was on her knees by the packing boxes. She had pulled open a box containing video cassettes and was reading the labels. They were marked with a combination of letters and numbers that meant nothing to me. She chose one but when she started to put it in the machine she discovered there was already a tape in it. She turned the television on and pushed the play button on the VCR. The tape must not have been rewound completely. It began in mid-scene. A young girl was in the throes of orgasm in a bathtub. Her partner was a detachable shower head set to emit a pulsating stream of water. Jessica hit the eject button and the screen went to snow.

The next tape was rewound and the screen flickered for several seconds before the picture started. This one was Jessica, naked and standing awkwardly with a long piece of sheer red fabric in each hand. Music started. The Jessica on the screen began to move slowly in a sensuous dance. I stared, mesmerized. As soon as she began to move, Jessica underwent a transformation. Her face seemed to become prettier, more defined, as if the camera could see beyond what was visible to the naked eye. She was no longer an awkward fourteen-year-old but the very essence of femininity, sexuality and innocence in an unbeatable combination. The red scarves floated about her as she moved to the music, her eyes firmly on the camera, full of promise and invitation. The screen flicked to snow as the real Jessica hit the eject button.

She inserted another tape. Jessica again. Sitting up in bed, blinking at sudden light, her eyes full of surprise and confusion. And then terror. The tape was ejected just as two naked men wearing ski masks appeared on the screen.

Jessica put the rape tape back in the box and sat on the couch, her dance tape clutched in her hands.

From the door, Nikki said, "What are we going to do?"

"I don't know. We need a phone."

"Beam us up, Scottie," Jessica said and we all laughed.

"Wait until morning and send smoke signals," Nikki said. "Maybe the cavalry will show up."

I went out to the porch and looked at the cars. The Buick, a Nissan hatchback, and a Cadillac big enough to bear the fat man's weight. Three sizes of tires, two flats on each car, and, presumably, one spare in each trunk. Slashing the tires had seemed like a good idea at the time. I looked down the road. The fat man had said Tony would be here with the van in a couple hours. I looked at my watch, Incredibly, it was less than an hour since I had first reached the house, just about three hours since I had first seen Nikki in the Buick. Portland seemed like a lifetime ago.

A van would be handy but did I want to wait? No. Did I want to meet Tony? Not particularly. *Smoke signals*. The Nova's explosion hadn't exactly drawn a crowd but the gas tank had been almost empty and the ravine was deep. The fire had burned out quickly without spreading to the wet brush and trees. I went into the kitchen and got a flashlight

I had seen on the counter then I crammed some paper into a packing box and told the kids to come with me.

We walked out to the barn. I flashed the light around inside it. Part of the roof was on the packed-dirt floor and there were several piles of wood and debris that had obviously been there for years. The walls were rotting, splintery wood. I put the box near a pile of wood scraps against the wall and touched the flame of my lighter to the paper.

Jessica was still clutching her dance tape. "You'll make a great Juliet," I told her. "You don't need that."

She held the tape briefly in front of her then tossed it into the box of flaming paper. We retreated to the corner of the house and watched as flames engulfed the side of the barn then spread to the front, turning the doors into sheets of fire. The flames leaped and soared, smoke and ash poured upward, lighting the sky. We went to the front of the house and sat on the porch steps.

I felt good. I had totaled my car, set fire to a kitchen, shot a radio, and torched a barn. I had killed three men — one with my bare hands — and wounded two others. I was sitting on the porch steps of an old house in the country somewhere in the state of Oregon, listening to flames crackle and snap. I had my left arm around a fourteen-year-old girl who was a rape victim and my right arm around a thirteen-year-old boy in a silver gown who was a kidnap victim. Back in Portland, a seven-teen-year-old murder suspect was sleeping with her arms around a bear she had named after me. What the hell, I still felt good.

Nikki yawned. Jessica yawned. I yawned. We all yawned again, simultaneously, then we laughed about it.

A set of headlights pricked the darkness down at the curve of the road. That was fast. Too fast.

CHAPTER THIRTY-THREE

I SENT NIKKI AND JESSICA INTO THE WOODS WITH orders to run like hell if necessary. I turned out the lights in the house and stood in the darkness just inside the door. The lights came steadily closer. When they reached the driveway, I could make out the shape of the vehicle. An old pickup with one occupant. The lights swept across me as the driver angled in beside the Cadillac. He left the motor running and got out, standing by the door of the truck. He was wearing old jeans, cowboy boots, and a western hat that shadowed his face. His right hand was in the big pocket of his denim chore coat.

I pushed the screen door open and stood in the doorway, holding my gun out of sight behind the doorjamb.

"Looks like you got a fire," the man said.

"Yeah, looks that way."

"You call the fire department?"

"There's no phone."

We had run out of conversation. We stood and stared at each other for a while. He kept his hand in his pocket.

I walked across the porch and down the stairs, my right hand down at my side, holding the gun behind my leg. The man used his left hand to rub his chin.

"It won't spread," he said. "Ground's too wet."

I nodded my agreement.

We were fifteen feet apart. Neither of us seemed to have any idea what to do so we just stood there looking at each other for a couple minutes. His jacket pocket looked too bulky to be holding nothing but a hand.

Some part of the barn collapsed, sending flames whooshing upward. The glow lit up the front yard, obliterating shadows. I could see the man's face clearly — a hooked nose, jutting chin, a shock of gray hair showing under the hat. He must have been able to see my face clearly, too, because he grinned and said, "Bundy told me you look like Superman."

The cavalry had arrived.

Within minutes, the old house was bustling with activity. The driver of the pickup was the local county sheriff and the four men who hopped out of the bed of the truck were his deputies. "Bundy didn't fill me in," the sheriff told me. "He just said we had rape and murder and Christ knows what-all going on up here. The place is so damn isolated we decided we better come in undercover, see if we could figure out what we were up against instead of barreling in with red lights and sirens."

He looked around the living room. "Looks like we missed all the excitement."

Two sheriff's cars arrived, closely followed by a fire truck and an ambulance. The firemen stood around and watched the barn burn safely to the ground while the wounded men were removed and I tried to give a coherent, chronological account of the night's events. I must have made some sense. The sheriff didn't ask many questions. Nikki filled in the missing part which I had already figured out. After he delivered his message to me in Portland, he had been accosted by the jock and the smoker and was hustled into the Buick at gunpoint.

Jessica sat close beside me while she told her story, her voice calm and clear, her nails digging scarlet crescents into her palms. She had gone to the Northwest Acting and Modeling School Thursday morning. After the discouraging reception at the Rose City School of Performing Arts, Virginia's interest and encouragement had seemed miraculous. Virginia had talked to her for a long time and had suggested a screen test for "art films." Jessica agreed and Blackbeard and Nikki's jock drove her out to the house that same morning. By the time Jason and Lily showed up in my office Sunday afternoon, their daughter had been at the house for four days and had been filmed performing a nude dance and had been raped on-camera.

When Jessica found out what type of "art films" the fat man made, she flatly refused to make a movie with any kind of sex in it, real or simulated, but the fat man's offer of a thousand dollars cash for a solo nude dance was too good for a girl on the run to turn down.

The dance was filmed on Friday and that night she woke to sudden bright lights and two naked men wearing ski masks. She fought and lost and spent the rest of the night huddled in terror on the bed. She thought at first that the rapists were intruders and that the fat man and his friends had been murdered. But sometime in that long night, Jessica put it all together, the locked room and the bright lights and the mirrored wall. She wasn't surprised when the fat man walked into the room the next morning.

He took her downstairs and made her watch both tapes, her nude dance and the recording of her own rape. He told her that if she went to the police, the dance tape would prove that she had known the rape was a movie scene.

"He was crazy," Jessica said. "They all were. No one would believe that was acting. No one can act that good. I couldn't believe they were going to let me go. How could they think I'd let them get away with it? I thought they were going to kill me."

Desperate to save her life, Jessica put on the show of a lifetime. She pouted for a while, then treated the rape as a good joke. She offered to make more movies and questioned the fat man at length about how much money she could make.

"The others were gone a lot of the time and I was alone with Edward — that's that fat pig upstairs. He was like a little kid. I don't think any girl ever acted like she liked him before or even talked to him. Well, who would? He's totally disgusting."

The fat man not only fell for Jessica's act but fell for her as well. "I flirted with him and sat on his lap and stuff like that. I would have thrown up if he wanted to . . . do anything else but he wasn't interested anyway. I think maybe he couldn't. I mean, he couldn't be very healthy, could he?

"I was hoping I could get him to trust me and then I was going to tell him I was bored out here and see if I could talk him into taking me out to dinner. I thought maybe I could get away or at least get to a telephone."

Jessica's plan to win the fat man's confidence went along just fine until I showed up at the Northwest Acting and Modeling School Monday morning. Virginia called the house. The fat man was furious because Jessica had lied to Virginia, claiming she was from Pennsylvania and had run away months ago. When they found out she lived in Oregon and her parents had enough money to hire a private detective, things got very tense at the old house. Jessica was locked in her room most of the time but she overheard enough conversations to figure out that at least one girl had been killed and that they were following me around.

The calls to Hank were Jessica's idea. She

thought if I stopped looking for her, things would calm down and she could eventually get away. The fat man told her to say she was in downtown Portland, hoping to limit my movements and keep me confined to an area where I could be tailed easily.

After she finished her story, the sheriff questioned her briefly about the rapists. She had heard their voices and was sure they were strangers, not the men in the house now. She described her attackers' bodies as well as she could. One of them had a big hairy mole on his groin. I almost threw up listening to her.

Jessica fell asleep with her head against my shoulder. Nikki was already asleep, stretched out on the couch on my other side with his head on my leg. One of the deputies came into the room and waved a small white telephone at me. He had found it in an oatmeal box.

The fire captain came into the house and crouched in front of me, clipboard on his knee. He was a freckle-faced redhead with eyes that had seen too many things go up in smoke.

"Any idea how the fire started?" he asked.

"I set it."

He jotted something on his report form, nodded, and said, "Why?"

"Signal fire."

"We got 911 out here," he said.

"I couldn't find a telephone."

"Uh huh," he said. "What about the fire in the kitchen?"

"I set that one, too."

He jotted, nodded, and asked why.

"Diversionary tactic."

"Uh huh. You know anything about the car down in the ravine?"

"It's mine. I headed it down the hill and jumped out."

"Why?"

"Uh…"

"Diversionary tactic?"

"That'll do."

He looked at the smoke-blackened wall by the ruined radio and didn't bother asking. "Busy night," he said and went back outside.

I was asleep with my cheek on Jessica's head when Bundy arrived. He shook me awake and said, "Jesus Christ Almighty."

He looked around the living room, shaking his head. The redhead was still on the floor where he had fallen, blood blackening the carpet around him. The smoker's body was on a stretcher by the door. There was a heated discussion going on about the best way to get a four-hundred-pound dead body down the stairs.

"Jesus Christ Almighty," Bundy said again.

"It got a little messy. I guess you found Virginia."

"We staked out the school and her apartment. She came home about thirty minutes after you called me. Her car was crammed with porno-graphic photographs of minors. Another of the school's sidelines. They were moving the whole operation. We had to wait for a lawyer but even-tually she talked. She's claiming all she did was recruit girls for movies and she doesn't know any-thing about rape or murder. But she told us about this place. Wilson and Garcia had called in by then, saying you'd given them the slip. I didn't know what the hell you thought you were doing but this seemed like a good place to start, so I called the sheriff and told him to get up here."

"They kidnapped Nikki."

"Yeah, the sheriff already filled me in. Featherhill's from California. He disappeared about eight months ago when the cops were closing in on a porno ring he was running down there. I need to talk to the sheriff then I'm taking you and the kids back to Portland. Finney's meeting us at the hospital."

"Featherhill?"

"The fat man. Edward Featherhill."

"That fat blob's name is *Featherhill*?"

"Go back to sleep."

It was four-thirty in the morning when Bundy shook me awake again. Nikki and Jessica and I stumbled out to his car. The kids fell asleep again immediately. It took us less than an hour to reach the outskirts of Portland. The Buick had taken a circuitous route, maybe to be sure I was lost or to avoid cops or maybe they needed to waste some time so the second car would be in place waiting for me. Whatever the reason had been, I had seen enough of rural Oregon to last me for a while. The lights of Portland were friendly and welcoming.

Jason and Lily were waiting in the emergency room at the hospital. I had been wrong about Lily. She didn't look better without the makeup, just older. The Finney family reunion was painfully awkward. Jessica seemed to be the oldest of the three, calmly reassuring her parents while Lily made clumsy, ineffectual mothering motions and Jason became very busy with paperwork at the admissions window.

Jessica gave me a quick hug and a whispered "Thank you," then she and her mother followed a nurse down the hall. Jason watched them go then turned to me and said, "Well, that's over. You'll be sending your bill, of course. Itemized, please." He walked off down the hall.

Bundy looked stunned.

"He doesn't like good-byes," I said.

"Or thank yous. Where did Nikki get to?"

I shrugged. Nikki had made a phone call as soon as we got to the hospital and the last I saw of him he was blowing me a kiss from the entrance. A long silver-gray shape was waiting at the curb for him.

Bundy shrugged, too. "We can find him when we need him," he said.

We went to the Justice Center. As soon as we walked into his office, Bundy picked up the Sunday *Oregonian* that was on his desk. He glanced at the headlines, then flipped the paper over to look at the bottom half of the front page.

"Well, I'll be damned," he said. "The Mackie cops figured out who done it."

Not now, I thought. But it was now. Bundy held the paper so I could see it. Allison, in living color, in a classic graduation pose, an off-the-shoulder black velvet drape contrasting beautifully with her hair, the diamond from her mother's wedding ring sparkling against creamy skin. I returned her smile weakly. "Pretty," I said.

Bundy scanned the story. "Mary Allison Vanzetti. Seventeen. Vanzetti's daughter. Jesus, how old was he? Sixty-eight? Must have been a change-of-life surprise. Ran away from a private school in Connecticut Sunday. The school made some discreet inquiries before it finally notified the police and hired a private detective who found out she flew from New York to Portland Sunday. Portland PB was routinely notified and, bingo, Mackie's got its killer. All they have to do is find her."

"Is there a warrant?"

"Being sought for questioning right now. Wonder why she killed him. Big time criminal and he gets killed by his own kid."

"Any chance of getting a cup of coffee?" I asked.

CHAPTER THIRTY-FOUR

It was almost eight o'clock when Bundy let me go. A uniformed cop dropped me off at the motel. Allison was awake and pacing. And furious.

"Where have you *been?*" she demanded. "You said you'd be back by three o'clock. I kept waking up all night and you didn't come home and I thought something awful happened."

She flung herself at me, sobbing. I patted her back and made comforting noises, thinking *"Home. Jesus, what have I done now?"*

With her face against my neck, Allison said, "Carrie called about six o'clock. She sounded worried. You're supposed to call her. And your answering service called just a few minutes ago." She stepped back and really looked at me for the first time. "What happened to your face?" she asked, then her eyes widened as she took in my ripped, muddy, bloody clothes. "What happened?"

"I lost a fight with some blackberries. I'll tell you all about it after I take a shower."

I made the phone calls first. I assured Carrie that she still had a brother and that I definitely did not want to hear what she dreamed last night then I called the answering service. Russell Garvey wanted to talk to me as soon as possible. I called the store in Allentown.

"Hey, man," Sarge said. "This is a murder investigation."

"Yeah, I know. What did they ask you?"

"Not much. They were out here yesterday evening. They asked if I saw the girl and what time it was and if she talked to anyone and if I saw how she left. They asked the people at the cafe the same things. They weren't interested in the customers, just asked the waitresses if any of them had talked to the girl. I didn't have to tell any lies, but look, this is murder, man. I'm withholding information. That's a fucking felony."

"It'll all be cleared up soon. It's been almost a week now. You could have actually forgotten I was there. There's no way they can prove you remembered."

"Yeah, I guess, but still . . ."

"It'll be cleared up soon. You won't get in any trouble."

Sarge still seemed uneasy but he agreed to keep quiet. I told him I'd explain the whole thing to him later.

I called the lobby and asked for a two o'clock wake-up call, then I took a long hot shower. I put on my sweatpants and joined Allison in her bed and told her the granddaddy of all why-I-didn't-come-home-last-night stories.

She listened silently, then said, "Well, you could have at least called."

I smiled against her hair. "I thought you'd be sleeping."

She raised up on her elbow and looked at me, her midnight eyes solemn. "Are you all right?"

"I'm fine. Just tired."

"Me, too."

I pulled her down against me. "You had a rough night," I said.

She nodded against my shoulder then we both started laughing and we laughed ourselves right to sleep.

I slept like the dead until the phone rang at two. So did Allison. Must have been a very rough night. Her day was going to be even rougher. While she was in the shower, I went down to the lobby and bought a newspaper. I considered getting her something to eat first but decided against it. She'd just throw it up.

I waited until she was dressed and had the tangles combed out of her hair then I motioned for her to join me at the table. I put the newspaper in front of her. She stared at her graduation picture, her face draining of color. "Oh, God, what am I going to do?" she asked. Then she got up and went into the bathroom. I listened to her retching and gasping. So much for keeping her stomach empty.

She got into bed when she came out of the bathroom. She was shaking and pale, clutching Mr.

Smith tightly. I sat beside her and stroked her hair. I couldn't think of any way to help except to keep her from doing something foolish.

After a few minutes, I got up and changed clothes. She was sitting up in bed when I came out of the bathroom. "Where are you going?" she asked.

"I have an appointment with the DA about last night. I thought I'd try to look respectable." I was wearing a gray three-piece suit that clashed badly with the scratches all over my face and hands. "You just stay here until I get back," I added.

She didn't say anything until I was at the door with my hands full. "What are you doing?" she asked.

"I'm afraid you'll panic and try to run."

"Please, Zachariah, don't take my things. I'll stay here, I promise."

"Then you won't need these, will you?" Something soft hit the door behind me as I closed it. Mr. Smith, probably. Like hell she'd stay there.

I called a cab from the lobby and directed the driver to take me to a car rental agency. I needed a trunk so I could stash Allison's things. I had the feeling the DA might look a bit askance at me if I showed up in his office carrying a pair of white leather sandals, a pair of women's Adidas, a floppy-brimmed straw hat, and a big white leather purse. As it was, the cab driver looked a bit askance at me. He kept sneaking peeks at me in the mirror, no doubt committing my face to memory for when the cops came around looking for a serial killer with a shoe fetish.

Only an attorney could turn a night fraught with danger and sudden death into two hours of sheer boredom. Bundy finally rescued me. I knew by the look on his face that the news was bad. We went to his office without speaking.

He sat behind his desk. He had been at work for close to twenty-four hours by then and looked it. "Peggy died late this morning," he said. "Never regained consciousness. Her family will never know what happened to her."

I nodded. There wasn't anything to say.

Bundy filled me in on the latest developments. Tony, who had been picked up by the sheriff on his way up to the old house, claimed he had been hired to help Featherhill move and denied knowing anything about the fat man's business. Nikki's jock and Blackbeard were alive and talking. They both claimed to be completely innocent of any major wrongdoing and were more than happy to spill their guts about the fat man's operation, placing all the blame on each other and on the dead men.

They both said that only Featherhill had known the identity of the rapists. When a girl was at the house, the rapists would arrive, strip, do their job, collect their pay, and leave without ever removing the ski masks. Telephone records from the house were being checked but Bundy wasn't optimistic.

Featherhill had been cautious enough to drive Jessica to a pay phone to make the calls to Hank so he probably hadn't called the rapists from the house either.

Richard Bolin, the man I shot under the Burnside Bridge, had been hired to keep me under surveillance while the fat man tried to decide how much of a threat I was. Bolin was the ideal choice for the job. Besides having no objection to committing cold-blooded murder, he could recognize the girls who posed a threat to Featherhill because he had spent a month out at the old house earlier in the summer and had entertained himself with marathon viewings of the rape films. According to Blackbeard, Bolin had lost me several times. It was just sheer bad luck that he happened to be around when both Brandy and Peggy contacted me. As Bundy had guessed, the fat man had ordered Bolin to kill Diane Dobbs and Karen Baylor simply because they were easy to find and he was worried about them talking.

After I killed Bolin, I was tailed by the smoker, whose name was Bill Thompson. He wasn't good at it, even with Virginia setting me up for him, and the fat man came up with the alternate plan of kidnapping Nikki and leading me out to the country. Since they were moving their operation, getting rid of me seemed unnecessary but evidently Featherhill had taken a strong dislike to me. I was relieved to know it was Thompson who tailed me in Portland. Neither of the men in the hospital had seen me running around with the notorious blonde who was on the front page of the paper.

"There are twenty-three rape movies," Bundy said. "Ten of them were made somewhere else, maybe back in California. Thirteen were made out at the house. Thirteen girls — Dobbs and Baylor, Brandy, Peggy, and Jessica. Two of the others are known prostitutes here in town. Four are complete unknowns. And two are a couple of our unsolved homicides. We probably can't prove it, but I'm betting Featherhill had them killed because he didn't trust them to keep quiet. That leaves eleven girls who were raped so the fat man could make a profit off the S and M crowd, and not one of them reported it."

"They're young. They were scared. Jessica might have told. I think she would have."

Bundy rode down in the elevator with me. When the doors slid open on the ground floor, I came face to face with Virginia Marley who was waiting to enter the elevator. She was flanked by a woman cop and a man who was probably her lawyer. Virginia didn't look at all cute.

"You fucking prick!" she screamed. "You're lousy in bed!"

I smiled down at her. "You're perfect. Comes from practice, I hear."

Bundy yanked me one direction and the cop yanked Virginia the other direction and Virginia's claws raked harmlessly through the air in front of my face.

CHAPTER THIRTY-FIVE

I PICKED UP SOUP AND SANDWICHES AND HEADED back to the motel to set in motion my plan for returning Allison to the scene of the crime. Trying to keep her from jumping out of a moving car for over two hundred miles didn't appeal to me so I had decided to be devious.

She managed to eat a little soup and keep it down but I had to eat both sandwiches. As soon as we finished, I called my office number. The line was picked up by Harriet Smith — no relation — who had been working at the answering service since before I was born. Her voice quavered, "Arrow Investigations, good afternoon."

"Hi, Harriet. How are you?"

"I'm just fine, Zack. No messages. How are your parents, dear? I suppose they'll be coming up when Carrie has her new little one."

"What time did he call?"

"Oh, my, are we being sneaky?"

"Let me have the address."

I scribbled a made-up address on a notepad while Harriet said, "This is so exciting. It's just making my poor old heart go pitty-pat, pitty-pat."

"Call him back and tell him I'll meet him there. I'm going to be out of touch for a while. Hold my messages. If any desperate clients call, refer them to someone in Pendleton. If any rich clients call, tell them to try to cope until I get back to town."

"Oh, you devil, you," Harriet said. "If only I were thirty years younger. Well, forty."

I laughed and told her good-bye. I hung up the phone, frowning at it, trying to look like a man who just encountered an obstacle.

"Well, hell," I said to Allison. "There's been a new development in a child custody case I've been working on for months. I have to meet the father in Washington late tonight." That was the sum total of the cover story I had concocted but I trusted that Allison's burning desire to get out of Oregon would keep her from asking questions.

"Washington? DC?" she asked.

"No, the state. Walla Walla." I looked her right in the eye and added, "It's up in the northeast part of the state. Almost to Canada." Walla Walla is, in fact, in southeast Washington, not far from the Oregon border. "I guess I'll have to take you with me."

She didn't quite manage to hide her relief. "I didn't think that was a real place. Walla Walla, Washington."

"It's real. They grow good onions there."

"Are we leaving now?"

"No, I don't want to get there early and have to

sit around waiting for my client." I did some quick figuring. Drive north until the sun was down then head southeast. I never met a woman yet who knew what direction she was facing unless the sun was rising in front of her. And some of them don't know then. "We'll leave about seven," I said.

The phone rang just then. It sounded innocent enough so I answered it. It was the last person on earth I wanted to talk to. Bundy had already screwed up my plan to claim I didn't know about Allison but I still didn't want to talk to Phil.

"So whatcha think?" he asked.

"I don't know. I've been busy. What do you think?"

"We got her getting off the bus at eight o'clock Sunday evening. We got her walking across the lobby at the Arms a few minutes later. We got her sitting in Sparky's drinking tea right after the murder. We got an old geezer who gave her a ride out to Allentown. We got her trying to gag down an English muffin at the Allentown Cafe and we got her leaving there about six-twenty.

"Nobody noticed how she left but we know she made it to Portland. The Portland cops have been getting calls all day. She's been seen all over town and out at Clackamas Town Center. There's a shoe salesman who swears up and down he sold her a pair of tennis shoes. Says some man paid for them. A white man. End of description. White male adult really narrows it down, huh? Couple other people say she was with a man, too, which seems a little funny since I talked to her school and they say she's the sweetest, most innocent little thing that ever lived. Didn't even date except for some dances when they bused in the boys from another school. Of course, after murder, picking up a stranger and cozying up to him enough to get him to buy you a pair of shoes is pretty tame. And, get this, Bucky. She spent Friday at the zoo and Saturday at the Saturday Market. I think maybe little Miss Vanzetti is a few bricks shy of a load. Commits murder then goes off to play tourist in Portland."

"Maybe she didn't do it."

"So what the hell's she doing? She was at the hotel. She's gotta know he's dead. If she didn't do it, why the hell isn't she here burying the son-of-a-bitch? Goddammit. She looks like one of them angels Botticelli or somebody was always painting. Not that I got any trouble with her pulling the trigger. Anyone can kill. We had that babyfaced sweetheart just last winter, took an axe to her stepdaddy. Anyone can kill. I got a little trouble with her be-bopping over to Sparky's for tea and crumpets afterward, but what the hell, she wouldn't be the first cold-blooded bitch with the face of an angel."

"You have a motive?"

"Yeah. She was mad at him. The woman I talked to at the school says Allison — she goes by her middle name — was in a real tizzy Saturday.

Vanzetti called her. She hadn't heard from him in months and she was pissed as hell because she graduated in the spring and wanted to leave school and she'd been waiting all summer to talk to him about it. So he finally calls and says no way is she leaving school until she's eighteen which is next April. So she was crying and carrying on something fierce, saying her father didn't love her and how could he be so mean and on and on and on. Then the next morning she's cool as a cucumber and asks permission to go to some art exhibit. Waltzes right out of school and hops a plane to Portland.

"I figure she tells him she isn't going back to school and he says oh, yes, she is, on account of the last thing a man running from the Feds needs is some little girl slowing him down. And they have a big fight — although why the hell they pick four-thirty in the morning for it, I don't know — and Vanzetti's gun is lying around somewhere handy and she picks it up and bang, bang, bang. How many was that? Bang. Four shots.

"Or, who knows? Maybe she had a damn good reason to kill him. She might have been his daughter but the man hardly knew her. Maybe the sight of that sweet young thing prancing around the room in her nightie got to him and he tried some funny business."

"Has anyone ever told you you talk too much?"

"Who, me?" Phil laughed uproariously.

"You seem to be in a better mood."

"Harkins took off early today. I been working forty-eight hours a day and that bastard takes the afternoon off. Ain't no justice in this world."

"No rest for the wicked anyway," I said, which set Phil off on another laughing fit. He broke off abruptly and said, "We got a notification from Portland PB this morning to the effect that one Jessica Finney, missing person case number such-and-such, has been recovered intact and turned over to her loving parents. I reckon you know all about that?"

"I found her last night."

"So are you coming home tonight?"

"No, I have some loose ends to tie up."

"Okey-dokey. Well, I gotta go. See you when you get here, okay?"

I said okay and told him good-bye.

I checked my watch and turned on the television just in time for the news. Someone had been slow releasing information. There was just a brief mention that the Portland police had been involved in breaking up a major pornography operation in which young prostitutes were hired to make movies and were then raped while the cameras rolled. The anchorman promised more details during the eleven o'clock broadcast. Jason Finney was going to love the bit about the young prostitutes.

I turned the television off and stretched out on my bed. Allison joined me. "What did he say?" she asked.

"Who?"

"Your policeman friend. That was him you were talking to, wasn't it?"

"He thinks you did it."

She didn't say anything for a while then she asked, "What are you going to do with me?"

I smiled and said, "Maybe I'll just keep you."

"Finders, keepers?"

"Mm hm."

She moved into my arms just as if she belonged there and after a moment she said, "I wish I could stay here forever." I had the feeling she didn't mean in a motel room in Portland. We spent the remainder of our time there cuddled up on the bed. I kept thinking about Virginia Marley who had seemed to enjoy the things we did together just as much as Allison seemed to be enjoying the much more innocent things the two of us were doing now. Virginia put on a good show. Allison was putting on a good show. April had put on a good show. I really knew how to pick them.

CHAPTER THIRTY-SIX

Shortly after seven o'clock on the last Sunday in August I drove the most wanted blonde in Oregon across the Columbia River and across the state line. I tried to figure out how many laws I was breaking, then gave up. I couldn't count that high.

I drove north on I-5 until the sun was completely down. I had checked a map in the motel lobby and plotted a course that would take us east across Washington then south. It was a long, slow route. Allison had to be asleep before we got close to the state line and since she had slept most of the day, I didn't expect her to doze off early.

Considering the circumstances, it was a pleasant journey. We stopped frequently, usually at moonlit roadside parks. A minor problem occurred to me, and at a stop for snacks I called Carrie and told her to put a set of my house keys in her mail box so I could pick them up.

There were frequent news flashes on the radio informing us that Mary Allison Vanzetti was still being sought in connection with the shooting death of her father. Mary Allison Vanzetti seemed untroubled by them. She entertained me with stories of her classmates' escapades and with gossipy tidbits about the school staff. The trip to Walla Walla had obviously seemed like a reprieve to her. I was positive she planned to make a break for it whenever the opportunity presented itself, but I began to wish she would act like a young woman who had killed her father and was sorry and was scared to death of the consequences instead of like a schoolgirl enjoying an unexpected holiday. Possibly I had my priorities backward but I could cope with Allison being a killer better than I could cope with her being crazy enough not to care that she was a killer.

I assured myself she wasn't crazy. It was just that any show of remorse on her part would contradict her claim of innocence. I had no doubt that the casual chatter concealed a frantic desperation. She was waiting for her chance, praying she could get hold of the keys to the Chevy with its nice little automatic transmission, praying my business in Walla Walla would distract me enough for her to get away, with or without the car, with or without any money. Time was running out for her. She was going to run and she'd do it barefoot and broke if she had to.

For once, one of my plans went according to plan. We had passed several signs giving the mileage to Walla Walla when Allison fell asleep shortly after midnight. My down jacket was gone with the Nova but she had Mr. Smith for a pillow and was sleeping soundly when we passed through Walla Walla and when we crossed the border into Oregon shortly afterward. She slept through Milton-Freewater and Pendleton and Pilot Rock and Mackie and the brief stop at Carrie's mailbox. I got the car into the garage and even got her out of the car without really waking her up. She murmured something against my shoulder and I murmured back comfortingly and carried her into the house.

If I had ever burped the damn waterbed, she might have stayed asleep. As it was, she rolled over when I put her down then sat bolt upright as the mattress bucked and sloshed loudly beneath her.

"Where are we?" she demanded.

"Just a place to sleep."

She looked wildly around the room and when she saw the photographs she hissed, "This is your house. You brought me back to Mackie. You lied to me. You tricked me. I hate you." The last words were accompanied by a kick to my ribs. She swung her legs off the bed and stood up.

"Just go back to sleep," I said. "We'll talk about it in the morning."

She wasn't in the mood to sleep. She preferred to fight. It was an unfair match. I outweighed her by at least a hundred pounds but I didn't want to hurt her and she was out for blood. I fended off blows for a while waiting for her to tire herself out.

She didn't get tired. I wrestled her to the floor and straddled her hips, holding her wrists tightly. Her legs thrashed impotently behind me.

I shifted my grip and got both her wrists in one hand and used the other to brush my hair back from my eyes. It suddenly didn't seem so hard to imagine her picking up a gun in a moment of rage. If one had been handy now, she'd have used it on me.

"Shut up and listen to me, Allison." I waited until she got tired of telling me how much she hated me. "You're going to be all right. Nobody gives a shit about your father. He was an ex-con, he did time for murder, for Christ's sake. He was peddling drugs all over the country. Nobody's crying over him. It's your word against his what happened at the hotel and he isn't talking. If you claim any justification at all for shooting him, even if you just say you were sick and confused, nothing at all is going to happen to you. People are convicted of felonies every day of the week and get a slap on the wrist. All you have to do is cooperate. The press'll love you. They'll drum up so much sympathy for you that no judge in his right mind will do anything but pat you on the head and say 'poor baby'."

"I didn't kill him."

"I'm turning you in to the police, Allison. If your mystery man exists, you'd better tell me right now who he is."

"I can't."

"Why? Who is he? A hit man? The head of the mob? Tell me who he is and I'll find him and put him out of commission until after you've talked to the cops and I'll be sure you're hidden away where he can't find you."

"You couldn't. You're hurting my wrists."

I let go of her. "Why couldn't I? Look at me, babe. Give me the element of surprise and I can put Godzilla out of action. There's nothing for you to be afraid of."

"No one will believe me."

I gave up. "I'm going to let you up and you're going to go to bed and go to sleep. The house is wired. If you open a door or a window, you'll set off an alarm that will wake up most of Oregon. There's also a silent alarm and the cops will be here in five minutes. And you won't find the car keys, so don't bother looking."

"You can't keep me here against my will. It's . . . kidnapping or something."

"Jesus Christ. There's a phone in almost every room in the house. Call the cops. I'm sure they'll be happy to come to the rescue."

I got off her. She got into bed, sobbing, and buried her head in a pillow. I carried the luggage in from the car and locked the keys and my gun in the room beneath the stairs. Allison refused to get up and undress so I pulled her shoes off and lay down beside her, leaving my jeans and T-shirt on.

I managed to get a corner of the comforter away from her and pulled it over my shoulders.

As Allison's sobs abated, I started drifting. I jerked awake. Would I notice if she got out of bed? Didn't matter. She couldn't get out of the house without setting off the alarm. She wouldn't get far on foot and I could catch her easily enough. I drifted again. And was jerked awake again by a vision of Allison holding a knife dripping blood. My blood. Ridiculous. She wouldn't kill me. I rolled onto my other side and drifted again. Jerked awake. Allison with a knife dripping blood. Her blood. Even more ridiculous. She wasn't suicidal, she was hell bent on surviving. I rolled over again. Drifted. Jerked awake. Knives in the kitchen. Razor blades in the bathroom. An old bottle of codeine pills in the medicine chest. Drain opener under the kitchen sink. I rolled over. Fireplace poker, drapery cords, electrical outlets, picture-hanging wire. I rolled over. Allison sat up and looked at me and lay down again. Rope in the garage. Axes. Gasoline. Kerosene. Insecticide. Weed killer. Chain saw. Screwdrivers. Hammers. A thousand blunt instruments and sharp objects. The whole house was lethal.

I sat up.

"What's the matter?" Allison asked.

"Nothing. I'm crazy."

She muttered something, probably an agreement, as I got out of bed. I rummaged around in a drawer, placing a key on the bureau before I returned to bed. She was lying on her right side, her back to me. I found her left wrist and slipped the cuff on it then clicked the other one around my own left wrist. She sat up, staring in disbelief at our hands.

"You can't handcuff me," she wailed.

"I just did. I can't get any sleep worrying about what you're doing."

"You can't handcuff me," she said again, shaking our joined hands. After a moment, she said, "What if I have to go to the bathroom?"

"I've seen women pee before. Go to sleep."

She lay down, turning away from me and yanking my arm across her waist. Otherwise, our bodies weren't touching. I closed my eyes. I was drifting again when she backed up into the curve of my body. I pulled her closer and kissed the back of her head. I fell asleep feeling bad for her. She had no one to turn to for comfort but the son-of-a-bitch who was going to hand her over to the police.

CHAPTER THIRTY-SEVEN

I WAS AWARE OF SOMEONE ENTERING THE HOUSE the next day, but whoever came in knew how to turn off the alarm so my subconscious registered the sounds as harmless. I didn't really wake up until Allison kicked me in the shin with her heel and stage-whispered, "Someone's here."

She yanked the covers up over her head just as Carrie appeared in the doorway, Melissa at her side.

Carrie said, "Oh, sorry," then stood there looking confused. She knew I never brought women to the house. She looked more confused as she took in the fact that I was dressed. She frowned at me then stared at the lump beside me.

I sat up, my left hand pulled across me and hidden beneath the blankets. "She's shy."

Carrie raised an eyebrow. "Evidently, so are you." She jerked her head toward the door. "I need to talk to you."

"This really isn't a good time."

She didn't go away. She stared at the lump some more then looked at me. It was her "oh-my-god-what-have-you-done-now-you-idiot" look. I sighed.

"There's a little key on the dresser. Hand it to me, will you?"

She found the key and gave it to me. I pulled my hand and Allison's clenched fist out from under the blankets and disconnected us.

"There's a perfectly logical explanation for this," I said.

"Uh huh," Carrie said. She clapped a hand over her mouth and left the room in a hurry, dragging Melissa with her.

I patted Allison on the backside and told her not to go away. I left the French doors slightly open so I could hear if she tried to go out the sliding glass door that led to the patio out back.

Carrie was standing in the middle of the living room. "You're all over the front page," she said. "People died. I thought you might want some company."

"I have more company than I can handle already. The men I killed were responsible for the deaths of at least four girls and were going to douse my client's daughter with gasoline and burn her to death. I'm not having any trouble coping with it. Is my picture in the paper?"

"Your picture? No. Why?"

We stood there looking at each other for a couple minutes. Neither of us bothered to look at Melissa, who suddenly shoved the French doors wide open. My sister and I turned toward the bedroom. Allison was standing by the bed, her hair in wild tangles, a pillowcase wrinkle imprinted on her cheek.

Very quietly, Carrie said, *"Allison* Wonderland."

I introduced them. Carrie said, "How do you do?" and Allison said, "Fine, thank you. How are you?"

"Fine, thank you," Carrie replied.

Melissa climbed onto the waterbed and started bouncing.

Carrie said, "Um."

Allison burst into tears.

I took Carrie's arm and pulled her away from the doors. She resisted, looking frantically over her shoulder toward the room where her beloved first-born was bouncing and squealing a few feet away from a sobbing cold-blooded murderess.

"She's fine," I said. "I want you to go home. I'll talk to you later."

"Do you have any idea what you're doing?"

"Not really. Have bail money ready."

"This isn't funny, Zachariah. She's wanted for murder. What are you doing with her? Where did you find her? The whole state's looking for her."

"I told you. I found her down a rabbit hole."

In the other room, Melissa suddenly broke off in mid-squeal. I trotted after Carrie, who was moving fast for a very pregnant woman. Allison, her face tear-streaked, was holding Melissa who had fistfuls of long blond hair and was chortling happily. Allison smiled tentatively at Carrie. "She's very pretty," she said.

"Thank you," Carrie said.

"Come on, Missy," I said. "Mommy's taking you home now." I pried her fists open and took her from Allison. Carrie followed me to the front door. I handed Melissa to her. "Everything will be fine," I said. "Go home. If you see Chief Harkins, give him a shit-eating grin for me."

She smiled, the creases in her cheeks appearing. "I'd like to see his face when you turn her in." The creases disappeared. "You are turning her in, aren't you?"

"Yes. Go home."

I waited until she headed her car down the long drive, then I went back into the bedroom to see what Allison was doing. She was curled into a tight ball on the bed. She refused to get up, refused to talk to me, and denied being hungry. I turned the alarm on and took a quick shower.

I had coffee brewing and was trying to decide whether I wanted breakfast or lunch when Allison wandered in and asked me what time it was. There were more clocks than telephones in the house. She had passed at least four of them on her way to the kitchen. I looked pointedly at the clock on the microwave and said, "It's eleven oh four. What would you like to eat? There's no milk unless you can stand powdered. I have some hot chocolate mix."

"I don't want anything."

"That's easy enough." I made a cheese and onion

omelet and ate it while she stood across the counter and watched me. When I finished she said, "There's no tub in the bathroom."

"That's the powder room, babe. There's a shower in the bathroom off the laundry room. That way." I pointed toward the back hall. "If you want a tub, you'll have to go upstairs. There are two of them up there. The rooms aren't finished, but the plumbing works."

"You have four bathrooms?"

"Seems a little excessive, doesn't it?"

She headed off down the back hall. As soon as I heard the shower start, I called the police. Phil Pauling wasn't there. I left word for him to call me then called his apartment and left a message on his answering machine.

Allison stalked past me, wrapped in a beach towel. I gave her enough time to get dressed then I went into the bedroom. She wasn't dressed. She was sitting at the bureau, her wet hair combed smooth, the beach towel tucked beneath her arms. She looked as if she'd been hatching up a plot and when her eyes met mine in the mirror I knew what it was. The oldest trick in the book.

She walked over to me. When she was very close, she dropped the towel and slid her arms around my neck, pressing her body against me. Five feet ten inches of sheer heaven. I kissed her forehead and said, "If you wanted anything else at all this would work just fine."

She jerked away from me, slapped my face, stooped for the towel and held it one-handed in front of her while she slapped me again. I grabbed her wrist. "Calm down. This isn't doing any good."

She re-wrapped the towel and flung herself down on the bed. It sloshed.

"Get dressed and come into the living room. I want to talk to you."

She rolled over and sat up. "I don't want to talk to you. I hate you. You lied to me. You're going to call the police. I hate you. You said you cared what happened to me and now he's going to kill me. I shouldn't have stayed with you. I should have left while we were in Portland. Oh God, why didn't I leave."

"Get dressed."

She took her time but eventually she appeared in the living room, wearing her jeans and a blue T-shirt I had bought for her at the Saturday Market. "Somebody in Oregon Loves Me" was silk-screened across the front in rainbow colors.

She sat in the middle of the couch, her hands clasped in her lap, and said, "I want you to let me go."

"I can't. Too many people know for one thing."

Her eyes widened. "Will your sister tell anyone?"

"Just her husband. That's as far as it will go. But they aren't the only ones." I told her about Sarge and watched her fear deepen into panic. She paced in front of the couch.

"You can still let me go. He already lied to the police. You can make him keep quiet."

"It wouldn't do any good. The paper is full of the story about the pornography bust. It's a nice sensational story full of sex and violence and the press is going to milk it for all it's worth. I bet anything that by the time tomorrow's paper hits the street someone will have dug up a picture of me. A lot of people saw us together in Portland. No one remembers me well enough to give the cops a good description, but if my picture's in the paper, someone will recognize me."

"You can say I left days ago, before you knew who I am."

"I've been pumping Phil Pauling for information all week. He'll never believe I didn't know."

"I don't care. Just let me go. Say I got away from you on the way here. You don't care about me, you're just worried about yourself."

"Allison, I wouldn't do it even if I could get away with it. It isn't fair to Tom and Carrie. They wouldn't tell anyone but it would put them in an awkward situation. They know most of the cops in town. The Chief of Police lives next door to them. I can't ask them to do it. Besides, I don't want to let you go. You can't spend the rest of your life running."

"I hate you! I hope you do get in trouble. I hope they put you in jail for the rest of your life."

We covered the same ground several more times

with Allison pointing out at length what a mean, heartless, selfish, et cetera bastard I was. I left the room when she got wound up in a lengthy threat about all the things she was going to tell the cops I did to her if I turned her in. For a virgin, she knew a lot of perversions.

I carried a telephone upstairs and called the police station again. Just as the line was answered, the house filled with a painful whooping shriek. I slammed the phone down and swore all the way down the stairs. Allison was standing at the open front door, hands over her ears, screaming something about the police. I silenced the alarm and called the alarm company. The only neighbors close enough to hear the alarm weren't due back from Europe for a few more weeks.

"Do that again," I said, "and I'm letting them come."

The afternoon passed with teeth-grinding slowness. Allison alternated between sulking and sobbing. She asked once why I didn't just call the police and get it over with. I told her to mind her own business which offended her sense of fairness so badly that she stomped her foot at me.

I left a dozen messages for Phil at the police station and a dozen more on his answering machine. No one seemed to know if he was on duty or off.

By five o'clock the house had become oppressively claustrophobic. The soft hum of the air-conditioning swelled to the sound of a swarm of angry bees. I collected Allison's belongings and locked them in the room beneath the stairs. She watched me duck into the closet with my arms full then come out empty-handed. She padded barefoot over to the closet and peered inside then shoved the jackets on the rod aside and looked some more. She glared at me and went into the family room to stare at the television, which wasn't on.

I turned off the alarm system and opened doors and windows. Heat and sunshine poured into the house. I changed into cut-off jeans and a T-shirt and went out back to the patio. The bricks were hot against my feet and the sun spread its warmth over me as I stretched out in a redwood lounge chair. After a while, Allison joined me, lying back in the matching chair beside me.

"I wish I had some shorts," she said.

"Just take your jeans off. There's no one here but me. You've been running around half-naked all week."

"It didn't work."

I sat up and smiled at her. "If it had worked, it wouldn't change anything. It would be all the more reason for me to want you to get this mess cleared up so you can get on with your life."

"He's going to kill me. I won't have any life." She got up and went into the house. When she came back, she was wearing a sleeveless undershirt of mine over her bra and panties. She lay down again after angling the chair so her face would be partially shaded by a tree. Her hair gleamed in filtered sunlight. Dancing shadows played across the planes and angles of her face. The sun glistened on her long slender legs. I watched the movement of her dark eyes as she tracked the flight of birds far overhead.

I considered methods of torture. It wouldn't take much. Twist her arm up behind her. Sometime before the point of agony, she would blurt out the truth. If the mystery man existed, she would tell me his name. More likely, she would confess to murder and once she admitted it to me I thought I could convince her to talk to a lawyer. I looked at the graceful line of the arm she had raised to shade her eyes and felt faintly nauseated. Not her arm. Thumbs are good. They hurt like hell. But they don't always heal properly. Okay, not her thumb. Her little finger. That would do it. Bend it back to the breaking point and she'd tell me anything.

I crouched beside her chair and took her left hand. She watched me solemnly as I studied her fingers. They were long and slender, fragile, half the thickness of mine. I kissed her palm and released her hand.

"Why can't you let me go?" she asked.

"Because," I said, sounding a lot like Melissa. But I finished the sentence in my mind. *Because I would never see you again.*

I lit the coals in the barbecue. When they were ready, I went inside and put two potatoes in the microwave and opened a jar of three-bean salad. I put the steaks I had removed from the freezer earlier onto the grill then set two places at the picnic table.

"I'm not hungry," Allison said.

"You haven't eaten anything all day. You're going to make yourself sick again."

"I'm going to be dead," she said. "It doesn't matter if I'm sick."

I ate. She didn't. I sat quietly after I finished, watching her. She seemed to be asleep but I didn't think she was. I thought she was lying there awake, gathering courage, storing strength, waiting — like a cornered wild thing — for a chance to make one last desperate bid for freedom.

I carried the dishes inside, putting Allison's dinner in the refrigerator in case she wanted it later. I made another call to the police station. I had talked to several people during the day and none of them had any idea where Phil was. This time the line was answered by Sam O'Connell. He asked me to hold on while he went to a different phone. I waited, curious because I barely knew O'Connell. He had reversed the usual procedure, putting in several years with the Portland Police Bureau before hiring on with Mackie PD shortly after I resigned in a blaze of shattered pumpkin shell.

"Smith?" I could tell by the lack of background noise that he was in an interrogation room.

"What's wrong?" I asked.

"I'm worried about Phil. He's supposed to be working but he got into it with Harkins this morning and he slammed out of here and hasn't come back. The Chief is pissed as hell and is threatening to fire him as soon as he shows up."

"Christ. What were they fighting about?"

"What weren't they? Harkins has had a bee up his ass ever since this murder went down and Phil's catching the worst of it as usual. I've never seen either of them so mad before. I thought they were going to pull their guns and shoot it out. I know Phil's been on the wagon for a long time, but the way he looked when he walked out of here . . . I'm afraid he may be out drinking. You think you can look for him?"

I couldn't explain why I couldn't leave my house. "I'll do what I can. If he shows up, tell him to call me right away."

I spent thirty minutes trying to track Phil down by telephone. He wasn't in a bar drinking soda and lime or anything stronger. He wasn't out at the firing range pretending the target was the Chief of Police. He wasn't at Sparky's flirting with the waitresses. I left messages for him with two of the regulars who would be attending the AA meeting at eight o'clock. The anonymity bit doesn't work well in a town the size of Mackie.

All else having failed, I called Patsy. The phone rang six times before it was finally picked up. There was a breathless "Hello," then the receiver thunked against something hard. After several softer, diminishing thunks, Patsy said, "Sorry, I dropped —." She broke off with a laugh. Then, her voice muffled, she said, "Stop it! Don't! Get off me, you idiot. Don't *tickle*!" The last word was a shriek. I hung up during some sustained out-of-control giggling. I had no desire to find out who was tickling the fancy of Phil's ex-wife.

I sat and stared at the phone for a while. If Patsy was fooling around at seven in the evening, Philip the Second wouldn't be in the house. He was probably with his father and the two of them were out in the country somewhere with a couple fishing lines trailing in the water. Shit.

I tapped out Phil's number and listened once more to his recorded voice drawling out an interminable message. At the sound of the beep, I said, "Where the hell are you? I have Allison Vanzetti. If you want her, get over here." I slammed the receiver down. Never a goddamn cop around when you need one.

I went outside and stretched out in the chair beside Allison. We went inside after the sunset had faded to a soft diffuse light beyond the hills. Very meekly, Allison told me she was tired and asked if it would be all right if she took a bath and then went to bed. When I said it would, her face flooded with relief. Reprieved again. She thought I was going to give her another night. But I wasn't. I couldn't. Long before dawn, the early edition of *The Oregonian* would hit the newsstands and if my picture was in it, Mackie cops and county sheriffs and state troopers were going to be banging on my door.

Allison asked for her nightgown and followed me to the hall closet. I blocked her attempt to watch me open the inner door. She glared at me then went upstairs. After a moment, I followed. I stood outside the bathroom door and listened to the water running and then to the light splashes as she bathed. When the water started draining from the tub, I went down the hall to the master bedroom and looked at the wall by the door. There was a ragged hole in the sheetrock where some fool had put his fist through it three years ago. Three years, three months, and . . . how many days? It seemed important to know so I stood there until I figured it out.

The bathroom door was still closed. I walked past it and went downstairs. I used the phone in the kitchen. O'Connell answered again and I asked for Harkins.

"He isn't here," O'Connell said. "He went home about an hour ago. Phil hasn't shown up."

"Thanks," I said and hung up. I could hear Allison walking around upstairs. She was in the master bedroom. There was nothing in there to look at except the hole in the wall and a stack of photo albums that tracked three years of marriage to an abrupt end.

I picked up the telephone receiver again. I wasn't one of the privileged few who had Harkins' unlisted number. Well, if the son-of-a-bitch didn't want me to know his number, he shouldn't live next door to my sister. I called Carrie and heard the relief in her voice as she gave me the number.

I punched the buttons and Harkins answered immediately.

"I have Allison Vanzetti," I said.

There was a long silence. If the bastard asked who I was I was going to reach right through the telephone and rip his tongue out.

"What do you mean?" he asked.

"She's here. Out at my place."

There was another long pause, then Harkins said, "At your house? She's there?"

"That's right. Listen, Harkins, she's young and she's scared. Handle this quietly. Don't call the press. You can get your picture taken tomorrow."

Another long silence. He was probably already trying to figure out how he could take full credit for apprehending her. Finally he said, "What did she tell you?"

"She said she didn't do it. Nothing else. And she isn't saying anything else until she has a lawyer. Don't try any grandstand plays on this one. If you lean on her, I'll kill you."

After another lengthy pause, Harkins said, "I didn't bring a city car home. Better go by the book and not transport her in a private vehicle. I'll call the station and send someone out in an unmarked unit. You can ride in with her and I'll meet you at the station. The place was dead when I left. There won't be any reporters hanging around. We can take her in the back way. I'll call the county and have them send a woman from the juvenile division and you can get a lawyer for her. How did you find her?"

"I picked her up on the road. Hurry up."

"Right," he said and hung up.

I looked at my wrist, which was bare, then at the clock on the microwave. It was 8:51.

I went to the bottom of the stairs and watched Allison come down. She descended slowly, her eyes on mine, her face solemn. The light at the top of the stairs cast an aura of gold around her hair and silhouetted the shape of her body beneath the thin nightgown. My throat ached. She stopped on the last step, her face level with mine, and put one hand behind my neck and one on my shoulder and kissed me, a long, slow kiss that was totally devoid of passion, sweet and sad and very final. A good-bye kiss. From A to Z.

Without a word, she walked away from me and went into the family room. After a moment the sweet sound of violins filled the air. I went into the room beneath the stairs and selected some clothes for her, the dark blue pants and the blue blouse, underwear, her sandals. I slung her purse over my shoulder and carried the clothes into the family room. She was standing at the counter, staring into the kitchen.

"Here," I said. "Put these on."

She looked at her clothes as if they were unidentifiable foreign objects. "What?" she said.

"Get dressed. I called the cops. They'll be here in a few minutes."

"What?" she said.

I tried again. "I talked to the Chief of Police. He's sending a —"

Allison went berserk.

She screamed, a less than human scream that stopped as abruptly as it started. She grabbed the clothes from me, dropping them all over the floor. She snatched up the pants, thrust one leg into them and fell, landing hard on her butt on the floor. Her face didn't register any pain. She shoved her other leg into the pants and had them pulled up and zipped by the time she was on her feet again. Her nightgown was ballooning around her waist, tucked loosely into the pants. She was sobbing loudly, harshly, and yet her eyes were completely dry.

She slid one foot into a sandal, bent to buckle it, then wriggled her other foot into the second sandal, leaving it unbuckled. She picked up her bra, dropped it and picked up her blouse, holding it in front of her as if she didn't know what it was for. She said "I need my purse" in a voice as calm as if she were asking me to pass the salt. She snatched her purse from me and ran, her blouse gripped in her hand. I caught her arm as she was rounding the counter into the kitchen. She spun around and attacked me with hands, feet, nails and teeth. When I finally got my arms around her, pinioning hers to her side, she used her hair, whipping her head around, the long strands flailing, lashing at my face.

I finally just let her go because I was afraid she was going to hurt herself the way she was arching her back and swinging her head around. She stood stock still for an instant then thrust her foot back into the sandal that had fallen off. I was blocking the entrance to the kitchen. With her shoe flapping wildly, she ran toward the front of the house. I caught her before she reached the hallway to the entry. She swung her purse, catching me on the side of the head. The strap jerked out of her hand and the purse flew across the room. I gripped her wrists tightly and she pulled hard away from me. All the time, she was breathing in those loud dry sobs and all the time I was telling her to calm down, to listen to me, to let me help her.

We were making a lot of noise. I didn't hear a car but, over the sound of music and Allison's sobbing, I heard the compressed-air sound of the screen door opening and I heard the footsteps in the entry.

I turned toward the sound, dragging Allison around with me, thinking, good, Phil finally listened to his messages. It had to be Phil. Anyone else would have knocked.

Anyone else but the man who walked into the room.

Chapter Thirty-eight

I PROBABLY WOULDN'T HAVE BEEN FOOL ENOUGH to rush a man with a gun anyway and as it was, Allison was in front of me, stepping back against me, stepping on me, trying to step through me. I gripped her arms above the elbows and felt fear jolting through both our bodies and, just beneath my own fear, shock and disbelief followed by an incongruous rush of relief. Allison didn't kill her father.

For a brief moment the only sound in the house was the swell of violins from the stereo. Then Allison spoke. Her body shielding mine was trembling steadily but her voice was glacial.

"He doesn't know. I didn't tell him anything."

Her words set me and the gunman into motion. I moved her to my side. He took a few steps farther into the room and made a quick upward gesture with the gun. I interpreted the movement as "put your hands up" and laced my fingers across the top of my head, moving my elbow awkwardly back to get it behind Allison's head, moving my head just enough to see the VCR. It was 9:07. Sixteen minutes since I called Harkins. The cops would be here any minute.

Allison put her right hand behind me and grabbed a fistful of my T-shirt. "He doesn't know," she said again, her voice calm and steady. "He found me and brought me here. I was trying to get away. I was trying to make him give me money. That's all I need, just some money to get away and I'll never come back. I'll never tell anyone. I don't care what you did. My father . . . I didn't know him very well. I'll go someplace far away and change my name and . . . I haven't told anyone. You can help me get away. I'll never tell anyone."

While Allison was speaking, the gunman stood still, the gun steady on me, then he pulled a length of rope out of his jacket pocket and tossed it. It hit Allison in the stomach and fell to the floor.

"What?" she said. "Tie him up?"

He nodded and she stooped down, her hand still clenched on my shirt. The fabric strained across my back as she used it to pull herself up again. I lowered my hands and crossed my wrists behind me. Her fingers were icy, bloodless, but she tied me up as if she had done it a hundred times before, tightly, crisscrossing the rope between my wrists, making no attempt to leave it loose. I was breathing a little better. He wouldn't tie me up if he planned to shoot me. At least, I didn't think he would.

While Allison was busy behind me, I studied the

man in front of me. He was overdressed for an August night in eastern Oregon. A tan ski mask was pulled over his head. The eyeholes were hidden behind cheap black plastic sunglasses. A white handkerchief, folded into a triangle and tied behind his head, concealed the mouth opening of the mask. He was wearing baggy blue overalls — the kind people pull on over their clothes to work on their cars. He was also wearing a maroon down jacket — wrinkled and lumpy — and black leather gloves and navy blue moon boots with bright orange stripes across the insteps. All I could tell for sure was that he was about six feet tall. His gun was just like mine only his was in his hand and mine was locked in a room beneath the stairs.

Allison gave a little tug on the rope, checking her handiwork, and moved to my side. Her body was vibrating. Her voice was ice-cold. "Shall we go?" she asked her father's killer.

I tried to keep my face expressionless and willed her to read my mind. *Shall we go? For God's sake, Allison, stall him. The cops are coming.* Her eyes met mine, briefly, blankly.

The gunman made a "turn-around" gesture with the gun. I turned and felt another, rougher, tug on the rope. It was followed by a slap across my shoulder. I turned again. He had backed a few feet from me. He gestured "come here." Allison went. He spun her around to face me, twisting his left hand in her hair. The gun jabbed in the direction of the kitchen. I went.

They followed close behind me, shuffle-footed, out of step. Allison's loose sandal slapped softly on the carpet then loudly across the kitchen tile. I stopped in the middle of the room and turned slowly to face them. The darkness outside was complete and the kitchen was dimly lit by the lamp at the front of the family room. The numbers on the microwave glowed bright red. 9:11. They'd be here any second now.

The gunman shoved Allison against the kitchen counter, long golden strands clinging to his glove as her hair was jerked out of his hand. He pulled a small bottle from his pocket and tossed it at her. She had the reflexes of a sleepwalker. Like the rope, the bottle hit her and fell to the floor, rolling back toward him. He kicked it toward her and she picked it up.

"You want me to take these?" Her voice was shaking. She seemed more afraid of the pills than of the gun. He must have nodded. I was trying to get a good look at the bottle. It was a clear, unlabeled prescription bottle full of tiny round pills. White or maybe pale yellow.

"How many?" Allison asked.

He held up four fingers. She looked at his hand for a long moment, her lips moving slightly. I could swear she was counting fingers, as if the concept of four was beyond her comprehension. She nodded slightly then twisted the lid back and forth several times, her lower lip caught up in her teeth, a small dot of blood appearing on it. Finally she pressed her palm flat against the lid and twisted and it came off and dropped to the floor. She dumped the contents of the bottle into her left hand, most of it spilling onto the floor. With her palm flat she flicked excess pills off with her index finger until four were left. She held them toward the gunman for inspection then tossed them into her mouth. She ran some water into a glass, took a big gulp, and dropped the glass into the sink. The sound of it cracking was very loud. I checked the microwave. 9:12. Where the hell are the cops?

The gunman was suddenly in a hurry. He shoved Allison to the floor by the sink and began pulling out drawers, glancing at the contents, keeping the gun on me. When he yanked the silverware drawer open there was a loud crack and the whole drawer came out in his hand. A service for twelve — April's pattern — hit the floor with enormous noise. He threw the empty drawer behind him and pulled open the next one. It was the one he wanted. He tossed dish towels onto the counter.

He made a downward motion with the gun in my direction. I dropped to my knees. Evidently that wasn't far enough. The back of his left hand slammed across my face and before I could get my eyes open again, his boot landed in the pit of my stomach. I can take a hint. I fell over onto my side, gasping for air and choking on the blood welling up in my nose and mouth.

Allison said, "Don't."

I lay on the floor, spitting blood, while he gagged her with two dish towels and tied her hands in front of her with another. The gun jerked upwards at me. He had to be kidding. Probably not though. I struggled awkwardly to my knees, got one foot flat on the floor, and pushed myself to my feet. 9:15. Where the goddamn hell are the goddamn cops?

The gun jabbed toward the family room. We filed into it, me first, then Allison, then the gunman. He pushed her roughly to the floor in front of the recliner. Then he put his gun in his pocket and headed my way.

"Don't cry," I said to Allison. "You'll plug up your nose." They were the only words I spoke the whole time Carl Vanzetti's killer was in my house.

His fist landed just beneath my ribs and was followed by another in the same place. I staggered backward, staying on my feet but sending a spiraling wrought-iron plant stand crashing to the floor. I followed it a few blows later, landing on my face in a mess of plants and dirt and cracked pots. His foot rammed into my side. I got my knees under me and then the next kick sent me sprawling again.

The thick padding in the moon boots probably helped but after the first few kicks it didn't seem to make much difference. He put his weight behind each swing and got a pretty good rhythm going. I made it to my knees a couple times but all I managed to do was give him new targets. A kick to the side of my head slammed me into the wall and I slid down it, coughing blood all over a broken-stemmed golden pothos. My face hit the floor.

The kicks stopped.

Here lies Zachariah Smith, done to death with moon boots.

I raised my head and turned it slowly until I found Allison. Above the gag, her eyes were wide and dry and pleading.

I couldn't help her.

I blinked away blood and sweat and tears and looked at the VCR. 9:21. Where the goddamn fucking hell are the goddamn fucking cops?

The moon boots came into view and Allison was jerked to her feet and out of my line of sight. All that was left was her sandal, upside down on the floor.

The black dots hovering in front of my eyes all joined together and I went away to some place where it didn't hurt.

CHAPTER THIRTY-NINE

I CAME TO SLOWLY, SURFACING TOWARD LIGHT AND
the low, slow beat of music and the clean-earth
smell of potting soil. My heart was thudding in
jackhammer strokes, out of sync with my mind
which came sluggishly to the realization that I was
on the floor and that I hurt all over and that the
feather-tickle on my face was blood dripping across
my cheek. I wiped it off on the carpet and inhaled
dirt. The sneeze fragmented the overall pain into
separate and distinct points of agony. It also
brought me back to full consciousness.

I looked at the place on the floor where Allison
wasn't anymore. By lifting my head a bit, I could
see the glowing LED clock on the VCR. I stared
until the gray-blue blur came into focus then mum-
bled the numbers out loud through swollen lips,
trying to make sense of them. Nine two five. 9:25.
Was that possible? It meant I had been out for less
than five minutes, that Allison was less than five
minutes away from me.

If the cops would just get here. Where the fuck
were they? It had been over thirty minutes since
I called Harkins. They should have been here,

could have been here twice by now. Never, ever, a goddamn cop around when you need one.

I thought about moving. My right eye seemed to be half closed and my nose and mouth kept filling with blood. The inside of my right cheek was ragged and I had spit out hard bits of something that I hoped was bridgework and not real teeth. My wrists were burning, scraped raw from my instinctive efforts to free my hands and protect myself. The right side of my body felt as if I'd been trampled by a whole herd of rampaging elephants. The left side wasn't too bad, just a generalized bruised feeling from being slammed against the wall. My rib cage was a fiery ache. I'd had broken ribs before and knew how to tell if they were broken now. All I had to do was sit up. If I screamed, they were broken.

I checked the clock. 9:27. Where the fuck were they? Maybe something big had gone down in town. No, it was Harkins' perverted idea of a power play. *"You have the girl we've been busting our asses trying to find? Ho hum, big deal. We'll get out there when we're damn good and ready."* No hurry. If Allison Vanzetti was in Zachariah Smith's safekeeping, she wasn't going anywhere. I laughed harshly, snorting against the carpet, breathing dirt again. The third sneeze gave me the impetus to roll onto my side. I got my back against the wall and pushed myself up to a sitting position. Without screaming.

I felt better sitting up, so much better that I thought about getting to my feet. Thinking about it was as far as I got. When the cops got here, they could help me up and untie me and I could tell them . . . tell them what? It didn't matter if they ever came now. Allison was gone and I didn't know who took her. I didn't see a car and any description of the man I could give them was useless. He wouldn't be driving around in a ski mask and sunglasses with a handkerchief tied train-robber fashion across his face.

I checked the clock. Still 9:27. I watched until the seven flicked into an eight. Time was dragging. Time was wasting. Time. Timing. He had good timing. He must have been waiting until dark to make his move. If Phil had just checked his answering machine. If Harkins had just sent someone out right away. If I had just called Harkins earlier. If I had just taken Allison to the police as soon as I got her back to Mackie. If I had just turned her in in Portland. If I had just, for once, not fucked up. But I had, royally, and Allison was paying for it.

I looked at the telephone, five feet from me on a small oak chest. I could punch buttons with my hands tied behind me but getting the receiver to my ear might be a little tricky. Fuck it, I already called them. God damn Harkins anyway. Why didn't they get here? 9:29. Any minute, they would be here any minute now. .

I leaned my head against the wall and closed my eyes, trying to visualize the gunman, instead seeing Allison walking slowly down my staircase, backlit by the light at the top, her hair a golden halo, her body . . . I pushed the thought away and concentrated on the man. Ski mask. Sunglasses. Handkerchief. Overkill. A ski mask is a good disguise, a favorite of bank robbers the world over. And baggy overalls. Jacket. Gloves. Boots. Christ, he must have been hot. Overkill. Why the overkill? Easy. He didn't want to be identified.

Kicking me half to death. That was overkill, too. Why? To put me out of action long enough for him to get away, of course. Still, there were better ways to do it. Tie me up better. Tie me to something. Feed me some of the dream-bringers he had forced Allison to swallow. Be sure I was out for a good long time. Why kick the shit out of me? What good is a battered witness? Less reliable, uncertain about details, confused about time. Time. I looked at the VCR. 9:30. God, let there be a hell, just for Harkins. Time. Timing. He had good timing.

I closed my eyes again. And saw Allison, floating down my staircase, hair a golden halo, body . . . A good-bye kiss. From A to Z. Beginning to end. *"Don't cry, you'll plug up your nose."* My last words to Allison.

Words. He didn't talk. That was overkill, too. Identifying someone by voice isn't easy. I opened my eyes, feeling the sudden kick of adrenaline, feeling pain lessen as my body geared for fight or flight, feeling my mind clear and focus sharply. He didn't talk.

Identifying someone by voice isn't easy.

Unless you already know the voice.

9:31. I pressed my back hard against the wall and pushed myself up it until I was standing.

He wasn't worried about Allison identifying him. He had to know she had seen him at the hotel. The overkill was for me. He didn't want *me* to identify him. No, not *identify*. *Recognize*. I knew him. He was someone I knew, someone I would recognize. By sight and by voice.

Who knew she was with me? Why didn't I think of that before? Figure out how he knew where she was and I'd know who he was.

Who knew?

Sarge. Sarge knew. Sarge, cleverly disguised for twenty years as a double amputee, rising up on magically restored legs to kill Vanzetti and kidnap his daughter. I took a deep, ragged breath to stop some laughter I knew would be hysterical. All right, it didn't have to be Sarge himself. He could be involved somehow and he told the killer, who came out here and took Allison away from me.

It didn't make any sense. Sarge hadn't asked the right questions. He didn't try to find out for sure if Allison was with me or where I was then or when I was coming home. All he was interested in was staying out of trouble for withholding information in a murder investigation.

Okay, not Sarge. Who else knew? Carrie. And Tom. She would have told Tom. Tom was a doctor. Vanzetti dealt in black market pharmaceuticals. Made a nice connection. But Tom was Carrie's husband. Tom was Melissa's father. Tom was one of the few people I would willingly die for. Tom wasn't a killer. Besides, I didn't think he could hit like that.

So who else knew? Nobody. Well, Phil would know if he ever bothered to check his messages. And Harkins, I told Harkins.

No one else knew. So maybe I was all wrong. Maybe he wasn't someone I knew. Maybe he was just overly cautious. Maybe he was cold. Maybe he had a bad case of acne. Maybe he had laryngitis. Maybe he found out where Allison was through some flukey set of circumstances I couldn't even guess at. It didn't matter. The bottom line was the same. Allison was gone and I didn't know who took her.

9:32. I rolled along the wall to face it and wiped blood from my face onto the wallpaper.

I didn't know who took her.

Yes, I did — Carl Vanzetti's killer.

I didn't know who killed Vanzetti.

Nobody knew that.

Allison knew.

I stumbled away from the wall, my right knee

buckling, white hot pain shooting through it. I hobbled to the kitchen, hitting walls and furniture and setting a lot of hanging planters in motion. The kitchen was dark. I stepped all over pills and silverware, fork tines jabbed my bare feet. I hit the light switch with the side of my arm. The sudden bright light made my eyes water and burn. I backed up to the knife drawer and pulled it open, grabbing the first handle I touched. I turned the long butcher knife awkwardly until it was against the rope and started sawing.

Allison knew who killed her father because she saw him do it. And her father had told her the man's name. What did she say? What the hell did she tell me?

Not much.

Allison, in a dreamy, faraway voice *"I know who he is."*

"You mean you know his name?"

"I know his name." Dreamily, dreamily.

"I asked Daddy who the man was and he told me. Maybe he thought it would reassure me."

Allison would be reassured.

I would recognize him.

The knife slipped upward, slicing into my back. My hands were slick with blood and sweat. I repositioned the blade and sawed faster.

She was sure Vanzetti told her the right name.

Had you seen the man before?

I never saw him before.

She knew his name but she hadn't seen him before. That was the truth. Everything she told me was the truth. No, not everything. She lied when I asked her where the killer had his gun. I thought I had tripped her up, caught her off-guard, caught her unprepared with a pat lie to add to the lies she had already told me. But the rest of it was the truth. Why did she lie about the gun?

I stabbed myself in the back again. And sawed faster. The rope loosened, fell away. I wiped my bloody hands across the front of my T-shirt.

"When a person witnesses a murder the usual reaction is to scream or faint or run for help or pick up the phone and call the cops."

Allison didn't scream or faint or run for help. And she didn't pick up the phone and call the cops. She stood in the dark behind a curtain and watched her father die. And then she walked away.

I picked up the phone and called the cops. Phil Pauling answered, saying, "Local Good Guys, at your service."

What was he so cheerful about?

Where the hell had he been all day?

What did it matter where the killer had his gun? What difference did it make if he had it in his pocket or stuck in his waistband or in a . . .

". . . scream or faint or run for help or pick up the phone and call the cops."

But Allison didn't.

Phil was rattling on and on, something about obscene phone calls to the police.

I hung up on him.

I ran to the closet beneath the stairs, fear and urgency obliterating pain and caution. I got my gun out of the cabinet, jerked my holster on, grabbed a light blue windbreaker off a hanger and pulled it on. Keys. I grabbed the keys and ran to the garage and hit the switch. The big door started its upward glide. Before it reached the top, I was backing the Chevy out.

The clock on the dash said 9:38.

Fuck the cops.

I knew who killed Vanzetti.

I knew who kidnapped Allison.

I even knew where to find him.

CHAPTER FORTY

At the end of the driveway, I stubbed my left big toe on the brake pedal trying to find a clutch, then I hit the brake and brought the car to a squealing, fishtailing stop. I fumbled the shift into Park and stared hard across the street at the trees which were floating, swirling, disintegrating. I looked in the rearview mirror and watched my house rise from its foundation, become transparent, disappear in a churning darkness.

I crossed my wrists on the steering wheel and pressed my forehead against them, willing the vertigo to pass. From somewhere far away I heard Allison, with a voice like a winter wind, say *"He doesn't know. I didn't tell him anything."* She had saved my life, exchanging my freedom for hers, and I didn't do anything but stand there like a fool, waiting for the cops to come to the rescue. *"Shall we go?"*

I raised my head and looked in the mirror. My house was there, solid and stationary. It was dark upstairs. It was always dark upstairs except when no one was home. Light streamed from the open door and windows. It looked just like a goddamn pumpkin shell.

I felt the dizziness returning and thought of Allison with an empty stomach full of pills and a dish towel stuffed in her mouth. Out loud, in case anyone was listening, I said, "Please don't let her throw up." I shoved the shift into Drive, turned onto Bunyard, and pressed the accelerator down.

I was around the first curve when a dark sedan with a whip antenna sped past me in the westbound lane. The cops had arrived.

I reached Franklin Street in under five minutes and hit the brake, slewing the car across the intersection. Something soft bounced across the seat and hit my leg. I glanced down and saw Mr. Smith's glassy eyes gleaming at me. Carrie's house was brightly lit. Her car was in the drive. Tom's wasn't. Beyond their place, Harkins' house was dark. I drove on into town, staying close to the speed limit. I didn't want any cops now.

It was 9:49 when I pulled into the parking lot behind the police building. I looked over the cars quickly, not seeing what I wanted, then abandoned the Chevy in the middle of the parking lot, blocking cars into parking spaces.

The pavement still held the sun's warmth. Bits of gravel and debris pricked my bare feet. I walked down a flight of dark stairs at the rear of the building. I no longer had a key to the basement door of the police building but there was always someone hanging around the locker room. I pounded on the metal fire door with the side of my fist. The door was yanked open. Dan Fogel squinted out at me. His uniform shirt was unbuttoned and untucked and he had a hand on the butt of his gun. "Holy shit, what happened to you?" he asked and took his hand off his gun.

"Nothing." I brushed past him into the building. "Is Harkins here?"

"Beats me. You're supposed to use the front door."

"I didn't want to bleed all over the carpet."

"Nice bear," Fogel said. I looked down and realized I was carrying Mr. Smith.

We walked a few steps down the hall. Fogel stopped at the locker room door. I said, "See you," and kept going. Halfway down the corridor I looked behind me. The hall was empty.

I backtracked a few feet and went into a dark room, closing the door before I turned on the light. The overhead fluorescent bulbs flickered then steadied, buzzing loudly. The room was used for storage and for Police Association meetings. Folding chairs leaned in untidy rows against the left wall. The right wall was lined with metal shelves crammed with cardboard boxes and sloppy piles of police forms. In front of the shelves, a battered card table held some pads of yellow lined paper and two overflowing ashtrays. PA posters and notices were tacked randomly on the walls and the floor was littered with wadded paper and chewed pencils from a recent meeting. High in the wall opposite the door, a narrow horizontal window was cranked open a couple inches. It didn't help much. The room smelled dankly of stale ashes and old sweat.

An old black desk phone sat on the floor beneath the window, its long cord snaking across the room and disappearing behind the shelves. I squatted beside the phone, propping Mr. Smith up against the wall, and dialed three numbers. Phil Pauling answered.

I said, "Don't say anything." The line was silent except for the amplified sound of my breathing. "I'm in the basement, in the PA room. Don't say anything to anybody. Just get down here."

"Okeydokey, artichokey," Phil said. Cheerfully. I turned the light out and opened the door, standing back from it so I was out of the light spilling in from the hall.

There was a low drone of voices and a sudden burst of dirty-joke laughter from the locker room, then I heard Phil whistling his way down the stairs. He walked into the room, saying "What's with the cloak-and-dagger bit, Bucky?" as he hit the light switch. His eyes widened during the flickering. "Jesus goddamn. Was I you, I wouldn't go looking in any mirrors any time soon. You look like you jumped without a chute."

"Where's Harkins?" I closed the door and leaned against it.

"Upstairs, chewing off his fingernails. He took it real hard when Malcolm called from your place and said you and the Vanzetti child were gone on arrival and your house looked like the aftermath of the Texas Chainsaw Massacre."

"Call —"

"Shook me up just a little bit, too. I was about to take a ride out there myself, see if maybe I could find your bloodsoaked body lying in a ditch somewhere."

"Phil —"

"I sure was dreading having to tell Carrie that her baby brother by four minutes was —"

"*Phil,* goddamn it, shut up. When did he get here?"

"Who? Harkins? Hell, I don't know. I don't keep tabs on the bastard. He came in after I got here, ten minutes ago maybe. Said you had Allison Vanzetti. He'd already called from home and sent Malcolm out to your place. You want to sit down? You look a little shaky."

"I'm okay. I want you to —"

"Did you really have little Miss Vanzetti or was that one of those attention-getting devices?"

"I had her."

"Yeah? And you lost her? She beat the shit out of you and you were too much of a gentleman to fight back?"

I shook my head, more to clear it than to answer him. I wiped blood from my face onto my T-shirt and slid my hand inside my jacket.

"So how did you lose her? And just how did you happen to have her in the first place . . . and what the fuck are you pointing that gun at me for?"

"Take your holster off slowly and put it on the table."

"What?"

"Do it."

"Why?"

"Jesus Christ, because I'm holding a gun on you and telling you to."

Phil looked amused. "Am I supposed to believe you're going to shoot me if I don't? Well, I don't believe it and neither do you, even if you are suffering from some obvious brain damage."

"Take it off."

We had a brief staring contest. I won. Phil's gaze dropped to my hand. Even cops are scared of guns. Especially ones in trembling hands.

"Shit," Phil said. "All right, but you better have a goddamn good reason for this." He took his shoulder rig off, not particularly slowly, and put it on the card table. "Happy?" he asked.

I motioned him away from the table, picked the holster up and shoved it behind a box on a shelf. Blood from my nose was tickling my upper lip. I rubbed at it with the back of my left hand then wiped my hand on the seat of my cut-offs. "Call

Harkins. Tell him to come down here. Don't tell him anything else."

Phil gave me a long, speculative look. "I got a better idea, Zachariah. How's about you and me kinda mosey over to Mackie General. Maybe get you a nice little CAT Scan or something."

"Call him."

"You don't want Harkins down here. That man can get a hard-on just thinking about running your PI license through a paper-shredder."

I took a deep breath. "In case you haven't noticed, you're a hostage. Just do what you're told and shut up."

"A hostage for what? Why don't you just tell me what's going on?"

I didn't answer and after a few seconds Phil ran both hands roughly through his hair. Looking up as if he could see Harkins through the ceiling, he said, "Man, are you gonna be pissed." He hunkered down by the phone, telling me all about how he could hardly remember how to use a phone with a rotary dial. His conversation with Harkins was mercifully brief. He stood up, his knees cracking loudly. "Damn, old age setting in already. Now what?"

"Look at that poster behind you. Don't turn around or do anything else unless I tell you to. And keep your mouth shut."

Phil, without a word for once, turned to face the poster that was tacked crookedly on the wall beneath the window. He shoved his hands in the back pockets of his jeans and rocked back and forth on his heels. I turned the light off and opened the door to a ninety-degree angle from the wall and stood behind it, watching Phil. I leaned against the wall and tried to slow down my breathing. My nerves jangled when Phil spoke.

"Maybe a good lawyer can get you off on account of diminished capacity. You're acting like a goddamn nut case. How about putting the gun away before he gets down here." The Texas twang had disappeared from his speech.

"Don't talk."

He sighed loudly. There was a metallic slam and a murmur of voices from the locker room then heavy footsteps, first on the stairs then on the tile in the corridor. Harkins walked into the room. He flipped the lights on and stopped about a foot from the edge of the open door. He was wearing dark pants and a pale blue shortsleeved shirt. His gun was in a shoulder holster. He said, "What's up, Pauling?"

Phil didn't answer. I pushed the door closed and Harkins spun around, crouching automatically, his hand going to his gun. He drew a deep breath and dropped his hand, straightening up. His face had drained of color. "What the fuck are you doing?"

I leaned against the door. "Put your hands on your head."

He laced his hands on top of his head and said,

"What's going on here, Pauling?" He didn't look away from me.

Phil didn't answer.

I stepped away from the door, then changed my mind and leaned against it again, fighting an incredibly strong urge to sit down on the floor. "Take his gun, Phil — *slowly* — and put it on the table."

Phil followed my instructions. I stashed the gun with the other one and leaned against the door again. "Stand there beside him, Phil. Hands on your head."

Phil obeyed. There was a long moment of silence in the room. I was holding the two top cops in Mackie at gunpoint. Phil looked like a man watching his best friend's life pass before his eyes. His expression changed when he looked at Harkins who looked like a man seeing his own life pass before his eyes and end with the clank of a jail cell closing.

"Where is she?" I asked him.

"You crazy fucking bastard. I don't know what you're talking about." Harkins' face was pasty white. A tremor ran across it as I raised the gun and sighted on the bridge of his nose.

"You didn't have much time. I could make Phil send someone to search your house and find your car. Did you bother to change guns? We could sit here for hours waiting for a ballistics report, but I'm not waiting. Tell me where she is or I'll kill you and find her myself."

"Jesus Christ," Phil said.

Harkins drew a jagged breath.

"I didn't mean to kill him. I didn't . . ."

"Jesus Christ," Phil said.

"Where is she?"

"Jesus Christ," Phil said.

"In my car. In the trunk. It's in the City Hall parking lot."

"Jesus Christ," Phil said.

"You have your keys?"

Harkins nodded and pulled them from his pocket.

"Give them to Phil."

Phil took the keys. "Jesus Christ," he said. "You want me to go?"

"No. Yell down the hall. Fogel's in the locker room. Tell him to bring whoever's with him."

I moved away from the door and Phil opened it and shouted, "Hey, Fogel." There was a distant "Yeah?" then Phil said, "Get down here. You, too, Andy."

"Send them both to the car," I said to Phil. "One of them stays with her and one comes back here."

Phil nodded and stepped out in the hall to give the two cops their instructions. They left running. The fire door at the end of the corridor clanged against the wall.

Phil came back in the room. "Call an ambulance," I said.

As soon as he made the call I told him to stand beside Harkins and put his hands on his head again.

"Why don't you just let me —"

"You're still a hostage. If she's dead, I'm killing him."

"The pills were just to knock her out," Harkins said. "I didn't give her enough to kill her."

I stepped forward and put my left hand on his chest and shoved hard. He staggered backward and hit the wall, then slid down it, sending Mr. Smith skidding across the floor.

"You gagged her, you bastard. She has a weak stomach. If the pills made her sick . . ." I stopped. The image of Allison choking to death on vomit was overwhelming.

Phil said, "Take it easy, Bucky."

Harkins got slowly to his feet and stayed out of reach, leaning against the far wall with his hands on his head.

The room was silent except for the buzzing of the light and Harkins' rasping breaths which made mine sound calm. Phil was looking at Mr. Smith. The wail of a siren wavered on the air, crescendoed, and died. After another long noisy silence the fire door clanged against the wall again then there were running footsteps in the hall and Fogel burst into the room, skidding to a halt. He looked uncertainly at me, even more uncertainly at his two superior officers with their fingers laced on their scalps, then back at me.

"What did you find?" Phil asked.

Fogel spoke to me. The man with the gun is

always in charge. "The Vanzetti girl," he said and shot a quick curious look at Harkins.

"Is she alive?" Phil asked for me.

"Yeah," Fogel said to me. "Tied and gagged and sleeping like a baby. We took her out and undid her. She threw up all over and tried to talk. Didn't make any sense. Looks like she's doped up pretty good, but she's breathing okay and everything." He paused for a second, glancing at Harkins again. "The ambulance is there," he added.

Phil stepped toward me, holding out his hand. "Okay, Bucky?"

"Yeah," I said and handed him my gun. I picked up Mr. Smith and headed for the door. Phil started to say something to me but I brushed past him. No one stopped me.

CHAPTER FORTY-ONE

THE AMBULANCE WAS GONE WHEN I REACHED THE City Hall parking lot so I stood at the curb and watched the cars passing by. Within five minutes, I spotted a familiar one and flagged the driver down. Small towns have their advantages. Another five minutes and I was up on the hill at the north edge of town, where Mackie General Hospital shone antiseptically white in the moonlight.

In the lobby, a year-old sign announced that Mackie General's emergency department now had a physician on duty twenty-four hours a day. A smaller sign next to it announced that the physician on duty tonight was Thomas R. Harry, M.D.

The woman behind the admissions window was busy at her computer. Police Officer Andy Riggs, in civvies, was using the phone on her desk. He kept saying, "Harkins? *Harkins?*" in stunned disbelief into the receiver.

I walked past them and went into the only examination room that had its door closed. I ignored the nurse inside who told me I had to wait outside. Tom was in his doctor persona and his expression was a masterpiece of clinical detachment as he looked me over.

Allison was on the examination table, looking as pale as the hospital gown she was wearing. Her eyes were half-open but she didn't see me when I bent over her. I put Mr. Smith beside her and stood at the head of the table, smoothing the long fall of hair spilling over the edge of it.

"She'll be fine," Tom said. "Have you been admitted?"

"I'm okay."

"If you aren't admitted, I can't bill you. Go do it."

I went and got admitted. By the time the paperwork was done and I had been pushed in a wheelchair to and from the X-ray department, Allison had been taken upstairs. I sat in the same examination room for the obligatory thirty-minute wait. Tom finally came in with a big folder of X-rays in his hand.

"So where does it hurt?" he asked.

"I don't want any Popsicle sticks up my nose."

"We don't use Popsicle sticks. Your nose isn't broken, just bent a little. Nothing else is broken either. I was on the phone with Carrie. She fell asleep in front of the television and had a terrible nightmare about you."

"Christ. I wish she'd stop that. I don't have bad dreams when she's in trouble."

Tom grinned. "She's never in trouble. Look over there."

I looked over there and he flashed his little light into my eyes, then told me to open my mouth. "What a mess," he said.

"Don't try to impress me with doctor talk."

"Halsey can put a down payment on a new Mercedes." Halsey was my dentist. A nurse came into the room and I lay down and perfected my macho act while Tom stitched and poked and prodded and made everything that had stopped hurting start hurting again.

"How'd you get these cuts on your back?" he asked when I was sitting up again.

"Self-inflicted knife wounds."

"The wrist is a bit more traditional."

There was a moment of silence while I felt guilty about Carrie and Tom felt guilty about making me feel guilty.

"I should keep you for observation but I'm not in the mood to argue. Don't drive and don't go off by yourself. And no sex for six months."

I promised him two out of three and headed off to find Allison. Three nurses stopped me on the way. One told me I couldn't walk around a hospital barefoot. The others asked what I was doing out of bed. I charmed my way past them, which was no small feat considering what I had seen when I glanced into the mirror in the examination room.

Allison was in a private room on the second floor. Mr. Smith had been tossed on the bedside table.

I tucked him into bed with her and pulled a chair close.

Phil shook me awake a couple hours later. I straightened up and yawned, immediately regretting it. My mouth had felt better before Tom went to work on it.

"Right off hand," Phil said, "I can think of about a hundred other ways you could have handled this, like maybe just telling me what was going on."

I shook my head. "I meant what I said. If she was dead, I was killing him. You would have stopped me."

"Well, that's true, I guess."

"Is Harkins talking?" I asked.

"Can't shut him up. He didn't even wait for his lawyer. I reckon he figures his only chance is to cooperate and hope the judge sends him some place where an ex-Chief of Police can survive prison life. Ex-Chief of Police. Damn, I like the sound of that."

"How do you like the sound of Chief of Police Philip J. Pauling?"

He grinned. "I'm Acting-Chief right now. The mayor about keeled over when I told him I arrested Harkins. I don't know though — too damn much pencil-pushing. I'll have to think about it." He walked around the bed and stood looking down at Allison. "He sure kept her a secret, didn't he? The Feds turned green when they found out about her. Kinda shot the shit out of their Big Brother image."

He pulled another chair away from the wall and sat down across the bed from me. "How'd you find her?"

"She left Allentown on foot and I picked her up down the road."

"*What?* You mean last Monday? She's been with you since right after the murder?"

"She didn't tell me her last name."

Phil's eyes narrowed dangerously. "Malcolm found her purse out at your place. Plenty of ID in it. Big hot-shot detective, you never thought of searching her purse?"

"She hid her ID. I found it Wednesday night."

"Wednesday. This is Monday. That's five days. What the fuck have you been doing with her for five days?"

"I behaved myself."

"That's not what I mean and you know it. Goddammit, what did you think you were doing?"

"She was sick. I'd already spent a couple days with her when I found out. I thought she killed him and didn't think a few days would make any difference. It seemed —"

"— to make sense at the time. That's what you always say, every goddamn time you do something stupid. Well, I know exactly why you did it and it's the only reason and don't you go trying to tell me there's any other reason. You did it because you went and fried most of your brain cells back when you were dipping into every illegal substance you could get your hands on and the few piddly little brain cells you have left are the ones in charge of your hormones and they go ga-ga every time you get within a hundred feet of a pretty face and that's why you did it. You have been nothing but a royal fuck-up since the day I met you. I swear to god, if there was a law against stupidity, you'd be about ten years into a life sentence by now. If I didn't need you to be my best man, I'd throw you in a cell and drop the key down the nearest sewer. I just might do it anyway."

"Your best man?"

"Yeah, I'm getting married next week."

"You're getting *married?*"

Phil craned his neck upward, checking all the corners of the room. "Seems to be an echo in here."

"I'll do it, sure, but who are you marrying? You haven't even been going with anyone. That red head at City Hall?"

"Why would you think I want to marry *her?* Oh, I remember. No, that was just a business date. I owed her a dinner because she put in some unpaid overtime looking for some papers in those old files in the City Hall basement. Patsy knew all about it."

"Patsy knew about it?"

Phil did his echo-seeking look again.

"You and Patsy are getting married again?"

"Well, yeah. Damn, this is embarrassing. I been

wanting to tell you but Patsy made me promise not to say anything until she made up her mind for sure, which I guess she did because we went and got the license this afternoon. And I don't need anyone telling me it's a mistake. Her parents already covered that. As far as they're concerned, the only bright point is she isn't pregnant this time."

"I never thought you should get divorced in the first place. When did all this happen?"

"We been working up to it for a while and then this past week everything went to hell at work and I've been over there crying on her shoulder every day and, damn, that woman does have fine shoulders. Not to mention a lot of other perfectly nice body parts."

"That's where you were. Damn it, I spent half the day trying to find you. I even called Patsy."

"You did?"

"Yeah. I hung up."

"That was you, huh? Well, Patsy'll be glad to hear it. She's been going crazy trying to figure out who it was that caught us in *flagrante delicto* over the phone."

"When I couldn't find you, I finally decided to call Harkins. You know what's really scary? He could have just shot us both out at the house. No one ever would have known what happened. She convinced him I didn't know anything. Which was true.

I figured it out afterward from some things she had told me."

"I want to hear the whole story but it'll wait till tomorrow. You want to hear Harkins' story?"

"Yeah."

"Okay, well, Harkins says he never heard of Vanzetti until a week ago Friday when Vanzetti called him and said they needed to talk. Vanzetti was pretty vague but I guess he threw a scare into Harkins because he agreed to go to his hotel room late that night. I need to backtrack a bit. Vanzetti had got himself between a rock and a hard place. Not only were the Feds after him but so was his ex-boss. It seems that when Vanzetti left Chicago one step ahead of the law, he was a little low on traveling money so he liquidated some assets that weren't rightfully his. To the tune of almost two hundred grand. He wanted to get out of the country but he was afraid to use his passport with a federal warrant out for him and his cohorts in the drug business had a contract out on him and he figured they'd get the word out and tip off whatever contacts he had who might have got him out illegally. A real double-whammy. So Vanzetti spent six months wandering around the country trying to figure out how the hell to get out. At some point in his travels, he remembered that he knew where to find a crooked Chief of Police and decided that was just the ticket he needed. So, he came to Mackie and contacted Harkins, made a lot of threats, said if he went down he was taking Harkins with him."

"What did he want from Harkins?"

"Wanted him to get him out of the country."

"How the hell was Harkins supposed to do that?"

"Vanzetti had this bright idea that Harkins could rig up some phony papers and take him out as a prisoner being extradited. Harkins kept saying there was no way he could do it and Vanzetti kept saying he better come up with a way. Harkins never met him in public, always went to the hotel room late at night. He says he never meant to kill him. He just went back one more time to try to talk some sense into him and he saw red and pulled his gun and fired away."

"Harkins must have had a key to get in the back door, right?"

"Shit, he's — was — the Chief of Police. Right after Vanzetti called him the first time, Harkins stopped by the Arms, asked the manager to look up some records for him and when the guy's back was turned, he helped himself to a spare key to Vanzetti's room, which wasn't likely to be missed until he checked out. Then, Monday morning Harkins showed up at the hotel right after the murder and put the key back. Hell, who's going to watch what the Chief of Police is doing, right? So when we got around to counting keys, they were all there." Phil laughed suddenly. "There it is — the flaw in the perfect murder and I missed it. I didn't want Harkins getting in my way that morning so I made sure nobody called him. And the son-of-a-bitch showed up anyway. Got there a few minutes after I did. I just shrugged it off, figured some busybody at the hotel called him."

"There was no reason for you to suspect him."

"True, but maybe if I'd put it together with the fact that he's been acting like a crazy man all week and maybe if I'd given a little more thought to just why Vanzetti was in Mackie in the first place . . ."

"Hindsight's twenty-twenty."

"That's a song. Don't you have a good Bible quote to cheer me up?"

I thought about it for a while and finally said, "'If the goodman of the house had known what hour the thief would come, he would have watched.'"

"You want to decipher that for me?"

"Hindsight's twenty-twenty."

Phil yawned. "Well, anyway. Harkins isn't saying much about just what pie he's had his fingers in, but he did say no one else in the Department is involved. I think he's hoping to bargain with his information about the drug business. As near as I could figure out, he isn't directly involved with anyone in Mackie. He has a contact in Chicago and helps arrange safe passage and fucks up as many busts as he can. That was him three years ago when our big bust went sour and you started yelling about police corruption. You were right. You remember who was on the investigating committee?"

"Harkins' golfing buddies."

"Yeah. "

Allison suddenly began thrashing around in her sleep. I stood up and took her hand and told her everything was okay. Her eyes opened.

"Did you like what I wrote?" she asked.

"What you wrote? What did you write?"

"On the tree."

"From A to Z? Yes, I liked that a lot."

"My legs are gone."

"They'll be back. Try to sleep now." She didn't hear me. She was already asleep.

Phil was staring at me. He said, "Oh, shit," very quietly. He stood up. "I gotta get going. I'll be back in the morning. Tom says she should be able to talk by then." He walked to the door then turned and said, "She's seventeen, Bucky."

"I know that."

Chapter Forty-two

THE ROOM WAS FILLED WITH THE GRAY LIGHT OF early morning when I woke. Allison was still sleeping soundly. There were muffled sounds of the hospital coming awake and I knew I wouldn't be able to sleep again so I took advantage of the difference in time zones and made some phone calls. I had just finished the last one when a nurse came in and ordered me out.

I walked slowly down the hall to a visitors' lounge. I watched my reflection in a set of double glass doors I was approaching and realized I was walking the way my great-grandfather walked in the months before he finally died of extreme old age. At the lounge, I got a cup of coffee from a machine and managed to get a few sips of it past my swollen lips. I wondered if I'd ever kiss again. Or eat. Eating was a more urgent need at the moment but everything in the vending machine was solid and salty.

I went back to Allison's room. A different nurse was just closing the door on her way out. She said she hoped my name was Zachariah. I said it was.

"You better get in there," she said. "She seems to think you're dead."

Allison was sitting on the edge of her bed holding the telephone receiver up to her ear. When she saw me, she replaced the receiver. Her chin trembled. I sat down beside her and put my arm around her.

"I'm sorry," I said. "You talked to me last night. I thought you'd remember me being here."

She shook her head. "I just remember . . . being in the trunk." We sat quietly for a minute then I asked who she'd been calling. "Nobody. I was trying to decide who to call. Tell me what happened."

Her breakfast arrived and I filled in the missing parts while she ate.

When she was finished I rolled the tray out of the way and pulled a chair up close to the bed.

"Tell me something, babe. I understand why you couldn't call the police in Mackie. For all you knew, every cop in town was mixed up in it. But why not tell the Portland police? Or the state police? Or the FBI?"

She smoothed her blankets and settled Mr. Smith comfortably at her side. "At first, all I could think of was getting away. After you picked me up, I didn't really think at all for a few days. I was so tired and felt sick all the time. I just wanted it all to go away. Then, when I felt better, I realized everyone thought I killed Daddy and I didn't think anyone would believe me. I was afraid they'd think

I just picked the Chief of Police because I saw him
on television and he was from Mackie. I didn't have
any way to prove he was there and I thought he
would have someone, maybe another policeman,
claim to have been with him at the time Daddy was
killed. I kept hoping he'd confess or get caught
somehow else and then I wouldn't have to do anything."

"Allison?"

"Yes? You look terrible."

"I know. Why not tell me?"

"I did. You didn't believe me."

"But if you'd told me who it was, even if I didn't
completely believe you, I sure as hell wouldn't have
handed you over to him. I would have believed you
anyway. There was something important I should
have given a lot of thought to that I didn't."

Allison batted her eyelashes dramatically. "Innocent until proven guilty?"

I smiled as much as I could without undoing Tom's
handiwork. "That, too. But what I meant is that
there had to be some reason why your father was
in Mackie. He wasn't just passing through.
Mackie's had a major drug problem for years and
it made sense that he'd be here to contact someone
who was involved in it. I've suspected for a long
time that someone in the police department was
mixed up in it. Harkins never occurred to me for
some reason."

"There's another reason why I didn't tell you, but

you aren't going to like it. The thing is, I thought you were a little crazy."

"You thought I was crazy? Why?"

"Honestly, Zachariah, you thought I murdered my own father and you didn't do anything about it. You didn't turn me in to the police. And you seemed to like me."

"I did like you. I do like you. And as far as you being a murderer, well, there are murderers and then there are people who happen to commit murder. I never thought you were a murderer at heart."

"Well, it seemed a little strange to me."

"Phil Pauling will be coming to talk to you this morning. He's the cop I was always calling from the motel. He's the Chief of Police now. He'll be more than happy to explain my behavior to you. He's an expert on the subject."

"Why do I have to talk to the police? I thought it was all over."

"You're an eyewitness to a murder, babe, and a kidnap victim. The DA should be around with a stenographer later on to get your statement. Don't worry about it. Harkins confessed and there won't be a trial."

"Okay. Zachariah? Where's my father?"

"He's . . . nothing's been done yet. I talked to the FBI this morning. He was in the army during World War II. We could arrange for burial at a national cemetery. How does that sound?" She said it would be fine. "I also called Fanhaven Academy. Mrs. Mayhew wants you to call as soon as you feel up to it. I called the IRS, too. Your dad had a lot of money with him but I don't think you're going to get it. The IRS has staked a claim to it and they usually get what they want."

"I don't want his money. It's from drugs." Her voice was tight with anger. She picked up Mr. Smith and hugged him tightly. "I suppose I'm being hypocritical. After all, that's how he supported me all these years. My clothes, my jewelry, Fanhaven, everything was paid for with drug money."

"Don't hate him, babe."

"I don't hate him. I don't feel much of anything for him. I'm sorry he's dead but I can't mourn for him. He was never there. How can I miss someone who was never there? I just wish I knew why he stayed away from me."

"My dad's fifty-two. Yours was almost that old when you were born. I don't imagine fatherhood comes easy at that age and when your mother died, he was faced with raising you alone. Maybe he just didn't think he could handle it. But I think it probably had more to do with his being involved in crime. Maybe he didn't want you mixed up in that kind of life. Maybe he thought staying away from you was the best thing he could do for you."

Allison didn't say anything and after a moment I said, "Mrs. Mayhew said he already sent the money for your tuition and expenses for another year at school."

She held Mr. Smith in front of her, staring intently at him as if he held the answer to an important question, then she hugged the bear to her and said, "He did take care of me, didn't he?"

"Yes, he did," I said and then I held Allison for a long time while she cried for the first time for her father, whose dying thought must have been fear for his daughter standing in the dark behind the curtain. I hoped he could somehow know that she had survived.

She was calm, if a bit red-eyed, when Phil arrived. He said, "Hey, there, little darling. You're looking better this morning." He looked at me. "Carrie's waiting for you downstairs. Good-bye."

Allison was looking at me frantically, her eyes pleading for me to stay and protect her from the big, bad policeman. I lingered by the door, not so much to reassure her as to watch Phil in action. He took her limp hand in his and very quietly said, "My mama died when I was six."

Allison's hand tightened on his and I knew by her expression that she had just bonded for life with a man she'd never seen before.

I left her in good hands.

CHAPTER FORTY-THREE

FOR THE FIRST TIME IN ITS HISTORY, MACKIE made the national news. All three networks had great fun juxtaposing the tape of Harkins' "We're trying to solve a murder here" speech with footage of Harkins, handcuffed, ducking into the back seat of a patrol car.

Allison was caught by the cameras as she was leaving the hospital flanked by the Chief of Police and a battered PI. In response to the questions thrown at her, she politely thanked the media for understanding her reluctance to discuss her father's death and for respecting her right to privacy. Phil Pauling's fingerprints were all over that little speech.

With typical fickleness, the media lost interest in the case a couple days later when gang violence erupted in Portland. We were left in peace to enjoy the warm, lazy days of the first week of September, during which a number of minor events occurred.

In the throes of collective guilt, the citizens of Mackie inundated Allison with enough flowers to make a Rose Festival float and with offers of jobs, homes, and money. She declined everything but the flowers.

Two tabloids offered her tidy sums of money for exclusive interviews. She turned them down but they ran stories anyway. The term "lovenest" was never actually used but much was made of the number of days — and nights — she had spent in Portland with me. She laughed herself breathless reading the stories aloud to me.

She stayed at Carrie's house, spending her nights in the spare bedroom upstairs and her days delighting everyone. Melissa dubbed her "Owie" and followed her everywhere. Tom cooked all his specialties for her while I sucked disgusting, supposedly nutritious concoctions through straws. After checking out Allison's meager wardrobe, Carrie raided my safe and took her on lengthy shopping sprees. Phil Pauling proposed to her several times. Allison finally accepted one evening but it was too late by then.

Phil and Patsy had been remarried that morning in a brief ceremony memorable mostly for the bloodshed. Phil wore his best faded jeans and a nearly new blue chambray shirt. Patsy's red hair was vibrant above her white tennis dress. Her sister had three kids in tow and hissed reprimands at them throughout the wedding. Old Judge Callahan droned through the brief ceremony, ignoring the fact that the happy couple's nine-year-old had a bloody nose and the two of them were having a whispered argument over whether he should bend his head forward or backward. The judge had to "ahem" loudly to get their attention for the "I wills" but they seemed to enjoy the kiss and beneath a wad of bloody Kleenex Philip the Second's grin was ecstatic. After the papersigning, the judge stomped out of his chambers and everyone hugged and kissed and Patsy elbowed Phil in the ribs when he stage-whispered to me, "Hot damn, no more child support payments."

A private courier tracked me down at Carrie's house and asked me to sign for two envelopes. I took them out to the picnic table where everyone was lingering over lunch. I opened the small envelope first. Carrie stood behind me and leaned on my shoulders to read the letter with me, secure in her belief that people who had shared the womb could have no secrets from one another. In a round, childish hand, the note said: "Dear Zachariah, My friend says I'm not worth the price of a Maserati. You'll have to settle for another Chevy. Love forever and ever, Nikki."

"Hmm," Carrie said. "Who on earth is she?"

"He. The boy who was kidnapped."

"Oh, yes. You forgot to mention his sexual orientation."

Any further discussion was forestalled when I ripped open the larger envelope. Old money fell out. Hundred dollar bills. Lots of them. I counted them out into fans of ten bills each. When I finished, I had ten fans. There was a moment of awe-stricken silence.

"My god," Tom said. "Tax-free, too."

Carrie said, "Did I happen to mention I have a birthday coming up?"

"No kidding." I gathered up five fans and handed them to her, saying, "Happy birthday." I said "Happy belated birthday" to Allison and gave her the other five. She protested, but Tom and Carrie overrode her objections with a detailed explanation of the foolish ways I would squander the money if I kept it. Pretty soon the conversation turned to a discussion of the price of backyard swimming pools.

I had a phone call from Jefferson Bundy. Our conversation consisted largely of his saying "you son-of-a-bitch" in between laughs. He hung up after extorting a promise of free paperhanging the next time I was in Portland with time on my hands.

I received an exorbitant bill from the wrecking company that had hauled the Nova out of the ravine. They offered to ship my toolbox to me C.O.D. upon receipt of payment.

I sent Jason Finney a bill I felt sure he would consider equally exorbitant. It was carefully itemized and included the wrecking company's charges. I received payment in full by return mail.

My bruises went through an impressive spectrum of color changes. Eventually, I began to feel that I might reach the solid-food stage before Melissa's new brother or sister did.

I bought a car, a Camaro a few years younger than the Nova. No wing windows, but its previous owner had lavished money and attention on it. The cash he had poured into its care and feeding came from kiting stolen government checks and his dad didn't want to store the car for the next five to seven years so he gave me a good deal on it. It was gleaming black with orange flames on the hood. I promised Carrie I'd have it painted.

A janitorial service got the blood stains out of the carpet but I was going to have to re-paper the family room walls. I figured I might as well do the upstairs while I was at it so I assigned Carrie the task of picking out paper

I bought Allison a one-way ticket home.

Her decision to return to Connecticut was made late one night when she came downstairs in her blue nightie and joined me on the couch where I was spending the night. I didn't leave a lot of extra room so she solved the space problem by stretching out on top of me. She put her fists one on top of the other on my chest and rested her chin on them.

"Hi," she said.

"Hi."

"Do you remember the promise I made you?"

"Uh huh."

"I think I broke it."

"Both parts of it?"

She studied my face for a long moment then said, "Yes, both parts."

She flattened her hands and lay her cheek on them. I twined my fingers through her hair and tried to think about the problems inherent in a relationship between two people separated by more than a dozen years in age and by an even greater disparity in experience. Coherent thought was difficult with Allison where she was. I had a sudden, vivid image of the look on my mother's face if I showed up at my thirtieth birthday party with a seventeen-year-old on my arm. Allison raised her head and asked what I was laughing about.

"Nothing. Get off me, babe. We need to talk."

She got up and watched expectantly as I sat up, throwing off the covers. I was wearing gym shorts. She looked disappointed.

I took her hand and led her into the kitchen. We sat at the table with the room lit only by the moonlight streaming through the window. Moonlight became Allison.

"You're going to make me go home, aren't you?" she asked.

"Not *make you*, no, but I think you should. The people at school may not be your family but they're as close as you come to one. They care about you. Running away isn't fair. If you don't want to stay, at least go back and tell them good-bye properly."

"What if I don't want to stay?"

"You have friends in Oregon. Allison, these last couple weeks haven't been exactly ordinary. I think you need some time to put things into perspective and I think you can do that better back at school."

I had neatly sidestepped the major issue. Allison got right down to the nitty-gritty. "How old is Tom?" she asked.

"Thirty-nine, almost forty. It isn't the number of years between us, babe. It's *your age*. I don't think you're old enough to be sure what you want. You've never even dated. I don't want you to stay and then find out your feelings for me were based on a need for security and a sense of gratitude."

"You think I'm suffering from hero-worship?"

"If you are, it's a bit misplaced. I seem to remember handing you over to a killer."

"But you came to my rescue in the end, just like a knight in shining armor."

I laughed. "If you're confusing me with a knight, you definitely need to take some time to think things over. When Carrie was seventeen, she fell in love forever at least once a month."

"Did you?"

"By the time I was seventeen, I was an ex-drug addict, an ex-thief, and an ex-husband. And an ex-father-to-be. I wasn't innocent enough to fall in love easily. I've done a lot of things in my life that aren't particularly admirable, Allison."

"That reminds me, I've been meaning to ask you

if you slept with the lesbians one at a time or both together."

I opened my mouth, closed it again, and finally said, "I think I'll take the Fifth on that one."

"Both together." Allison gazed over my shoulder with a funny look on her face as if she were trying to picture that scene and finding it hard to do. She looked back at me, smiling. "Are you saying you're too corrupt for me?"

"I'm not sure corrupt is the word I would choose but, yes, something along those lines."

"I think the real problem is that you're afraid you'll be left again."

"I think the real problem is that *you're* too old for *me*."

"What would you do if April came back?"

"I don't even know April any more. I don't want her back. I'd like to know why she left. I'd like to know . . . that it wasn't my fault."

We sat quietly for a moment, then Allison said, "Okay. I'll go home. For a while."

I made her travel arrangements the next morning, booking a flight out of Portland so I wouldn't have to worry about her making a connection if I sent her off on a puddle-jumper out of Pendleton. Tom and Carrie had wisely refrained from questioning me about Allison's plans but I had intercepted a lot of worried looks passing between them. After I told them she was going home, they treated me with the stifling over-solicitousness usually accorded only to the terminally ill.

Phil Pauling told me I was crazy if I let her go and crazier if I let her stay. I already knew that.

Nineteen days after we met, I drove Allison back to Portland. For what were, no doubt, very good reasons of her own, she wore her blue dress. It wasn't necessary. The trunk of the Camaro was loaded down with luggage. She had arrived in Oregon with a nightgown stuffed in her purse and was leaving with excess baggage. Among other things, she had three of my white T-shirts. Mr. Smith rode to Portland on her lap. We held hands across the seat, speaking only of unimportant things.

At the airport, we stood close together with our arms around each other until it was time for her to board. I walked her down to the end of the boarding tunnel. She hugged me, whispered in my ear, kissed me quickly, and was gone.

I waited long enough to see the airplane safely off the ground then I retrieved the Camaro and headed home, holding tight to the last words she had said to me.

"I'll be back."

I drove all the way back to Mackie with my fingers crossed.

— THE END —